IN THE STILL OF THE NIGHT

Lindsay's cell phone, perched on her nightstand, rang just after midnight and jerked her awake. Accustomed to being awakened in the middle of the night, she sat up and answered it. "Hello?"

No answer.

She shoved back her hair and glanced at the clock on the bedside table. Sam had dropped her off more than three hours ago and she'd fallen into bed exhausted. "Hello?"

There was breathing on the other end. Normally, when she got late-night calls, it was a frightened woman hiding out from her abuser, too afraid to talk. Often she had to coax the woman into speaking.

But tonight, she didn't sense someone in trouble. She sensed danger. Her voice harsh, she demanded, "Who is this?"

There was a moment's pause. And then the line went dead.

Lindsay hurried past her roommate's closed door and went down the carpeted stairs to check the lock on the front door. She peered out the peephole. Nothing. Then she went to the back sliding door. Locked. She moved from window to window checking them. All locked.

She flipped on the floodlight and it shone over her backyard garden. She stared into the yard looking for any sign of movement.

Nothing moved.

And yet she had the feeling that someone was watching. . . .

I'M WATCHING YOU

MARY BURTON

ZEBRA BOOKS
Kensington Publishing Corp.

ZEBRA BOOKS are published by

Kensington Publishing Corp.
850 Third Avenue
New York, NY 10022

ISBN-13: 978-0-7394-9161-4

Printed in the United States of America

Chapter One

Richmond, Virginia,
Monday, July 7, 4:10 A.M.

Thou shalt not kill.

The shadowed figure squatted in the darkness by Harold Turner's lifeless body, amazed that excitement, not shame, surged.

The sense of power and righteousness was nearly overwhelming. God's calling to be the Guardian had never been clearer.

Placing the .45-caliber handgun and silencer into a black duffle bag, the Guardian eyed Harold's body, propped against dented metal trashcans.

Even in death, Turner appeared pompous. Arrogant.

A neat part divided Harold's thinning black hair. Manicured nails glistened in the moonlight. His double-breasted suit and white shirt still looked crisp, and his yellow silk tie matched the handkerchief packed in his breast pocket. Gold monogrammed cuff links told anyone worth knowing that Harold had money and taste.

But beneath the expensive suit that Harold always wore were track marks on his arms and behind his knees. It was an open secret that Harold had been a drug addict for years.

The Guardian adjusted Harold's tie over the growing plume of blood staining the attorney's shirt. Countless hours had been spent planning this first murder, strategizing and worrying to near exhaustion. And in the end, luring Harold here had required only the promise of drugs. Firing the bullet from the .45 into his chest had been effortless.

"A fitting place, don't you think? I mean, a battered women's shelter. Your wife certainly would understand why I chose this place."

The shelter behind them was housed in a white Colonial, and it blended so seamlessly into the middle-class subdivision that most neighbors didn't know the home's true purpose. Soft moonlight washed over the shelter's grassy backyard. A six-foot privacy fence corralled assorted kick balls, bicycles, and rusted wagons—all donated toys used by the children staying at the shelter. There was a swing with a long yellow slide surrounded by mulch.

Thoughts of the children stirred anger in the Guardian. "There shouldn't be places like this. It's not right. Children should feel safe in their own home."

The Guardian leveled an accessing gaze on Harold. The high-and-mighty attorney had stood up in federal court this morning to defend his drug dealer client, speaking with authority, visibly comfortable with his ability to manipulate "reasonable doubt."

The Harold Turner who had appeared in the county courtroom was a far cry from the man who'd stood here just minutes ago with tears running down his face begging for his life. *That* Harold had never understood a fear so sharp it burned.

But *this* Harold had.

This Harold had dropped to his knees. He'd offered money and promised lavish favors—anything to buy back his miserable life.

"But fancy appeals don't work on me, do they Harold?" the Guardian had said. "There is no redemption for you."

A slight breeze rustled through the thick canopy of leaves above. Soon the sun would rise and with it the heat. This had been one of the hottest Julys on record and the heat was drying up yards, draining water tables, and straining tempers.

In the distance a dog barked. A cat screeched. They ran through the dark yards, their sounds vanishing in the night.

The Guardian stared up at the shelter, searching for any sign that the animals had awoken anyone. A light on the second floor came on but it just as quickly went dark. In the last hour of the night, the people in the shelter and the neighborhood slept.

This was a sacred and blessed time. Predawn's quiet and peace conjured feelings of invincibility and invulnerability.

The Guardian unfastened the gold cuff link on Harold's left wrist and carefully tucked it in the attorney's pocket before neatly pushing the shirt and jacket sleeves up to his elbow. A platinum wedding band squeezed the ring finger on Harold's left hand.

"His power is great, and He never lets the guilty go unpunished." The Bible verse had given the Guardian comfort during the darkest days after Debra's death. Sweet, sweet Debra, dead at thirty-nine, her life stolen by her own husband. Like Harold, Debra's husband had been a respected man in the community, but a violent man at home. His tyranny had trapped Debra and her daughter in hell for years.

Memories of Debra and her child brought sadness and regret. Debra had cried out for help. She'd wanted out of her marriage. She'd wanted a fresh start. But no one had come to her rescue. No one had cared what happened behind the closed doors of her house.

And then Debra's husband had killed her. He'd violently beaten her to death and then, like the coward he was, had retreated and killed himself. Debra's only child had found her mother. The violence of that day had left its mark on the girl and she'd run away.

Many a night the Guardian had dreamed about Debra and her child and prayed for their forgiveness.

Twelve years had passed. And then the sign from God came a few months ago. The sign was an article in a magazine. It was so clean and pure and it made the Guardian weep. There had been no question then that the time for revenge had come.

Debra was gone forever, as was her child's lost innocence, but those who hurt their families could be rooted out and severely punished. They could be made to pay for their sins against their families.

The Guardian removed a machete from the black duffle bag and raised the blade high overhead. The edge was razor sharp, finely honed on a whetstone until the blade could slice paper.

Moonlight glinted off the blade before it came down in one slicing blow that severed the flesh and bone of Harold's left hand.

Blood splattered onto Harold's face and shirt as well as the Guardian's jumpsuit and gloved hands. The blood looked brown in the moonlight as it oozed from the stump and pooled in the dry earth around Harold's body.

Primal energy surged through the Guardian. For a moment, life had never felt sweeter.

Retribution is mine.

After wrapping the hand in a plastic zip-top bag, the Guardian shoved it into the duffle bag along with the machete, still dripping with blood.

Satisfied that no one had seen, the Guardian zipped the duffle bag closed and then jogged across the back-yard, slipped though the privacy fence gate, and sprinted to the waiting van parked halfway down the block.

Opening the van's front door tripped the dome light. Blinking against the brightness, the Guardian quickly got in and closed the door. Darkness shrouded the cab once again. For several seconds, the Guardian sat in the darkness scanning the homes around to make sure no one had seen. The homes remained dark.

Finally, satisfied that no one would intrude, the Guardian shifted his attention to the open flower box on the passenger seat. The box was filled with purple irises. Each individual stem had been capped with a vial of water to preserve freshness.

After removing Harold's hand from the canvas duffle bag, the Guardian reverently wrapped it in green tissue and nestled it under the flowers.

The choice of irises was inspired. She would under-stand their meaning.

Friendship. Hope. Wisdom. Valor.

After replacing the lid back on the flower box, the Guardian tied the red silk ribbon around it into a pre-cise bow, removed a prewritten card from the glove box and slipped it under the knot.

The Guardian switched on the ignition. The dash-board light washed over the box and the thick, bold handwriting on the card.

It read, *"For Lindsay."*

Chapter Two

Monday, July 7, 8:10 A.M.

Lindsay O'Neil was late for work. Desperately late. She was running so far behind because a power outage had silenced her alarm clock and she'd overslept by almost three hours.

She glanced down at her Jeep's speedometer. It hovered just above thirty miles per hour, but she'd gladly have doubled that speed if Broad Street's four lanes of westbound traffic hadn't been so clogged with commuters.

Tension squeezed her chest. Normally, it took fifteen minutes for her to make the ten-mile trek from her apartment to the women's shelter where she worked. But normally, she didn't sleep as soundly as she had last night. Most nights dreams woke her frequently and she had no trouble rising early and leaving by five A.M.

Lindsay turned on the radio. She punched the "scan" button several times before finally settling on a song she liked. The music and lyrics calmed her and enabled her to take a few deep breaths. Some of the tension released from her body.

For the last year and a half, Lindsay had worked as the

director of Sanctuary Women's Shelter. Her schedule was always jam-packed with counseling sessions and administrative meetings, and most days she barely had time to eat.

And today's schedule was going to be busier than most. In the last two and a half hours, Lindsay had missed the seven A.M. group-counseling session that she held each Monday. The meeting was mandatory for all shelter residents. She'd also missed an eight A.M. conference call with the chairman of the shelter's board of directors, Dana Miller, who expected weekly updates.

Missing the teleconference was a problem, but she could talk her way out of it. However, sleeping through the group session with her residents was inexcusable. The women who attended that meeting were all in abusive relationships. Many hadn't worked in years, and most were more afraid of the unknown that lay ahead than they'd been when they'd lived with the threat of physical violence. Often Lindsay did little more than listen, dispense tissues, and offer hugs. What was important was that she was always there to bolster them up—*no matter what.*

And today she'd let them all down.

She flipped open her cell phone. She'd rushed out so quickly this morning, she'd not thought to call the office. However, the phone's screen was blank. The battery was dead. Hadn't she set it on the charger? "The power outage. Damn it."

Lindsay stopped for a red light and tossed the phone onto the passenger seat. Heat spiraled up from the road's black asphalt. Even though she had the air-conditioning on full blast, the heat rose up through the floorboards. The Jeep's engine fan came on and within seconds the motor hesitated and threatened to cut off.

"Damn it," she muttered.

She'd been promising herself for months to take the Jeep in for a tune-up but kept putting it off. There never seemed to be enough time. Now the engine balked in the high temperature. She shut off the air conditioner and rolled down the window. Thick, heavy July air rushed into the car.

Without the strain of the air conditioner, the engine settled down.

She started to perspire.

"God, I hate the heat."

It coiled around her. It made her temper rise. It made her remember. . . .

"Mom," she whispered, closing her eyes.

Twelve years ago a seventeen-year-old Lindsay had come home early from her lifeguard job on a hot, stormy afternoon. Usually, she worked until closing time, past nine in the evening. But on that hot day, thunderstorms had sent streaks of lightning across the cloudy sky. The manager had closed the pool around two and had sent the lifeguards home.

Her lifeguard buddy from the club, Joel, had given her a ride home. "Hey, are you sure you don't want to catch a movie?" Joel was a skinny kid with blotchy skin and braces. "It's my treat."

She knew Joel had a crush on her and she didn't want to hurt his feelings. "Thanks, but I don't get a chance to spend much time with my mom. But I promise we'll go next week?"

"It's a date." He dropped her off at the top of the circular drive in front of the green framed house built almost a hundred years ago by her great-grandparents.

Lindsay waved and with her pool bag dashed past her mother's prized flower beds filled with daylilies, begonias, and marigolds. The front screen door wasn't locked, which bothered her. She'd warned her mother about keeping the door locked.

Her mother had forced her father out two months earlier, because she could no longer endure the verbal and physical abuse. Since his departure, the house had taken on a lighter air. Her mother had begun singing again and she'd taken to wearing makeup. Now Lindsay no longer searched for excuses not to come home. In fact, she looked forward to it.

Lindsay dropped her pool bag by the front door and checked her watch. Her mother's waitress shift at the Ashland Town Restaurant wouldn't start for a few more hours so it gave them time to hang out together.

Thunder boomed and shook the windowpanes in the house. Dark clouds hovered over the corn fields and the distant trees. Gusty breezes inverted the oak tree leaves, making the tree line look more silver than green. The storm was heading east fast and soon it would be all around them.

"Mom?"

No answer.

From the kitchen, the radio crooned *California Dreamin'* by The Mamas & the Papas. It was her mother's favorite song. Lindsay smiled, recalling how the two of them had danced to the tune just a few weeks ago. Her mother dreamed of going to California, of seeing the Pacific Ocean and visiting Universal Studios in Hollywood. Lindsay had promised to drive her mother cross country next summer right after she graduated from high school. For fun, they spent their spare time mapping the route west.

"Mom!"

The song's chorus repeated the verse about churches, kneeling and pretending to pray.

Lindsay started to hum and grabbed a soda from the refrigerator, popping it open.

That's when Lindsay spotted her father's worn work gloves on the kitchen table. Suddenly, her stomach churned. What was her father doing here?

He'd called her mother once or twice in the last couple of weeks. The calls had worried Lindsay, but when she had questioned her mother about them, her mother had downplayed everything and told her not to fret.

Everything looked as it should. The linoleum floor was swept clean. Dishes drained in the strainer. White lace curtains fluttered in the window. The Formica-topped table had two place settings arranged across from each other. Her father could be charming when he wanted to be and most likely had convinced her mother to fix him lunch.

Now a stir of cold air brushed the back of Lindsay's neck. The house suddenly felt different. Wrong. Apprehension squeezed her heart.

Lindsay glanced around. "Mom!"

She crossed the kitchen, pushed the back screened door open, and glanced at the swing and glider by the toolshed in the backyard. Dark clouds covered the horizon.

"Mom, where are—"

Lindsay turned to the right side of the yard. She stopped abruptly. Her mother lay on her back near the trash cans by the fence.

She rushed toward her mother and stopped just inches from her. Her mother's face was so beaten, so swollen, it was nearly unrecognizable. Blood pooled around her head. Beside her body lay a bloody hammer that looked as if it had been hurriedly discarded.

Dropping to her mother's side, Lindsay reached out to her mother but hesitated. She was afraid to touch her.

Afraid to touch the woman who'd loved her, cared for her, and refused to abandon her no matter what.

A honking horn wrenched Lindsay from the memory

and brought her back to the present. She glanced up at the green light. Sweat beaded on her forehead. Her hands trembled. Cursing, she punched the gas.

Twelve years and her hands still trembled when she remembered that day. Twelve years and she still had nightmares. Twelve years and she felt that if she didn't have a white-knuckle grip on her life it would all slip away.

"Stop it, Lindsay," she muttered. "It's long over. *Done.*"

Purposefully, she shifted her mind from the past to her to-do list that she made certain never ended. The first thing she needed to do was call her boss Dana and apologize for missing their conference call. The second must-do job was to write the summation for the grant application, which, if they won, would pay the salary for a full-time counselor. Then there were the fund-raiser ideas, the notes for her talk to a local church group tonight, and the hospital intervention awareness seminar. . . .

A therapist had once called Lindsay's jam-packed schedule an avoidance device. He'd said it was easier for her to stay busy than to think about her losses. Lindsay hadn't argued, because she knew he was right. But she didn't know how to slow down and keep the dark thoughts at bay.

When she turned into the quiet residential neighborhood where Sanctuary was located, she slowed to the twenty-five-mile-per-hour speed limit. She was so far behind schedule today that she'd be working late into the night just to break even.

She downshifted to first gear when she spotted the two police cars and the unmarked Impala parked in front of the shelter.

Her fingers tightened on the steering wheel and tension nearly choked her breath away. "Oh, God, what's happened now?"

The last time the cops had been to the shelter's secret

location, one of the residents, Pam Rogers, had broken strict protocol and called her abusive husband. Pam had divulged the shelter's location and asked him to come get her. He'd arrived fifteen minutes later. She'd run out to him, begging him to take her back. Instead of welcoming her, he'd hit her and then ordered her into his car. When the hysterical overnight volunteer had called Lindsay at home, Lindsay had immediately contacted the one brother Pam had mentioned. He didn't know where his sister was so Lindsay had called in favors hoping to find Pam.

The woman was found dead the next day behind a convenience store. She'd been badly beaten and strangled. The cops had tracked down the husband two weeks later and arrested him. Jack Rogers had shown no remorse but had talked about his rights as a husband.

His rights. What about his wife's right to live a life free of fear?

Lindsay pulled her Jeep into the paved driveway. She jerked the parking brake up, grabbed her satchel purse, and hurried up the concrete sidewalk to the glass front door.

Sanctuary was on a corner lot and wasn't distinguished by signage but by a wide front porch furnished with weathered white rockers. A collection of planters that Lindsay had filled with red geraniums over the Fourth of July weekend added a splash of color. The yard was neatly cut and edged and the beds had been freshly mulched. It had been her experience that people in the neighborhood didn't pay much attention to those who kept their yards in good shape. And going unnoticed was vital to Sanctuary's success.

The shelter's first floor had four main rooms that were divided by a center hallway. The first room on the right didn't serve as a living room but her office. It was closed off by French doors and filled with stacks of files, manuals, and sacks of unsorted donations.

A conference room, a dining room in a conventional home, adjoined her office. In its core there was a circle of chairs that reminded her of the counseling meeting she'd missed that morning. The walls were decorated with posters that denounced domestic violence.

Across the hallway was a den furnished with a large television, a couple of secondhand couches covered with white sheets, and huge throw pillows on the floor. At the back of the house was a kitchen she'd painted yellow last month. Upstairs there were five rooms, each having two sets of twin beds. Often women moved here with their children and she tried to put the entire family in one room together. She even had a couple of cribs and a bassinet.

The house was normally teeming with the women and their children who made Sanctuary their temporary home. The chatter of women and children often mingled with the TV and ringing phone.

But now, the place was silent and it appeared deserted.

Silver bracelets jangled on Lindsay's slim wrist as she pulled the rubber band from her blond hair and released the too tight ponytail that was already giving her a headache. Blunt, straight hair fell around her shoulders.

Lindsay started toward the kitchen, unable to suppress the growing panic as she searched for last night's volunteer. "Ruby!"

A heavyset black woman rushed out of the kitchen, a phone in hand. Ruby Dillon, when she wasn't working at the nursing home as an aid, volunteered nights at the shelter. About fifty, Ruby was a big woman who wore her hair short and her pants and shirts oversized. Her dead-on honesty about her own past mistakes, including time in prison and drug use, had earned the residents' respect.

"It's about time you got here. I've been calling you for an hour," Ruby said, shaking the phone at her.

"My power went out last night. The house phones didn't work and my cell phone didn't charge. What's with the police? What's going on?"

"They came because of the body."

Images of her mother lying dead in her backyard flashed in her mind. "Body? Please tell me it wasn't one of ours."

Ruby touched Lindsay gently on the arm. "No, no, honey. It wasn't one of our residents. All our people are off to work or school."

Relieved, Lindsay closed her eyes. She had to choke back a sudden rush of tears. "Who?"

Ruby shrugged. "I don't know. But the body is male. I found him when I was taking out the garbage this morning. He was propped up against the trash cans behind the toolshed, his suit buttoned up and his hair combed as if he were headed to Sunday church."

Lindsay moved down the hallway into the kitchen and looked out the window over the sink. The backyard was filled with a half dozen cops gathered at the yellow tape. Most were uniformed but in the center stood a plain-clothes detective. His back was to her.

The cops blocked Lindsay's view of the corpse. "Did you recognize him?"

Ruby folded her arms over her chest. "Who? The dead guy? No, ma'am. And I didn't look in his face either. The devil can steal your soul if you look the dead in the face."

Lindsay dropped her purse on a well-worn kitchen table that was covered with nicks and flecks of paint from a child's weekend craft project. "I've seen my share of death. Maybe the devil has stolen my soul."

"Don't even kid about that."

"Do the police know who the dead guy is?"

"If they do, they're not telling me. A detective just arrived minutes ago. I told him everything I know, but he was pretty tight-lipped when I asked questions. He's the one who said to stop what I was doing and track you down." Ruby's sharp gaze traveled over Lindsay. "Are those the clothes you wore yesterday?"

Lindsay glanced down at the faded jeans and pink cotton top. She smoothed a wrinkle from her shirt. "Yes."

Ruby cocked a dark eyebrow. "Where have you been? Lord, I hope you've been with a man."

The idea made Lindsay blush. "Nope."

"Too bad. You certainly could use a man in your bed. That no-account husband of yours hasn't paid you any attention this last year."

"We're separated, remember?"

"No man in his right mind would leave you."

Lindsay was unwilling to get into another discussion about her failed marriage or her monastic, workaholic life. "I taught a yoga class yesterday afternoon and then went home to work on this grant. I fell asleep in my clothes on the couch. The power went out sometime last night and the alarm didn't go off." If not for her roommate, Nicole, who'd been awakened by a barking dog, she could have slept a couple more hours.

Ruby grunted. "Well, if you ain't got a man, I'm glad you at least got a good night's sleep. You work too hard. You're burning the candle at both ends, if you ask me."

This last year, since she'd separated from her husband, she had stayed particularly busy, even by her own standards. "You'll be glad to know that I slept like the dead."

Ruby grimaced and glanced toward the heavens. "Don't be making fun of the dead. The devil will come and get you."

Lindsay pushed her hand through her hair. "Sorry. Morbid jokes are a holdover from having lived with a cop."

Ruby frowned. "Your husband is a cop?"

"Yeah." This was another topic she did not want to explore. "I'm going to talk to the police. I want to get those squad cars away from my house before everyone figures out we're a shelter."

Ruby's heavy feet trailed behind Lindsay. "Don't waste your breath. I tried a couple of times to talk to that 'detective.'" The word *detective* sounded like an expletive. "He said to stay out of his crime scene. He even locked the back door and pocketed the key from the deadbolt so no one would go in or out that door."

That ticked Lindsay off. Sanctuary was her creation. "This cop is on my turf now and he is going to tell *me* what's going on?"

Grinning, Ruby shook her head. "Sometimes I think you'd rather fight than eat."

She smiled. "Somebody's got to lead the charge."

Ruby snorted. "Honey, you've got too many causes. About time someone worried about you."

"I'm better off taking care of myself." She'd said those words so often in the last year that she almost believed them.

Lindsay headed out the front door and went around the side of the house to the loose slats in the privacy fence. She bent the slats back and slipped through unnoticed.

The closest cop to her was a patrolman. He stood at the lip of the yellow tape and faced the crime scene, his back to her. He was slender, a little gawky, and appeared fresh out of the academy. He couldn't have been much more than twenty-one.

A humid breeze tunneled through the backyard's still,

hot air and carried with it a host of smells. Blood. Waste. Gunpowder. Death.

From this angle she couldn't see the body beyond the circle of six cops who stood around it.

She approached the uniformed cop. She cleared her throat. "Do you know anything about the victim?"

The young cop whirled around and glared down at her. "Where'd you come from?"

"That house." She crooked her head toward Sanctuary and then nodded to the crowd of cops. "Do you know who was murdered? I hear it was a man."

The young cop started to answer, then caught himself. He puffed out his chest. "Ma'am, this is a police crime scene. You are not supposed to be here."

His attempt to intimidate her barely registered on her radar. She'd stared down far scarier people than this kid. "Look, Officer . . ." She glanced down at the bronze name badge on his chest. "Bennett. That house is Sanctuary Women's Shelter and I'm the director."

"I don't care who you are. You can't be here."

Her tone had sounded brittle and she was reminded of Ruby's frequent advice to soften her delivery. She remembered something about catching more flies with honey than vinegar.

With a conscious effort, she smiled and relaxed her stance. "I really need to know who was killed in case it involves one of the women staying here. It's my job to keep them safe."

The cop's frown deepened. "Even if I knew, I couldn't tell you."

His attitude annoyed but didn't deter her. "How'd the guy die?"

"I can't say."

"Do you know the time of death?" She edged around

the cop. If she got a little closer she might find out more about the victim.

He shifted and blocked her path. "No one gets in that crime scene."

She leaned around him. Even from this angle, most of the crime scene remained blocked by the broad shoulders of the detective, who had now removed his suit jacket, rolled up his sleeves, and donned rubber gloves and booties. She couldn't see his face but noted his military short black hair and crisp white shirt. His hands rested on his narrow hips.

He must be the bossy detective Ruby had mentioned. Lindsay summed him up in a nanosecond: an alpha male, a by-the-book tight-ass, and a bully.

She suddenly felt very weary. She'd been dealing with bullies far too long. But if he was the one she needed to talk to, then so be it.

Reading her thoughts, the officer said, "The detective in charge is going to talk to you when he's ready."

She pushed her hand through her hair. "This detective got a name?"

"Detective Kier."

She swallowed. "Zack Kier?"

A smug smile lifted the edge of the officer's lip. "That's right."

Zack Kier was her estranged husband. They'd not spoken in almost a year.

She glanced toward the plainclothes detective again. Since when had Zack moved from undercover narcotics to homicide? When had he cut his hair, shaved the beard, and taken to wearing suits? Her Zack had worn his thick, long hair tied at the nape of his neck. He had preferred faded jeans, T-shirts, worn boots and a well-worn black leather jacket.

Everything about him had changed in the last year. And nothing had changed.

She should have recognized the rigid, controlled stance, which had always announced his unwavering commitment to police work. He also still tapped his index finger against his belt buckle when his hands rested on his hips.

Raw emotions she'd struggled to bury this last year enveloped her in a rush. Love. Hate. Fear. Betrayal. All ripped through her and for a moment left her speechless.

Lindsay's knee-jerk reaction was to retreat. She'd have preferred avoiding this meeting with Zack and sidestep the messy tangle of emotions that were sure to follow.

Then she caught herself. Her therapist had pointed out that she had a habit of running from emotions that were personally painful. He had told her she had to learn to face her feelings for Zack. When she'd expressed her doubts, he'd reminded her that she'd risen above her father's brutality and her mother's death. Zack and their marriage should be no exception.

Still, Lindsay had to swallow before she could shout, "Zack!"

All the other cops turned first and stared at her while Zack's body stiffened. For a moment he seemed frozen, but then he turned slowly and stared at her from behind aviator sunglasses.

Instinct screamed *run*. She stood her ground.

The sunglasses hid Zack's sharp blue eyes, but she knew even without the shades his expression would have been unreadable. He'd always been so good at hiding his emotions. It's why he'd made a great undercover cop and a lousy husband.

"Zack, can you tell me who the body is?" Her voice sounded surprisingly controlled—a minor, but appreciated miracle.

For a moment, Zack tensed and she expected him to walk toward her. Their relationship was unconventional and damaged, but they had a history and that had to be worth something.

He drew in a breath but didn't move toward her. "I'm not ready to interview you yet, Lindsay. Go back inside and wait for me."

Zack sounded so controlled. So together. He'd anticipated seeing her.

That realization angered her. He could have given her a heads-up and called her on her cell. *Crap.* She remembered her cell was dead and so was her home phone. Maybe he had tried to call.

Still, the insight didn't soften the sharp emotions digging at her. "Well, I'd like to talk to you now, detective." She'd laced the words with attitude, knowing he'd hate it.

Zack's left hand flexed. She recognized the gesture. It signaled he was irritated. Good.

Speaking to the young cop, Zack said, "Officer Bennett, escort Ms. O'Neil away from my crime scene now."

The curt dismissal had her squaring her shoulders. "This is shelter property, Detective Kier. You can't shut me out. Whoever was killed on my property affects my residents."

Zack didn't answer. Instead, he turned back toward the body.

Honey not vinegar. Honey not vinegar.

With effort, Lindsay drew in a breath and softened her tone. "Look, Zack, my assistant found the body and it's in our backyard. Can't you give me any information?"

"Not now, Lindsay," Zack said. He crouched by the body, pulled off his sunglasses, and chewed the earpiece as he stared at the body.

Barely a few moments together and already it was clear that the emotional wall between them was as thick as it had been a year ago. It was hard now to believe that they'd ever been close.

Lindsay always felt most alone when she tried to connect with him and he shut her out. "Detective, can you at least move the marked police cars?" she asked. "Sanctuary doesn't need any more bad publicity."

He didn't respond.

Officer Bennett took Lindsay's arm. "Ma'am, you need to leave this area."

She snatched her arm free. "Yeah, yeah, yeah. I'm going."

Chapter Three

Monday, July 7, 9:25 A.M.

For the past two days, Detective Zack Kier had been running down leads on a suspicious murder in the county's east end. He'd pieced together enough information to prove that the woman who had fallen to her death had committed suicide, and that it was not a murder. He had been ready to clock out and start a stretch of three days off when dispatch had reported a homicide at Sanctuary Women's Shelter.

He'd taken the assignment without hesitating or clearing it with his supervisor. The action would no doubt come back to bite him in the ass but he didn't care. He'd needed to make sure Lindsay was okay.

He'd not only seen her, but he'd also managed to piss her off.

Now, it wasn't even ten o'clock and Zack was juggling what was going to be a high-profile murder and Lindsay. *Shit.*

Zack decided to focus on the lesser of the two evils—the crime scene.

The responding uniformed officer had roped off a

generous perimeter around the body and had done a good job keeping everyone out and the area secure until Zack had arrived.

A monthlong drought had left the ground bone dry, so the chances of retrieving footprints, DNA, weapons, the victim's hand, and anything else left behind by the killer were all good. But they'd have to work fast. Thick rain clouds that looked ready to burst hovered above.

"Officer Watt," Zack said, speaking to the older officer behind him. "What do you have so far?"

In his midfifties, Watt's gray crew cut emphasized a perpetual scowl. Usually, he had little to say, but when he did speak smart detectives listened. "Call came in from a Ruby Dillon. She found the body just after eight. Ms. Dillon spent the night at the shelter. She was in charge of supervising the overnight residents and getting the four female residents off to work and the two male children to summer school. The place was empty when she came outside to dump the trash and discovered the body."

Zack patted his shirt pocket in search of cigarettes. The pocket was empty. He'd quit smoking nine months ago, but cravings still plagued him. "Did she hear or see anything last night?"

"Not a word. And none of the residents mentioned anything out of the ordinary to her before they left for the day. It was an unusually quiet night."

Zack studied the corpse's bloated features. He didn't need ID to know who he was: Harold Turner.

Turner was well known at headquarters, because he wasn't particular about whom he defended as long as the case translated into cash or media attention. Turner had been in the news this past week for his defense of drug dealer Ronnie T., who, after numerous delays, was on trial for tax evasion. Now that Turner was dead, Ronnie

T.'s trial could be compromised. That worried Zack. Eighteen months ago, he had been one of the under- cover cops who'd gathered evidence against the affable Ronnie T.

Zack rose and removed a notebook from his breast pocket. He jotted notes: interview Quinton Barlow, Harold's law partner. Examine Turner's client list. Talk to Mrs. Turner.

He glanced left and right at the surrounding houses. With his partner on vacation, he would also be knocking on a lot of doors today. "Any other witnesses?"

Officer Watt shook his head. "Not yet."

Zack was careful to stay clear of the blood-caked grass and dirt around the body's mutilated arm. The scent of decaying flesh made his stomach clench. He'd been a cop for thirteen years, could look at any grisly sight with- out flinching, but the smells always got to him.

"Do you have an ETA for forensics?" Zack asked Watt.

"They've been called twice and should be arriving any minute."

"The sooner the better. We're not going to have much time with this one and I don't want any evidence com- promised by the weather, curious cops, or reporters."

"Understood."

Zack glanced at the shelter. "Also, make sure Ms. Dillon and Ms. O'Neil don't leave the shelter unless I know about it. I want to talk to them both."

"Sure."

Ms. O'Neil. Lindsay.

Zack had not seen his wife since the meeting at the lawyer's office almost a year ago when she'd served him with divorce papers. She had let the attorney do her talk- ing and had refused to acknowledge him, because he had been drinking.

Hell, who was he kidding? He'd been drunk. *Shit.*

Zack had worked undercover narcotics for three years before he met Lindsay. Drugs had been a part of that world. He'd been careful to stay clear of the drugs, knowing he got tested by the department regularly. But he had started drinking more heavily during that time. Ego had had him believing he could handle the booze. He'd been wrong.

When he'd met Lindsay, he'd cut way back on his drinking. But then he'd started working more undercover assignments. The stress of hiding his private life from the drug world grew along with the cravings for booze. Soon he was chasing beers with shots of bourbon.

Lindsay had figured out what was happening very quickly. She had begged him to stop drinking and to consider AA meetings. He'd assured her he didn't have a problem. He'd seen the hope in her eyes. She'd wanted to believe him but when he hadn't quit, she'd tossed him out. He'd felt betrayed, furious, and he'd done the dumbest thing he could have. He'd slept with another woman. Lindsay had found out and there'd been no going back after that.

That day in the lawyer's office, he'd been royally pissed because she'd not returned any of his phone calls. He'd said terrible things to Lindsay, hoping to wound her the way her throwing him out had hurt him. His words had found their mark. Unshed tears had glistened in her eyes when she'd fled the attorney's office.

Zack would like to have said he'd joined AA right after that meeting. But he hadn't. He'd stayed drunk another month before his brother, Malcolm, had threatened to expose his drinking to the department if he didn't get sober. Zack had agreed. With the help of his family, he had sobered up.

After he'd been sober sixty days, he'd known he'd have to leave narcotics. So he'd parlayed his arrest record and gotten a transfer out of narcotics to homicide. He'd been in the new job eight months.

Zack had wanted to call Lindsay after he'd gotten sober and apologize for all the crap he'd put her through. But he'd been afraid she'd reject him and he didn't fully trust his sobriety those first few weeks. Days turned into weeks. Weeks into months. He got stronger, more in control of the cravings that would never really leave him. But now, nearly a year had passed since that day in the lawyer's office, and here they were: married strangers.

He wasn't sure what he expected when he saw Lindsay, but he did know that their first meeting wouldn't be easy under the best of circumstances—nothing with his wife had ever been uncomplicated. Intruding into his crime scene was classic Lindsay.

What he hadn't anticipated was her pale skin and the veil of bravado that was as thin as her frame.

This past year had been hard on her too.

Zack's head throbbed. He shoved out a breath and buried the remorse. He had a job to do.

The snap of rubber gloves had Zack turning toward the forensics tech, Sara Martin. Tall, slim, and in her early thirties, she wore her long auburn hair in a tight ponytail at the base of her neck. She'd slid crisp blue coveralls over her clothes and booties over her shoes. In the three years he'd known her she was always immaculate, always contained no matter what the situation.

"Sorry it took me so long." Sara's sweet perfume drifted above the blood's pungent rusty smell. "When my beeper went off I was still in the shower. So what do we have?"

"Harold Turner."

She didn't look surprised. "It's a wonder he lived this long. Guy had a ton of enemies." A digital camera dan-

gled from her neck and she switched it on, then started
to snap pictures. "Jesus, his left hand is gone."

"Yeah."

"What can you tell me about the murder?" Sara said.

"I just got here myself. But from the looks of it, Harold
was shot point-blank in the chest and his left hand severed. In which order, I don't know yet. The medical examiner should be able to tell me."

Sara nodded, lowered the camera. "Blood-splatter patterns suggest he was shot where he fell. The bullet to the
chest would have been enough to kill him."

She squatted and studied the body. "There seem to be
no bruises, no scratches, and no signs of trauma. And
there'd be signs of all that if the killer tried to take the
hand first."

"Harold was a street-savvy guy and didn't trust easily.
But it looks like he came of his own free will with the
killer. His car isn't parked on the street."

That caught her off guard. "He rode here with his
killer?"

"I think so. But that only narrows the search to about
a million people," Zack said.

"What would make him get into the car with a killer?"

"Look at his left arm."

She frowned. "Track marks. You think he came for
drugs?"

Zack understood the power of addiction. "Wouldn't
surprise me."

She snapped more pictures. "With all the blood it will
be a miracle if the killer didn't get any on his feet. I'll
search for footprints." Sara glanced up at the sky and
frowned before she lowered her lens back to Harold's
wrist. "Any sign of the hand?"

"Not yet. I've got officers walking the backyard searching for it."

"Why take the hand? Some kind of trophy?"

"Maybe."

She glanced around at the houses. "I'm guessing a silencer was used. Gunshot residue will tell me if the killer was close."

"Work fast. I don't think the weather is going to hold."

Sara nodded. "Morning news says late morning thunderstorms coming out of the west."

Not good. A scene like this could take days to process and it appeared that they might only have hours.

"I'll leave you to your work. Thanks." Zack stepped back, aware that tension had settled in his lower-back muscles. He wanted a beer but that was out of the question. He'd have to settle for a long run along the river.

"Hey, Zack."

"Yeah?"

Sara flipped her bangs out of her eyes, which were bright with anticipation. "I'm having a party this weekend to celebrate my promotion. Care to come?"

Over the last couple of months Sara had asked him out a few times. He'd made the mistake of sleeping with her a year ago. Since then, he had made a point of keeping their relationship professional and sidestepping all of her invitations. He couldn't explain why but he felt he owed fidelity to Lindsay until the divorce papers were signed. "Thanks, Sara, but I don't think I'll make it."

She didn't hide her disappointment. "You sure you can't come? Everyone at headquarters is going to be there. The party should be a real crush."

"Sorry. I'm going to have to pass, Sara." He offered a wan smile and took a step back.

Sara nodded thoughtfully and let her gaze drift from him to the shelter. "When you see Lindsay, tell her I said hello."

Chapter Four

Lindsay leaned over the sink in the shelter's kitchen, staring out the window toward the crime scene. Zack had expanded the crime scene to include the entire backyard. No doubt, he'd seal it for days, months. If anything, he was thorough.

Any hopes she'd had of preserving the shelter's anonymity had vanished when she'd spoken to Zack. He wasn't going to cut one corner on this investigation. She'd asked Ruby to call around to other shelters to find beds for her six residents.

Lindsay watched as the forensics technician brushed her bangs off her forehead as she stared up at Zack. The tech leaned toward him a fraction, her smile subtle but flirty. One hundred dollars said the chick was wearing perfume.

A familiar knot burned in the pit of her stomach. Was she the one Zack had slept with the night she'd thrown him out of their apartment? Painful memories compressed her heart. She turned from the window. It took a moment before she could breathe deeply.

Lindsay's fingers tightened into fists. "I don't care who he sleeps with now."

Ringing phones startled her from her mood. All at once three lines lit up on the phone on the kitchen wall.

Lindsay slid open the pocket door that separated the kitchen from the conference room. Ruby sat at a small desk, the phone cradled under her ear. She mouthed "line two."

"Got it." Lindsay picked up the line in the kitchen. "Sanctuary Women's Shelter."

"Lindsay?"

It was Dr. Sam Begley, chief resident in emergency medicine at Mercy Hospital. Immediately, the pressure in her shoulders relaxed. Sam and Lindsay had met six months ago when she'd given a seminar on domestic violence to the hospital staff.

"Sam, what can I do for you?" She leaned against the sink, her back to the murder scene.

"You might want to come down here," he said in a sober tone. "I've got a woman in cubical six who's been badly beaten. Her story has changed a couple of times. I think the abuse is domestic."

A protective urge welled inside her. "How bad are her injuries?"

"Cracked ribs. Bruised arms. Sprained wrist."

She rubbed her temples with her fingertips. A headache was starting to pound behind her eyes. "Did she say who did it?"

"No, but she exhibits all the signs you outlined. No bruises on her face. Whoever did this didn't want anyone to know she'd been slapped around."

"Did she say anything about what happened?"

"She said she fell down some stairs. I was hoping the shelter had a bed available."

Lindsay turned toward the window facing the cops

crowding her backyard. "I don't think we'll have a bed for a few days. But I could talk to her, try to get her in another place if she'll take it."

He sighed into the phone. "Good. She needs someone to talk sense into her."

"You sound tired. Did you pull another eighteen-hour shift?"

He chuckled. "No rest for the wicked."

Lindsay admired Sam. He was one of the hardest-working people she knew. She checked her watch. Better to stay, deal with Zack, and be done with him. "I'm stuck here at the shelter for another hour or so. Can you hold on to her?"

"She's over eighteen and can walk out of here any time she wants." He dropped his voice a notch. "But you know how slow the paperwork moves around this place. It could easily take a couple of hours before she's discharged."

Lindsay couldn't help but smile. Sam made life easy. "I'll be by as soon as I can."

"Good."

"You're one of the good guys, Dr. Sam Begley." She imagined his face turning red.

"You're the one who does the real work." He hesitated. "I had fun at the movies last week. We should do it again sometime soon."

"Sounds good." She hadn't really thought of their outing as anything more than a friendly trip to the movies until Sam had kissed her. The awkward moment underscored the fact that she'd not been out with another man since she'd left Zack.

"How about tonight?" he said quickly. "I'll buy you a slice of birthday cake."

Her birthday was in two days. She'd almost forgotten. Leave it to Sam to remember.

"I'm going to be working late tonight." She was grateful

to have a real excuse. "Rain check? Maybe next week? And make the cake carrot."

He laughed. "Consider it done."

She glanced at her phone console, noticing two other lines blinking. "Hey, look, I've got other calls. Lots of stuff going on here today."

"Everything all right?"

"It's a long story. I'll tell you when I see you."

"No problem. See you in about an hour."

"Thanks." Lindsay hung up and caught Ruby's gaze.

Ruby cupped her hand over the receiver. "Line three. Dana Miller."

Lindsay's stomach knotted with tension. "Thanks."

Dana, the shelter's board chairman, was essentially Lindsay's boss. Had Dana already heard about the murder or was the call about the missed teleconference? Neither topic boded well.

She punched line three. "Hello, Dana."

"What's going on over there? First you miss our phone meeting and then the director at Riverside Shelter calls and tells me Ruby requested bed space for some of your residents."

Lindsay sighed. No beating around the bush with Dana. "A body was found behind the shelter."

"What!"

"It wasn't one of our residents," she rushed to say.

"Who the hell was it?"

"I don't know. The police aren't telling me much right now."

"Damn it, Lindsay. This is not good."

Lindsay pictured Dana sitting in her high-rise office wearing her trademark red Brooks Brothers suit. On her desk there'd be a half-full cup of coffee and a cigarette burning in a crystal ashtray. Dana had made millions in real estate and had built a reputation as a hard-driving ball buster who distained sloppy emotions. Lindsay never could figure why she'd decided to champion battered women or Sanctuary.

"I know the victim is a man, and as soon as I know anything else I'll call you," Lindsay said.

"Do you know how the guy died?"

"No."

Dana exhaled. "We don't need bad press, Lindsay. Not after what happened before with that other woman."

"Her name was Pam Rogers." Dana may have forgotten the woman's name but Lindsay never would.

Dana blew out a lungful of smoke into the receiver. "Handle this, Lindsay. I don't want to defend the shelter again to the media. It's not good for me or you."

Handle this. "Consider it done."

The line went dead.

Ruby poked her head into the kitchen, clearly having overheard the conversation. "Sorry about that. I wanted to call Riverside first thing. If we can get Aisha Greenland and her boys transferred there, the boys won't have to switch schools."

"The children's well-being comes before politics. You did the right thing. Did they get bed space?"

"Yes. I've also put a call in to Michelle Franklin over at Hayden House." The shelter was in the east end of the county. "They've got two beds."

"We've got six people here now." Lindsay mentally went through the list of residents. "Greenlands to Riverside. Tracy and Cindy to Hayden House. Call the Y and see if they have a bed for Barbara."

"I'll take care of it."

"I'll contact the women at work and tell them what's happening. The last thing they need is to hear about this on the news."

Ruby shook her head. "What a mess."

"Yeah."

Lindsay called each of the women, did her best to down-play the situation, and promised to transfer their goods to the new shelters so they wouldn't have to return to Sanctu-ary. Ruby would pick the Greenland boys up at school and take them directly to Riverside.

By the time she hung up the phone, Lindsay's head was really pounding. She needed caffeine.

At the kitchen sink, she rinsed out stale coffee from the coffeemaker carafe, refilled it with tap water, and dumped it in the machine's reservoir. She tossed out the old grounds, scooped fresh into the metal filter, and switched the machine on.

A flicker of movement caught her eye. She turned in time to see Zack step through the front door, a cell phone cradled under his chin. He'd loosened his tie. Thick stubble covered his chin, as if he'd been up all night. His gun rested on his narrow hip.

He spoke into his cell. "Ayden, you and Warwick need to see this. Yeah, well, tell him his vacation is over."

The deep timber of Zack's voice swirled around Lind-say, raking over her frayed nerves. Just having him close made her nervous.

Zack had a strong profile and Lindsay found herself liking his hair short. It suited him. Unexpected desire flickered to life. A part of her still wanted Zack. Probably always would. Damn. Her fickle libido was the last thing she needed to deal with right now.

"I need to talk to the shelter director first," he added.

She turned back to the hissing coffeepot, in a sudden rush to have something to do. She pulled the half-full carafe out. Hot coffee dripped down on the machine's burner as she quickly poured a cup, then replaced the pot. Coffee spilled over the edge of the burner.

She grabbed a handful of paper towels and started to mop up the mess. "Damn."

Footsteps sounded behind her. "Patience never was your specialty," Zack said.

Lindsay ignored the greater meaning behind his words and swallowed a tart retort. "No, I guess not." *Be nice,* she thought. Turning, she held up a mug. "You want a cup?"

"That would be great."

She filled a Styrofoam cup with black coffee and handed it to him. He thanked her. The forced civility didn't fit them. Their relationship had never been luke-warm. When they fought, laughed, or made love the intensity could have shaken the rafters. And she'd been proud of that. She'd never figured that that same intensity would also rip them apart.

Lindsay nodded toward her office door. "We can talk in my office."

Tension snapping at her, she headed past him, down the center hallway to her office. Her office, like every other room in the shelter, served many purposes. The public health nurse used her desk when she visited, residents used the space for private meetings, and donations were usually left there before they were sorted.

Stacks of papers covered her desk but she could, at any given moment, find anything she needed.

Lindsay removed a donated clothes bag from a chair and set it behind her desk. She motioned for Zack to sit as she took her chair behind the desk. Here she felt safe.

Zack took a seat and flipped open his notebook. "Are you going to tell me who was murdered?"

In no rush, Zack sipped his coffee and then set it on the edge of her desk before settling his gaze on her. "You had any trouble here at the shelter lately?"

That was so Zack to answer a question with a question.

"Not lately. You know about Pam Rogers, the woman who revealed the shelter location to her husband. He picked her up and later he killed her."

"Nine months ago, right before I joined homicide. I read the file."

"Since then, we've had no trouble."

"No threatening phone calls? No messages in the mail?"

"No, nothing out of the ordinary." She sipped her coffee. It tasted bitter. "So who was murdered?"

He watched her face closely. "Harold Turner."

Stunned, Lindsay dropped open her mouth. "The attorney?"

"That's right. You know him?" He stared at her, gauging her reaction.

Yeah, she knew Harold. He liked to slap his wife around, a fact few knew. Lindsay had found out about the abuse when Jordan had cornered her in the ladies' room at the Race for the Cure fund-raiser two weeks ago. Jordan had told Lindsay everything: Harold's drug use, the beatings, and the verbal abuse. Lindsay had comforted Jordan and begged her to come to Sanctuary. But Jordan Turner had refused. She had admitted that she enjoyed Harold's wealth far too much to abandon it. She had wiped her tears away, fixed her makeup, and assured Lindsay she could handle Harold. She'd called her tears a momentary lapse and then downplayed the entire incident.

Lindsay had likened Jordan's emotional outburst to a leak in a dam. Eventually, the water would widen the dam wall, erode the foundation, and rush out with devastating force.

My God, had Jordan shot Harold? Had she lured her husband to the shelter and killed him as some kind of message to Lindsay? *I can handle Harold.*

If convicted, Jordan could spend the next thirty years in jail for ridding the earth of human slime. The need to protect Jordan overrode Lindsay's responsibility to tell Zack what she knew.

"Sure, who doesn't know Harold? He's in all the news-papers. He's defending some drug dealer."

"Have you ever met him in person?"

"Sure. We crossed paths at different fund-raisers. Two weeks ago, as a matter of fact, at the Race for the Cure gala at the Virginia Museum."

Blue eyes narrowed. "That's it? You've never spoken to him any other time?"

She didn't look away. "Nope."

His gaze held hers as if he were waiting for her to say more. When she didn't, he frowned. "You're not telling me everything."

Uncomfortable, she leaned forward. "Are you some kind of psychic?"

"I know you."

She noticed his ring finger. The absence of a wedding band wasn't a surprise. Because of his undercover work, he'd rarely worn it when they were married. "You *knew* me, Zack."

His face hardened. "I know when you're holding back information, Lindsay."

She stiffened. "As I remember, you were good at hiding things."

His jaw clenched slightly, but otherwise he looked un-affected by her comment. "Lindsay, I'm here to investi-gate a murder, not rehash our marriage. We'll save that gem for another day. Right now, I want to know if Harold Turner had a connection to the shelter."

"You're right. Harping on ancient history is foolish." She shifted in her seat. "He's never been here before, if that's what you're asking."

"I'm going to need to see your files."

She had started a file on Jordan. Only a few notes, but

it was enough to prove a connection. She wasn't going to make it easy for Zack to arrest Jordan. "My files are confidential. If you want to know what's in them, you're going to have to get a court order."

"Consider it done." He studied her with more intensity. "Why not just tell me all that you know?"

"You know why. The women who come through my doors or who talk to me are frightened, battered, and often humiliated. Some go on to better lives. Some go back to their husbands. Either way, they know I'll guard their privacy. They count on me. I can't betray their trust unless the court orders me to."

"Did Jordan Turner ever visit the shelter?"

"No."

"You ever meet her?"

She folded her hands in front of her. "She was at the fund-raiser two weeks ago. We spoke briefly." She sipped her coffee. "How was Harold killed?"

"Not ready to release that yet."

"Harold had a lot of enemies. He'd sell anyone out for a buck."

"Then why was he murdered behind the shelter?"

"I don't know."

"Any of your residents have a drug problem?"

"No. We test all who want to stay here. They're clean."

Always one to play his cards close to his vest, Zack simply nodded. "I think his body was positioned behind the shelter for a reason."

Jordan. "Just because Turner's body was found behind the shelter doesn't mean his death had anything to do with me."

"I've never put much stock in coincidence." He ran his hand down his tie as he leaned back in his chair. "Where were you last night and this morning?"

His proprietary tone rankled her nerves. He didn't

have any rights to her time now. "I was home asleep. And I overslept this morning."

He lifted an eyebrow, amused. "As I remember it, you rose at five every morning come hell or high water."

"A power outage knocked out all of electricity in my row of town houses. My alarm didn't go off."

"I also never remember you sleeping through the night."

"I did last night."

"Can you prove you were home last night?"

He didn't trust her and that hurt more than it should. "Do I have to?"

"It would be nice."

Very few knew Lindsay had taken on Nicole Piper as a roommate. Her former college roommate had shown up two weeks ago on Lindsay's doorstep begging for a place to stay. Nicole had left her abusive husband and was hiding from him. Lindsay had taken her in without question. If Zack knew she had a roommate, he'd start checking into Nicole's past. And that could tip off Nicole's husband as to her whereabouts.

"Sorry, I can't prove anything. I was home alone. You'll just have to take my word for it."

He studied her and then deliberately glanced around the office. "How many women does the shelter serve each year?"

She rolled with the change of topic. "We saw about a hundred women last year."

"Impressive." He scratched a few words in his notebook.

"Sadly, business is booming."

He nodded thoughtfully as if remembering that afternoon in Byrd Park when she'd confided her own horrific past to him. She'd told him of her mother's murder, of her father's suicide, and of her running away. He, better than anyone, understood her drive to protect the women and children under her care.

"I want a list of everyone who was here last night," Zack said. "I want to see records of all the women who've been through the doors since you opened."

"Only when the warrant arrives."

He looked annoyed. "You always have to be so stubborn."

With an effort, Lindsay kept her tone light. "It's what I do best."

His lips flattened as he rose. "Thanks for the coffee."

She stood. "Always happy to help."

At five ten, she stood eye to eye with most men. Zack had a good six inches on her. "Is it all right if I leave the shelter? I received a call from Mercy Hospital to counsel a battered woman. The doctor is trying to delay her, but he won't be able to hold her more than an hour, which leaves me about twenty minutes."

He seemed to gauge the truth of her words. "Keep your cell phone on this time. I want to be able to reach you easily."

"It's always on."

"Not this morning."

He had tried to call.

"As I said, there was a power outage in my town house complex. I'm sure you can verify it with maintenance. And I put my phone in the charger as soon as I arrived here."

Zack studied Lindsay again as if trying to pry into her brain.

Lindsay folded her arms over her chest, matching his glare.

"I'll be back this afternoon or tomorrow at the latest with the warrant."

Thanks to Harold's murder, she would have to deal with all the agonizing baggage she shared with Zack and had done her best to ignore this past year. "I can't wait."

Chapter Five

On the way to the hospital, Lindsay called Jordan Turner twice. The first time she got her voice mail. She didn't bother to leave a message. What was she going to say? Mrs. Turner, did you murder your husband?

Thanks to light midday traffic, Lindsay made good time driving downtown. Still, the Mercy Hospital parking deck was crammed with cars, forcing her to drive to the bottom level, where she found an open spot in a darkened corner.

She shut off the car engine, waited until it shuttered off, got out, and locked the car. Her sandals clicked against concrete as she moved along the line of parked cars. A horn honked, the sound echoing from the level above. A car door closed.

She'd parked on this deck a thousand times before, always cautious but never afraid. However, today, the hairs on the back of her neck prickled. She scanned the rows of parked cars around her. The air-conditioning system whirred overhead and condensation dripped from the ductwork.

The deck appeared deserted. On a deck below, a car horn honked again. There was no need to be nervous yet her nerves tightened, as if someone were close.

Watching.

She tightened her hold on her purse. "Is anyone there?"

No answer.

It wasn't like her to be so jumpy. Crossing quickly to the elevator, she punched the button, careful to keep her back to the doors. She dug in her purse fishing for her mace and cursed when she couldn't find it in all the clutter. When the elevator doors whooshed open, she rushed into the empty car. Her heart pounded in her chest.

As the doors closed, a nearby car door slammed shut, the sound echoing from an unseen corner.

Lindsay punched level four, the lobby level. She dragged a shaking hand through her hair. "Get a grip."

Within seconds the elevator doors opened to the muted sounds of gurneys rolling past, carts clattering, and telephones ringing. The smell of antiseptic cleaner blended with the bright hospital lights. Her nerves settled and the parking garage was forgotten.

She walked up to the nurses station and smiled at the familiar face behind the counter. "Hey, Jennifer."

Jennifer Watkins glanced up from a chart and grinned. Red hair scraped back in a tight bun accentuated green eyes that sparked behind wire-rimmed glasses. "What's shaking, Lindsay?"

"I missed you at yoga on Friday night." She didn't want to talk about the murder. It would be headlines soon enough.

"I know. I'm sorry I missed your class. It had been a long day and I was beat."

Lindsay taught yoga at a small studio near her town

house. She'd gained a reputation as a patient but exacting instructor. "You'll be better for it if you make the time."

"I know, I know. If anyone needs yoga, baby, it's me. I'm about as flexible as a piece of plywood."

Lindsay smiled. "You carry too much stress in your shoulders, but if you keep at it, your body will open."

Jennifer held up her hands in mock surrender. "Okay, okay, I promise to be there Wednesday night."

"Good. Hey, I'm here to see Sam."

"He's just finishing up rounds. He should be passing by in just a second."

"Great."

Jennifer leaned forward. "I hear you and Sam had a date last week."

Color rose in Lindsay's face. Jennifer knew everyone and their business. Hospital staff jokingly called her "Jenni-dot-net." "I wouldn't call it a date at all." The idea that Jennifer and likely now everyone else was calling her evening with Sam a date didn't sit well.

Jennifer wagged thin eyebrows. "What would you call it?"

Lindsay shoved fingers through her hair. "A friendly night out."

"Friendly?" A smile twitched the edges of Jennifer's full lips, made her eyes spark. "I've seen the way Sam looks at you."

Since Lindsay was a child, she'd been careful to keep her private life private. Her home life shamed her and she didn't want anyone to know about it. But the days of hiding a violent home life had long passed and there was no need to keep secrets. Yet the habit of hiding persisted.

Her evening out with Sam wasn't shameful or dark, just fun, and it had been exactly as she'd described it—

friendly. "Movies. Dinner at a burger joint. Home by nine. Very pleasant."

Jennifer looked disappointed. "That can't be it."

"It is."

"Ah, come on, there must be more details," Jennifer said.

"Nope. Sorry."

Sam's voice drifted down the hallway as he gave orders to a nurse.

Lindsay sighed her relief.

Jennifer laughed. "The cavalry has arrived."

"See you around. I've got to run." Lindsay tossed Jennifer a grin and hurried down the hallway toward Sam.

Sam stood in front of a curtained cubicle wearing his green scrubs, a patient's chart in hand. An inch taller than her, Sam was trim but not muscular. He looked like a tennis player who belonged at a country club. Blond hair curled at the edges above his ears. Horn-rimmed glasses accentuated intelligent brown eyes.

"Sam."

He peered over his glasses and smiled warmly as he closed the chart. "I was beginning to think you'd forgotten me."

Her smile came easily. "Sorry, we had some trouble at the shelter."

Worry creased his forehead. "What?"

She lowered her voice and leaned close to him. "This is not for anyone else to hear right now, but Harold Turner's body was found in the shelter's alley this morning."

"What?!" His voice raised in shock.

Lindsay glanced around and noticed several nurses staring at them. "I don't have many more details than that. The cops were at the shelter this morning interviewing me. In fact, they'll be there for days."

"No one else was hurt?"

"We're all fine."

He let out a long breath. "Damn. Harold Turner. His wife came through here two months ago with a sprained arm and bruised ribs."

"I know. She cornered me at a charity party two weeks ago and told me about her marriage. I offered her a bed at Sanctuary but she refused."

Sam shook his head. "Sanctuary is a big step down from a mansion on River Road."

"Yeah." *I can handle Harold.* Jordan's words replayed in Lindsay's head. "I can't imagine her sleeping in a bunk bed or sharing kitchen duties."

"I'd say your morning ranks high on the stress meter."

"You've no idea."

Sam laid his hand on her shoulder. "You look like hell."

Lindsay couldn't help but smile as she leaned into him. "You know how to make a girl feel good."

He grinned. "It's a talent."

She rubbed the back of her neck.

Sam studied her closely. "What gives with your neck?"

"I fell asleep on my couch last night. I must have slept crooked."

Sam captured her elbow in his hand. "Exam room three is open."

"I don't need to be checked out. And I need to see that woman you called me about."

"You've got a minute or two to spare."

Aware Jennifer hadn't missed a second of their exchange, she hesitated. "Sam, we are quickly becoming grist for the rumor mill."

He didn't look worried. "Since when do you care what people think?"

She glanced at the nurses. Their eyes gleamed with laughter. "Let's just say I've been gossiped about enough in my life. I don't like it."

"It's harmless." He pushed her toward the exam room and nodded toward the table. "Sit."

She stood stock straight. "I just need to talk to that woman and get back to the office. I've got cops crawling all over the shelter."

"For a moment, take the advice you give your yoga students and the women you counsel. Sit. Take a deep breath."

He was right. She'd been running on adrenaline since she'd been startled awake. She climbed up on the table as he closed the curtains behind them.

He moved behind her and began to massage the muscles around her neck. "My God, you're tense. It's a wonder you haven't collapsed yet. Your schedule is more insane than an intern's."

"I'm fine." His gentle touch soothed but didn't excite, like Zack's, which was a good thing. Excitement was overrated.

"So you're the doctor now?"

"I know my own body." She took several deep breaths.

His fingers worked up the back of her neck. God, it felt good. She closed her eyes. She could let her defenses down, if only for just a moment. "I'm so tired of holding it together all the time."

"You want to talk about it?" He leaned a little closer. His breath felt warm on her cheek. "I've been told I'm easy to talk to."

"Maybe another time."

Sam's fingers stilled and she feared this would turn into a tug-of-war. When she'd first met Zack, he hadn't been content until he'd known everything about her present and past. To her surprise, Sam leaned forward and kissed her lightly on the side of her neck. "Have dinner with me tonight."

Awkwardness replaced worry. Nearly thirty and she still turned knock-kneed when a man got romantic. "Uh, Sam, we've been through this. I'll be working late tonight."

"So we'll have breakfast at the diner. We'll grab coffee." When she hesitated, he added, "It wouldn't kill you to live a little."

Something she'd done very little of since she and Zack had separated. "I suppose not."

"That's a yes?"

She nodded. "Yes to dinner *tomorrow* night."

"What time?"

"Six."

"Done. I'll pick you up at the shelter."

"Better make that my town house. The cops sealed the area off."

"Will do."

Sam's cell phone vibrated on his hip. Groaning, he yanked it off and flipped it open. "Dr. Begley."

Immediately, his light expression darkened. He glanced at Lindsay and cupped his hand over the phone. "I've got to take this, Lindsay. See you tomorrow night?"

"Right." Lindsay slid off the table, thankful for the interruption.

He managed a strained smile.

"Where is that woman you told me about?" she whispered.

"Number six." Already he was turning from her.

"Thanks." She scooted around the curtain.

"Yes, damn it, I'm still here." Sam's angry whisper caught her attention and made her stop.

In the few months she'd known Sam, he'd never uttered a harsh word. He seemed to be the nicest guy on the planet.

"I told you I'd do it and I will," Sam said. "I've got to go."

Lindsay hurried down the hallway toward room six, surprised that there was something more to Dr. Sam Begley than just his quick smile and great bedside manner.

Chapter Six

Monday, July 7, 11:45 A.M.

Lindsay checked the name on the chart. She scanned Sam's notes. Cracked ribs. Contusions on the arms. A sprained right wrist. The injuries were classic. Her stomach knotted. She closed the chart and shoved aside the curtain to cubical six.

She found a petite woman sitting on the exam table wearing neatly pressed jeans, tennis shoes with double-knotted laces, and a white long-sleeved shirt. Small manicured fingers were clenched into tight fists.

Over the years, Lindsay had seen hundreds of battered women like this, but the sight always enraged her. Careful to keep her face neutral, she managed a smile. "Gail Saunders?"

The woman's tired gaze held a hint of anger. "Yes. Do you have my discharge papers?"

Irritation was a good sign. It meant spirit. She hadn't given up.

Lindsay closed the curtain behind her. "No, I'm not with the hospital. Dr. Begley asked me to talk to you for a few minutes."

Understanding dawned in Gail's gray eyes. "You're a social worker, aren't you?"

Lindsay dug a Sanctuary business card out of her purse and handed it to Gail. "My name is Lindsay O'Neil. I'm the director of a women's shelter."

Gail snatched the card, studied it. "Sanctuary. A haven for battered women." She tossed the card on the floor. "I don't need this."

Lindsay picked it up and laid it beside Gail. "That's right. We shelter women who've been abused. The number on the card is the hotline." She pulled out a pen and wrote her cell number on the back. "You can always reach me at this other number, day or night."

Gail slid off the exam table, wincing when her feet hit the ground. "I'm not abused. I told that stupid doctor that I fell down the stairs. What's the big deal?"

"He was concerned."

Her lips flattened as if she were barely holding on to her control. "Well, I'm fine."

Lindsay remained by the curtain so Gail wouldn't feel crowded. If she didn't tread carefully, the woman would bolt. "There are old bruises on your neck and they look like they were made by fingers."

Color flooded Gail's face. "I hit my neck on the banister as I fell down the stairs."

"Why the long sleeves and pants in July?"

"I'm cold natured."

Lindsay's voice remained soft and calm, but sadness and anger welled inside her. "Gail, I think you've been bullied enough already. So I'm not going to debate the issue with you. Experience has taught me that victims can be excellent liars."

Gail bristled. "I'm not a liar. My husband is a good man. He loves me. He works hard and would never hurt me on purpose."

"But he did hurt you," Lindsay said quietly.

Gail crushed the card in her hand. "I didn't say that!"

"Honey, the bruises did."

Tears welled in Gail's eyes, and for a moment Lindsay thought she would open up. She looked so small, so beaten down by life. Instead, the woman straightened her shoulders and grabbed her purse off the exam table. "I don't have to listen to this."

Lindsay pressed her card deeper into Gail's hand. "No, you don't. Just know you can reach me twenty-four/seven."

A tear rolled down Gail's face and she angrily brushed it away. She moved toward the curtain and shoved it open. "I won't be calling."

"I hope you do." She laid her hand on Gail's shoulder. "If things do get bad, remember to run to a room with soft furniture. Stay away from the kitchen and the bathrooms. They can be dangerous."

Gail hesitated, then left the room.

Lindsay listened to Gail's footsteps meld into the confusion of the hospital. For a moment her knees felt weak and she had to sit in the metal chair by the exam table. How many times had her mother made excuses for the bruises that had marked her body? How many times had she forgiven her father and stayed when she should have fled?

Like Gail's, her mother's lies were rooted in fear, shame, and the desperate hope that the abuse would really stop. But it never did.

What Lindsay hadn't understood was why everyone had accepted her mother's lies over and over again. No one had stepped in and no one had cared. And her mother had paid with her own life.

Jennifer appeared, her expression grim and angry. "Room number six looked pissed when she stormed past."

Lindsay straightened her shoulders, clinging to the hope that kept her going. "Yeah, but she kept my card. I see that as a hopeful good sign."

Jennifer frowned. "Is she going home?"

"That would be my guess. It's human nature to return to places we know best."

"But she's not safe there!"

Lindsay clung to the bright side. "I have to have faith that she'll survive until she finds the courage to call me or someone else for help."

"Damn it! That just doesn't seem good enough. Isn't there anything we can do?"

"Don't underestimate a victim. They know how to survive. They've learned how to walk on eggshells."

"This really sucks, Lindsay."

"Jen, I've been down this road too many times. Just pray that she finds the courage to leave. Or better—that bastard husband of hers drops dead."

The humidity and temperature had risen the heat to an almost unbearable level. Black thunderclouds thickened in the western skies.

Zack and several of the uniforms, including a canine unit, had combed every inch of the shelter's backyard and the surrounding yards for Turner's hand, the murder weapon, or anything that might connect to the murder. They'd found nothing.

Sara had photographed the crime scene from every angle and sketched it. She and her assistant had collected hair and fiber samples from the corpse and then given the go-ahead for the body removal company to take Turner to the medical examiner's office.

Zack and Sara had watched as officers had lifted the dead man into the body bag. After zipping the bag closed, Sara had sealed the zipper with a plastic tie. The seal wouldn't be broken until the corpse arrived downtown at the state medical examiner's office on Jackson Street.

The attendants now placed the body bag on the gurney as Sara glanced at the dark sky. "I'm going to keep working the scene until the weather forces me out."

"Good. You don't have much time." Zack followed the gurney around the side of the house to the hearse waiting in the driveway.

A dozen neighbors, most of them retirees and stay-at-home moms pushing strollers, had gathered near the front yard, which he'd also taped off. Three television news trucks were now parked in the street with reporters lingering close by. Soon the rain would drive them all back inside their homes and vans, but for now he had to contend with an audience.

Zack eyed the crowd, paying close attention to the people's expressions. Killers sometimes returned to the scene to witness the chaos created by their handiwork.

As the body was wheeled through the privacy fence gate, everyone's gaze shifted toward it. Film cameras started taping and following the body. Even some neighbors snapped photos. By this evening, the area would be crawling with curiosity seekers.

Zack had spoken to the police department's public relations officer and told him to ask the press to keep the address and location of Sanctuary a secret. For now, the reporters had agreed. If he could close this case sooner than later, the press would move on to their next story and Sanctuary would be forgotten.

He wanted to protect the shelter. Not only would it be a shame to lose it as a resource, but the place meant so much to Lindsay. When they'd been together, she'd just received the grant application to purchase the property.

She had been so excited and had spent long days fixing
up the place and transforming it from a run-down rental
property into a place that felt like a real home. A month
after she'd opened the place, they'd separated and he'd
not seen the house since then.

Now, looking at this place, he could see how much
work she'd done. She'd had the exterior repainted and
she'd replanted the yard, which had been a dust bowl
when she'd bought the property. There were traces of
her everywhere. The brightly painted walls inside, the
potted plants on the porch, the manicured lawn, and a
collection of toys in the backyard testified to her commitment.

Too bad she couldn't have invested the same time and
energy into their marriage.

An unmarked Crown Vic pulled up in front of the
house. In the front seat sat Zack's boss, Captain David
Ayden, and Zack's partner, Jacob Warwick.

Annoyed, Zack checked his watch. It had taken Ayden
two hours to track Warwick down. Warwick had been on
the State Police force for thirteen years, before taking a
job with the county's homicide division two years ago.
Ayden had paired Zack with Warwick, believing the two
would make a good team. Professionally, they did just
fine, but personally, they'd not hit it off at all.

Somehow Warwick had found out about Zack's drinking problem and had made it clear he didn't think
drunks stayed sober long. Zack could be a hothead who
had no trouble sharing his thoughts. But this time he
had swallowed his frustration. His drinking had caused
a lot of damage, and he knew actions, not words, were
going to win his partner over. That had been ten months
ago, and so far, he'd not impressed Warwick.

Ayden got out of the car. His muscular build hadn't
softened in the last couple of years even though he

logged more time behind the desk than he would have liked. His thick hair grayed slightly at the temples and deep frown lines marred his forehead. He was a stubborn guy who had seen his late wife through cancer and now was raising two teenage boys on his own. He had little patience and didn't like being jerked around.

Warwick followed Ayden toward the house. He was built like a wide receiver and carried himself like an athlete. But football hadn't been his sport. Boxing was his specialty. As a teenager, he'd been a Golden Gloves fighter before entering the army, where he'd been in the Special Forces.

Today, Warwick was dressed in jeans and a T-shirt, a sign that Ayden had cut his vacation short. Normally Warwick leaned toward sports jackets and khakis. His hair looked in need of a trim, and though he was clean shaven, he'd have a five o'clock shadow by three.

Warwick nodded to Zack but the men didn't shake hands. "Kier."

"Warwick."

"Can you give us a rundown on the murder?" Ayden said.

"Follow me. I'll walk you through what we know right now."

Zack led the two men to the backyard, pulled a notepad from his breast pocket. Sara was by the back fence shooting more pictures. "The body was discovered over by the trash cans. He was shot point-blank in the chest. A wallet found in the victim's pocket identified him as Harold Turner."

A hiss of air escaped Warwick's lips. "Damn. Are you sure it's him?"

"I don't have a print match yet but it's Harold," Zack said.

Ayden rubbed the back of his neck with his hand. "Any ideas on who might have done this?"

"Nothing solid yet," Zack said. "But there are plenty of leads to run down. It could take weeks to talk to everyone."

"Why didn't you hold the body until we arrived?" Warwick said.

Zack resented Warwick's tone but kept his own tone even. "The skies are about to open up and I didn't want to lose trace evidence."

Warwick frowned. "Why didn't you call me earlier?"

"I didn't know what I had until I got here. When I did, I had Ayden track you down."

Ayden rested his hands on his hips. "What else do you know?"

Zack let his gaze scan the yard. "The backyard looks clean so far. Sara is going over it inch by inch."

Warwick studied the pool of blood caked in the dirt by the tree. "You said his wallet was still in his pocket?"

"Yeah, and it still had a couple hundred dollars in cash and a dozen credit cards in it. His briefcase was set neatly beside him and it also appeared untouched."

"What's the pool of blood from?" Warwick said.

"It's from his left hand. The killer severed the hand at the wrist."

"Shit," Ayden said. "Any sign of it?"

"No."

Warwick's eyes narrowed. "Was Turner left-handed?"

"Don't know," Zack said.

"Do you think this is some kind of ritual thing?" Ayden said.

Zack pointed to the trash cans. "The victim's body was positioned near the cans. His tie was straight and his hair looked as if it had been combed. The killer didn't appear in a rush to leave the body."

Warwick rested his hands on his narrow hips. "Like

you said, it'll take weeks to interview everyone who had a beef against Turner."

"My gut tells me that this killing was personal," Zack said.

Ayden shrugged off his coat and loosened his tie. "Turner pissed off a lot of people. But none of them would be likely to stop and fix his tie after they'd shot him."

"No. This murder has a different feel to it," Zack said.

The three were silent for a moment.

"You have anything else?" Warwick said.

"I talked to the shelter staff," Zack said. "Ruby Dillon, an assistant to the director, was on call last night. She didn't see anything until this morning when she found the body." Zack didn't relish what he was about to say. "You might as well hear it from me. The director of Sanctuary is Lindsay O'Neil. She's my wife."

Warwick frowned. "I didn't realize you were married."

"I thought you were divorced," Ayden said.

"Not officially," Zack said.

Warwick's gaze sliced across him. "How long have you two been separated?"

The question reiterated how little the two men knew about each other. "About a year."

"You shouldn't have taken the call," Warwick said.

Zack refused to lock horns with his partner now. It was more important that Ayden keep him on the case. "I want this case, Ayden."

Ayden frowned. "Why?"

Zack couldn't even explain his reasons to himself, let alone his boss. "I just want in on it."

"The last damn thing I need is a conflict-of-interest issue," Ayden said. "A body in the suburbs is going to generate a lot of media coverage. And everyone in the county government is going to be all over this by lunchtime."

"Where was O'Neil last night?" Warwick said.

Zack straightened. "She was home last night."

"Can she prove it?" Ayden said.

"She says she was home alone. No witnesses. She was also late this morning, because a power outage shut off her alarm clock." He knew she hadn't told him everything. There was more going on with her. But still his gut told him she was no killer. One way or another, he'd find out the truth. "There are a lot of people who could have killed Harold."

Warwick exhaled. "You're too close to this case."

Tension rose in Zack's body. He'd had about enough of Warwick's attitude. "Are you questioning my judgment?"

Warwick met his gaze. There was no hint of apology. "Yes."

Ayden raised his hand. His expression allowed for no argument. "Jesus, you two sound like my boys. Cut this crap out." He tightened his jaw and released it. "Fight later. Solve this case now. Turner may have been slime, but he got himself killed in a nice suburban neighborhood. The public is not going to be happy. If you two can't work this case, I'll get Vega and Ricker to handle it."

Zack didn't want to get pulled from the case. "We'll be fine."

Warwick nodded in agreement. This was a case he didn't want to lose either. "We've got it under control, sir."

"You'd better," Ayden warned. "Because if I get even a whiff that you two aren't working well together, you're off this case." Ayden ducked under the tape. "Keep me posted." Without a good-bye to either officer, he disappeared around the side of the house.

"As long as you stay sober, I'll be fine," Warwick said.

"Don't be an ass."

Warwick shrugged and crossed the yard. He crouched in front of the bloodstain and studied it. "Word is Ronnie

T. and Turner fought after court yesterday. I heard Turner presented a plea deal to him. The deal required that he do five years in the state penitentiary."

Zack shifted his gaze to his partner with a measure of respect. "How'd you hear that?"

"I box with guys in the Justice Department. We talk. Harold and Ronnie T.'s argument caused quite a stir yesterday."

"What was said?"

Warwick pulled off his sunglasses and leaned closer to the stain. "Ronnie T. apparently was paying Harold big bucks in exchange for a promise that he wouldn't have to do jail time. Ronnie T. thinks of himself as a family man. He wants to see his three kids grow up."

"The son of a bitch got his start selling drugs to kids and he's worried about being away from his own. Priceless."

A fat rain droplet fell and hit Zack on the shoulder. "Damn." He glared at the sky and then at Sara. She nodded and picked up her pace. "This doesn't look like Ronnie T.'s work."

"I agree. A drive-by is more his style, but he's got to be checked out." Warwick rose. "Do you have Turner's home address?"

Harold's wife was at the top of Zack's list. "Yes. His home is about twenty minutes from here."

More rain droplets started to cut through the leaves above and hit the ground around their feet. "Let's go talk to Mrs. Turner and then we'll have a chat with Ronnie T."

Chapter Seven

Monday, July 7, 12:02 P.M.

Zack took off his suit jacket as he and Warwick moved toward Zack's Impala. Several reporters and cameramen rushed toward them but neither paused before getting into the car. Zack fired up the engine and wove through the neighborhood and out onto the main road that fed into the interstate. He gunned the engine and pulled onto the ramp into traffic.

Scattered rain droplets peppered the windshield. He flipped on the windshield wipers. The rain came down harder.

A hand on the steering wheel, Zack glanced toward Warwick, who was staring out his window. Zack had tried small talk with Warwick when they'd first been partnered up, but the guy simply wasn't interested, so he'd given up.

Craving a cigarette, Zack reached in his pocket and found gum instead. He pulled out the pack, unwrapped a stick, and popped it in his mouth. He offered one to Warwick, who declined.

Ten minutes later, Zack had gotten ahead of the rain, which was moving in from the west. He maneuvered the

Impala off the interstate and down River Road. This was the high end of town where pedigree was just as important as a fat wallet. Turner hadn't been born into the right family, but he'd married into one of the oldest in the state.

Zack pulled onto a tree-lined side street and into Harold Turner's circular driveway. The enormous brick Colonial was bordered by manicured beds filled with boxwoods, daylilies, and a rainbow palette of annuals. The house, like the man who'd remodeled it, screamed *money.*

Warwick whistled as his gaze traveled over the home's exterior. "Look at this place. It's worth more than I'll make in five lifetimes. This is a far cry from Harold's subsidized housing days at Randolph Court."

Zack didn't feel envy, just a curiosity for the well-bred woman who had married a man like Turner.

The fixer-upper he'd just bought could fit in one of Turner's garages. However, this house was cold. His house, which Lindsay had spotted shortly after they'd married, had character and was full of possibilities. Yeah, it had dents and dings—just like their marriage—but that's what made it interesting. Or so he kept telling himself.

He stared at the ivy-covered house willing it to reveal its secrets. "I called Ricker about an hour ago and had her do a quick rundown on Mrs. Turner. She's a Georgetown grad and in her midthirties. She and Turner married about five years ago. They have no children, but she's a member of a children's hospital board and a member of several other children's charities."

Warwick flexed his fingers. "How did those two hook up?"

"He was her father's attorney."

Warwick raised an eyebrow. "Her old man is not so squeaky clean?"

"He was charged with investment fraud. Turner got him off."

"So he kept the old man out of jail and married the daughter."

"So it seems." It was amazing how much dirt could be hidden behind such regal walls.

Zack opened his door and was struck by the humidity, thick with the promise of rain within minutes. As Warwick got out, Zack pulled on his suit jacket. The worsted wool felt scratchy against his skin. The suit was classified as a "nine months suit," and he'd bought it figuring he'd get the most wear out of it. He now realized July was one of the three months it was not intended to be worn. He straightened his tie.

Warwick studied a large iron planter filled with ivy. "If she's such a class act why marry a shyster like Turner?"

"Love's a fickle thing." Crushed gravel crunched under their feet as they walked up the walkway. Eight months in homicide and he'd not gotten used to the grim task of delivering news of a death.

"Love ain't got nothing to do with this union. It's all about the money." A shadow darkened Warwick's face.

"Are you completely cynical?"

Warwick shrugged. "Just calling 'em as I seem 'em. Women gravitate toward the coin. Saw it a million times when I worked undercover. Go into a club dressed as a bum, and none of the chicks talk to you. Return to the same club dressed as a player, and it's like bees and honey."

Money didn't motivate Lindsay. She had walked away from their marriage without a dime. In fact, she had given the money from their joint savings account to his mother and asked her to put it toward Zack's recovery.

He'd used that money a month ago to put the down payment on that fixer-upper that Lindsay had loved.

"When we get to the door," Warwick said, "let me do most of the talking."

"No problem."

"Don't say we're from homicide. I don't want her shutting down. Once anyone hears homicide, they start gauging their words carefully."

"I know the drill." Irritated, Zack rang the front bell.

Within seconds footsteps sounded on the other side. The door opened to a young Hispanic woman dressed in a maid's uniform. "Yes?"

Warwick held up his police badge. "We're here to see Mrs. Jordan Turner."

The young woman frowned. "Just a moment, please." The front door closed with a soft click.

"Do you think she'll show?" Zack said.

"I don't know."

The door opened a second time. This time a tall slim woman appeared at the threshold. She was dressed in a simple black sheath that accentuated full breasts and a narrow waist. A gold cross dangled from a chain around her neck. Long black hair grazed the top of slender shoulders and framed a lovely oval face that could have been classified as angelic if not for the sharpness behind her violet eyes.

Behind her, polished wood floors gleamed. Walls papered in cream and black stripes served as a backdrop to eighteenth-century portraits. A crystal chandelier hung from the vaulted ceiling, twisting sunlight into rainbows.

"Mrs. Jordan Turner?" Warwick said.

"Yes?" A crease formed between neatly plucked eyebrows as her gaze shifted between the two of men. "I understand you're with the police department."

Both men reached in their pockets and pulled out badges.

"We're with Henrico County Police," Warwick said.

"What can I do for you?" Her tone turned cautious.

"Is there anyone else in the house with you?" They didn't want her alone in case she took the news of her husband's death badly.

She glanced behind her. Feminine laughter sounded from inside the house. "I've a few ladies from the church here. What's this about?"

"Have you seen your husband this morning?" Warwick said.

Answering a question with a question often led to more information.

"Harold and I had dinner together last night. After that we went our separate ways. I had a late church meeting and didn't get home until after eleven. I'm not sure what plans Harold had scheduled on his calendar."

"What time did your husband come in last night?" Warwick said.

She frowned. "What's this about?"

Warwick ignored her question. "I would appreciate it if you would just confirm his arrival for me."

Jordan drew in a breath. "We have separate bedrooms." Color rose in her cheeks as if she was embarrassed by the admission. Appearances were clearly a priority for her. "Harold has terrible back problems and he needs a special mattress."

Zack tucked the badge back in his pocket. "What time did you have dinner with him last night?"

Her lips flattened. "Six. We left *La Mer* at seven. Is Harold in some kind of trouble?"

"May we come inside?" Warwick said.

Jordan stepped out onto the front porch, softly closing the door behind her. "As I said, I've a group of women visiting from the church. Now is not a good time to hear about Harold's latest indiscretion."

"It's more than an indiscretion, ma'am," Zack said.

She fidgeted with her five-carat wedding ring with her thumb. "What has my husband done this time?"

"This time?" Zack said.

"A month ago he was arrested for drunk driving in the city."

Warwick's gaze didn't waver from Jordan's face. "Mr. Turner was found dead this morning behind Sanctuary Women's Shelter."

For a moment, she just stared at them, her eyes blinking slowly as if her brain couldn't process. She raised her hand to her mouth. Finally, she found her voice, which possessed surprising steel. "Are you sure it was Harold?"

"Yes, ma'am," Warwick said. "We found his wallet in his breast pocket."

Sudden tears glistened in her eyes. But Zack couldn't tell if they were born in sadness or relief. "What happened to him? How did he die?"

"He was shot." He wasn't telling her anything that wouldn't appear on the six o'clock news. Details about the mutilation and the caliber of the gun would remain confidential until the case was solved.

She flexed her French-manicured fingers. "Where exactly did you say you found Harold?"

"Behind Sanctuary Women's Shelter," Zack said. Shock was natural, but this calm reaction wasn't. Normally, when a loved one was reported dead, strong emotion followed.

But Jordan Turner didn't show much sign that she was upset. In fact, she looked confused. "This doesn't make any sense. Harold wouldn't ever go to a women's shelter."

"There's no reason Mr. Turner would be at Sanctuary Women's Shelter?" Warwick said.

Amusement softened her features, as if he'd just said something funny. "No, Harold would never go to a place like that."

"Why not?" Warwick said.

"He doesn't support any charity unless it advances his standing with the media. And even if Santuary was a media darling, he wouldn't support it. He doesn't like quitters."

"Quitters?" Zack said.

"Women who give up on their marriages."

Zack's tempter rose. "They're abused women, Mrs. Turner."

The censure in his voice had her shoulders stiffening. "Until death do we part, detective. Those are the vows we all take when we marry in the church. We may not like the way our marriages turn out but that doesn't mean we abandon our promise before God."

"You don't believe in divorce," Warwick said.

She released the cross she had been holding. He could almost hear her defenses slamming into place. "I don't. I also don't believe in murder."

"No one says that you do," Zack said.

She raised a brow. "Please, I've been married to a defense attorney for five years. I know how it works. The spouse is always at the top of the suspect list when there is a murder."

"No one's a suspect yet," Warwick said. "These questions are standard procedure. Right now we're just trying to establish a time line."

A fat rain droplet leaked through the porch roof and landed on Zack's shoulder. He didn't need to glance up to know the sky was about to open up.

Jordan turned, dismissing them as she reached for the front door handle. "I will contact my attorney and he'll be in touch with you. If you have more questions, you can ask them of me in front of him."

"There a reason you need an attorney?" Zack said. More droplets hit him on his broad shoulders.

She met his gaze head-on. "Harold said you always, always need an attorney when cops are around. Now I must go."

Warwick stopped her retreat by asking, "Know of anybody who would want to kill your husband?"

The question made her smile again. "I'll draw up a list. My attorney will submit it." She opened the door, then closed it in their faces as she went inside.

Warwick planted long hands on his hips. "Smooth, controlled, and not exactly torn up," he said, summing her up.

Zack turned up his collar as raindrops peppered the ground. "I'll subpoena phone records and get a full background check on her."

Rain greeted Lindsay's Jeep as she pulled out of the Mercy Hospital parking garage. She flipped on her headlights and windshield wipers to cut through the river of water falling from the sky. Slowly she merged into traffic and followed the procession of red taillights onto I-64 West. The downpour made drivers hesitant and slow. The trip back to shelter was going to take longer than she'd planned.

Seeing Gail made her think of Jordan. Unable to resist, she picked up her cell and dialed Jordan again. She doubted Jordan would pick up, but she felt as if she had to try although she wasn't sure what she'd say to Jordan when she got her on the phone.

After the third ring, the call connected.

"Jordan?"

"Yes. Why are you calling me, Lindsay?"

"Because we need to talk."

"I've said all I'm willing to say to you."

"Don't hang up. Please, we need to talk about Harold."

"There's nothing to say. The police were just here. They told me about him."

Harold Turner may have abused his wife but that didn't mean Jordan didn't love him or wasn't feeling a great sense of loss. "Are you okay?"

"I'm fine. Now, leave me alone. I can't talk to you anymore." Jordan's voice sounded brittle, more tense than usual.

"We need to talk about Harold."

"I have nothing to say about him."

The questions had to be asked. "Jordan, you said a couple of weeks ago that you could handle him. Did you kill him?"

There was a long pause. "Why would you ask me a question like that? Harold was found behind *your* shelter."

"Because I think whoever put him there was sending me a message. I think you might have been telling me that you'd handle him by killing him."

"He was worth more to me alive than dead. And I was handling him." A heavy silence followed before she added, "Did you kill him?"

Lindsay felt dizzy. "No."

"It makes sense that you would. I saw the way you looked at him at that charity party. You hated him."

"Jordan, I didn't kill Harold."

"Who else would? Harold was right about you. He said you hate men."

"I don't hate men, Jordan. I hate it when men hit the women they say they love."

"Harold did love me."

"Jordan, you told me he held a gun to your head and played Russian roulette."

"I also told you the gun was empty. If he'd wanted to kill me he would have, but he didn't. He said he was just kidding."

Lindsay nearly cried out her frustration. "Jordan, you have to understand that a man shouldn't treat a woman that way."

"Don't tell me any more of your lies. I don't want to hear them. Harold and I would have been fine if you'd just stayed out of our lives."

"Jordan, you're the one who came to me."

"You killed my husband."

"I did not!"

"I'll never forgive you for what you did to me." The line went dead.

Lindsay shoved out a breath and closed the phone. Frustration ate at her. Jordan had decided Lindsay was the cause of her problems.

Lindsay tapped her pinky ring—her mother's high school ring—against the steering wheel. She clicked on the radio, hit "scan," and hoped for some kind of news about Harold. Nothing. Each station played a collection of songs and advertisements, but no news.

Aware that her breathing had grown shallow, she drew in deep breaths. Slowly the muscles in her chest eased.

What had Harold been doing behind the shelter? Sanctuary was the kind of place he despised and he had no reason to be there—unless Jordan really had lured him to the shelter and killed him as some kind of message to Lindsay.

"Jordan, please tell me you didn't do anything stupid," Lindsay whispered to herself.

The deluge of rain slowed. Streets glistened with rain.

Steam rose from the hot pavement. Puddles collected on the shoulders of the road.

Lindsay flipped open her cell phone and redialed Jordan Turner's number. The phone rang once and then went straight to voice mail.

"This is Jordan. Leave me a message and I'll get back to you."

"Jordan, it's Lindsay O'Neil. I need to talk to you again. You've got my number."

Lindsay clipped the phone back into its holster on her waistband. Ten minutes later she parked in front of Sanctuary. The downpour had just stopped but it had chased away the forensics team and the curiosity seekers. A squad car with a lone officer in the front seat remained parked in the driveway and two television news trucks lurked across the street. The reporters huddled inside the front cabs.

A streak of lightning shot across the sky. Lindsay flinched. She counted to five. Thunder boomed. Another storm was close.

Grabbing her purse, she hurried across the muddy front lawn and climbed Sanctuary's front steps. She darted in the front door.

The morning calm had been replaced by a buzz of video games and children's chatter. Jamal and Damien Greenland had arrived home from summer school. Damn. They shouldn't be here. Ruby should have picked them up at school.

"Ruby!" Lindsay shouted. She pushed open the pocket door that portioned off Ruby's small office.

Ruby sat behind her desk, a phone cradled under her chin. When her gaze met Lindsay's she hung up. "How was the hospital?"

Lindsay brushed the rain from her face. "Time will tell. Planted a few seeds. Why are the Greenland boys still here?"

"The school wouldn't release them to me and I couldn't get hold of their mother. I had no choice but to let them ride the bus home. The bus just dropped them off. I decided to plant them in front of a video game until you got back."

Lindsay sighed. "Now that the rain has let up, the cops are going to return soon to salvage what they can from that backyard. I'll run the boys over to Riverside now. I don't want the kids around when they return."

"Are you sure?"

"Yeah, I'll be back in an hour."

Lindsay headed into the front family room, where the boys were playing the video game on the television. Ruby had closed the shades to block all views of the police car and news vans parked out front. "Hey, guys, how's the game going?"

Damien glanced up from the screen. "This game is kinda lame, Lindsay. No guns, no bombs, no fun."

The video game system had been anonymously donated to the shelter two months ago. She was grateful for the donation but had immediately sifted through the stack of games that came with it and tossed the violent ones. The kids who lived there saw enough violence in real life. "That hasn't stopped you fellows from playing it nonstop."

Damien had a concerned look on his face. Usually during the day she was too busy to chat. "Is Mom okay? I saw the cop outside."

She could have sugarcoated the whole issue, but she'd hated it when adults had condescended to her after her mother's death. *It's going to be fine, dear. Don't you worry.* "Your mom is fine but we're going to have to move you, your brother, and your mom to another shelter today."

"Because of *him*." Damien's voice wavered even as he

jutted out his chin. His brother set down his video controller and looked at her.

Him was their father—Marcus Greenland. He'd been a star linebacker in college. During his junior year, he'd gotten involved in drugs and trouble with the local police. He'd been suspended from the team. Then he'd hooked up with another college but hadn't lasted the season. From then on, he had been on a downward spiral. Frustrated by his own failures, Marcus took out his anger on his wife and children.

Lindsay laid her hand on Damien's shoulder. "No, your father has nothing to do with this."

Suspicion narrowed Damien's eyes. "Are you being straight with me?"

"I promise, Damien. I can't give you details but I swear that this has nothing to do with you, your mom, or your dad."

Finally, the anxiety eased from the boy's shoulders. "Thanks, Lindsay."

"No problem, kiddo."

"Can I save the game to the memory card?" Damien said.

"I thought it was lame," she teased.

"Not too lame," he added.

Unless this murder was resolved quickly, the shelter would close, and she had no idea if and when it would open again. "You can take it and the game with you."

He grinned. "For real?"

"Absolutely."

"Thanks!" Jamal exclaimed.

As the boys finished up their game, she grabbed a plastic grocery bag from under the kitchen sink. Jamal pocketed the disc and memory card as Damien unplugged the game and tucked it in the bag. The three headed outside.

"We can really keep this?" Jamal said.

"Until you and your brother get settled in a real home with your mom. When you guys are feeling comfortable in your new place, I'd like it back for the next kid."

Jamal frowned. "Damien and I aren't the last kids?"

Sadly, there would always be a next kid in her line of business. It was the main reason why she was there. But Jamal didn't need statistics or grim predictions of the future. He needed hope that his life would one day be happy and normal. "I sure hope you are."

Lindsay ushered the boys outside to her car. They buckled in and soon were headed across town. Fifteen minutes later, they rolled into the Riverside parking lot. The shelter was also in a residential neighborhood and looked much like the other trilevel houses around it. Toys now damp from the rain littered the front yard. The front door was open. Inside, lights glowed.

Aisha Greenland came outside, her shoulder-length braids brushing her wide shoulders. She grinned when she saw Lindsay and the boys. The boys scrambled out of the backseat and ran up to their mother. She hugged them close.

Lindsay followed with the video game system in hand. "How'd the interview go?"

Aisha grinned. Hazel eyes flashed with genuine happiness. "I got the job."

Lindsay knew Aisha had been terrified of the interview. It had been eight years since she'd worked out of the home. "That's great."

Jamal cupped his mother's face in his hands. "You got a job?"

Aisha kissed her son. "I sure did, baby. I sure did. I'm gonna be working as a cashier at the supermarket." She lifted her gaze to Lindsay. "Thank you."

"Happy to help." Moments like this made all the bad stuff fade.

"I have just a little something for you," Aisha said.

"You don't need to give me anything."

Aisha shook her head and from her pocket pulled out a small wrapped box. "I heard Ruby saying it was your birthday on Wednesday."

Emotion tightened Lindsay's chest as she slowly opened the box. Inside was a plastic butterfly. Clearly it wasn't expensive, but that didn't matter. "You know butterflies mean rebirth."

Aisha shook her head. "I just liked the pretty colors."

Lindsay hugged her. "So do I. Thank you." Unshed tears burned the back of her throat. "Good luck. You guys take care. I've got to get back to Sanctuary."

Inside her car, Lindsay turned on the radio, found a good song, and cranked it. She felt good and wanted to savor this small victory. To celebrate, she went to a drive-thru to treat herself to a milk shake, burger, and fries. The delicious smells made her stomach rumble for she couldn't remember the last time she'd eaten.

Twenty minutes later, when she parked in front of Sanctuary, she'd eaten the fries and drank half the milk shake. A little food on her stomach had settled her nerves and she felt steadier.

The cop car was still parked out front, as well as the forensics van. Only one news van remained. And that was a good thing as far as she was concerned. She prayed the press would lose interest and this whole thing would just go away.

She was halfway up the shelter's front steps when she heard a woman shout, "Lindsay O'Neil!"

Turning, she saw a tall woman with dark hair pulled back into a low, tight ponytail. She was wearing a sleek sapphire silk blouse that accentuated flawless porcelain skin expertly made up and black pants that showed off long legs and a narrow waist. Kendall Shaw, former cover model and now a reporter for Channel 10, was perfectly dressed as always.

One look reminded Lindsay that she'd barely had time to run a brush through her hair this morning. "Hey, Kendall."

Kendall grinned and held out her hand. "It's good to see you again. I guess it's been a couple of months."

Lindsay shifted her fast-food bag and drink to one hand so she could shake Kendall's with the other. "Since you interviewed me a couple of months ago for that free-lance article for *Inside Richmond.*"

Kendall's grin broadened. Her grip was strong and firm. "That article was well received. The paper said that their sell-through for that month was eighty percent. You were a hit."

"It wasn't me. The other gals you profiled were pretty amazing."

Kendall let her gaze travel over the white vinyl siding and the trimmed boxwoods. "So this is Sanctuary. I always wondered what Sanctuary actually looked like. Those couple of times we met at the coffee shop, you never said where it actually was."

"That's the idea. We need to keep our location secret. We still do."

She nodded. "Oh, don't worry about that. I won't talk location. None of the news stations are." She slid manicured hands into her pocket and pulled out a slim notebook. "But I was hoping you could tell me more about what went on here this morning. The cops' public relations guy said Harold Turner was killed here but won't say much else. Any thoughts why?"

That was the million-dollar question. "I don't know anything else. I'm just as much in the dark as you are."

Kendall didn't look convinced. "Oh, come on, you must have an idea." She'd dropped her voice as if they were somehow coconspirators. "Detective Kier was in your office for over a half hour. And he was very tight-lipped when I tried to talk to him. He must have told you something."

Zack hated the press. He never spoke to them unless he absolutely had to. "I really don't know anything, Kendall."

"I thought he was your husband?"

Lindsay didn't ask Kendall how she'd found out about her marriage. No doubt she'd done extra digging while working on the article. "I can't add anything." She inched past Kendall up the stairs toward the door.

Kendall followed. "Harold's death didn't have anything to do with the Pam Rogers case?"

Tension snaked up Lindsay's back as she reached for the doorknob. She'd never considered the two could be linked. But Kendall thought more like a cop.

"Kendall, I'd help you out if I could." Another lie. "But I don't know anything."

Kendall's smile was smooth as she laid her hand on the front rail. "Oh, come on, you must know something that you can share with me. I mean, I figure you owe me."

Lindsay dropped her hand from the doorknob and faced the reporter. Whatever goodwill she'd felt toward Kendall had vanished. "You want to run that one by me again?"

Kendall didn't look intimidated. "You were quite the 'it' girl there for a few weeks after the article came out. I'd heard that donations to the shelter had soared."

Donations had risen for a while but that didn't mean Lindsay liked being pushed. "Right now I can't say a word."

Kendall's eyes hardened but she maintained her trade-mark smile. "But when you can you'll give me a call."

"Don't count on it." Lindsay escaped inside the shelter but the well-being she'd felt on the drive back had evaporated. Kendall Shaw's questions had set her teeth on edge and reminded her that no matter how hard she worked on the pending grant applications, the specter of another shelter-related murder could shut her down permanently.

Lindsay headed to her office. Carefully, she laid the butterfly in the center of her desk as she studied a long white flower box sitting on her chair. It was wrapped with a thick red ribbon. There was a card on the box. It read, "For Lindsay."

No one ever sent her flowers.

"Hey, Ruby," she shouted, "what's with the flowers?"

"They just came." Ruby rounded the corner, a big grin on her face. "They're for you."

"Do you know who sent them?" Had Zack remembered her birthday? Could he have sent the flowers?

Ruby grinned. "Open the card and find out."

Tenderly, she touched the ribbon that seemed to have been wrapped with care. "There must be some kind of mistake. I've never gotten flowers." The truth was she didn't like flowers, because her father always gave her mother flowers after he hit her.

Ruby shrugged. "No mistake. And if you've never gotten flowers, it's high time you did."

Her curiosity rising, Lindsay opened the card. "*Lindsay, you are not alone anymore. The Guardian.*"

Ruby came around behind Lindsay and glanced over her shoulder and read the note. "'Lindsay, you are not alone anymore.' What does that mean? And who is the Guardian?"

Lindsay also was puzzled. "I've no idea."

Ruby cocked an eyebrow. "I hate it when men play games. There a name?"

"No."

"There's no man in your life?"

"No."

"What about your husband?"

"He knows I don't like flowers. Besides, romantic gestures aren't his thing."

Curious, Lindsay untied the crisp bow. She laid it carefully aside before opening the lid to reveal purple irises. They'd been one of her mother's favorite flowers and, consequently, she loved them as well. "They're beautiful."

Ruby leaned over her shoulder, admiring the bouquet. "Maybe it's from that doctor."

"I bet you're right. I saw Sam this morning. He knows I was having a rough day and he's one of the few who knows where the shelter is located."

Sadness coiled inside her chest. It was foolish to want or expect anything from Zack. But for a brief moment she had. "I think we have a vase or a large jar in the kitchen."

"I think it's under the sink. I'll be right back with it." Ruby disappeared down the hallway.

Lindsay lifted the flowers out of the box. As she raised the blooms to her nose she saw a bundle wrapped in green tissue paper. She laid the flowers aside on her desk and opened the second package.

Bile rose in her throat. For a moment she thought she'd throw up as she dropped it and backed away from her desk.

Cradled in the tissue and wrapped in a zip-top bag was a severed hand.

No one noticed delivery people. Some might glance at the name *Joe* embroidered over a breast pocket, but few would gaze under the bill of a hat or look beyond a nondescript magnetic florist sign stuck on a van.

That was the problem with people, the Guardian thought. They were selfish and far too wrapped up in their own lives to notice what didn't directly concern them.

That's why it was easy to feel safe moving past the unmarked police car and the cop now distracted by a well-timed cell phone call from his kid's day care.

And the Guardian smiled at the ambitious reporter as she tamed a strand of hair and practiced smiling as her cameraman began taping her intro for the six o'clock news report.

Like everyone else, the cop and reporter were blind. Blind to the delivery. Blind to the pain and suffering around them. Blind to everything but their needs.

The only one who could truly see was Lindsay.

She reached out to others in need. She put the lives of others in front of her own.

The Guardian closed the door to the van and started the engine and pulled out. She would get the flowers soon. Soon she would know she wasn't alone. "Happy birthday, Lindsay."

Tightening fingers on the steering wheel, the Guardian slowed at an intersection when the light turned yellow. The car in the left lane darted through a red light and he frowned.

"No respect."

Today had been a good day.

The rains had purified the killing ground and signaled the beginning of a long overdue holy cause.

Together, Lindsay and her Guardian would destroy The Evil Ones.

Chapter Eight

Monday, July 7, 2:59 P.M.

Richard pinned Christina's hands down over her head as his heavy body pressed her into the mattress. She could feel his erection pressing against her skin and knew what would come next. His breath smelled of stale cigars and whiskey. She felt dirty and so unclean when he touched her.

She didn't want his idea of lovemaking. She didn't want him.

But she was careful to hide her revulsion and fear. The last time she'd tried to resist him, he'd slapped her hard across the face, and after he'd raped her he'd locked her in a dark closet all night long.

Richard thrust inside her, using as much force as he could.

She couldn't suppress a wince.

He smiled and pushed into her again and again until tears spilled down her cheeks and stained the silk pillow under her head.

He slipped his hands under her buttocks and gripped hard. He was enjoying her suffering.

"You love this, don't you?" he whispered against her ear.

Christina swallowed. She couldn't bring herself to respond.

He straightened and slapped her hard against the face. "Say you love this."

She tasted blood. "I do."

Richard smiled, satisfied. He cupped her full breasts with his large hands. "I want us to have a child, Christina. I want a child to bind us together forever."

Fear burned inside her. She begged God not to give her a child.

How had her life gotten so messed up? How had she slid from independence to this?

He moved inside of her, faster and faster. He fisted his fingers in her long dark hair and pressed his cheek to hers. His beard scratched her skin. His breath was hot against her face. Sweat dripped from his body.

"Say you love me," Richard commanded.

She didn't speak. Saying the words always made her ill.

"Say it!" he urged. He tightened his hold on her hair and pulled until sections started to come out.

Pain seared Christina's scalp. She started to weep again. "I love you."

He grunted, satisfied. Even in his own twisted way, he needed assurances. He released her hair and kissed her lips. "I love you, Christina. We'll be together forever. Until death do us part."

The words were heartfelt. He did love her. And at one time she had loved him.

Richard found his release. He collapsed on top of her, his body damp with sweat. Tenderly he stroked her hair.

"We are destined to be together forever."

Nicole Piper awoke with a start. Her mind was still clouded by the dream and for a moment she was confused and afraid.

She didn't know where she was as she swung her legs over the side of the overstuffed couch. A book that had been in her lap fell to the floor. Sweat dampened her brow. Her heart raced.

Drawn window shades bathed the room in near darkness and added to her disorientation. Overwhelmed by the sensation that she wasn't alone, she frantically searched the living room's shadowed corners for any sign of her husband, Richard.

A chill prickled her skin. "Who's there!"

No one answered.

"Richard, are you there?"

Still nothing. And yet the feeling that someone watched lingered.

Seconds passed. No phantoms appeared. Her heart slowed.

Nicole's mind cleared. "He's far away, three thousand miles away. Richard is in San Francisco. Christina is dead. I'm Nicole now." She was in Virginia and living with her friend Lindsay O'Neil.

"I'm safe. It was a dream." Nicole switched on the lamp by the faded floral couch. As she hugged a colorful pillow, her gaze traveled over the living room's hodgepodge of antique and modern furniture. An assortment of clocks ticked and chimed on the mantle. A large area rug warmed the scuffed parquet floor. The room should have looked disjointed, but Lindsay had united the salvaged pieces and given them a new life and purpose.

She'd done the same for Nicole.

Without question, Lindsay had taken in Nicole when she'd fled her abusive marriage. She'd given her safe harbor and was helping her to regain control of her life.

Nicole curled trembling hands into fists and said aloud, "He can't find me. I've covered my tracks well. I'm safe." But the helpless fear still remained.

A clock chimed four times. Other clocks joined in, creating a symphony of sounds. Four o'clock.

It was time to get ready for her evening shift at the studio.

Just a week ago, Nicole had told Lindsay she had to get back to work. Lindsay had tried to convince her to just hang out for a while and give herself time to heal, but Nicole had refused. She needed to work so that she could push the past from her mind. Lindsay had understood and had gotten Nicole a new Social Security number. Nicole wasn't sure how Lindsay had accomplished the feat so quickly but she hadn't asked.

Within two days, Nicole had gotten a job at a mall portrait studio. She'd only been on the job about a week and knew that snapping photos of babies and high school graduates was a far cry from the artistic photography she'd done in San Francisco. But right now she didn't have the luxury of being a snob. This job was about making money, which equaled the means to run if Richard found her.

Nicole moved through the dimly lit apartment to the kitchen and got a soda from the fridge. She popped it open and savored the cool liquid on her dry throat and uneasy stomach.

She was afraid all the time and that made her angry with herself. She'd been a fool to love Richard, a man who had ruined her life.

Richard.

He'd been the man of her dreams and she'd loved him so much in the early days. But behind the kindness and flowers lurked a man who was evil incarnate.

Two years ago when he'd burst through the front door of her San Francisco photography studio, he'd been dodging an onslaught of rain. Dressed in jeans, a white linen shirt, and Gucci loafers, he had immediately captured her attention with his dark good looks. They'd hit it off. He'd been so charming. She'd been enthralled. They'd married less than two months later in a sunset ceremony on the beach. Her parents had passed away by then but she'd had a collection of friends to stand by her side. She'd worn a silk halter dress that had shimmered in the light of a hundred torches. Flowers had adorned her head. She'd worn no shoes.

Richard had held her hand as they'd stood before the minister. His hand had been cold and she knew he was nervous. She'd been charmed that such a sophisticated man could be nervous. He'd sworn that they'd be together forever.

Forever.

The word haunted her now.

They'd been married less than six months when the problems started. She'd been late coming home one night because she'd spent extra time in the darkroom, burning and edging the print of a mother and child until it was perfect. When she'd left the studio, she'd felt so proud of the work. She was finding her voice as an artist. And commercially, she was on the brink of something big in her career.

When she'd arrived home, Richard had accused her of seeing someone else. The idea was so ridiculous, she'd laughed. His temper had snapped. He'd called her a whore. A cunt. He'd said he despised the sight of her.

The words had cut through her like knives. She'd started to cry.

Instantly contrite, Richard had begged for her forgiveness and poured her a snifter of brandy to settle her nerves. He'd sworn he'd never lose his temper again.

Stunned and shaken, she'd allowed him to hug her. And God help her, she'd clung to him.

Each day for the next month, he'd sent her flowers: large and lavish displays of roses, tulips, rare orchids.

Slowly, she'd dropped her guard. She'd believed his words of love.

But as her success grew so did Richard's resentment. He didn't like the demands her work made on her time. And like a fool, she'd confused his need to control with love. And so she had tried to appease him. She'd downplayed her successes and awards. And when that didn't work, she'd cut back her hours. Seen her friends less so she could be with him more. Each time she gave up a piece of herself, he seemed to be mollified. But he was never content for long. She realized she could never sacrifice enough to make him truly happy.

Nicole began to despise her marriage. Increasingly, she'd felt trapped. Angry. Alone. She'd even gone to a local community center to hear a woman, Claire Carmichael, speak about abuse. But at the time, Nicole just couldn't believe that her marriage was that bad.

Then, almost three weeks ago, Richard had lost his temper because he'd not liked the dress she'd chosen. It had looked cheap to him and in his eyes a poor reflection of his standing.

She'd tried to explain it was the latest fashion. But she had been silenced by the anger and venom that had erupted from him. He'd beaten her so badly that she couldn't leave the house for days. He'd told her if she ever tried to leave him, he'd kill her. With great relish, he'd spoken of drugs that could keep her alive for days as he'd slice away at her flesh with a knife.

She'd been terrified, knowing he would do exactly what he'd threatened to do.

Confident that he'd totally trampled her spirits, he'd given her a lavish display of roses and then left their San Francisco home for an overnight business trip to New York.

Nicole had known, as she'd stared at the roses, that if

she didn't get out, he would eventually beat her to death. The next flowers she'd receive would be placed on her grave.

Her body still aching, she'd packed what clothes could fit in a large purse. She couldn't leave their home without his driver, Jimmy, who was always there watching. Donning dark sunglasses, she had asked Jimmy to take her across town and drop her near the waterfront. She had vanished into a restaurant bathroom and climbed out the window.

Near the restaurant was Claire Carmichael's small New Age bookstore. She'd raced to Claire's and told her she needed to be hidden. Claire had remembered her and offered her a bed at the local shelter. Nicole had known she had to get farther away from San Francisco than a local shelter. So, Claire had given Nicole $200 cash and the keys to a beat-up Honda. In gratitude, she had given Claire her wedding bands and told her to hawk them.

Grateful and terrified, she'd headed east, not sure at first where she was going. In Denver, she had bought a hat and tucked her hair up inside it. She also had calmed enough to sit and think where she'd go next. She had remembered Lindsay. They had been roommates at the University of Southern California but had lost touch over the years. Nicole had remembered a notation in the USC alumni magazine. Lindsay had returned to her native Virginia. She worked with battered women.

So, Nicole had called information from a pay phone and gotten the number of the abuse hotline in Lindsay's area. She'd begged the counselor to find Lindsay and have her call Nicole at the pay phone. The counselor hadn't made any promises, but five minutes later the pay phone had rung. It was Lindsay.

Lindsay hadn't hesitated. She'd given Nicole directions to her house, and when she'd arrived two days later, Lindsay had opened up her home to Nicole.

Sunlight peeked around the edges of the shaded kitchen window. Nicole set her soda can on the counter and opened the blinds. Afternoon light made her squint, but the sun warmed her face. The rain had stopped.

Men like Richard didn't have the right to walk this earth. They stole dreams and lives. They nurtured humiliation and fear. They all deserved to die.

Somewhere along the way, she'd lost herself. But she'd corrected the mistake. She was in control now.

San Francisco, 1:00 P.M. PST (4:00 P.M. EST)

Jimmy Quinn had endured a lot of pain during his career in the boxing ring, weathering split lips, broken bones, and bruised knots the size of goose eggs. Long after a damaged right hand had forced him from the ring, the boys on the street respectfully called him Iron Jim, because he could take a licking better than anyone. He was the toughest of the tough.

However, never during his sixty-four years had he ever, *ever*, hurt so bad that he wanted to die.

Now, the pain ravaging his body made him wish he were dead.

Someone splashed ice water on his face and his head snapped up. But he couldn't see so well. Both his eyes were swollen shut.

"One last time, Jimmy. Where is Christina Braxton?" The calm, even voice came from the shadows. Jimmy couldn't see the speaker's face anymore, but he knew it was Vincent Malone.

"I don't know," Jimmy whispered.

He tried to flex his swollen fingers, now numb from the too-tight ropes that secured his hands behind his back. Blood caked his well-lined face and stained the white button-down shirt he'd pressed himself this morning. Or was it yesterday? The beatings had robbed him of any sense of time.

His last clear memory was of entering the waterfront warehouse to meet his former boss, Richard Braxton. Only, Mr. Braxton hadn't been there. His right-hand man, Vincent, and a couple of his goons had been waiting for him. There'd been no conversation as the goons had strapped him to a chair. To set the tone, Vincent had taken a billy club and smacked it hard against Jimmy's knuckles. And then the questions about Mrs. Braxton had started.

"Don't make me hurt you, Jimmy. I don't like hurting you," Vincent had said.

"I don't know where she is. I ain't seen her in two weeks." Pain had burned every muscle in Jimmy's body.

Jimmy didn't want to give Vincent Mrs. B. He had liked her from the moment he'd first laid eyes on her. Pretty didn't come near to describing her. She was a stunner. And Mrs. B. was a kind soul. She'd treated him with respect from the get-go, always calling him "*Mr.*" Quinn. No one had called him "*Mr.*" anything in his entire life.

This past year Mrs. B. had been his responsibility. It was his job to drive her where she wanted to go, wait for her until she finished whatever it was she was doing, and then take her home. And it was his job to report to Mr. Braxton every move she made. The boss wanted to know everything his wife did, who she saw and even what she read.

Jimmy hadn't been proud of the work but he'd done his job, figuring it didn't hurt anybody. Who was he to say what went on between a man and his wife?

Two months ago, everything had changed. Mrs. B had gotten into the black Lexus wearing a vicious shiner. She'd said it was an accident. He'd accepted the excuse, because he liked the pay his job brought in and didn't want any trouble. But more bruises followed. He wasn't so punch drunk or stupid to see what was happening. Braxton had started to beat his wife.

Jimmy had begun to hate Mr. Braxton.

Through it all, Mrs. B. had been nice to him, always calling him Mr. Quinn. But he could see the light in her eyes was fading, bit by bit. He'd have quit the job, but Mrs. B. needed him and he needed the money.

"Remember the last time you saw her, Jimmy? You dropped her off somewhere. Where was it?" Vincent now leaned close to his ear. "Tell me, Jimmy, and I'll make the pain stop. She isn't worth this kind of trouble. She's a lying whore."

Rough hands shoved his head back against the chair. A sharp blade pressed against his cheek. It cut into the tender flesh under his eye.

Jimmy screamed. Blood streamed down his face.

"Next come the eyes, Jimmy."

"I dropped her near the water at a restaurant." He gave the address. "I think she slipped out the bathroom window."

"Where'd she go?"

The blade slid over his eyelid. "The restaurant owner said north."

"Did you see anyone else? Did she meet another man?" He jabbed his thumb into the fresh cut under Jimmy's eye.

Jimmy screamed. "I didn't see no one, I swear."

"That's all?"

Jimmy figured he'd burn in hell for what he was about to say. But what could Satan do to him that Mr. Braxton hadn't already done? "He hurt her. Made her cry. She had bruises on her face."

"I believe you, Jimmy." The voice he heard now was Richard Braxton's. Terror flooded his broken body. He tried to open his eyes but couldn't. God, but he hurt. "You got to believe me, Mr. B. I didn't know she was planning to run."

He heard a cigarette lighter snap open, then smelled the scent of a freshly lit cigarette. Braxton liked his smokes when he was tense. "You shouldn't have let her get away."

"I know."

The tip of a gun pressed against his temple and fired.

Chapter Nine

Monday, July 7, 4:02 P.M.

The law offices of Turner and Barlow were located in a suburban office park twenty miles west of Richmond. The five-story building had a shiny, reflective exterior and was nestled next to a large lake surrounded by pristine park benches and tree-lined jog paths. Tall front doors led to a foyer capped with skylights that magnified sunlight down on polished black marble floors.

Zack and Warwick checked the business directory posted on the wall and rode the elevator to the fifth floor. The elevator door dinged opened to muffled shouts. It was impossible to make out what was being said, but the tone was unmistakably angry.

Wordlessly, the detectives bypassed the stunned receptionist and cut around the maze of cubicles toward the corner office on the building's south side. The name on the office door read Quinton Barlow.

"I want to see my damn attorney! Where is he?!" the male voice thundered behind the wood paneled door.

Zack hesitated. "That sounds like Ronnie T."

Warwick nodded. "He's either one damn good liar or he doesn't know what happened to Harold."

"My money's on one damn good liar."

Ronnie T. had built a drug empire that stretched up and down the I-95 corridor. He'd evaded arrest on drug-trafficking charges; however, thanks to Zack's under-cover work, the Feds had been able to make a case for income tax evasion.

Without announcing himself, Zack opened the door and strolled into the plush office. "I thought I heard a familiar voice."

Warwick was a step behind him. "What's got everyone so upset?"

Ronnie T. stood in front of Quinton Barlow's desk, his right hand clenching an ornate walking stick that coordinated with his white jumpsuit and custom Nikes. He sported a ball cap cocked at a jaunty angle and wore a thick gold chain worth more than most cops made in a year.

Across the desk, a composed Quinton Barlow faced him. Short and pudgy, he wore a white monogrammed dress shirt, red silk tie, and dark suit pants. Barlow had been practicing criminal defense law for thirty-plus years. Dealing with men like Ronnie T. was standard.

Barlow met Zack's gaze and smiled pleasantly. "Gentlemen, what can we do for you?"

Ronnie T.'s eyes narrowed before he smiled at Zack. "Five-O. Shit. Before you ask, I ain't done nothing wrong. My hearing was canceled this morning, because my damn attorney didn't show. I was just asking Quinton here where the hell Harold is hiding."

Zack pulled a slim notebook and pen out of his pocket. "So where is Harold?"

Ronnie T. flashed a signature grin even as his grip tightened on his cane. "Quinton isn't telling."

"Ronnie only just burst into my office," Barlow said.

Zack raised an eyebrow and looked at Barlow, unsure of what he really knew about his law partner. "Do you know where your partner is?"

Barlow didn't flinch. "I've spoken to Jordan. She told me about your visit."

"She didn't waste any time," Zack said.

"She understands even the innocent need an attorney when dealing with the police," Quinton said.

Ronnie T. leaned on his cane. "Someone mind filling me in on what's what?"

Zack studied Barlow's guarded expression before he shifted his gaze back to the dealer. "Harold's body was found this morning behind Sanctuary Women's Shelter. He was shot point-blank in the chest."

Ronnie T.'s eyes widened and his mouth dropped open. "Shit."

Zack wasn't fooled by Ronnie's surprise. "When's the last time you saw your counselor?"

Barlow cleared his throat. "Don't answer any of their questions."

Ronnie T. shrugged. "I don't mind answering, Quinton. I ain't got nothing to hide. I saw Harold yesterday after court."

"Word is you two fought," Zack said. "Fact, I hear it was nearly a knock-down, drag-out fight in the courthouse."

"Ronnie," Barlow warned, "keep your mouth shut."

Ronnie T. waved Barlow off. "Yeah, we mixed it up. He wanted me to take a plea agreement. I told him I was paying him the big bucks to keep me out of jail. The deal was no time spent behind bars."

"What time was that?" Warwick said.

"About three."

"Do you know where Turner was headed?" Zack said.

"Said something about dinner with his old lady."

"And where were you last night, Ronnie T.?" Zack said.

Ronnie T.'s full lips split into a wide grin. "I was at a swim meet. My kid was swimming the butterfly for the first time at the community pool. He's on the Mite team. And he won his heat."

"I'm assuming you have witnesses," Warwick said.

"I do." Ronnie T. sounded amused. "They are some of Richmond's finest—all white folks. I can give you a list of names."

Zack flipped to a clean page in his notebook. "Let's have them."

Ronnie T. rattled off a half dozen names. He looked pleased with himself. Whatever had gone down last night, Ronnie T. had made certain that he was in a very public place.

Barlow picked up a letter printed on the firm's stationary. "I too have an alibi. In this letter is the name and phone number of the manager of my country club. He can verify my alibi for last night. You'll also find Mrs. Turner's alibi contacts on that sheet."

"Can those witnesses vouch for where she might have been at four or five this morning?" Warwick asked.

"As a matter of fact one can vouch for her at that time. Her sister and she were talking on the phone between three A.M. and six A.M. Her sister lives in Australia. There is also a maid who lives in the house who says she heard the women talking until almost five."

Zack took the paper but didn't bother to read it. He'd call all the names on both lists but already knew each contact would verify the stories he'd been given.

Warwick picked up an engraved crystal paperweight off of Barlow's desk. He tossed it between his hands. "How was the Turner marriage overall? Happy? Tense?"

"I wasn't privy to their personal life until just minutes ago," Barlow said, frowning at the paperweight in Warwick's hand. "However, Jordan did tell me that she confided the details of her troubled marriage to Lindsay O'Neil two weeks ago. Jordan said Ms. O'Neil was quite angry and upset when Jordan refused to leave her husband."

Zack bit back an oath. Lindsay had been holding out on him. "Why would Mrs. Turner share that bit of information?"

"She said Harold's body was found behind Sanctuary, which, if I'm not mistaken, is the shelter your wife oversees."

What kind of angle was Jordan Turner working?

"Did O'Neil and Jordan Turner have any other contact after that meeting?" Warwick said.

The question was necessary but nevertheless annoyed Zack.

Barlow shook his head. "Mrs. Turner said that Ms. O'Neil called her this afternoon."

Zack swallowed another oath. "And they talked about?"

"Mrs. Turner was concerned that Ms. O'Neil had killed Harold," Barlow said.

"Did she have proof?" Zack asked.

"No."

Amused, Ronnie T. raised a finger. "What a minute. Lindsay O'Neil was your wife, wasn't she, Detective Kier?"

Zack's jaw tightened. "She still is."

Ronnie T. cackled. "I thought she divorced your sorry ass a year ago."

Warwick set the paperweight down, stepping between the two men. "We'll want to interview Mrs. Turner again."

Barlow moved the paperweight out of Warwick's reach. "We'll be happy to help in the investigation in any way."

"I'd be happy to ask my associates if anyone hated ole Harold enough to kill him," Ronnie T. offered.

"The last thing I want is your help," Zack said. The dealer's favors always had strings attached.

Ronnie T.'s smile didn't fade but his eyes hardened. "Is my help too good for you now that you're sober, Detective Kier?"

Zack got right in Ronnie T.'s face. "Stay out of the investigation."

Ronnie T. laughed. "But I want to help."

Warwick nudged Zack. Zack reined in his temper and backed up. "Neither of you leave town."

When Barlow and Ronnie T. both agreed, the two cops walked out of the office. Zack pushed the elevator button. His temper seethed. The doors opened. They got in. Neither spoke until they were outside by the car.

Warwick glared up at the building. "Ronnie T. really pisses you off."

"I crossed paths with him during several narcotics investigations. That million-dollar smile hides a ruthless heart." He'd tried several times to supply Zack with drugs. Once after Lindsay had moved out, he'd been tempted, but he'd refused, as always.

Zack's cell vibrated. He checked the number. Ayden. He flipped open his phone. "Kier."

"Get over to Sanctuary." Ayden's sharp voice jumped through the phone. "Someone delivered Harold Turner's hand to Lindsay."

The police had ordered Lindsay into the shelter's family room across the hallway from her office. She'd been told to wait for the detectives. She sat on the couch, her arms folded and her stomach knotted. She tapped her foot, believing she was going to jump out of her skin.

A half dozen uniformed officers had taken over Sanctuary. One was posted outside Lindsay's office, two on the front porch, and three in the kitchen. They spoke in hushed tones laced with nervous excitement.

With each flash of a camera bulb, she knew Sara, the forensic tech, was in her office shooting pictures, no doubt from every conceivable angle, of the hand and the boxed flowers. Lindsay lost count how many times the digital camera had flashed.

News vans now from all three local television stations were parked out front. She noticed that Kendall Shaw was talking with her cameraman. A frown furrowed the tall brunette's brow as she jabbed her finger in the air. Kendall was angry that there was no film of Lindsay running hysterically out of the shelter toward the unmarked police car. Too bad for Kendall, Lindsay thought bitterly. That bit of film would have made great news.

This day was churning memories that she'd thought were long buried. Running out of the shelter today reminded her of a similar July day twelve years ago when she'd found her mother. She'd bolted from the house. Screaming, she'd run a half mile to the neighbor's house and pounded on the door until a befuddled Mr. Jenkins had answered. Words had rushed from her mouth. Most had been unintelligible. And she'd nearly hyperventilated. But her neighbor had pieced together enough, figured out what had happened, and called the sheriff. She never went back in her parents' house again.

Lindsay shoved a trembling hand through her hair. Rising from the couch, she moved to the window. She'd been almost as rattled today.

Jesus. Someone had sent her a severed hand.

Ruby came around the corner from the kitchen with a cold soda. She pushed the can into Lindsay's hand. "Why don't you come into the kitchen so I can make you something to eat? I've got turkey and bread."

Food was the last thing on Lindsay's mind. "No thanks, Ruby."

"Milk shakes don't cut it, honey. You're going to get sick. I should make you a turkey sandwich."

Lindsay's argument died on her lips when she saw concern in the older woman's eyes. She knew Ruby wasn't so worried about food, but the entire situation. She needed something to do. "You know what, turkey sounds great to me. Extra mustard?"

Ruby nodded. She was obviously relieved. "I'll have it for you in two shakes. Now, come away from the window and sit down."

"We're going to have to move the shelter," Lindsay said. "I thought this morning that maybe, just maybe, we could dig our way out of this, but not now. The press aren't going to sit on our location much longer."

Ruby planted meaty fists on her wide hips. "Don't borrow trouble, Lindsay. Let's just take it one step at a time."

"We don't have the cash reserves for a move. And Dana is going to be furious." She closed her eyes and pictured her boss's tight angular face. She sensed an invisible tide had turned against her.

Ruby laid a hand on Lindsay's shoulder. "Honey, you're good at what you do. The board knows that. You'll find a way out of this."

One way or another, she would fight for this shelter. But she'd been in enough uphill battles to recognize one. "Thanks for the vote of confidence, but in the meantime, you'd better see if you can pick up extra hours at your other job. I know we've never been able to pay you much, but we may not have much to offer for the near future."

Ruby had a teenage daughter to support. "I hate leaving you."

She didn't want Ruby to worry. "I'm going to be fine."

Frown lines formed around her mouth. "I'll be back as soon as you can have me."

Lindsay squeezed her hand. "I know."

Tears in her eyes, Ruby disappeared into the kitchen as the front door opened.

Zack strode in the foyer, his stern expression sweeping clockwise until it landed on Lindsay. Behind him stood a tall, grim-faced man dressed in jeans and a T-shirt. Even if he'd not been wearing his badge on a chain around his neck, she'd have guessed by his demeanor he was also a cop.

Zack made no move toward Lindsay but stared at her long and hard before he released a deep breath. "Are you all right?"

Unexpected relief flooded Lindsay's body. She wanted to rush to him, let him take her in his arms and assure her everything would be okay. But she didn't run to Zack. She stood her ground, her back stiffer than wood.

"I'm great. Never a dull moment, is there?" She tried to sound glib but instead sounded brittle. So be it.

Zack was deadly serious. "You look pale."

"I'm fine." She put steel behind the words, knowing if he showed her any pity she'd break. "Just figure out who sent me that little present in there and I'll be even better."

His expression reflected his disbelief. He knew stress made her bitchy. Knew this shelter meant everything to her. Knew about her mother's death. Knew *her.*

Tension knotted her lower back. She folded her arms over her chest. This was not the time to have unwanted feelings rolling to the surface.

Zack cleared his throat. "This is my partner, Detective Jacob Warwick. This is Lindsay O'Neil. She's the director of the shelter."

Warwick nodded. "Ma'am."

Lindsay prided herself on reading people, on being

able to size up anyone in a nanosecond. But this guy was a blank slate. Tight, controlled, he reminded her of Zack during his undercover days when life and death depended on cloaking emotions.

"I'll bet you worked undercover at one point," Lindsay said.

Warwick didn't seem to appreciate her hard tone. "That's right. That a problem?"

Shrugging, she feigned disinterest. "Nope. I can just spot you guys a mile off."

"Tell us what happened," Zack interjected.

Lindsay drew in a deep breath. "I had just returned from taking the last of my residents to the Riverside shelter and was headed into my office. Ruby told me someone had sent me flowers. I opened the box and saw the irises."

If Zack had remembered that he'd once sent her irises he gave no indication. "And?"

"And I picked up the flowers. That's when I saw the second package. I opened it and saw the hand. I dropped the package. I ran straight to the police car outside." No need to mention her scream could have shattered glass.

"Do you know who might have sent the flowers to you?" Warwick said.

"If I had an idea I would have shared it with the other six officers who asked me the same question in the last fifteen minutes."

Warwick let his doubt show. "Would you have told the police?"

The challenge caught her off guard and irritated her. She stepped forward. "Yes, I would have. Do you think that this is fun or that I want this kind of drama in my life?"

"That's a good question," Warwick said.

"What about Jordan Turner?" Zack countered.

Her defenses rose. "What about her?"

"Harold Turner was smacking her around. Not only did she run into you at that charity fund-raiser, but apparently you two had a long conversation about Harold's abuse at the party. And you called her today."

"I'm not about to apologize for doing my job. I consider her a client. Our conversations were—are—privileged."

"Not legally," Zack said.

She raised her chin. "Morally."

"Do you think she could have done this?" Warwick asked.

She shifted her gaze from Zack to Warwick. "No."

"But you thought she could have killed her husband," Zack said. "That's why you didn't share the details about your conversation with her two weeks ago. It's why you called her this morning."

No sense denying what Zack already knew. "I wasn't sure what she'd done at first." She sighed. "When I realized it was Harold, I was afraid she'd snapped. But after seeing the hand, I know she didn't do it."

Zack's eyes narrowed. "Why do you say that?"

"Because cutting off Harold's hand was some kind of public declaration. The killer is making some kind of statement."

"And Jordan wouldn't do that?" Warwick said.

"She wouldn't. Above all else, Jordan Turner is a very private woman. Appearances are important and this kind of drama is not her style. She'd find it tacky, for lack of a better word."

Neither cop looked convinced.

"Unless she thinks we'll never catch her," Zack said.

Zack knew Lindsay put her heart and soul into her work. It didn't make sense that she'd trash it all. But he'd come across crimes before that made little or no sense.

He and Warwick walked into Lindsay's cramped office, made more claustrophobic by Sara as she snapped pictures of the scene with her digital camera.

Sara glanced up at them and smiled at Zack. "So we meet again."

Stoic, Zack pulled out his notebook. "Yeah."

She raised the camera to hide her frown.

"What do you have?" Zack asked.

"I've rolled prints from the flower box but have yet to run them through AFIS." AFIS, the Automated Fingerprint Identification System, would compare crime scene fingerprints with millions of others across the country in hours. If the murderer was in the system, they'd find him.

"Anything else?" Warwick said.

"No hair fibers so far, but I've yet to take the hand out of the bag. I'll do that when I get back to the lab."

Zack glanced at the note, now sealed in a plastic evidence bag. He picked it up, holding the bag by the corner. The bold script was large and covered most of the white card with embossed edges.

"*Lindsay, you are not alone anymore,*'" he read. Zack handed the note to Warwick.

Warwick glanced at the note and then at Zack. "Who the hell is the Guardian?"

"I have no idea. Lindsay comes in contact with hundreds of different people in a week. Some are pretty rough characters." Zack had never liked the idea of her dealing with thugs. In his mind, she took too many chances. "And then there was that damn newspaper article in May. How many thousands read it?"

"I'm going to need Lindsay's fingerprints," Sara said.

As a husband, Zack wanted to defend his wife and tell everyone she was no killer. As a cop he couldn't rule anyone out as a suspect at this stage of the investigation.

"She had a police background check when she applied for this job. Her prints are on file."

She nodded. "I'll pull them."

Warwick studied the hand positioned neatly in the box. "He wrapped the hand in a plastic bag. That explains why we didn't have a trail of blood leading from the crime scene."

"He's meticulous," Zack said. "The crime scene this morning suggested he's an organized killer."

Warwick stared at the hand's bloated fingers with blackening nail beds. "Why the left hand?"

Zack didn't like the scenario forming in his head. "Turner's wedding band is still on his ring finger. Mrs. Turner was abused. The left hand is supposedly the one that leads to your heart. I'd bet it's symbolic in some way."

"The killer doesn't like abusive husbands," Warwick said.

"Maybe. Or maybe Ronnie T. killed his attorney and set all this up to throw us off the trail. Ronnie T. also knows Lindsay is my wife."

Warwick nodded. "Why go after you?"

"Payback. When I worked narcotics, I put one hell of a dent in his operation."

"Ronnie T. is smart and dangerous, but I don't see him going to this kind of trouble. Like I said, a drive-by is more his style."

"Maybe. But for now it's a theory we've got to consider."

Zack left Warwick and returned to Lindsay, who stood in the family room by the French doors that faced out back. Yellow crime scene tape, pelted by the rain, drooped in mud puddles.

"Who is the Guardian?" Zack said. He watched closely for any reaction.

She looked puzzled. "I don't know."

"Why would he write you a note?"

She hugged her arms around her. "I've no idea."

"Have you received any unusual phone calls lately, notes, contributions, anything out of the ordinary?"

"Nothing that jumps to mind. That May article generated several donations."

Zack could have pressed Lindsay about sharing her case files, but he didn't. He was going to wait for the warrant. The delivery of Harold's hand had officially bumped this case to high priority. From here on out, each step of the investigation could have huge ramifications, so he'd do everything by the book.

Lindsay flexed her fingers as if trying to release the tension knotting her muscles. "I have a grant application due in three days. Can I at least grab that file so I can work at home?"

Stress always did send her running in to work. "Nothing leaves the office for now."

She stabbed long fingers through her hair. "The grant has nothing to do with this. But it means everything to the shelter."

Despite it all, she was still trying to hold on to this place. "It's in the office so it stays."

A helpless sigh shuddered from her. "What about my purse?"

"Nothing leaves the office."

"I need my car keys."

"I'll drive you," Zack said.

"I'm supposed to speak to a local church group tonight."

"Cancel it."

She took a step back. "No, thanks."

"Lindsay, there's a guy running around town who's left a dead body in your backyard and sent you a severed hand. It's not safe for you."

She stiffened. "Bullies don't scare me."

But he saw fear in her eyes. "This one should."

"Is it my safety that you're so worried about or are you afraid I'll skip town because I'm the killer?"

She was going for the jugular, trying to throw him off balance. Two could play that game. "Honestly, I can't rule you out yet."

Her mouth dropped open. "You're kidding."

"I'm not. You have motive and no alibi."

"I didn't do it."

"Prove it."

She paled and turned away.

Satisfied he had the last word for now, Zack left and found Warwick talking to Ruby in the kitchen. The older woman was smiling and stared up at Warwick with a twinkle in her eye. Damn, what had he said to soften her up? When Zack entered the room, Ruby's smile vanished.

Ruby's simmering resentment suggested she knew about his and Lindsay's separation.

"I'm going to run Ms. O'Neil home." Zack had made a statement, not a request.

Warwick's eyes narrowed. "I'll ride along."

"Suit yourself."

"She doesn't need you," Ruby said. "She can drive herself just fine."

Zack dug his keys out of his pocket. "Not with her car keys sealed in a crime scene."

"I'll take her," Ruby said. "She's got enough stress right now without you adding to it."

The older woman had painted him as the bad guy in the marriage. And truthfully, she wasn't off base. "Thanks, but I've got it covered."

Ruby frowned but wasn't in a position to argue.

Zack found Lindsay by the front door. "Do you have spare keys to your house?"

"Yes. Hidden under a pot by the front door."

He'd lectured her enough about safety when they'd been married. He'd always feared his undercover work would spill into his personal life and put her in danger. "That's not too safe."

Her face colored as if she remembered what he'd said. "It's handy."

As soon as they emerged from the house, the reporters who'd been on the front lawn lunged toward them. Zack shielded her from the cameras and hustled her to his car while Warwick ran interference with the press. Zack opened the backseat side door. She was half inside the car when Kendall darted around Warwick and caught up to them.

The reporter shoved a microphone toward Lindsay's face. "Lindsay, can you tell me why you were so upset earlier? Why did the police return? Has someone else been killed?"

Zack waited until Lindsay was fully inside before he closed the car door. "No statements now, Ms. Shaw."

Kendall looked annoyed. "I'm just trying to do my job, detective. Lindsay, tell me what happened."

Warwick moved beside Kendall, using height and size to intimidate her. "Talk to the department's public relations guy."

Kendall didn't look threatened, but annoyed. "When I'm interested in the party line, I will. Right now I'm looking for real answers."

Warwick frowned. Clearly he didn't like the woman. "No comment." He slid in the front passenger seat.

Cameras rolled as Zack got behind the wheel and started the car. In silence, they drove through the neighborhood to the main road.

Lindsay stared out the window. From the rearview mirror, Zack could see her jaw was tight and her body tense. She needed a friend right now.

But Zack couldn't be that for her. Not if he was going to figure out who killed Turner and who now harbored an obsession for her. He merged onto the interstate.

"Tell me about that charity function and the Turners again," Zack said.

She fidgeted with the bracelets on her wrist. "Like I said, I didn't kill Harold. And neither did Jordan."

Warwick stared out the side window as if he were a million miles away, but he wasn't missing a syllable.

Zack couldn't let her off the hook. "There's no need to protect Jordan. She's got an attorney and an alibi for the time her husband was killed."

Her lips flattened. "Like I said, I met them at a charity function two weeks ago. Jordan was on Harold's arm, smiling radiantly. They looked like the perfect couple." She hesitated. "I should have known then that something was up."

"Why?"

"No such thing as a perfect couple." She sighed and recapped the encounter with Jordan. "A half hour later, Harold approached me at the party. He told me to stay away from Jordan. I told him to stop hitting his wife. We got into a big fight. Then I left the party."

"Witnesses?"

"No doubt. I noticed several people were staring, but I couldn't tell you who."

Zack tightened his hands on the wheel. "That's it? You never saw Harold again? You never communicated with him?"

Disgust darkened her face. "Not Harold. But I did call Jordan several times. I hoped I could help her. And I did call her this morning after I saw you."

"To tell her about Harold?"

She hesitated. "To try to figure out if she'd crossed the line." She dug fingers through her hair. "The last time I talked to Jordan, she told me not to worry about Harold. She said she could take care of him."

"And you figured that meant murder."

"Not at the time. A lot of women believe they can handle their abusive husbands. They think that if they always smile, that if the house is immaculate and sex is always available, everything will be fine. But no matter what they do, it's never enough. Sooner or later the guy snaps again and hits her."

They'd only talked about her mother's death once. As a husband he'd let his unanswered questions lie. As a cop he couldn't. "Did your mother think she could handle your father?"

Lindsay flinched, glancing to Warwick. He met her gaze in the rearview mirror. It was one thing for Zack to know about her past; quite another for Warwick. Humiliation washed over her.

"My mother has nothing to do with Harold Turner's murder."

Zack didn't enjoy opening a painful wound. He'd always avoided discussing the subject with her because he knew it bothered her. "Your family life was beyond rough, Lindsay. That changes a person."

Warwick glanced in the rearview mirror at her, as if trying to peer into her mind.

Lindsay lifted her chin. "I went into social work and opened Sanctuary because of Mom. I didn't become a murderer because of her."

Zack shot her a glance in the rearview mirror. "The Commonwealth's attorney could argue that because you couldn't have it out with your old man, you picked the next best target—Harold."

"That's crap. Remember the killer sent *me* Harold's hand."

"You could have sent it to yourself," Warwick said.

She leaned forward, fingers gripping the seat. "And written myself a creepy note?"

Warwick turned toward her. "You wouldn't be the first to try something like that."

"I can't believe we are having this conversation." Her voice sounded loud, angry.

Warwick kept his tone even, calm, but the menace was unmistakable. "Whoever killed Harold did it in anger. He *cut off* Harold's left hand. If that isn't a statement about shattered vows, I don't know what is."

"I didn't kill him."

"You don't have an alibi," Zack said.

"I can't help that. It's not my fault the damn power went out." Arms folded, she dropped back in the seat and turned toward the window. She swiped away a tear.

The only time Zack had seen her cry had been that day in the attorney's office. Tension twisted his gut.

Five minutes later, they reached her town house development. Well-manicured lawns jutted out from near identical row houses that looked as if they'd been stamped from cookie cutters. This kind of development was very un-Lindsay. She'd always leaned more toward the older, quirky homes that needed more attention than a full-time job. Why had she chosen such a place? Zack kept his question to himself as he parked in the numbered spot she directed him to. A sprinkler system whooshed in the background and a dog barked.

"Thanks," she said ironically, opening her car door. She walked to the planter, tipped it back, and retrieved the front door key.

Following, Zack didn't bother to hide the frustration in his voice. "From now on, don't hide the key there."

Lindsay shoved the key in the lock. "I can take care of myself."

He flashed a smile that looked more like a snarl. "Humor me."

A flicker of movement caught his eye. A man dressed in a green maintenance uniform moved toward them. Blond, pudgy, and short, he was smiling as he held hedge clippers in his hand.

Zack moved his right hand to his belt closer to the .22 holstered on his hip.

Warwick got out of the car and leaned against it. His demeanor stated he was ready to intervene if necessary.

"Lindsay," the maintenance man said. "What are you doing home in the middle of the day?"

Zack and Warwick watched the man very closely.

Lindsay seemed to relax around him. "Hey, Steve. How's it going?"

Steve glanced at Zack and Warwick. His eyes narrowed. "You friends of Lindsay's?"

Ole Steve seemed a little territorial when it came to Lindsay. "Detective Zack Kier," Zack said as he flipped open his wallet and showed his police badge. "This is my partner, Detective Warwick."

"Steve Hess. I manage this property. Everything all right?"

Zack watched Lindsay smile at Steve. She had resented his interference about the key but seemed to appreciate Steve's protective tone.

"It's fine, thanks," she said. "Did you want to tell me something?"

Steve was distracted by Zack and Warwick's presence. "Oh, I was just headed into your place to check the AC unit. You said it wasn't working well."

"Did I?"

"You put in a maintenance request about three weeks ago."

She smiled. "Right. Thanks. Do you mind if we do this another time?"

"No problem. Oh, and the cable guy came by to check on your television. Your reception is all cleared up."

"Thanks," she said.

Steve's gaze flickered between the cops. "Why the police escort home?"

Lindsay unlocked her front door. "There was a little trouble at work today. It's nothing to be worried about. Detective Kier is just being extra careful."

Steve's smile turned brittle. He didn't seem to like cops. "Tax dollars at work."

"Something like that," Zack said. "Can you tell me anything about the power outage this morning?"

Steve rubbed the back of his neck with his hand. "It was a real mess. The whole east side of the development was out from about midnight last night to eight this morning."

At least Lindsay hadn't been lying about that. "What happened?"

"Transformer blew late. It took Virginia Power until this morning to get it up and running."

"Does that happen often?"

"Been fifteen years since the last transformer blew and that was in an electrical storm," Steve said. "Must have been some freak power surge."

An outage caused Lindsay to be late to work. Across town Harold was murdered. The two incidents weren't necessarily related, but that didn't mean they weren't.

Zack glanced back at Warwick, still positioned by the car. "I'll be back in a minute."

Warwick pushed away from the car. "No rush. I have a few more questions for Steve."

Zack left the nervous maintenance man with Warwick and followed Lindsay inside her town house. She flipped the lights on. The ticktock of clocks jived with the hum of the AC unit.

He saw far enough into the town house to see a floral couch. The pillows on the couch were straight and neatly fluffed. If the outside was cookie cutter the inside was vintage Lindsay. The clocks, the restored second-hand furniture, and the stacks of books were all her. The place smelled of linseed oil, which, he remembered, she used to dust her furniture.

Standing this close, he caught the soft scent of her soap. He'd forgotten how good she smelled.

Lindsay lifted her gaze and for a moment a connection sparked between them. She sensed it as much as he did. He leaned forward, testing. She drew back.

"Mind if I have a look around?" he said.

She blocked his path. "As a matter of fact I do."

"Why?"

"I don't want you here."

His gaze narrowed. "What are you hiding?"

"Nothing."

He took a step back. "You're hiding something. And I'll figure out what it is."

Chapter Ten

Lindsay was fighting a headache when she arrived at the church just before six. Without car keys, she'd had to borrow a car from her neighbor. The gal had been a little reluctant at first, but Lindsay had promised to drive carefully and have the car back by nine.

She'd considered canceling this speaking engagement to the church's group. Despite the extra sleep last night, she felt wrung out and exhausted after the day she'd had. But Nicole was at work and the idea of staying home alone didn't sit well.

Besides, this church's pastor was one of the shelter's best supporters. He had called her after the *Inside Richmond* article and offered his congregation's support. For several months since then, there'd been a stream of clothes, some money, and food donations.

She didn't want to let him down tonight. So, she made a double espresso and pushed through the fatigue.

The Methodist church was located on Shady Grove Road in an affluent tree-lined section of the city. The church had been constructed less than five years ago. It had a tall A-line roof and tall windows that let the sun shine in. The church also had an education building that was joined to the church by an arched breezeway. This building had a more streamlined look and was suited strictly for function, not worship.

The day's heat hadn't cooled much and the sun was still bright. The large gravel parking lot was nearly deserted. There were only a half dozen cars, including the one that filled the *pastor*'s slot. It looked as if it was going to be a low turnout tonight. Not surprising. Low turnouts weren't uncommon. Few wanted to give up their evening to hear about grim domestic violence stats.

Lindsay grabbed her laptop with her PowerPoint presentation and made her way to the education building. She opened the side door and started down the long red-carpeted hallway to the minister's office.

Halfway down the hall, a man came out of a side parlor. He was tall and thin with dark thinning hair. He looked to be about fifty and was dressed in a golf shirt and khaki pants. He had a "father knows best" way about him that made you glad he was in charge.

He noticed her immediately and smiled warmly. "Ms. O'Neil?"

Lindsay nodded. "Pastor Richards."

"How are you doing?"

The evening news hadn't hit yet so he didn't know about the murder. "Great," she said. She didn't want to discuss the murders. After the evening news, she'd be answering a lot of uncomfortable questions.

Pastor Richards moved toward her and shook her hand. He had an extension cord in the other hand. "Thank you for coming out this evening."

"Happy to. Thank you for having me."

He nodded toward the parlor. "I've got you set up in the green room. In fact, I was just going to see if I could find a longer extension cord. You said you needed power for your computer."

"Yes. I've a PowerPoint presentation."

"Go on in and get yourself set up. I'll see if I can't find a longer cord."

"Sure." She moved into the room. It was elegantly decorated with silk swag curtains on the tall windows; a Chippendale sofa and chairs; and, in the corner, a baby grand piano. Pastor Richards had set up a podium and table for her, a white projection screen, and a dozen chairs. In the back of the room was a small round table set up with coffee, lemonade, and cookies.

She removed her computer from the case and set it up just as the pastor returned.

"I can't find the longer cord," he said, scratching the side of his head. "Our church secretary is on vacation and, honestly, she is the brains behind this operation. When she's away, the church and I just stumble along until she returns."

Lindsay smiled. "It's fine. I should have enough battery power to get through the presentation. And if not, I'll do what I do best—talk."

Chuckling, he checked his watch. "Most of the folks should be here any second. They're just wrapping up their Monday night supper down the hall. It's a summer Bible study program and they decided to turn it into a pot luck. They're four weeks into a six-week program."

"Great."

"Help yourself to coffee."

"Thanks."

She moved to the back table and filled a Styrofoam cup with coffee. "So tell me a little more about the group I'm speaking to tonight."

"It's a ladies circle group and their husbands. They're studying references to marriage in the Bible and I thought it would be interesting to discuss a modern take on marriage. Domestic abuse is just one of the topics we're looking at this summer."

"Right." She sipped her coffee. Compared to the espresso, it tasted like water. "I want to thank you again for all the help the church has given Sanctuary. We've really appreciated it."

Pastor Richards's smile was warm and there was a kindness about him. "Oh, we're just happy to help." He shoved his hands into his pockets and looked a tad embarrassed.

"A friend of mine works for the police department," he said. "He told me a body was found behind your shelter."

"Yes. It was Harold Turner." She didn't want to talk about the murder but knew it had to be addressed. "I don't know why he was murdered in our backyard."

The pastor nodded. "I've met his wife. Our church works with hers on several children's charities. Lovely woman."

She remembered her conversation with Jordan this morning. "I hope she has good support around her now."

"Oh, I'm sure she does. I want you to know this doesn't change First Methodist's commitment to the shelter. We believe in what you're doing."

Relief washed through her. "Thanks. That does mean a lot to me."

Within minutes the group of couples gathered in the room. They all looked to be in their fifties and sixties. Each wore a wedding band. The minister made introductions and soon Lindsay stood before the group.

Lindsay had spoken to groups like this many times before. In fact, she had never turned down an opportunity to speak, believing that if she did, she might somehow miss the one person who needed her help.

"I'm not going to give you a bunch of statistics or talk to you about the problem of domestic violence," Lindsay began. She smiled and tried to look relaxed and comfortable. "I'm here to tell you a story."

She didn't like to stand behind podiums. She liked to feel a connection with her audience, no matter how small it was. She clicked on the first slide. A picture of a young, smiling, dark-haired woman appeared on the white projection screen.

"This is Pam when she was a senior in high school in Henderson, North Carolina. Pam was a smart girl. She made all As in high school and she married her high school sweetheart. His name was Matt. Pam got a good job as the executive secretary to an insurance president, and he would later say that Pam was hardworking and diligent and that everyone at the insurance company liked her. Five years ago, Pam and Matt moved to Richmond. She didn't get another job, because Matt wanted her to stay home. They were trying to have a baby. Pam was thirty-five.

"In December of last year, Pam showed up at work wearing dark glasses. And underneath the lenses was bruising. The company president asked Pam about her eyes and she explained that she'd been in a car accident. Two days later, police were called to her residence. The neighbor had heard shouting. But when police arrived Pam assured the officers that she was fine."

Telling the story always made her sad. "Two days later she ended up in the emergency room. I met with her then and was able to convince her to spend a few nights at Sanctuary. I took her to the magistrate's office and walked her through the protective order process. She seemed relieved."

Pastor Richards frowned. "Did I read about this case in the paper?"

Lindsay nodded grimly. "You did. About nine months ago. And, in fact, the husband was just sentenced about a month ago." She sipped her coffee as she searched her notes for the spot where she'd left off.

"We'll say a prayer for them at the end of the meeting," the pastor said.

Lindsay smiled, not sure what to say to that. Maybe wherever Pam was now, the prayers would help. "We can offer board in our shelter for only thirty days. As the thirty days ticked away, Pam began to worry that she wouldn't have a place to live. Her parents were gone, she'd made no friends, and she wasn't close to her brothers, who had never liked her husband. Matt had seen to it that she'd stayed isolated. Anyway, Pam called Matt. And he came to the shelter and picked her up." She paused. "We found her body the next morning. She'd been beaten to death."

A woman with short gray hair folded her arms over her chest. She glanced at her husband, a short, stocky man with a ruddy face. "I can tell you I wouldn't tolerate that kind of behavior from my husband."

Lindsay shrugged. "None of us knows what we'd do."

The woman grinned as if she had all the answers. "I know what I'd do if my husband ever hit me—I'd shoot him."

Nervous giggles rippled through the room.

Lindsay smiled. "Do you know how to boil a frog alive?"

Everyone sobered. "You put it in cold water and then you very slowly start to turn the heat up under the pot. When the frog realizes it's too late and is about to be boiled alive, the heat overcomes the frog and kills it."

Few in the room took the analogy that seriously. But when she raised her gaze, she realized Pastor Richards was staring at her with a renewed intensity that made her uncomfortable.

Zack and Warwick returned to the shelter. It was past six. Ruby had gone home and Sara was still processing the crime scene in Lindsay's office.

The two detectives questioned neighbors but learned little other than Lindsay kept a nice yard. Few knew the house was a shelter, though none worried about the number of cars that came and went during any given day. No one noticed anything unusual around five that morning.

After several hours, Zack and Warwick called it quits with the promise to meet again at headquarters by seven the next morning.

By the time Zack pulled into his driveway, he was bone tired. He turned off the car and just sat. His last encounter with Lindsay played in his head as he stared at the salt-box house he'd just bought. He took in the broken windows, peeling paint, overgrown shrubs and, for the hundredth time, wondered why he'd purchased the damn place. He knew the answer.

Because Lindsay had loved it.

He'd passed the house a dozen times in the last month, each time pausing to see if the FOR SALE sign had been pulled up. It hadn't. In this waning real estate market, the house required more work and attention than most were willing to give. Yet, he still kept coming back, staring past the decay and rot to the possibilities Lindsay had once envisioned.

Zack got out of the car and slung his coat over his shoulder. After climbing the front steps, he unlocked the door. He prayed his beeper wouldn't go off before the morning briefing. He needed downtime and sleep.

Inside the house, plaster walls had trapped the day's heat, leaving the foyer stuffy and humid. The supplies from the hardware superstore had been delivered a couple of days ago, but the job had kept him on the run and he'd barely had enough time to stack the supplies into the empty living room.

Late-afternoon sun streamed through the transom above the front door. His footsteps echoed as he moved over scarred hardwood floors toward the kitchen. The place felt unwelcoming.

He dropped his keys on the gray kitchen counter and laid his coat on a stack of boxes by the back door. From the kitchen window above the sink, he stared at the back-yard. It reminded him of the surface of the moon: barren, lifeless.

Zack went to the new, starkly white refrigerator. When he and Lindsay had been together their refrigerator had been covered with pictures of them, schedules, and drawings from the kids at the shelter.

He opened it. The bright bulb illuminated two boxes of Chinese food, a half-full carton of orange juice, and a couple of cans of soda. He craved a beer right now but tried not to think about it as he snatched a soda and headed back out to the front porch. He sat on the front step, loosened his tie, and popped the soda's tab. Maybe he'd go for a run and then order a pizza.

Zack downed the last of the soda and crushed the can just as a black SUV pulled up in front of the house. The car belonged to his brother, Malcolm.

This wasn't Malcolm's part of town. He must be doing recon for their mother.

Malcolm wore a loose, white T-shirt, faded jeans, and flip-flops. He strolled around the side of his truck, a brown paper bag tucked in close at his side, sunlight bouncing off his chrome aviator glasses. Malcolm was a year younger than Zack and, at six one, a couple of inches shorter.

"Tell Mom I'm fine," Zack called.

Malcolm shook his head. "That won't be good enough. She's going to want details." He stopped in front of the house, pulled off his glasses, and studied the exterior. "Were you sober when you bought this piece-of-crap house, Zack?"

"Sober as a judge."

"Now I'm really worried about you. Do yourself a favor and bulldoze it and start fresh."

That coaxed a grin from Zack. "It's a great investment. The realtor said lots of potential and charm."

Malcolm's gaze scanned the peeling paint on the front porch and the dry rot by the front door. "Lots of work. Lots of money to fix it up."

"Consider it therapy." Zack nodded to the bag. "What's in the bag?"

"Mom sent food." Malcom handed him the bag.

Zack opened the bag and found a large tinfoil container of ziti, cellophane-wrapped bread rolls, two cookies, and a plastic fork. He was starving. "Bless you."

Malcolm sat down on the porch and studied the house. "Why'd you pick this place?"

Because Lindsay had once looked at the house and talked about filling it with babies. Instead he said, "It's an investment. I paid next to nothing for it." He was nostalgic but not stupid.

Sighing, Malcolm glanced down the street at the collection of half-century-old homes. Most had been renovated. "Fixed up, it could be worth a fortune," he said.

"That's my thought. If it doesn't work out I can always flip it for a profit."

He sighed and didn't seem convinced. "Oh, Mom said to remind you about the party."

"Party?"

Malcolm looked at him as if he were dim-witted. "Damn, Zack, Eleanor's birthday party. Saturday. Mom's been planning it for months. Be there or suffer the consequences."

"Oh yeah, right." He opened the tinfoil container and savored the blend of ziti, tomatoes, oregano, and basil. His sister, Ellie, had talked about the party for weeks, and he'd cut off his right arm before he'd disappoint her. "I won't miss it."

"Mom would have come but the restaurant is packed tonight. She couldn't get away."

"No sweat."

"I saw the six o'clock news. I guess you saw Lindsay today." Malcolm didn't hide the fact that he disapproved of Zack's *un*marriage to Lindsay.

"Yep. And I'm in no mood for lectures about Lindsay, our marriage, or unsigned divorce papers."

Malcolm held up his hands. "You'll get none from me today."

"Good."

"Still, this investigation is going to be a hornet's nest. Is Ayden going to let you stay on the case?"

"Yes, but Warwick's taking the lead."

Malcolm frowned. "He eased up on you at all? Or is he still being an ass?"

"Like always, he's expecting me to screw up." Zack bit into a slice of warm, buttery Italian bread. "Warwick will have to wait until hell freezes over before I drink again."

The comment pleased Malcolm. "Any leads on the Turner case?"

"No forensic evidence on the body. Turner's wife has an ironclad alibi, as does his number one drug-dealing client and his law partner."

"What about *your* wife?" Malcolm kept his voice neutral.

"Lindsay doesn't have an alibi. She says she was home alone. Frankly, her alibi is so lame, it could be true. But I need to be sure. The judge should sign my search warrants in the morning, and then I'll work my way through her phone, computer, and office records."

Malcolm traced a callus on the palm of his hand. "Lindsay can be tenacious when it comes to protecting battered women."

"But I'm betting she's no killer. She hates all kinds of violence."

They sat in silence for a moment as Zack ate.

"So what are you two going to do about your marriage?"

Zack jabbed his fork into a cluster of ziti. "We're not talking about that, remember?"

Malcolm stretched out his legs and crossed them at the ankles. "Cut the crap and answer the question."

Zack chewed his ziti slowly. "I'm going to do my best to save our marriage."

"Shit, Zack, have you lost your mind? She left you." Malcolm was a man of strong opinions. During Zack's recovery he'd been a rock. But even though Zack had regained his balance, his brother remained overprotective.

The truth behind his failed marriage shamed Zack. "She had good reason."

"She should have stuck by you when you got sick."

Sick. Zack shook his head. "It's not like I had cancer, Mal. I was a drunk. I let her down."

Malcolm shook his head. "Marriage is for better or worse in my mind. Sickness and health."

"I guess this is the worse part."

"How can it ever get better between the two of you? Lindsay is obsessed with work. She can be abrasive. And she is now a suspect in a murder investigation. No one in their right mind would want her."

Zack grinned. "And your point is?"

Malcolm's eyes darkened. "This isn't funny."

Zack sobered. "No, it's not. My marriage is sloppy. Sucks right now. But once, it was pretty great. I want that back."

Malcolm shook his head. "Will she have you back?"

"I don't know."

The Guardian clicked off the television, irritated by the evening news reports. Harold's name had been released to the press, but the stations had given the murder little airtime. All three stations had screwed up the story, but that dumb bitch reporter from Channel 10, Kendall Shaw, had missed the point completely. She'd prattled on about the county's low murder rate and domestic violence statistics. She seemed more worried about her own image than reporting the story.

That was the problem with people. They were selfish and far too wrapped up in their individual lives to notice what didn't directly concern them.

The only one who could truly *see* was Lindsay.

She reached out to others in need. She put the lives of others in front of her own.

Her warrior spirit should have appreciated Harold's hand nestled in a bed of irises. Like the flowers, which telegraphed Friendship, Hope, Wisdom, and Valor, the hand was rich with symbolism. It not only bore Harold's platinum wedding band, but it was the left hand and it was well known that the attorney was a lefty. It was his dominant hand. His power center. He'd always struck his wife with his left fist.

One click of another remote and a very different image snapped on the TV. This in full color as well, but it was an image of Lindsay's living room.

The cameras had been placed in her apartment thirty days ago. It had been appallingly easy to gain entrance. A work order and a report of fuzzy cable was all it had taken. The cameras had been easy to install. Several weren't bigger than the size of a dime, and the transmitter, which boosted the signal up to seven miles, was easily wired into an outlet behind the AC unit.

The Guardian settled back in a chair and studied the television screen. In the background, Lindsay's favorite Sugarland CD crooned. The country western song was upbeat, fast paced. In the background he heard Lindsay singing.

Seconds later Lindsay emerged from the kitchen. Her hair was damp from a shower and she wore an oversized, well-worn T-shirt that said "USC." She had a large bowl of popcorn and a diet soda. Her favorite evening ritual before bed.

Lindsay's habits were so predictable. Two cups of coffee before work. An hour of yoga in the morning. Glasses only when she read. Weekends when she wasn't on call meant refinishing the chest of drawers that would be a showpiece. Insomnia when she was troubled.

Lindsay sat on her carpeted floor and switched on a cable news station. Silently she watched and ate her popcorn.

Her phone rang and she leaned over and grabbed the receiver off the cradle. "Hello."

Late calls never boded well. They always meant a crisis that pulled her away, and she'd already had a long enough day. She shouldn't have gone to the church. But then she wasn't one to quit on a promise.

A flipped switch and the call broadcasted over the speakers.

"Hey, Aisha," Lindsay said. "Is everything all right?"

Aisha sighed. "The shelter is fine. Everyone is real nice."

"And the boys are settled in?"

"Yes. We're all in the same room. They like that."

"What's wrong?"

"Marcus called me again this evening on my cell phone. He keeps telling me how much he loves me."

Lindsay's expression tightened. *"We've been through this before, Aisha. He wants to control you. What he feels for you isn't healthy."*

"I know, I know. And I told him I wouldn't be coming back to him no matter what. And I meant that. I really did."

"Good girl."

Lindsay and the Guardian spoke the two words in unison.

"But he wants to see the boys. He says they're his sons and he has a right to them. I don't want to keep Damien and Jamal from their dad."

"The boys are afraid of him."

"He hasn't hit them in a while."

Lindsay gripped the telephone, struggling with her temper. The children always got to her. *"He is talking about his rights as a father but you have rights, too, Aisha. You and the boys have the right to a safe home."*

"I know, but . . ."

"Have you called my friend at Legal Aid about the divorce and custody?"

"Not yet."

Lindsay pressed fingertips to her temple. *"We've been through this before. Call the woman at Legal Aid whom I told you about. She's very nice. She'll tell you about your rights."*

"Okay."

"Are you going to call?"

"Yes."

"Good. You're doing a good job, Aisha. I'm proud of you."

A sob escaped Aisha. *"Are you really?"*

"I really am."

"Thanks."

They talked a few more minutes about the legalities of divorce and custody before Lindsay hung up. The Guardian switched off the phone speaker.

Lindsay turned back toward the television and rubbed her temple. She scooped a handful of popcorn and took a bite. But she no longer seemed to enjoy her snack. Frowning, she tossed what remained in her hand back in the bowl.

Absentmindedly, she pushed away the bowl. She had a tendency not to eat when she was upset. And at the rate she was going, she was going to make herself sick.

Lindsay rose, then began to pace. She moved around her town house like a caged animal.

The Guardian touched the television screen and traced the profile of her face.

Harold's death, the hand, even the note hadn't been enough to assure her that she wasn't alone in her Holy Cause. She needed to know she had an ally. She wasn't alone.

But words didn't matter to Lindsay. Only deeds mattered to her.

The real way to prove to Lindsay that she had a true friend now was to ferret out more Evil Ones. The more men who died now meant that many fewer battered wives whom Lindsay would have to care for.

As the bodies would begin to stack up, she would see the pattern. She would see that she had a true Guardian.

Chapter Eleven

Tuesday, July 8, 12:00 A.M.

Kendall Shaw was pissed. She stopped the recording of her eleven o'clock news report and climbed down off the elliptical trainer she kept on the sun porch of her mother's house.

The story she'd filed had been nothing short of lame. Murder in the city's west end. Identity of victim. A brief recap of his career and murder stats in the metro area. Domestic violence. *Ya, ya, ya.*

It was all very bland, very ordinary, and not the kind of story that was going to get her to a bigger television market like L.A. or New York.

But her boss had given in to pressure from Dana Miller, the shelter's board chair, and had ordered her not to mention Sanctuary or its location. For now, all stations were protecting the shelter's identity. And unless something broke soon, Dana would see to it that the story faded away.

As Kendall had stood outside Sanctuary today, she had sensed she'd stumbled upon a big story. She'd wanted to linger and remain on hand with her cameraman, Mike.

Something was going to break—she could feel it in her bones.

But the evening news producer had felt otherwise. He'd wanted film of a warehouse fire. She'd argued. He'd denied her request to stay and had pulled her cameraman.

Minutes after Mike had left and Kendall was packing up, Lindsay had run screaming out of the shelter. Her terrified screams had the cop in the patrol car scrambling toward her. Within minutes, the place was swarming with more cops.

Something *big* had happened in the shelter.

And if she'd had film, it was the kind of *something* that would get her a better job.

Mike did return, but by then it was too late. The cops didn't release any details and she'd had to file her original story.

From her briefcase she pulled out a CD of the raw footage from this morning. She swapped it out for the other CD in the tray and hit "play."

She fast-forwarded through the morning interviews with neighbors. The last interview of the morning was with Mrs. Young, the neighbor across the street, who kept going on and on about how nice Lindsay's yard was and how no one knew the house was a women's shelter.

Blah, blah, blah.

Kendall slowed the tape to just before Mike had shut off his camera. This time she didn't focus on Mrs. Young but the background just to the right of the shelter.

A cat chasing a squirrel. Thunder clouds. And then in the bottom-right corner, the bumper of a van pulled into the frame. At the time, her back had been to the shelter and she'd been on the phone with her producer. She'd not noticed the driver. Hell, who ever noticed delivery guys?

Now as she reviewed the footage, she watched closely.

The driver, head tucked low and a box of flowers in hand, got out of the van, ran up to the front porch, rang the bell, and set the box down. As the driver turned, the tape turned to static. Mike had switched off the camera.

"Damn it!" Kendall rewound the tape. She watched the footage again. Lindsay had returned to the shelter around two. She started screaming minutes later. Whatever had freaked Lindsay out had to be the box.

"What the hell was it? What was sent to her?"

Kendall had good instincts and she had learned to listen to them. Whatever had gone on at the shelter today had to do with Lindsay. She couldn't prove it, but she'd bet money that Harold had been killed for Lindsay.

She dashed upstairs to the stack of files in the corner of the living room. She kept all her interview notes filed away in case she ever needed to reference them again. Since she'd moved into the house last December, she'd not taken the time to put the notes away, convinced that she was here only temporarily.

Flipping through the manila folders, she pulled the file containing her article about Lindsay.

Scanning the pages, she read her notes from her late April interview. There seemed nothing out of the ordinary. She had notes on Lindsay's day-to-day routine at the shelter. She had stats on domestic violence in the county and the country. All this was strictly background.

Kendall flipped to her notes on Lindsay's past. She was a graduate of the University of California. She entered school at the age of nineteen and attended on a full scholarship and was an honor student. Lindsay worked for a landscape company to pay for living expenses. And she made it through in three years so that she graduated with her class. Originally she was from Ashland, a town in Hanover County, Virginia.

That notation had Kendall pausing. She'd forgotten Lindsay was a Virginian. Lindsay had only mentioned it in passing and had spoken of herself several times as a California girl.

It wasn't unusual for a kid to go so far from home for school, nor extraordinary to take a year off between high school and college. Still, something nagged at her.

Kendall dug her Blackberry out of her briefcase and looked up the number of the *Herald Progress*, the local paper that covered the town of Ashland and Hanover County.

Last year, she'd done a very nice piece on the *Herald Progress*' anniversary celebration. The paper's assistant editor had always said to call if she needed anything. Well, she needed a favor.

Unmindful of the time, she dialed his number.

The phone rang five times before a groggy male voice answered, "Hello."

"Barry. Kendall Shaw. I need a favor."

"Kendall?" She heard fumbling with what must have been a light switch. "It's midnight. Can't this wait until the morning?"

"Not really. And I'm sorry for the late time, but I'm working on a story. Can you do a search for me?"

"*Now*?" he groaned.

"Yes."

"You are insane. I'm not digging up anything for you at this time of night."

She rushed to say, "You said you owed me big for that piece I did on the paper's anniversary."

Grogginess mingled with irritation. "Kendall, it's midnight."

She twirled her finger in her hair as she paced. "Look, do this search for me and I'll *owe* you."

"What's that mean?"

"Name your price."

He cleared his throat. "Cover my book signing at the Book Nook next week?"

Kendall had received and read his press release on the signing of the self-published book of homespun stories. She'd tossed the release and hadn't given it a second thought. Damn. "Deal. But I need my information now."

"I want to be on the morning news."

"I'll make it happen."

"Swear."

"Swear."

Barry chuckled. "What do you want?"

"Anything and everything you have on Lindsay O'Neil. She would have lived in your area about eleven or twelve years ago."

"O'Neil. That name doesn't ring a bell."

"I wrote an article on her for *Inside Richmond* back in May. She's about thirty. A very pretty blonde."

"Oh yeah, I remember her. That article caused a bit of a buzz up here."

"Why?"

"I don't think her name was O'Neil when she lived up this way. Anyway, a few of the old guys at the paper remember when she was tangled up in some murder."

Kendall straightened. "What murder?"

"I don't remember."

Impatient, she tapped her foot. "You've got to get me more information, Barry."

"I'll see what I can dig up."

Lindsay was the key to this story. "Do that."

Chapter Twelve

Tuesday, July 8, 5:05 A.M.

Jacob Warwick had loved the smell of a boxing gym since he was a kid. The leather. The sweat. The liniment. He also loved the rhythmic sound of gloves hitting the speed bag, the thump against the heavy bag, and the skipping rope scraping the floor.

All conjured feelings of *home*. Not so surprising since he'd grown up in Myers's Gym.

He drove his fists into the punching bag suspended from the ceiling, savoring the burn in his muscles, the rapid pumping of his heart, and the sweat on his body. There wasn't anyone else working out at this early hour. The gym didn't officially open until six, but because Pete had given him a key he could come and go as he pleased. Often he boxed early.

By seven, the place would be full of men training and fighters sparring in the ring.

"Let me adjust those laces for you," Pete Myers's familiar rusty voice said behind him.

Jacob wiped the sweat from his eyes with the back of

his glove. "What are you doing here this early? I'd have figured you wouldn't get here for another hour."

Pete flashed a grin. "Ah, you know me. I'm not much of a sleeper and I like it here better than at home." Barring a few extra gray hairs, the sixty-nine-year-old man looked exactly like he had the first day Jacob had met him twenty years ago. He stood a few inches under six feet, kept his body fit by sparring daily, and always wore a wide grin. "Let me see your glove. The laces look loose."

The tension in Jacob's body eased as he held out his gloved hands. "Thanks."

When Jacob had first found Myers's gym, he'd been twelve and his mother had been on a weeklong drunken binge. Angry and wanting to wreck something, Jacob had stolen a dozen eggs from the market and made a beeline for the gym, which was celebrating its grand opening. Jacob had covered the freshly painted exterior with yolk. It had been a real laugh until a pissed Myers had come looking for him. Jacob hadn't figured the old man could run so damn fast or that he'd chase Jacob two blocks before catching him. The ex-boxer's grip had been like iron.

Myers had dragged Jacob home, taken one look at Jacob's drunken mother, and then called Social Services. Jacob's mother hadn't fought for her son, and within two weeks, Jacob was living in the small apartment above the gym with Pete. The two had clashed a lot in the beginning, but Pete had never given up on Jacob.

That was twenty years ago. And a day never passed when Jacob didn't thank God for Pete. The old boxer had saved his life.

Pete tightened the laces. "So why are you here so early?"

"I needed to break a sweat before work." Jacob hit

the long punching bag hanging from the ceiling, testing the laces.

Pete got behind the bag and steadied it. "Everything all right?"

"Yeah. Kier and I have a homicide."

"Who died?"

"Harold Turner. It was on the news last night."

Pete snorted. "I saw that. Can't say I'm too sorry. A dead attorney ain't gonna make me miss sleep."

Sweat dampened Jacob's T-shirt as he pounded the bag. "Yeah, he wasn't exactly a model citizen."

"You guys got a suspect?"

"Not yet."

"You're a smart kid. You'll figure it out."

Jacob hit the bag again. Normally, he didn't talk about cases but Pete was family. "This case could be a little dicey. Kier's wife is right in the middle of the investigation."

"Not good for Kier."

"Nothing is good when it comes to Kier. The guy is a disaster waiting to happen."

Pete frowned. "Is he drinking again?"

"No, so far I've not gotten a hint that he's had a drop. But once a drunk always a drunk."

"Your partner ain't your mother, kid. From what you've said over the last few months, Kier seems to be getting his shit together."

"We'll see."

Pete's gaze grew serious. "So how long you going to make the guy jump through hoops before you cut him some slack?"

"I'll let you know when he reaches it."

"The department was smart to pair you up with Kier. You'll keep him straight. He might even get you to lighten up."

The old man's confidence meant everything to Jacob.

"I don't want to baby-sit. And I sure as shit don't need a friend. I want a partner I can count on."

Pete nodded thoughtfully. "Until the guy screws up, cut him some slack."

Jacob knew he couldn't do that. "Sure."

Pete understood some of his foster son's scars ran deep. And he knew when to change the subject. "So when are you going to bring Sharon around the gym again? I liked her."

A twinge of regret nagged Jacob. "Sharon and I are history."

Pete shook his head. "Damn. The gal is built like a brick house and can cook. What the hell more do you want from a woman?"

"Sharon was fine. It just didn't work out."

The old man swore. "Bachelorhood ain't what it's cracked up to be. A man should have a wife and children."

Imitating Pete's raspy voice, Jacob said, "Dames are more trouble than they are worth. I do just fine by myself."

Wrinkles deepened in Pete's forehead as he smiled. "Don't you want a family of your own, Mr. Smart-mouth?"

"No." Jacob hit the bag. Truthfully, the idea made him feel backed into a corner. "Besides, you never had a family."

Pete shrugged. "Keeping you out of trouble wore me out."

Jacob frowned. "Did you ever regret taking me in?"

The old man grinned and shook his head. "You drove me to the brink of insanity more times than I could count, but I was never sorry I took you in. I'm only sorry your mother never let me formally adopt you."

Emotion tightened Jacob's chest. He hit the bag harder.

"If you don't ease up on that bag, the bones in your hand are gonna look like Swiss cheese," Pete said.

"I don't want to ease up. It feels good to push myself."

"It's not a matter of what you want, kid; it's a matter of what you need. Lay off for today. You've done enough."

Jacob stopped. His muscles ached with fatigue, just the way he liked it. But he always listened to Pete.

Pete grabbed a clean towel for Jacob and handed it to him.

"Thanks."

Pete started to unlace Jacob's right glove. "So I guess you'll be working this weekend?"

"Depends on the case." Jacob wiped the sweat from his eyes. "What do you have in mind?"

"I'm looking for a sparring partner for a fighter. I want to schedule a few friendly rounds on Saturday."

"I'd love to do it. I should know by late Thursday how the case is going."

Pete nodded, satisfied. "Great. I knew I could count on you."

Whoever said life was supposed to be easy?

The words Lindsay's mother had spoken to her so often played in Lindsay's head as she cradled a cup of coffee in her hands. She sat in an Adirondack chair on the back patio garden of her town house. The sun had crept up high in the sky but the air remained comfortable, thanks to yesterday's storms, which had banished a lot of the humidity.

The rains had been a welcome respite from the July heat for her gardens, which covered most of her ten-by-twelve backyard. Her yard was separated from the others by a tall privacy fence that looked like all the others in the development. However, her yard was completely unlike the others, which were little more than patchy plots of grass.

Her yard was an oasis. She'd only been in this town house eleven months, but already she'd filled the tiny land plot with numerous flower pots overflowing with brightly colored annuals, including marigolds and petunias. There were more pots filled with tomatoes, lettuce, cucumbers, and sweat peas.

Lindsay had learned to garden from her mother, who had always kept a lush garden. Her mother had always taken pride in her tomatoes, which frequently placed in the county fair, and her roses, which were once photographed for the paper. Her mother had spent hours in that garden, tenderly caring for her plants. Lindsay had loved digging alongside her mother in the rich soil. In the garden not only could they create, but they could escape her father's foul moods.

Sipping her coffee, Lindsay wished she had more gardening space and more land. One day, she'd have a real home with property around it to plant bushes and trees, and a vegetable garden. One day.

A flicker of movement caught Lindsay's attention. She turned as Nicole pushed open the sliding glass doors. Her friend wore an oversized T-shirt and long pajama pants that brushed her ankles. Blond hair swept high on her head in a rubber band accented clear green eyes and a high slash of cheekbones.

Nicole surveyed the garden. "You and your garden. I'm starting to think it's an obsession."

Lindsay stretched out her legs. "What can I say? I'm a sucker for greenery."

Nicole sat in a matching Adirondack chair next to Lindsay. She touched a bright yellow marigold blossom in a pot next to her chair. "Remember sophomore year in college when we had the room that overlooked a flat roof?"

"How could I forget? We lived next to that girl who liked to play Broadway tunes at five in the morning. I swear, if I ever hear the theme to *Cats* again I'll go nuts."

Nicole smiled. "I was thinking about your garden."

"I filled the windowsill with pots."

"And when the windowsill filled, you expanded your garden pots onto the roof. Inch by inch you took it over and filled it with every kind of vegetable imaginable. I'm surprised security didn't bust you."

Lindsay sipped her coffee again, hiding a grin. "Actually, they did. Mr. Wheeler, the head of security, found the garden and threatened to tear it down. I gave him a few tomatoes to try and he was hooked. I supplied him with vegetables all spring and he looked the other way."

"Bribery? I'm shocked, Ms. O'Neil."

Lindsay laughed. "I learned early on how to work the system."

Nicole's normally tanned skin looked pale, tired. At first, Lindsay had attributed it to her change in hair color. Lindsay had cut Nicole's dark hair and helped her dye it blond. It was a shame because her black hair had been so beautiful.

"Want some coffee?" Lindsay offered. "I just made a fresh pot."

Nicole held up a hand in surrender. "No, thanks. I'm a little queasy again. I think I've caught another bug from one of the kids I photographed. I had one yesterday sneeze all over me."

"So, how was work last night?"

She tucked her legs underneath her. "Good and bad. I actually got some great shots of the two kids I photographed. Their mother was thrilled and she ended up ordering twice as many prints as she'd planned."

"Good. What was the bad part?"

"My boss, Bill, loves my work too. He keeps raving about it. He keeps wondering how such a talented photographer landed on his doorstep."

"Why is that bad?"

She brushed her bangs out of her face. "He wants to enter some of my photography in a national competition. Says the publicity would be great for his business. I really was flattered. I'd gotten so used to downplaying my work. And it's been too long since someone has praised my photos. I'd forgotten how much I missed that."

Lindsay set her cup down on the arm of the chair. She understood living in secret was hard, but it was necessary right now. "Nicole, you can't enter a national competition."

"I know, I know. I'm not foolish enough to risk national exposure." She drummed her fingers on the chair's arm. "But I really hate living under the radar. I want my life back. And I want a divorce."

"You've only been here a couple of weeks. The bruises have only just faded and you're running on raw emotion. It's very natural that you'd be angry."

"I am angry. In fact, I'm furious. Last night I woke up and was so mad I couldn't get back to sleep."

Lindsay kept her tone even. She remembered how battered Nicole had been when she'd first arrived. And from what little Nicole had shared about her marriage, Lindsay knew Richard was a monster. "And if Richard were to find you, he would force you back to San Francisco. And I'm afraid he would treat you far worse than before."

Nicole picked at a loose chip of paint on the chair arm. "This is the twenty-first century. It shouldn't be this way. I have rights too."

"I know, I know. This isn't fair. But sometimes it's

better to be safe than right. Sometimes the only solution is to just vanish."

A heavy silence settled between them. "I'm starting to feel like Christina Braxton died. She's starting to feel like a distant memory."

"She became Nicole Piper. And Nicole Piper is going to have a wonderful life."

"But I'll always worry. I'll always have to look over my shoulder. Unless I get lucky and Richard drops dead."

Lindsay understood Nicole was in a no-win situation and didn't bother with platitudes. "What time do you work today?"

"Three." Nicole shifted in her seat and looked through the sliding glass doors at the wall clock. "Hey, it's almost eight. You're running late."

Lindsay had been up since six. She'd practiced her yoga for almost ninety minutes, trying to fill her time and to push the murder and Zack from her mind. "I don't have to be in the office until nine."

"Is today a shelter day?"

"No, I'm working out of the Mental Health Services building today." She hesitated. She didn't want to tell Nicole about the murder, because she didn't want her to worry. But better Nicole hear from her about what had happened. "We had some trouble at the shelter yesterday."

A deep crease formed on Nicole's forehead. "What happened?"

Lindsay chose her words carefully. "Ruby, the Sunday night volunteer, found a body behind the shelter near the trash cans."

Nicole lurched forward. "What!"

Lindsay held up her hands. "The cops have identified the guy. He's a local attorney who apparently had lots of enemies." She skipped the details about the flowers, the severed hand, and the Guardian's note. "It's nothing for you to worry about, because it has nothing to do with you or Richard."

Nicole's expression grew more serious. "Lindsay, don't patronize me. A dead body is something to worry about. How did he die?"

Lindsay picked at the chipping paint on her chair arm. "He was shot in the chest."

Nicole blew out a breath. "Who was it?"

"His name was Harold Turner."

"This isn't good."

Lindsay smiled, hoping to lighten Nicole's worries. "It's under control. The police are all over this case. I'm sure they'll figure out who did this. And I want you to know that I haven't told anyone that you're living here."

Nicole relaxed a fraction, as if Lindsay had touched on a secret worry. "Okay."

"This will blow over soon enough."

Nicole looked skeptical. "What can I do to help you?"

"Nothing. Everything is fine. If I need you, I promise to unload my troubles, okay?"

"I'm holding you to that. You've done so much for me." Nicole shifted, pressing her hand into her stomach.

"You aren't feeling well, are you?"

Nicole's skin looked sallow. "No. I can't seem to shake this stupid bug."

Lindsay studied Nicole's tight face. She knew her friend was under a terrible strain, but some topics couldn't be avoided. "I've been tiptoeing around this subject for a couple of days. But there seems to be no getting around it now. When was your last period?"

Nicole shook her head and held up her hands. "Don't even go there. I'm not pregnant."

Lindsay relaxed back in her chair. "So you've had a period recently?"

Slim fingers drew into fists. "No, but I've been under

a lot of stress the last couple of months. Things were getting pretty bad with Richard toward the end."

Lindsay's concern returned threefold. "How long has it been since your period?"

Nicole frowned, closed her eyes as she thought. "Two months."

Lindsay leaned forward and clasped her hands in front of her. "Have you ever gone this long before?"

Hope flickered in Nicole's gaze. "When my mother died, I missed one."

"But not two or three."

"No."

Lindsay blew out a frustrated breath. "You need to take a pregnancy test, Nicole."

"I don't need a test. I'm not pregnant." Anger etched her delicate features. "Richard said he wanted to have a baby. He said a baby would bind us together forever. But I was able to use some kind of protection almost every time."

Lindsay rose, then squatted in front of Nicole's chair and laid her hand on her arms. "I'd love to think this is just the flu. But you've been sleeping a lot and you've been nauseous too often to ignore it any longer. I know you don't like the idea of carrying Richard's child, but the possibility exists, doesn't it?"

Defiance burned in Nicole's blue eyes. "It was only just one time that he completely surprised me and I wasn't able to take precautions."

"When?"

"May."

The timing would be right. "Once is all it takes, honey."

Nicole pressed trembling hands to her cheeks. "I can't have Richard's baby. I *can't*."

"Hey, hey, don't panic or borrow trouble. Just pick

up a pregnancy test tonight. They have to be taken in the morning. By this time tomorrow, you'll know where you stand."

Nicole's voice was a hoarse whisper. Her gaze reflected fear. "Lindsay, what if I *am* pregnant?"

"Honey, let's just do the test first. Then we'll figure out what the next step is."

Nicole offered a weak smile, but her eyes still looked panicked. "You're right. One step at a time. You've been saying that since I arrived here."

Lindsay admired Nicole's strength. With only the clothes on her back, she had left a very powerful, very vengeful man. "Do yourself a favor and get out of the house today. Go see some of the city. Put that new camera of yours to work." Photography would give Nicole something positive to focus on temporarily.

A sigh shuddered through Nicole's body. "I have been itching to try out the vintage Leica I found at the flea market last week."

"Perfect. This apartment could use some real photographic art on the walls."

A clock in the hallway chimed eight times. "Now, I've got to get my act together. And my car is still at the shelter, so I'll have to call a cab."

"Why is your car at the shelter?"

She shrugged. "Long story."

Nicole rose, shaking her head. "You don't want to tell me."

Lindsay smiled. "Not right now."

"I get that we all have things we don't like to talk about. Okay, I'll drive you. Give me fifteen and I'll be ready to go."

Lindsay touched Nicole's shoulder. "It's going to be okay, baby or no." *It's going to be okay.* She was trying to reassure herself as well.

Nicole straightened her shoulders. "I know."

Both smiled.

But neither believed the other.

Minutes before seven, Zack arrived in the lobby of the Public Safety building. The modern building, located in the west end of the county, housed the homicide division and sat adjacent to the police training facility.

Zack headed past the guard at Reception and, instead of taking the elevator, climbed the steps to his second-floor office. In deference to the heat, he'd skipped the suit today and dressed in khakis and a white collared shirt. The way he figured it, he and Warwick would be doing a lot of legwork on the Turner case.

The homicide division consisted of five small offices, one for each detective, and a conference room with a long table that sat twenty. Fluorescent light made the industrial-blue carpet look gray and the ivory walls washed out.

His eyes itched with fatigue. Dreams of Lindsay had invaded him and kept him awake half the night.

Last night's dreams were different from the others he'd had this past year. They weren't a replay of the fights they'd had during the last days they'd lived together. These dreams had been purely sexual. Until yesterday, he'd almost forgotten how good the sex could be between them. When he'd awoken, a restless energy had been churned up. He'd gone for a long run, taken a cold shower, but neither had been enough to banish Lindsay.

"Damn." He grabbed a cup of coffee from the break room and headed to Warwick's office.

Warwick glanced up from his desk. "You look like shit."

Zack had come to recognize the tone. It meant Warwick was gunning for trouble. Normally, Zack ignored it, but today, he didn't have the patience. "I haven't been drinking, if that's what you're implying."

Warwick looked unrepentant. "This isn't the time to fall apart."

Zack hadn't even had his first cup of coffee and already he was pissed at his partner. "I'm not falling apart and I'm not going to drink again. The sooner you accept that fact the better our partnership will be."

Warwick didn't hide his skepticism. "We'll see."

Zack shook his head. "And I thought I had hang-ups. But I'm begining to believe you've got some real issues of your own."

Warwick rose abruptly. "What's that supposed to mean?"

"Was it your mother or father who was the drunk?"

Tension radiated from Warwick's body. "Don't try to lay your problems on me."

"As long as I'm sober, I don't have a problem. But you, you could be sober as a judge and still have demons chasing you." He sipped his coffee, enjoying the fact that Warwick was the one at a disadvantage. "I'd say it was your mother who was the drinker. Or was she a drug addict?"

Warwick tightened his jaw and released it. "Fuck off."

Zack shrugged.

Warwick snatched up a file from his very orderly desk. "I asked everyone in the division to meet us in the conference room at seven. They should be waiting for us now."

Zack knew he'd just opened a wound. If Warwick hadn't been such a prick these last eight months, he'd have felt bad about it. "Let's do it."

Warwick nodded stiffly. "Right."

The two went into the conference room as Detective Vega offered Detective C.C. Ricker Danish from a bakery bag.

C.C. glowered at Vega. The redhead stood just over five feet and had a compact, lean body. In her late twenties, she had come up through patrol, the domestic violence division, and for the last two years had worked homicide.

Catching sight of Zack and Warwick, Vega wiped his hands clean. Nick Vega was tall, had olive skin, and wore his black hair slicked back. Born in Cuba, he'd immigrated to New York when he was six. He spoke Spanish like a native and English like a New Yorker.

C.C. stood a little straighter. "So I hear you boys snagged yourself a juicy murder."

Warwick's frame dominated the space. "Lucky us."

Vega chuckled. "Tread carefully. C.C.'s on another diet. Low carbs this time. And she's mean as a snake."

Warwick sat down. All traces of the anger toward Zack had vanished. "What's the occasion and how long do we have to suffer before you can have a real meal?"

C.C. frowned. "My sister's wedding." They'd all seen the pictures of C.C. and her three sisters. The other Ricker sisters were tall and blond. C.C. had often joked she was a genetic throwback. "So how's Sharon?"

Warwick's smile didn't waver but his eyes hardened a shade. "No more Sharon. I'm a single man again."

C.C. didn't hide her sadness. "Sorry to hear that. I liked her."

"No biggie," Warwick said.

Zack wouldn't use any more armchair psychology to his partner again. Their exchange a few minutes ago, coupled with the fact that he'd broken up with another good woman, told Zack all he needed to know. His partner had been raised by a drunk and it had left its mark. No matter what he did, no matter how long he stayed sober, Zack would always be a drunk to Warwick.

Add that to the three detectives' camaraderie and Zack wondered if he'd ever live down the days he drank.

Ayden entered the room, silencing any other banter. He had rolled up his sleeves and loosened his tie. Under his arm, he held a stack of files. In his left hand, which still bore his wedding band, he gripped a mug that read "#1 Dad," a gift from one of his sons. He tossed the files on the table.

"Zack and Warwick. Phone records just arrived." He pushed the files toward them. "Harold and Jordan Turner's are included as well as O'Neil's and the shelter's records. There are hundreds of calls to wade through."

Zack thumbed through the records. He remembered the feeling he'd had yesterday that Lindsay was hiding something. God only knew what they'd find.

"Is Sara joining us?" Ayden said.

"I'm here," Sara said, breezing into the room. Her neat ponytail suited her khakis, crisp white shirt, and polished brown flats. "And please tell me no one expects DNA this morning."

They all laughed.

"Let me guess, your crankiness is a sign that you're scheduled to speak at the academy today. Am I right?" C.C. said.

"I was there last Friday. I've heard it said there are no stupid questions, but sometimes I wonder," she said, smiling, then opened her file. "Everyone under twenty-two thinks it takes the press of a button to get DNA results. The *CSI* craze is killing me."

Again everyone laughed.

"What have you found?" Zack said. He didn't mean to sound so abrupt.

Sara straightened. She was all business. "From the crime scene, I didn't learn that much. So let me start with the body. I spoke to the ME this morning. Harold was killed with a .45-caliber shot to the heart. We've got the slug but so far no matches to anything in the ballistic databases. I *can* tell you that Harold was dead before he hit the ground. The bullet shattered his heart. He had no defensive wounds or any other signs of trauma on his body. His hand was removed postmortem with the use of a very sharp object."

"Any theories on the instrument that was used to cut his hand off?" Warwick said.

"Machete or an ax. The ME and I are leaning toward a machete. The cut was narrow and did minimal tissue damage at the wrist. Bone was severed cleanly." She flipped a page over. "We won't have the toxicology screen on him for a couple of weeks, but there were track marks on both arms and behind both knees. This guy was a full-blown drug addict. Just the promise of drugs would be enough to get him to go almost anywhere."

"Which explains why he'd have gotten into a car with his killer," Warwick said.

"Exactly."

"And the crime scene?" Zack said.

"The killer was very careful and very methodical. He left no fingerprints, shell casings, or hair or fabric fibers; however, there was a footprint. I was able to get a very good footprint impression by the back gate. The ground had been softened by a leaking garden hose, so the soft soil created the perfect medium to make a mold." She glanced at her notes. "Men's size twelve running shoe. And I can tell you that his foot turned inward. My guess is that he has an excessively high arch, which can shorten a foot up to an inch. If the print belongs to the killer he has a slight limp. Also, there was an unidentified white powder on the heel. It's definitely not drugs and I'm having it analyzed."

"That's it?" Ayden said. He looked frustrated.

Sara nodded. "As I said, the killer was careful and, unfortunately, I only had a couple of hours to collect data before the rains came and literally obliterated the evidence. We returned after the rain, but the backyard was a mess."

"What about the hand sent to Lindsay O'Neil?" Zack said.

Sara nodded. "It's definitely Harold's. His prints match ones we had on file. I also checked the hand's nails, hoping for a partial print from the killer, but nothing. The flowers are fresh irises. They can be bought in fifty different places in the metro area."

"What about the flower box?" Ayden said.

Sara frowned. "The only prints on the outside and inside of the box were Lindsay's and her assistant's."

C.C. nodded. "I worked with a couple of robbery detectives last night and we called all the florists in the city. None had an order for the shelter address yesterday."

"Did anyone notice who delivered the box?" Ayden said.

Zack shook his head. "The cop parked in the driveway was on the phone with his kid's day care. He'd received a call that his child had been badly injured. Turned out to be bogus. And Ruby Dillon had three calls come in at once to the shelter. She was too distracted to notice the guy."

"You and Sara refer to the Guardian as a male, but do we know for sure that the Guardian is a man?" Ayden said.

Zack frowned. "Not for sure."

"What about the TV news crews?" Ayden said. "Think a camera might have picked up something? Shaw at Channel Ten had her cameras running all morning."

"I'll talk to Shaw," Warwick said.

"Do you think the killer delivered the flowers personally?" Zack said.

Warwick shrugged. "Who knows?"

No one spoke for a moment as the weight of what he'd said sank in. Did the killer return to the shelter to deliver the hand?

"And the note that was attached to the flower box?" Zack said. "What do you know about that?"

Sara glanced at her notes. *Lindsay, you are not alone anymore, The Guardian.* "I've sent it to a handwriting expert. At first glance, he says the Guardian likes control, as exhibited by the note's neat block lettering and the deep indention of the letters. He's going to look at it more and see what he comes up with."

"And the paper?" Zack said.

"The paper is extremely common and can be found in dozens of card stores."

Zack kept his voice neutral, trying not to hint at the fear he felt for Lindsay. "Lindsay's never heard of the Guardian and doesn't know why he's fixated on her."

"What's her connection to Turner?" Ayden said.

Zack recapped the facts as Lindsay had told him.

C.C. looked skeptical. "I saw Lindsay once in court. It was the trial of a woman accused of shooting her husband. Lindsay testified for the defense about battered victim syndrome. She said that a perfectly sane woman who has been badly battered can snap. On cross the Commonwealth attorney tried to get Lindsay to waver but she didn't. Lindsay is one intense woman."

"Lindsay *is* intense." Zack hesitated, dreading what he needed to say next.

"There's something we all should know about Lindsay, isn't there," Warwick said. "You hinted in the car yesterday that there was domestic abuse in her home when she was growing up."

Warwick was right. Everyone did need to know about Lindsay's past.

Zack folded his fingers together. "Lindsay had a complicated childhood." All gazes zeroed in on him. He felt disloyal even though the Department of Social Services had done a background check on her and knew her history. "She's from Ashland, about twenty miles north."

"I thought she came from California," C.C. said. "I remember talking to her about USC at some department Christmas party. She led me to believe she was from California."

Zack nodded. "She did go to school out there but she's from here."

"So why lead everyone to believe she's from the West?" Ayden said.

He drew in a deep breath. "Her mother was abused by her father for years, but it's worse than that. Her mother was murdered by her father. It was twelve years ago. Lindsay was seventeen. And her last name was Hines then." A hush fell over the room.

C.C. and Vega glanced at each other and Warwick sat back in his chair, his shock evident.

Ayden leaned forward. "Shit. I remember that case. The Hanover sheriff was a friend of mine. We talked about it a lot, because the murder scene was so bloody. It really shook him up."

"Lindsay's father beat her mother to death with a hammer," Zack said. "Lindsay found her mother."

No one spoke for several seconds.

"When did Lindsay change her name?" Warwick finally asked.

"When she turned eighteen," Zack said. "O'Neil is her mother's maiden name."

"For those of us who didn't live here then, what else can you tell us about the case?" Vega said.

Zack longed for a cigarette. "I don't know much more than that. I only know what Lindsay told me. I'd like to send a teletype to the Hanover sheriff's office and request the murder file. I don't know if the details are relevant but they could be."

Ayden nodded. "Do it."

"What happened to her after her parents died?" Warwick asked.

"She told me she moved to California. For a while she lived in shelters and in her car. Eventually, a social worker got involved with her and encouraged her to get her high school diploma. This woman also helped her earn a scholarship to the University of California."

Vega frowned. "No disrespect, Zack, but the more I hear about this the more I worry about how impartial you can be. Lindsay is your wife. Are you the guy who should be looking into this murder?"

Ayden tented his fingers. "Vega, we've already taken care of that. Warwick is taking the lead and Kier is backing him up. But I want everyone working this case."

Zack hid his satisfaction.

Warwick didn't miss a beat. "I'd like for C.C. to start going through the phone records. Look for any patterns, connections to the shelter, any unusual calls Mrs. Turner might have made."

C.C. nodded. "Will do."

"Vega, talk to Ruby Dillon, the woman who stayed at the shelter the night of the murder. Kier talked to her but she made it clear she doesn't like him. She might remember something if *you* ask the questions."

"Sure," Vega said.

Zack wasn't about to take a backseat to Warwick. "Also, C.C., once you've gone through the phone records, find out who sells machetes or anything sharp enough to cut bone."

She glanced at Warwick, and when he didn't protest she nodded. "Sure."

Warwick glanced at his watch. "I'll send the teletype to Hanover now and then Zack and I will head up there."

Chapter Thirteen

Tuesday, July 8, 9:15 A.M.

"We're with Henrico County Police," Warwick said to the clerk at the Hanover sheriff's office. "I'm Detective Jacob Warwick."

Zack showed his badge. "I'm Detective Zackary Kier. We sent a teletype an hour ago about the Hines murders."

The clerk was a short, round woman in her midfifties. She wore her graying hair in a tight perm that drew attention to a strawberry birthmark on her left cheek. "The sheriff and most of his deputies are in a staff meeting this morning, but the deputy who worked the case stuck around so he could talk to you personally. Let me buzz him."

She picked up the phone and told the person on the other end they'd arrived. "Deputy Graves will be right out."

"Thanks," Warwick said.

Zack knew the personnel turnover in this office had to be low. "You been here long?"

The woman nodded with pride. "Thirty years."

"You remember the Hines case?"

Her weathered face twisted into a deep frown. "I sure

do. It was one of the saddest cases I'd ever seen. Just about everyone in Hanover knew someone who knew the Hines family. And when their little girl ran away, it just about broke my heart. We said prayers for her at Sunday service for months."

Zack rattled the change in his pocket and tried not to pace. He thought about Lindsay at seventeen: young, alone, frightened.

The urge to protect her was so strong.

They didn't have to wait long for Graves. He pushed through a side door. He was a tall, stocky man with full, ruddy cheeks and thinning red hair. His protruding belly stretched the fabric of his brown uniform.

He offered his hand to Zack. "Deputy Marty Graves."

Zack shook his hand and discovered the deputy's grip was strong.

"You've come about the Hines murder?" Graves said.

"Yes," Zack said.

"I've got the file on my desk. Come on back."

They followed him through a pair of heavy security doors and down a narrow corridor to his cramped office. Both took a seat in front of his desk.

"Can I get you men coffee?"

Both declined.

Graves sat and put on his reading glasses. "I remember this case. Fact, I knew Frank Hines from Rotary. Nicest guy you'd ever want to meet. And Deb was in my wife's circle group at church. Both would give you the shirts off their backs." He cleared his throat. "We were all shocked at first when Frank did what he did. But then later, as folks started to compare notes, we started to piece together a few things. Life in the Hines house had to have been bad for years."

"What about the daughter? What can you tell me about her?" Zack said.

"Lindsay." A sad smile played at the corners of Graves's mouth. "She was a lifeguard at my grandkids' pool. She saved a child from drowning that summer. The youngest Thompson kid, a four-year-old, had gotten out of the baby pool and fallen into the deep end of the main pool. The *Herald-Progress* did a story on her. Both her folks seemed proud. And all the boys wanted to date her, but she kept them at arm's distance. My grandson, Joel, worked with her as a lifeguard at the pool. He always figured she was playing hard to get. Of course, none of us really knew what was going on at home. Her mother never reported any abuse and Lindsay never said a word."

Zack wondered what kind of hell Lindsay had witnessed in her home.

Warwick tented his fingers. "What happened to Frank Hines?"

Zack knew the short answer to that question but wanted to hear the deputy's version. He realized now how much Lindsay had downplayed the problems in her past.

"After he killed his wife, he fled the scene. Went to a local motel, downed a bottle of Jack Daniels, and then killed himself." Graves flipped through the file. "He left a suicide note for Lindsay. I never showed it to her." He found the note in the file and handed it to Zack.

Zack read it. Typical MO for a wife beater. "Shit."

Graves nodded. "There was no sense dumping that kind of crap on a kid. She had enough to deal with."

Zack handed the note to Warwick. "He blames his wife and Lindsay for his problems. Said if they'd been a better wife and child he'd have been fine."

"What a piece of work," Warwick muttered.

"You think you know a guy," Graves said.

Zack thought about the hell he'd put Lindsay through

when his drinking had gotten so heavy. No wonder she'd tossed him out.

Graves dropped his gaze to the file. "We did receive a 911 call from the Hines' house about three months before Frank and Deb died. Before the caller could speak the line went dead. According to the report, the dispatcher called the house back. Frank answered. He said it was a mistake."

"Only the one call?" Zack asked.

"Yes."

"Anything unusual happen recently to remind you of this case?" Zack said.

"Nope. Of course, I saw that article a couple of months ago about Lindsay. I recognized her the very instant I saw her. She's the spitting image of her mama. It did my heart good to see she's done so well for herself."

"That article didn't prompt any talk about the murders in town?" Warwick asked.

"Well, of course it did. We all remembered it. I talked about it with Joel at Sunday supper after the article came out. But nothing out of the ordinary came up. Why all these questions about a twelve-year-old murder?"

"Just following up on a lead," Zack said. "Lindsay have any relatives?"

"No one came forward after her parents' deaths." Graves shook his head. "There was no one to take custody of her, so the state stepped in. She was sent to a foster home."

"But she ran away," Zack muttered.

"Right," said Graves. "This got something to do with the murder at Sanctuary yesterday?" When they hesitated, he smiled. "I wasn't born yesterday, boys. You think that murder's tied to Lindsay's past?"

"We don't know," Zack said honestly. "Can you tell us where the Hines house was?"

"I can draw you a map to the lot. The house burned to the ground not one month after the murders. Fire department said it was arson, but we never did figure out who set it."

"Was Lindsay a suspect?" Zack said.

"No. She'd run off by then."

"We'll take a look at the lot then."

"Sure." The deputy drew a map, clipped it to a copy of the file, and slid it across the desk.

Five minutes later, Zack and Warwick left the building armed with the hand-drawn map and the Hines file.

Zack tossed his keys to Warwick. "Mind driving? I'd like to look at the file."

"Sure."

They got in the car.

Zack opened the file and studied the color photos of the murder scene. The victim lay on her back, her face discolored and swollen from the brutal beating. Her wide-eyed death stare reflected the panic she had to have felt those last few seconds of her life.

"My God," Zack said.

Warwick glanced at the map. "Never gets easy."

"No, it doesn't." His problems with alcohol abuse this past year had been a bitch, but through it all he'd had a solid family behind him. Lindsay had been alone when she'd lived her nightmare.

"The less personal you make this," Warwick said, "the easier it will be."

His partner's sudden empathy surprised Zack. "Autopsy reports on Lindsay's mother show that she'd suffered multiple factures over the years—nose, right arm, left hand." He flipped over a page and discovered a medical report on Lindsay. "Lindsay's doc reported that she was in a state of shock. He also stated that she'd suffered a spiral fracture of her right wrist."

"Someone twisted her hand so hard her wrist broke."

Zack tamped down his anger. "Yeah. Doctors reported that her and her mother's breaks occurred a couple of years before the murder/suicide."

"What does the report say about Frank Hines?"

"Died of a single gunshot wound to the chest. A forty-five."

"Like Turner," Warwick said.

Turner and Hines shared similar fatal wounds made by the same caliber gun. Another coincidence. Things weren't looking good for Lindsay. "Yeah. Autopsy reports show advanced liver disease, a by-product of excessive drinking."

Warwick shook his head. "Lindsay ever tell you this stuff?"

His wife had hidden her darkest secrets even from him. "Only the barest details. I tried to talk to her about it, but she always changed the subject. She said she'd put her past behind her and didn't want to discuss it."

Warwick tightened his hands on the wheel. "This is the kind of stuff that can really fuck with someone's head."

Zack flipped to a picture taken of Lindsay when she was a junior in high school. Challenge radiated from her eyes. "That doesn't mean she killed Turner."

"Turner smacked around his wife. Lindsay knew it. Maybe she'd had enough of bullies."

Zack stared at the more than decade-old crime scene photos. And then he noticed the date. "*Shit.*"

"What?"

"Yesterday was the twelve-year anniversary of the Hines murder/suicide."

Warwick tightened his jaw and turned down a country road. "This is a little too connected to be a coincidence."

"Yeah."

Another right and another left and they arrived at the Hines' driveway. As Graves's map indicated, it was marked by a tall oak tree that had been split down the center by lightning. The rusty mailbox had long fallen from its post and lay on the side of the road covered in weeds.

They drove down the rutted driveway until they reached the end. Before them stood the charred remains of the home Lindsay had grown up in. The only part of the structure left standing was the brick fireplace and the foundation.

They got out and walked toward the foundation.

"Who owns the land?" Warwick said.

"Lindsay said the county took it for back taxes about eight years ago. They tried to sell it to a developer, but the well water in the area turned up contaminated from one of Hines's underground storage tanks. Remediation was too expensive so the land has just been sitting."

Lindsay had said her mother had loved to garden, but there were only hints of the flower beds she'd told him covered the property. Soil mounds for vegetables cut through a portion of the field behind the house. A flowering vine twisted around a gazebo that had been ravaged by the weather and time. And on the back of the lot, there was a greenhouse.

"Let's have a look."

They walked around the house's foundation toward the greenhouse. Most of the windows had been shattered by vandals' rocks. The door hung on one hinge and it was easy to push open. Inside were rows of long-dead plants and a collection of clay pots. Zack picked up a stack of pots. Lindsay's birthday was tomorrow. If he had time, he'd clean these up for her.

"We'd better get back to town," Warwick said.

"Yeah."

As they turned, Zack spotted words carved over the

doorjamb. The letters were crude and looked as if they'd been carved with a knife.

He reached up and wiped the dirt free. The words read, *L and J forever.* "L and J. What was Graves's grandson's name?"

"Joel Heckman."

"Let's have a chat with Joel."

It wasn't hard to find Joel Heckman. He worked at a bicycle shop in the town of Ashland, the county seat. Zack and Warwick stepped through the shop's doors fifteen minutes later.

A lean man in his early thirties stood behind a glass display case filled with expensive bike accessories. He was holding a bike shoe and trying to fasten a clip to the bottom. "Welcome. Can I help you?"

Both detectives pulled out their badges as they approached the counter.

"Joel Heckman?" Warwick queried.

"Yeah."

"We came to ask you a few questions about Lindsay O'Neil."

He looked puzzled. "O'Neil?"

"You'd know her as Lindsay Hines."

Joel's eyes widened. "Lindsay. God, I haven't seen her in years. What's this all about? Is she okay?"

"She's fine," Zack said. "We're looking into her background."

Joel nodded. "Her mother's murder."

"Yeah," Zack said. "What can you tell us about it?"

He shoved out a breath and set down the shoe. "I wish I'd gone into the house with her that day. I always thought if I'd gone in I might have found her mother first and spared her the sight."

"But you just dropped her off," Zack said.

"Yeah. She was excited to be home early. It was Thursday and her mother's regular afternoon off. Her mom had started working at the diner in town and had to work all the time. They didn't see each other much."

"Know anything about her extended family? She ever talk about anyone?" Warwick said.

"Naw, she never talked about them at all. I think her mom had a falling out with her family. They didn't like Frank, I think."

"She talk about anything?" Zack said.

"She always kept the conversation light. She never brought friends home and spent a lot of time in the library. She could have graduated a year earlier because she had so many credits but she wanted to stay in town. I think now it was to be close to her mom. Maybe she thought she was protecting her."

"What about her father?" Warwick said.

"There's no nice way to say it—he was an asshole. He lost his temper once with her at the pool because she kept him waiting five minutes." Joel shook his head. "Lindsay had been giving a kid a swimming lesson. The kid was terrified of the water and Linz always spent extra time with her."

Linz. Joel's affection for Lindsay was clear. "She was your friend."

"Yeah. She was great. And I can tell you she didn't deserve her father's shit. I can tell you if Frank Hines hadn't killed himself, there were about a half dozen people in town who would have killed him. Myself included."

Chapter Fourteen

Tuesday, July 8, 10:00 A.M.

Vega and Ayden pulled up in front of Ruby Dillon's small brick house, located just a couple of miles east of Richmond International Airport. Crabgrass covered the front lawn, but there was a pile of neatly piled bricks, as if someone was planning to fix the place up. There were three cars parked out front. By the looks of the property, several people lived there.

This was Vega's neck of the woods. He'd grown up in the east end of the county. His old man had worked for one of the airlines and his mom had taught math at Highland Springs High School. His little brother, Michael, was a cornerback on the same school's football team. Both his folks were active in the church.

As Vega and Ayden got out of the car, a jet engine roared over their heads. Vega glanced up at the sky. He'd never gotten used to the noise. His roots were in this part of New Kent County, but he'd chosen to live twenty miles east in a rural section.

They strode to the front porch. Rap music blared

from inside the tiny house. The music was so loud that Vega could feel the bass in his chest.

Ayden rang the bell. "My boys like this crap. I bet they're cranking it just as loud at my house."

"I thought they were going to summer school."

"The oldest is. The younger one works afternoons at a hardware store."

"They doing all right?"

Ayden frowned. "We're all still stumbling through the motions. Carol has been gone a year and a half and we still can't get our shit together." He pounded on the door. This time a dog started to bark.

"At least the dog knows we're here," Vega said.

The sound of locks unlatching followed. Ruby Dillon opened the door. She wore a brown and orange uniform. Vega and Ayden knew that she worked as a nurse's aid at Virginia Commonwealth University Medical Center. They pulled out their shields as she faced them.

Ruby frowned and then turned to shout, "Brianna, turn that music down!" After a second's pause, the music stopped. She didn't open the screen door. "You come about that dead man, I suppose."

Ayden nodded. "Yes, ma'am. We'd like to ask you some questions."

Her jaw set. "I spoke to two other detectives yesterday. I've told them all that I know."

"We've got a few more questions, if you don't mind," Vega said.

Ruby pursed her lips. "I do mind, as a matter of fact. I've got to get to work."

The woman looked familiar to Vega. He'd bet money she knew his mother through the church. His mother knew everyone in this part of the county. "Excuse me for asking, but do you know Rita Vega?"

Ruby eyed him. "Maybe I do."

Vega smiled. He was good at shooting the shit and getting people to warm up. "You go to Third Baptist?"

"I do."

"Thought so. My parents attend. Mom's been a fixture there for twenty years."

Ruby's frown softened. "You're one of Rita's boys?"

"I am."

Her stance relaxed. "I haven't seen Rita in a few weeks. How she doing?"

"Fine. My brother, Michael, is giving her fits. He gets his driver's license in a week and can't wait to drive. Dad swears his heart won't be able to take Michael driving."

Ruby chuckled. "Michael's a good boy. Full of piss and vinegar, but he's good. Rita and George will get a handle on him." She was thoughtful for a moment. "Your mama was one of the few that was nice to me when I got released from jail. She even took Brianna shopping for her prom dress this spring."

Vega and Ayden had discussed Ruby on the way over. She had been hiding cocaine for her boyfriend when the cops busted her. She'd done six months in exchange for testimony against him. He was now doing ten years at Greensville Prison. But they had realized this morning that the boyfriend, as it turns out, worked for Ronnie T.

Ruby pushed open the screen door. "I got a couple of minutes before I got to go. Come on in."

Vega promised himself he owed his mother a big thank-you. If not for her, Ruby Dillon would have shut the door on them now.

Ayden didn't look rushed. He glanced at the surrounding yards before stepping over the threshold into the house. "We'll do our best to hurry things along."

Vega's gaze scanned the living room, which reminded him so much of his parents'. The furniture was old and worn, but the room was neat and organized. Off the living room at the kitchen table sat a teenage girl. She wore shoulder-length braids and an *Usher* T-shirt. No doubt that was Brianna, the one who had been playing the loud music.

Ruby didn't move from the small foyer nor did she offer them a seat.

"Tell me about yesterday," Vega said. "How did you find the body?"

Ruby sighed her impatience. "I told that Detective Kier yesterday that I got the shelter women off to work and the kids off to school. It was a regular day and nothing out of the ordinary. I loaded up the trash like I do each morning I work at the shelter and took it out to the trash cans. That's when I found him."

"You didn't see anyone else in the backyard?" Ayden said.

"Nope. And I didn't hear or smell nothing either."

"What about during the night?" Vega said.

"Quiet. But I did hear a dog barking around five. It woke me up. I got up and looked out the front window but didn't see anything."

"How many nights a week do you stay at the shelter?" Ayden asked.

"Three or four, depending on the schedule. My son stays with Brianna when I'm gone overnight. I generally show up around five and leave by ten. Yesterday was the exception. I stayed late to help Lindsay."

"You were there when the flowers were delivered?"

"I was."

"Did you see who dropped off the flowers?"

"I didn't. Lindsay's office is closer to the front door than mine, so it would be simple for anyone to come in the front door and drop the box on her desk. I thought I heard somebody but figured it was a cop. After I answered all those calls, I went into Lindsay's office, thinking she'd returned. That's when I saw the box."

"Did you open it?" Vega said.

"Well, yeah, I peeked inside. Lindsay never, ever gets flowers and I wanted to see what she'd gotten." She shuddered. "I had no idea what was under those blossoms."

"Did you look at the note?" Ayden asked.

"No. The note was private."

"Did the shelter have any trouble recently? Other than yesterday?" Vega said.

"One of our residents, Aisha Greenland, kept getting calls from her husband, Marcus, on her cell phone. He left her all kinds of nasty messages. Finally, Lindsay had Aisha change the number. And a couple of weeks ago, we had to toss a gal out for drug possession. She was pissed."

"She got a name?"

"Sally somebody. It's in Lindsay's records."

"I didn't see surveillance cameras at the shelter," Ayden said.

"We can't afford them right now."

Vega made a note. "Is there anything else you can tell us?"

Ruby's first response was to shake her head no, but then she stopped. "Well, I'll tell you, last week something did happen, here, at my house. It wasn't much and I didn't bother to tell Lindsay."

"What happened?" Vega said.

"I had a break-in. Someone came inside my home while I was at work and Brianna was at school. Nothing was taken but I knew someone was here."

"Any idea what they were looking for?" Ayden said.

"There was a time when someone might have found *something*, but I did my time and there is no more of that here."

"You report it?" Ayden said.

"No. Like I said, nothing was taken. But someone was in my house."

The detectives asked a couple more follow-up questions about Ruby's job and Lindsay's work. Nothing out of the ordinary came up and they left.

"So why break into a woman's house and not take anything?" Vega said as they walked to their car.

"I hate coincidences," Ayden answered.

"So do I."

Chapter Fifteen

Tuesday, July 8, 11:00 A.M.

Mental Health Services was in a one-story brick building that was curtained off from the main road by a row of trees. It had tinted windows and nondescript signage. Few noticed it when they drove by.

Lindsay was on staff at Mental Health Services as a full-time counselor. Tuesdays and Wednesdays, she worked eight-hour days. On Thursdays she worked a twenty-four-hour shift, manning the crisis line. The rest of her time was spent at the shelter.

Since the shelter location was a secret, she used this facility to meet with her shelter family members on Mondays and Fridays. The county also allowed her to host her shelter's board of directors' meetings in the main conference room and interview potential shelter staff here on her off days.

Today, like every Tuesday, her morning was insanely busy. She had held her regularly scheduled counseling sessions and had also ended up on the phone with her board director, Dana Miller. The conversation had lasted almost a half hour. Keeping her tone positive, she had filled Dana in on everything about the Turner murder investigation. Dana had reminded her that so far she'd been able to keep the press at bay. Lindsay had thanked her and promised that with luck they'd be back in business by the end of the week.

Dana hadn't sounded happy, but she hadn't complained too much.

Lindsay's last morning appointment was with Howard and Marilyn Jackson. The couple was in their late fifties, came from an affluent background, and split their time between Richmond and Boca Raton. Lindsay had first met the couple when she'd helped their twenty-six-year-old battle alcoholism. Brenda had moved in with the couple a few months ago, and all had seemed well—until last week, when Marilyn had discovered her daughter was using illegal drugs. Marilyn had called Lindsay on Sunday night for help. Lindsay had agreed to a Tuesday appointment.

Marilyn and Howard sat side by side across the conference table from Lindsay. Dark circles marred the white flesh under Howard's eyes. Clearly he'd not been sleeping. And the lines in Marilyn's face looked deeper.

"How long do you think she's been using?" Lindsay said.

Marilyn's large purse sat in her lap as if it were a shield. "I don't know. Years maybe. I'm starting to wonder if we ever knew her."

Howard remained silent, his arms folded over his chest. Deep wrinkles creased his temples and the corners of his mouth.

"Will she come and talk to me?" Lindsay offered. "I've dealt with my share of drug addicts and alcoholics."

Marilyn shook her head. "She refuses to talk to you or attend any AA meetings. She thinks she has all the answers. She thinks she's in control."

"Believe me, she's not in control," Lindsay said.

Howard nodded as if he was relieved to hear someone else say those words.

Lindsay understood firsthand how difficult and persuasive substance abusers could be. "What I'm proposing won't be easy."

Howard shifted forward as if needing a plan of action. "We'll do what it takes."

Lindsay nodded, saying, "Don't underestimate what it takes to help her get clean and sober."

Marilyn lifted her chin. "We're not afraid of hard work."

Hard didn't begin to describe what lay ahead. "You need to tell Brenda that if she doesn't get help there are going to be consequences."

"Such as?" Howard said.

"If she doesn't stop drinking and using, then you will withdraw all financial support. No access to your cash, definitely no use of your car, until she sees me or an AA counselor. And you can always ask her to leave your house."

Marilyn's shoulders slumped. "How can we ever ask her to leave? She depends on us so much. I don't want to see her suffer anymore."

"I understand the rough road you face," Lindsay said softly. "I'm not saying you put her out on the street today. But she needs to understand if she's going to stay in your house, she's expected to be clean and sober. It's your house and your rules." Lindsay kept her tone gentle. "The alcohol and drugs are eating her up. It's only going to get worse."

Tears ran down Marilyn's lined face. "But she needs our help. And I'm afraid if she doesn't have us, she'll go back to her ex-husband."

Lindsay thought back to the hour-long conversation they'd had on Sunday. "Brenda is twenty-six, and she doesn't have a job. She depends on you for cash, which she's using to buy drugs and alcohol. She's stolen from you. Marilyn, it's time to stop making it so easy for her to drink and use."

Marilyn started to weep.

Howard's frown deepened. "Have you ever been through anything like this? And I mean personally, not just professionally."

Lindsay nodded. "As a matter of fact, I have. I've been through the kind of battle you are going to fight."

Marilyn sniffed. "Who did you have this problem with? A brother or a sister?"

Lindsay usually was careful not to reveal too much about herself. It was important to keep barriers between her and her clients. But today her guard was down. Seeing Zack yesterday had brought a lot to the surface. "My husband. I was devastated when I realized he was an alcoholic, like my father had been."

Marilyn stared at her through watery eyes. "What did you do?"

"I begged him to stop drinking. And when he refused, I kicked him out of our house."

Howard stiffened. "That sounds drastic."

"It was. But he is a tough, arrogant man and I wanted to get his attention. I wanted him to understand he had to clean up."

"Did he?" Howard asked.

Her hope had been to save her marriage, not destroy it. "Yes. In the end, he got sober. But it was a very long haul."

Marilyn swiped a tear from her cheek. "Did he ever thank you? Did he ever understand what you really did for him?"

Sadness tightened Lindsay's chest as she remembered the morning after he'd left. She'd been guilt ridden after their fight, so she'd called his cell early the next morning to talk. A woman had answered. *He's in the shower right now. Can I have him call you?*

That's when she'd realized Zack had slept with another woman and their marriage was truly over.

Lindsay swallowed the emotions in her throat. "He's living a happy, productive, and clean life now. That's all I really wanted for him."

"So it was worth it," Howard said.

Lindsay tried to smile. She still loved Zack, but understood it was over for them. "Yes."

Howard and Marilyn thanked her, made promises to consider what she'd said, and left.

Lindsay had spent a long time talking to the couple, and she felt completely drained. Normally, she worked through lunch, but today, she had to escape the building and get fresh air.

She dug in her jeans pocket and counted out the money she'd scrounged this morning from the coin jar on her washer. It was only six dollars and twenty-five cents. Not a fortune, but until she got her purse back, it was enough to buy her lunch.

She pushed through the security doors separating the counselors' offices from the lobby, then swung by the receptionist desk. "Back in a half hour. Need anything, Madge?"

The forty-something woman peered over reading glasses. "A man who cooks."

Lindsay laughed as she signed out. "I'll see what I can do. Any particular type of cook you're looking for?"

"No, baby. Just as long as his food is tasty and hot, I'm good. It doesn't take much to make Madge happy."

As the phone rang, Madge handed Lindsay a stack of pink telephone messages before picking up the line.

Lindsay shuffled through the messages. Dana had called again. Ruby called once. And Zack called at 11:32.

Out of habit she reached for her cell in her purse. But

she had no purse and no cell. Both were in her office. She felt naked without them. "Damn."

She considered returning to the conference room to return the calls, but her stomach grumbled. Eat first, and then tackle the calls, she decided.

Outside, midday heat warmed her skin, which had been chilled by the hours in the air-conditioning. For a moment, she just stood and drank in the warmth. She opened her eyes and stared into the cloudless sky before returning her gaze to the pink message from Zack. The "Please Call" box was checked. A lightning quick image of Zack's piercing, unreadable gray eyes flashed across her mind. Her stomach clenched and her heart quickened. She wondered if his lips still tasted the same.

Not good. She crumpled her messages and shoved them in her pocket.

She started across the parking lot. A quarter mile down the road there was a fast-food joint where she could grab a burger. Not her first choice but it would fit the bill.

Halfway across the parking lot she heard, "Lindsay O'Neil!"

The gruff voice had her turning to find a tall man wearing faded jeans and a Redskins T-shirt. He weighed about 200 pounds and was losing his fine blond hair to age. He quickly closed the dozen feet separating them.

"Yes?" Lindsay said. The sun shone in her eyes, forcing her to squint.

The man's jaw tightened, released. "My name is Burt Saunders." He dug calloused fingers into his jeans pocket and tossed her rumpled business card back at her. It fluttered to the ground and landed near her feet.

Saunders. Gail Saunders. This man was married to the woman she'd seen yesterday at Mercy Hospital. So this was the creep who had beaten the hell out of his wife. Damn, he must outweigh his wife by a hundred pounds.

Bloodshot eyes glared at her as he advanced a step. "Where is my wife?"

She glanced back toward the building and wondered if anyone on the other side of the tinted glass could see her. Wasn't there supposed to be a security guard by the door? "I don't know."

He swayed as if he'd been drinking. And he reeked of beer and vodka. "She moved out last night. All she left me was a goddamned note that said good-bye and not to come looking for her."

Good for her! Lindsay would gladly have gloated over the victory but she wasn't a fool. Burt Saunders was a big man, he was drunk, and he was real pissed. "I don't know anything about your wife's whereabouts, Mr. Saunders."

"You know where she is. She had your card."

She took a step back. "I don't know anything."

He moved with lightning speed, wrapping his hands around her throat. With a violent shove, he ground her back into the hot metal of a parked car, which quickly started to burn through her cotton top. "Bitch, I'll kill you if you don't tell me where my wife is staying."

The pressure on her throat made speaking difficult. She thought about the mace she carried in the purse she didn't have. "Get your hands off me," she managed.

He snarled and put his lips to her ear. "I ought to choke the life out of you."

Lindsay grabbed his hands and tried to pry them from her neck, but his grip tightened. Black spots dotted her vision. She coughed and gasped for air. Soon she'd black out.

Without warning, Saunders released his grip and lifted his weight off of her. She staggered away from the car and fell to her knees. At the same moment, Saunders dropped to the ground with tremendous force. He was clutching his own neck.

Lindsay looked up, squinting into the sun.

Looming over Saunders was Zack, who was already removing cuffs from his waistband and reciting Saunders his Miranda rights.

Warwick was right behind Zack, gun drawn.

Zack didn't take his gaze off Saunders as he shoved the man down on the ground to his belly. Zack then wedged his knee into the man's back and forced his face to the ground. Cuffs clamped on wrists.

Saunders had regained a little of his composure and started to fight the cuffs. "Fuck you!"

Zack pressed his knee deeper into Saunders's back. "Don't you speak one more word." He glanced over at Lindsay. "Are you all right?"

Her throat burned as she straightened and coughed. "Yes. I'm fine."

Warwick didn't lower his weapon. "Do you have him, Kier?"

"Yes."

Warwick called dispatch. "This is Detective Jacob Warwick. I need a patrol car at the county mental health building on Woodman Road." He waited as the dispatcher responded, "Right."

Saunders struggled. "Let me go. That bitch won't tell me where my wife is."

Again Zack dug his knee into Saunders's back. This time the guy flinched. "Don't say another word." The menace in his voice chilled Lindsay and reminded her of a time when he'd been that furious with her.

Still, she'd never been happier to see anyone. "Thanks."

Zack shot her a glance, swiftly assessing her. "Are you sure you're all right?" His voice sounded brittle.

"I'm good."

Warwick moved beside her. "Your neck looks bruised."

The guy almost sounded concerned. "Like I said, I'm fine."

Zack studied her for another beat and then turned his attention back to Saunders. He informed him he was under arrest for assault.

Saunders's wrists strained against the restraints. "The bitch deserved it. She butted into my life."

Zack jerked on the cuffs. "Shut up."

Within seconds two blue-and-white patrol cars, lights flashing, pulled into the parking lot. The uniforms took custody of Saunders and put him in the back of one of the squad cars.

The reality of how close she'd come to a bad beating or worse sank in.

Zack rested his hands on his hips and stared at her. He kept his voice low but she heard the tension. "What happened?"

"The guy's name is Saunders. His wife was taken to Mercy Hospital yesterday. She had injuries consistent with a beating, so the doctor on call asked me to visit with her."

"That's the appointment at the hospital you had."

"Yes. I spoke to Gail, this guy's wife, and gave her my business card, but I didn't think she cared about what I was saying." She nodded to the car where Burt sat in the backseat. He was glaring at her. "Ole Burt said she moved out last night. He found my card and figured I knew where to find her. And for the record, I don't know where she is." She frowned. "She could have called me. But if she had, she couldn't have gotten me at Sanctuary or on my cell, which is in my purse in my office."

Zack tightened his jaw. "I'll get your purse back today."

"Thanks." Lindsay watched with satisfaction as Saunders struggled against his cuffs in the squad car's backseat.

"Gail might not have been willing to file assault charges against him, but I have no problem with it."

Zack moved away and spoke to Warwick. After several minutes of discussion, Warwick got in the front seat of the patrol car holding Saunders, and the car drove off.

The shrill of an ambulance siren had her cringing. The flash of red lights got closer and the ambulance turned into the parking lot. "Please tell me that ambulance isn't for me."

"It sure is," Zack said.

She dragged a shaky hand through her hair. "I'm fine."

He towered over her. "Easier to get an ambulance here than you to the hospital."

His proximity made her uneasy. She'd always had trouble thinking when he was close. "I'll go see my family doctor."

Even, white teeth flashed. "Time has not made you a better liar."

She tried to sound offended. "What's that supposed to mean?"

"I know you. You're not going to see a doctor. You'll retreat back to your office, maybe eat a pack of Nabs, and drown yourself in work."

Uncomfortable, she shifted. He'd hit the nail on the head. Still, pride had her denying it. "You're wrong."

The paramedics got out and shook hands with Zack. "Bill, good to see you."

Bill was medium height, muscular, with ink black hair and a Cary Grant cleft in his chin. "You too, Zack. So what's going on?"

Zack took Lindsay by the arm. His touch was gentle but unbreakable as he pulled her toward Bill. "Have a look at her. I just pulled a creep off her. He was trying to strangle her."

Strangle. It sounded more frightening when Zack recapped the incident. Adrenaline fading, she felt her knees weaken.

Bill lifted his sunglasses. His green eyes were sharp as he leaned forward to look at Lindsay's neck. "Some red marks that will likely lead to bruises. Come over to the back of the truck and sit down, so I can have a closer look."

Lindsay didn't argue. Saunders could have done real damage and she'd be a fool at this point to pass up a quick once-over from the paramedic.

Zack walked with her to the ambulance.

Bill opened the back of the truck and his partner climbed inside and removed a tackle box filled with medical supplies. With Zack behind her watching, Lindsay climbed inside and sat on the cot.

After donning rubber gloves, Bill turned her head from side to side studying her battered skin. "You've got some scratches and you'll have a couple of fingerprint-size bruises in a few days. Can you swallow?"

Lindsay nodded. "Yes. My throat is fine."

Bill pulled an alcohol swab packet from the tackle box and tore it open. "This might sting but I want to get those scratches cleaned."

She winced when the alcohol made contact with her raw skin.

"He grab you anywhere else?" Bill asked.

"No. Just the throat," Lindsay said.

"Who did this to you?" Bill asked.

"Some guy who took exception to the fact that I encouraged his battered wife to leave him."

Bill's lips flattened into a grim line. "I thought I recognized you. I've seen you over at Mercy Hospital in the emergency room. It was a couple of months ago. You showed up to talk to a woman who had been beaten."

"Good memory." Lindsay held out her hand. "Lindsay O'Neil."

Bill took her hand and grinned. The smile was warm, genuine, and she found her foul mood lifting. "Bill Kline." He wiped her neck a second time, his hand lingering close. "I work out of the station house down the road."

The guy was flirting with her. And she felt flattered.

Zack pulled off his sunglasses. Dark eyes flashed annoyance. "Does she need to see a doctor?"

Bill's gaze skipped between Lindsay and Zack. Realization that Zack wanted Lindsay to himself had Bill easing back a fraction from her. "A throat X-ray wouldn't hurt."

"No," Lindsay said. "I'm fine."

Bill took a last look at her neck. "If you have any trouble swallowing, get to a doctor immediately. Otherwise, aspirin and rest are the best medicine."

"Thanks," Lindsay said.

Zack nodded. "I'll keep an eye on her."

She scooted off the cot and hopped down onto the asphalt. "Thanks, fellows, I'm fine." As the paramedics packed up, she painfully started walking the quarter-mile toward the fast-food joint. She needed to sit down before her knees gave way.

Zack followed Lindsay as she made her way across the parking lot. She needed a cold soda and a couple of aspirin.

"I don't need a babysitter," Lindsay said.

Zack wasn't put off. He fell into step beside her. "When's the last time you ate?"

She faced him. "I was on my way to lunch when what's-his-name decided to turn my neck into hamburger."

Zack glanced down the road. "The closest place is a burger shop."

"Walkers can't be choosers."

"You need a real meal—the kind with plates, a table with a cloth, and napkins."

"I don't have time or a car for that kind of stuff."

"You can spare an hour. I'll drive."

He was right. She was hungry, shaken, and needed to collect her thoughts. "Fine."

Zack guided her to his car, opened the door, then closed it after she got in. He slid behind the wheel, put the car into gear, and pulled onto Woodman Road.

In the confined space, Lindsay was aware of his hands on the wheel, the width of his shoulders, the way he clenched and unclenched his jaw as he drove. Suddenly, she wasn't so sure this was a good idea.

"So where are we headed?" she said.

"An Italian place close by."

She tried to relax back into the seat. She needed to loosen the reins for a little while but feared if she did the energy would completely drain from her body.

Zack soon pulled into the parking lot of a small eatery, put the car in park, and turned off the engine. She had climbed out and was halfway around the car before she really looked at the restaurant. *Zola's.* The restaurant owned by his parents. "Aw crap, Zack. Not here. It's your parents' restaurant."

He had the nerve to look shocked. "Why not? It's the best food in town."

She shot him a frustrated look. "Zack, I'm not exactly on your parents' favorite person list. I haven't seen them in a year."

That seemed to surprise him. "They've nothing against you."

She blew out a breath. "Please, Zack."

He stood so close to her she could see he wore the shirt she'd given him. "They like you, Lindsay. It will be fine. Besides, they're not even here today. Mom's got Dad helping her with Eleanor's birthday party. It's Saturday."

His explanation didn't dispel her unease. "Eleanor must be excited."

"Mom's turning the party into a big thing. Dad is going along without a fight, which tells me he's having fun. They've invited half of Richmond."

Lindsay's heart clenched. When she'd eloped with Zack the Kier family had welcomed her with open arms. She'd fallen for the entire clan as hard as she'd fallen for Zack. And when she'd kicked him out, she'd desperately wanted to explain to his parents why. But they'd never called her and she hadn't felt right about calling them. As fast as she'd made a family, she'd lost one.

Lindsay managed a smile. "I'm glad for them. Don't they have an anniversary coming up soon?"

"Next month. Thirty-five years."

"Wow."

Zack stared at her as if trying to read her mind and then, placing his hand in the small of her back, guided her into the restaurant. Immediately they were hit with a blast of cold air. The interior was dark and it took a moment for their eyes to adjust. The place was deserted.

"Where is everyone?" she said.

"We don't open until four on Tuesdays."

"If they aren't open, why are we here? I don't want to put anyone out."

"You're not. And they've always got pots on the stove simmering for dinner. I know we can scrounge a decent meal."

The familiar smells of marinara and freshly baked bread swirled around her, and for a moment she was transported back to those few months when everything had been good between them. "The place is just as I remembered it."

"Mom wants to redecorate—she's even called in a few

contractors for bids. But Dad refuses. He says people like tradition, places that don't change."

Her gaze skimmed the small square tables covered with crisp white linens. Even the napkins were cloth, pressed neatly into rectangles. On each table was a small hurricane lamp with an unlit candle.

Oddly, the restaurant had always made her feel at home. "Your dad is right. I always liked the place just like it is."

"Don't let Mom hear you say that."

Audrey Kier was a force to be reckoned with. A former stage actress, she had a flare for drama, which was accentuated by her short silver hair and still-trim body. She was outspoken, generous, and fiercely loyal to her family. Cross one of hers and you crossed her.

Lindsay's unease returned. "Maybe this isn't such a good idea."

Zack grabbed his sunglasses and tucked them in his breast pocket. "You're not afraid are you?"

Challenge punctuated each word. "No."

He smiled. "Then stay and have lunch."

He was daring her. "Fine."

Zack's brother, Malcolm, pushed through the kitchen door. Dressed in black, Malcolm possessed the same gray eyes as his brother, but his build was more muscular. Zack was the runner; Malcolm, the bodybuilder.

Malcolm frowned, clearly not happy to see Lindsay. "Zack. Lindsay. What's up?"

Zack grinned. "Looking for some lunch."

Malcolm glared at Zack as if to say: *We'll talk later.* "There are a few things brewing on the stove."

If Zack noticed his brother's dissatisfaction, he ignored it. "Great. We'll have two plates of whatever you've got. What are you doing here today?"

"Mom's got Dad wrapped around the axle about the party. I had a few days off so I offered to fill in today."

Zack grinned. "You swore after high school you'd never work in the restaurant again."

Malcolm shrugged. "Never say never, right? Go ahead and pick a table and I'll send Eleanor out with bread. Pasta and marinara sound good?"

Zack looked at Lindsay, his eyebrow lifted. "Work for you?"

Malcolm could have offered rusty nails on a plate and she'd not have argued. She smiled. "Sure."

Zack guided Lindsay to a back table tucked in a corner. He pulled out a chair for her, waited while she sat, then took the seat nearest to the wall—he always liked his back to the wall, eyes facing the door. This quirk was a holdover from his undercover days.

"Well, that's a first," she said as she sat.

"What?"

This close she could smell his soap. She loved the simple, masculine scent. "You held out a chair for me."

He opened a napkin. "Even an old dog can learn a new trick." Extra meaning punctuated the comment, and she didn't know how to respond. An uneasy silence settled between them before he broke it. "How secure is your apartment?

She opened a pack of crackers. "K-bar in the sliding glass door. Dead bolts on front and back doors. Extra long screws in the doorjambs. Not real high tech but effective."

"Lose the key under the flower pot yet?"

Lindsay nodded. "I'm willing to admit it was stupid to keep the key under the pot. It is now gone."

Zack seemed satisfied. "Ever had any trouble with anyone connected to the shelter? Anyone ever follow you home?"

"No. That hasn't been an issue. But I've been called every name in the book by enraged husbands and boyfriends. Even the victims can get nasty when I push them to testify against their abusers. But that's all par for the course. Nothing new."

"What about the woman who was killed by her husband about nine months ago? What was her name? Rogers?"

"Pam Rogers. And I blame myself for that one."

He frowned. "Why?"

"I should have seen it coming. Pam was extremely codependent and terrified of living without her husband. I told her time and again not to call her husband, but she couldn't let it go. Thirty minutes after I left for the day, she called him. A half hour after that he picked her up. He was hitting her before they were in the car. The volunteer on call telephoned me. We called the police."

"She was found dead the next morning," Zack said.

"Yes. I went to her funeral. One of her brothers approached me. He was angry and blamed me for what had happened. I remember someone from the crowd dragging him away."

"She was an adult, Lindsay. You couldn't have stopped her."

"But if I'd been there I could have talked her out of calling." The *but-ifs* stalked her.

His voice softened. "You can't be there twenty-four/seven."

She shook her head. "I still remember the pain in her brother's eyes."

"What was his name?"

"Simon Palmer."

"Where does this guy live?"

"Richmond. Southside, I think. He's an accountant."

"You had any contact with him since his sister's funeral?"

"None."

The doors to the kitchen swung open and a young

waitress with honey blond hair swept into the room with a tray of water glasses, bread sticks, and plates of pasta. Lindsay recognized Zack's older sister, Eleanor, immediately. Eleanor was thirty-three years old, vivacious, and had Down syndrome. She had as much pride as the other Kiers and was determined to be as independent as possible.

Lindsay beamed. "Eleanor!"

"Hi, Lindsay," she said, grinning.

When Lindsay had met Eleanor, Eleanor had been living in her parents' house but had wanted a place of her own. Her fiercely protective family had vetoed the idea. It had been Lindsay who'd suggested that the room over the Kier family garage be converted into an apartment. The idea had been a hit, and within months the room had been turned into a fully functioning apartment. Eleanor had been thrilled. So had her parents.

Eleanor set her tray on a stand and served them.

Lindsay then stood and hugged Eleanor. "You look wonderful."

Eleanor grinned broadly and hugged Lindsay back. "You look skinny."

Lindsay laughed. Eleanor had no pretense and always said what was on her mind. The honesty was refreshing. "So everyone keeps telling me. I guess I'd better eat."

Zack stood. There was softness in his gaze when he looked at his sister. He was a year younger than her, but he'd always been her protector. He'd once told Lindsay that Ellie was the reason he'd become a cop.

"So what are you doing here this afternoon, Ellie? I figured you'd be helping Mom and Dad with the party."

Eleanor made a face. "No way. Mom is driving us all crazy. She wants the party to be perfect. And Dad is mumbling a lot under his breath."

Zack smiled. "What else is new?"

"Nothing." Eleanor waved for Lindsay and Zack to sit. "Can I get you anything else?"

Lindsay smiled. "No, this is great."

Zack nodded. "We're good."

Eleanor leaned close to Lindsay and said in a stage whisper, "Zack is real sorry about your big fight."

Zack coughed. "Would you beat it, Ellie? Lindsay and I have business to discuss."

"Marriage business?" Eleanor said, hopeful.

Heat rose in Lindsay's face. She didn't dare look at Zack, but she could feel his gaze on her. "Just business."

"Zack, you need to fix this marriage," Eleanor said.

Zack cleared his throat and glared at her. "*Ellie*."

She matched his glare. "What?"

"Butt out."

She grinned. "No way, José."

"*Ellie*," he warned.

"Okay, okay, I'm going. But I'm going to be listening at the door."

When Eleanor vanished into the kitchen, Zack said, "She can be a little outspoken."

Lindsay broke a breadstick in two. "I always liked that about her."

He laughed. "I do too, most times."

She took a bite of pasta. It tasted like heaven. She didn't realize how hungry she was. Before she knew it, she'd eaten half of the pasta on her plate.

Zack set down his fork. "Ellie's right, you know."

"About what?"

"Sooner or later, we're going to have to settle this marriage business."

Chapter Sixteen

Tuesday, July 8, 2:00 P.M.

These days it was the little things that reminded Nicole of how much she'd lost during her marriage and was only now regaining in increments. Walking through the park. Ordering an ice cream cone. Having money that she'd earned in her pocket.

She still felt shaky about life in general, but she was discovering how much she'd forgotten how good it felt to make decisions and to be independent.

She strolled down the Carytown district sidewalk. This was her favorite section of town. She loved the early nineteenth-century row houses that were painted bright colors and housed ethnic restaurants and curio shops as eclectic as their patrons.

Nicole moved past the smoothie store, the chocolate shop and into her favorite French bakery. She purchased a croissant and a café au lait and savored both before wandering back outside. Down here, she could almost pretend her life was normal.

Her gaze drifted to a familiar FOR RENT sign posted above a Pilates studio that was sandwiched between a jewelry store and a restaurant. Again, she imagined reopening her photography business.

Giving rein to impulse, she climbed the narrow steps of the building to the second floor. She followed a RENTERS INQUIRE HERE sign to a half-open green door. She knocked.

"Come in!"

Nicole pushed open the door and found a tall woman dressed in a loose-fitting pants-and-shirt ensemble. She had long black hair and dark brown eyes that reminded Nicole of a cat.

"Can I help you?" the woman said.

"I saw your FOR RENT sign."

The woman smiled and extended her hand. "That's wonderful. My name is Fiona Moore. I own the building."

"Nicole Piper." She shook Fiona's hand, grateful she hadn't stumbled with her new name.

"Would you like to see the space?"

Her throat felt dry. It really was madness to entertain owning a business. "Yes."

The woman grabbed keys from the desk drawer. "Follow me."

Nervous, Nicole tightened her fingers around the strap of her bag. "Great."

Fiona moved with the grace of a dancer as she walked down the hallway. She unlocked a door, pushed it open, and flipped on the lights. "So what kind of business do you have?"

"I'd like to open a photography studio." Soft scents of lavender and fresh paint swirled as she stepped into the all-white room distinguished by high ceilings, chair molding, hardwood floors, and a bay window that overlooked Cary Street. The space was small but the southern exposure lighting was exquisite. Immediately, she imagined furnishing the room with simple pieces that she could use as props for her portraits. The place had so many possibilities.

"The space is only about three hundred square feet," Fiona said. "But there is a kitchenette with a large sink that could be converted into a darkroom. That is, if you need a darkroom. So much photography is digital."

Nicole strolled into the center of the room. She pictured cameras on tripods, lights, and backdrops. "I can take digital, but I prefer film. There's a richness that comes through when I develop the photos individually."

Fiona smiled. "You're an artist."

At one time art was all she was about. Now it was a luxury she couldn't afford. These last two months she'd learned to be brutally practical and ruthless. "How much is the rent?"

"Seven hundred plus utilities."

Nicole tried not to wince. Once she could have afforded the price. "I'm just getting started and poverty is a fact of life right now."

Fiona wasn't put off by her honesty. "Do you have a portfolio?"

Nicole moved out of the room. No sense dreaming about what wasn't to be now. "I've a collection of recent work I've done since I came to Richmond. All portrait work."

"I'm looking for a photographer to take pictures of me and the studio. Big marketing push for the studio in the fall. I'd love to see your work."

Excitement rose inside her. "Sure."

"I can't pay much." Smiling, Fiona locked the door behind them. "You're not the only one on a tight budget."

Nicole mentally leafed through her pictures. Already she'd taken several dozen portraits. What she had to show didn't measure up to the caliber of her old stuff, but it was still good. "Might take me a couple of days. I could come by next Monday."

Fiona brightened. "Ten?"

She thought about her work schedule. "I can make that."

Fiona held out her hand. "See you on Monday at ten, Nicole Piper."

A wide grin tugged at Nicole's lips. "Great."

The thought of freelance work filled her with hope for the future. She didn't have the money to open a business now, but she'd taken the first step toward it.

Nicole hurried down the stairs but was so distracted she nearly bumped into a man. He had dark hair slicked back off his face and Rayban sunglasses.

For just a split second, she thought the stranger was her husband, Richard.

Heat from the sidewalk shot upward, and sweat began to trickle down her bare legs. "Excuse me." Her voice cracked.

The man nodded. "No problem." He kept walking.

She stared after him. He wasn't Richard. Richard was 3,000 miles away. Yet, her heart hammered in her chest. She started walking, but her gait wasn't as confident. The ease she'd felt just seconds ago had vanished.

She'd not seen Richard in nearly three months, but that didn't mean she was safe. She *knew* her husband. He was out there looking for her, and if she wasn't very, very careful he'd find her. She glanced back at the FOR RENT sign. What had she been thinking? A business was just too risky.

She opened the cell phone Lindsay had given her and turned it on. She usually kept the phone off because Richard had used her old cell to keep tabs on her.

Her hands trembling, she dialed the number of the woman who'd helped her escape Richard: Claire

Carmichael. As the phone rang, she wasn't sure what Claire could tell her. Maybe that Richard was still in San Francisco . . . that he'd forgotten about her.

Claire's voice mail picked up. When the beep sounded, Nicole panicked and couldn't speak. Lindsay had warned her about any contact with people from her old life. She closed the phone.

Let sleeping dogs lie.

Better to be safe.

For the millionth time, she wished Richard was dead.

San Francisco, 11:15 A.M. PST

Richard Braxton had chosen his home because of the stunning view of San Francisco Bay. The original house on the lot had been old, filled with "charm," according to the historical society, but it hadn't suited his vision of the home he deserved. So he'd had the house razed. There'd been an outcry, protests, lawsuits even, but he'd maneuvered through it all.

The showpiece house he'd created, with its steel and sleek modern lines, didn't suit the narrow-minded tastes of his neighbors, who preferred brick and boxwoods. But that didn't concern him. Richard Braxton did what *he* wanted, *when* he wanted.

Richard understood his greatest skill was his ability to see the potential; to know when a house, a market, or a woman was worth his attention.

Potential had been the reason he'd been drawn to the lot and it had been the reason he'd been attracted to Christina, his wife. Christina was a beauty, a stunner, and he had known from the moment he'd first seen her in that rundown photography studio that he could make her into something special.

Training her had not been easy. She had a fierce and spirited nature, and it had taken so many lessons to mold her into the vision he'd had for her. In the last few months they'd been together, he'd begun to believe that he had nearly succeeded. She no longer argued with him. She dressed perfectly in the tasteful Chanels and de la Rentas. She'd learned to be punctual, to keep her makeup perfect, and had tamed that thick mane of black hair.

Perfection had been in his grasp.

And then she'd vanished. That fool chauffer had let her slip away.

How long had she been planning to run from him?

The thought tormented him daily. He replayed every moment they'd shared those last couple of months. He thought about the books she'd read, the movies she'd seen, and the people she'd spoken to, looking for clues. He'd been insanely busy with work during that time and had been distracted. But he'd thought she'd been transformed and there was nothing to worry about.

For her to run, there had to be someone else. She had to have taken a lover.

A soft knock on his study door had him turning to find Vincent Malone standing at the threshold. Vincent wasn't a tall man, but his wiry body was compacted muscle. His Italian double-breasted suit complemented his frame, and his ice blond hair, pulled back in a ponytail, accentuated vivid green eyes. He was Richard's right-hand man. He knew all his dirty secrets. For the last two weeks, he'd done nothing but search for Christina.

"Anything come of that lead Jimmy gave us?" Richard said.

Vincent closed the study door behind him. "I've had men canvassing the area and showing her picture around. No one has seen her."

Richard moved to his large mahogany desk that he'd had specially made in Spain. "So that's it? She just vanished?"

Vincent smiled. Like Richard, he savored a good hunt. "Everyone leaves a trail, Mr. Braxton. The trick is being able to find it."

"Has there been activity on a credit card or cell phone?"

"No. There's been no activity on her cards, phones, or Social Security number. And I've had computer experts check every chip in her computer. Nothing. I've still got men looking in every airport, bus and train station, and car rental place. But there's been no sign of her."

Anger was nearly driving him insane. Killing Jimmy had made him feel good for a while. But his well-being hadn't lasted long. "So we've got shit."

"Not exactly."

Richard flexed his fingers. "So you've found something?"

"Claire Carmichael."

His patience wore thin. "I don't know her."

"She owns the New Age bookstore about five blocks from the restaurant where Jimmy lost Christina."

"Why do I care about her?"

"She's part of this network of people who help abused women disappear. She speaks regularly at community centers in your area."

Months of pent-up rage burned in Richard. "Abused women. Christina wasn't abused. I gave her everything. I love her."

Vincent nodded his head in deference. "I didn't mean to suggest she was."

Richard drew in a deep breath. "So you think this Carmichael woman helped Christina?"

"Yes. Your wife's driver remembered taking her to a

Bay Area church several weeks in a row. I checked. It was a support group run by Claire Carmichael. I want to talk to her."

Richard shook his head. "The bitch interfered with my marriage. Give me her address."

Vincent looked doubtful. "Wouldn't you rather I take care of it? Better to let me do the dirty work."

"I like the dirty work."

Richard downshifted the gears of his BMW and pulled into a parking spot in front of the New Age bookstore located near San Francisco Bay. The store was housed in an old row house that had survived the big earthquake a hundred years ago. Tall with a sharp roof, square bay windows, and lots of gingerbread trim, the building was considered a treasure, but by his way of thinking it was an old pile of junk.

He'd never have given the place a second glance if not for Claire Carmichael.

He shut off the car engine and got out. Inside the store, he spotted Claire. She was about thirty, olive skin, not tall. She wore a frumpy, flowing dress that hid her curves, and she had pulled back curly hair into a high ponytail that highlighted sharp cheekbones and bright eyes. Not his type, but loosen the hair and ditch the dress and she might be worth a spin.

Richard grew hard.

He imagined her eyes lighting with desire as he shoved inside her. And then he pictured the passion shifting to fear as he wrapped his hands around her neck and squeezed the life out of her. She'd fight to breathe. She'd kick, try to scream. But in the end, the life would fade from her body.

It was almost closing time and it didn't take long before the store emptied of customers.

Richard had all night to chat with Little Miss New Age about Christina.

When she disappeared behind a curtain into the back room of the store, he went inside, careful to keep the bells on the door from jingling. Softly he shut the door, locked it, and flipped the OPEN sign to CLOSED.

Richard moved behind the counter and unplugged the phone.

"Hello, is someone out there?" Claire called.

He reached into his pocket and let his fingers slide over the cold steel of his knife.

Claire heard the creak of footsteps in the store. The hair on the back of her neck rose. She'd had trouble with shoplifters in the last few months and didn't like to leave the store unattended.

She took off her glasses and laid them on the ledger on her desk. She stood and crossed to the curtain separating the back room from the retail portion of the store. She pushed through the curtain. "Can I help you?"

The man standing by the display of healing crystals wasn't what she'd expected. He was hardly a teen thug looking to grab up what he could. And he wasn't remotely like her regular patrons.

He was smartly dressed in a stylish suit that looked handmade. His white open-neck shirt was made of crisp linen. His nails were buffed and his short black hair was brushed off his face. Strong jaw. Tanned skin. Nice to look at.

The man raised his head and met her gaze. His eyes were so dark that the pupils all but disappeared. She'd never glimpsed the face of Evil but now she sensed she was looking right at it.

The man tossed her a quick smile. "I hope you can help me."

A lump formed in the pit of her stomach. "What do you want?" Her tone had grown hard, losing all hint of welcome.

He set down the expensive crystal he'd been cradling. "My wife. Christina Braxton."

Claire remembered the woman vividly. The bruises on her arms and neck testified to the trauma she'd suffered at the hands of her husband. Claire had sensed the fear and the goodness in Christina. It had been an easy choice to give her cash and the keys to the secondhand car. "I don't know what you're talking about."

Richard nodded almost as if he were pleased by her answer. He pulled the switchblade from his pocket and he flicked the blade open. "I was hoping you wouldn't talk too quickly."

Panic exploded inside Claire. She snatched up the phone and discovered the line was dead. She bolted to the back of the shop to the back alley exit.

Richard moved quicker than a cat. He reached her just as she made it to the door. He grabbed a handful of her hair and jerked her head back. He drew the knife blade along her cheek, slicing flesh as he went. Pain burned her face as warm blood oozed down her cheek.

"Where is my wife?" he whispered against her ear.

"I don't know."

Claire wasn't going to tell him where Christina was hiding. And she knew the cost of her silence was going to be her life.

Chapter Seventeen

Tuesday, July 8, 3:20 P.M.

Kendall was very pleased with herself. She and Mike had shot her evening report and it had gone better than good. Lindsay's past made great television. This newscast was going to get Kendall noticed.

Her phone rang. Without taking her eyes off the road, she pulled the phone from her purse and flipped it open. "Kendall Shaw."

"You're a hard woman to find." The deep male voice sounded smooth, confident, but she didn't recognize it.

"Who's this?"

"Detective Jacob Warwick, Henrico County Police. Your phone has been busy all morning."

Damn. She thought about the film footage of the delivery truck at the shelter. That was the kind of information she should have shared with the cops first thing this morning. An obstruction of justice charge would not help her career.

Kendall kept her voice smooth. "Sorry. Running down leads on a story. What can I do for you?"

"I'd like to chat with you about the shelter murder and review your tape from yesterday."

She kept her voice cheerful. "Sure. What time works for you?"

"Now would be nice."

The steel behind the words left little room for argument. And she wasn't about to piss anyone off at this point. "I can swing by the station and get a copy of the footage." No need to mention she had one at home. "It will take me at least a half hour to get the tape and meet you at my office."

"I'll meet you at the at station office."

Her mind turned. Maybe she could even score a quote or two from Warwick. "See you in a half hour."

Kendall arrived at the television station fifteen minutes late. When she rushed into the lobby, she spotted the detective immediately. He was staring into one of the station's trophy cases, his hands clasped behind his back. He had a relaxed way that she suspected was deceptive. "Detective Warwick?"

His smile didn't reach his piercing eyes. "Kendall Shaw."

Kendall crossed the lobby and accepted Warwick's hand. His grip was powerful. "Good to meet you."

"I appreciate the help."

"If you will follow me, I'll take you upstairs. I can burn a copy of that footage onto a CD for you." The west wing of the Deco-style building was littered with ladders and plastic tarps. "Excuse our mess. We're undergoing a huge renovation."

"No problem."

They wound down the narrow corridors. "Would you like a tour of our newsroom?"

"No thanks." He flashed even, white teeth. "Maybe another time."

"Sure." Under his easygoing demeanor was steel. "When the renovation is done, all this is going to be gone. From what I hear, it will all be very sleek."

"Really?"

So much for small talk. She led him to a news edit bay, a small glassed-in room off the hallway furnished with a computer station. She sat down on the swivel chair in front of the computer. "The station's new P2 cameras are equipped with hard drives, so there's rarely a tape anymore. With luck we still have the footage. Generally, when we've filed the story, we dump the raw stuff to clear space on the computer."

Warwick frowned. "Let's hope it's still here. The other stations didn't have anything."

Kendall punched a few buttons and opened a file. "You're in luck. The footage is here." She burned a CD and handed it to him.

"Thanks."

She rose and had to look up to meet his gaze. "No problem."

When he nodded and started to turn, she said, "I hear Lindsay had a rough past. Think there is any connection between this murder and her mother's death?"

The comment surprised Warwick. "You've been doing some homework."

"That's my job. Do you think the two killings are linked?"

His expression was unreadable. "We don't discuss the details of an active case."

"Just seems odd. Her mother is the casualty of a domestic murder and this latest body is dumped behind a women's shelter."

"Can't help you."

She'd have better luck getting blood from a stone than information from Warwick. "Thanks."

Chapter Eighteen

Tuesday, July 8, 4:25 P.M.

Lindsay stood behind Zack as she watched the uniformed officer crate up her office files. Impotent rage roiled inside her. She'd worked for a year to make this shelter into something worthwhile, and in twenty-four hours it had fallen apart.

"Do the cops have to mess everything up?" Lindsay asked, unable to remain silent.

Zack turned. "Lindsay, wait in the kitchen. When Warwick returns, we'll all talk."

Frustration ate at her. A few hours ago, they'd shared a meal. She'd laughed with his sister. Now, he was all cop again. "Can I have my purse? I'd rather go back to Mental Health Services. At least there I can be productive."

"I'll bring it out to you," Zack said.

The wall was back between them. "Great."

She went into the kitchen. This time of day the kitchen should have been teeming with activity. Kids would be running around, residents would be talking, and the phones would be ringing off the hook. Now it was dead silence.

Needing something to do, she went on the back deck to the potting table. There were four six-packs of marigolds, a pot, and soil. All the supplies were still damp from yesterday's rain. Careful to keep her back to the murder scene, she opened the bag of soil and poured rich, dark dirt into the pot. It felt good to have her hands in the soil. She gingerly removed a marigold from the plastic container and pushed it into the soil. She was reaching for the flower pack to get another when the back door opened.

"Ms. O'Neil," Warwick said, "could we talk?"

She shoved out a breath, wondering when he'd returned. "Sure." She headed back into the kitchen and washed her hands. Zack came into the room and the three sat at the kitchen table.

Warwick opened his notebook to a clean page. "We've got our warrant, which gives us open access to your files. You can help us by telling us those that should be red flagged."

Lindsay had thought about that a lot last night. "It's hard to say."

"We'll get the names with or without your help. But your help will make the investigation go faster."

She sighed. The sooner Harold's killer was caught the sooner the shelter would reopen. "We've had some rough cases the last few months. Give me your notebook and I'll write the top ten."

Warwick pushed the notebook and a pen toward her. She scratched out the worst of the abusive spouses she'd dealt with.

Once she'd finished, Warwick studied the names. "Do you think any of these men could be the Guardian?"

"I don't know. But they're all violent men. And none of them would want to help me."

Zack leaned forward but remained silent. Clearly this was Warwick's show.

"When is the last time you saw Turner?" Warwick asked.

She didn't like his tone. "I told Detective Kier all this."

Warwick flashed white teeth. "Again, please, for my benefit."

She reviewed the details of her encounter with Turner.

"And you confronted him at the party?" Warwick said.

She felt that evening's anger returning. "It wasn't my intention, but, yes, I did have words with him."

"Remind you of your old man?" Warwick said.

Angered that Zack must have discussed her past, she straightened. "Yeah, in a lot of ways Turner did remind me of him."

Warwick tapped his index finger on the table. "It's clear you love this place. The toys, the warm colors, and the flowers—they were all done by you, weren't they?"

"Sure."

"And you care about the women and children. I've leafed through a few files. Your notes suggest you really do want these women to succeed."

She sensed a setup. "Cut the compliments. What's your point?"

Warwick's expression hardened a fraction and she had a sense he'd mentally taken off the gloves. "I went to your folks's place in Hanover. It looked as if it had been a nice place at one time."

A sudden weight pressed against her chest. "You were there?"

"Kier and I read your mother's murder file. We see how rough you had it."

"Why are you telling me this?" Her voice was just above a whisper.

"You grew up with an abusive man and then you run into someone like Harold, who reminds you of your father." He met her gaze head-on. "He gets in your face and in essence threatens to close the place you love. It would be reason enough to kill him."

Zack said nothing, nor did he show any emotion. She'd never felt more alone.

"I didn't kill Harold," Lindsay said, teeth clenched.

"You have no alibi, Ms. O'Neil."

"I told you that I was home asleep."

"A fact you can't prove."

Jordan Turner may not have wanted her help but Nicole Piper did, and Lindsay wouldn't tell the cops about her. Richard had contacts in the San Francisco Police Department, and she couldn't risk inquiries from the guys on this end. She'd find a way out of this mess somehow. "No, I can't."

Warwick closed his notebook. "I suggest you get an attorney, Ms. O'Neil."

She glanced at Zack, expecting some kind of support. "I need an attorney?"

Zack showed no hint of emotion. "It wouldn't hurt."

Abruptly she rose. "I can't believe this," she said. "I've got some nutcase out there sending me body parts and now the cops are breathing down *my* throat. I didn't kill Harold. But I'm the first to admit I hated the guy and I won't lose any sleep over the fact that he's dead."

Zack stood but said nothing. He shoved his hands in his pockets and rattled change.

Warwick was unfazed by her outburst. "Get a lawyer."

"Are you going to charge me?" she demanded.

"Not yet."

Lindsay couldn't believe this. All she'd done was stand up for herself when Turner had tried to browbeat her and now she was a murder suspect. "Can I have my purse?"

Warwick slowly rose. "Yes. It's on the banister by the front door."

"Thanks." She started down the hallway.

"Don't leave town without calling me, Ms. O'Neil," Warwick said.

She didn't glance back. "Right."

She snatched up her purse and dug out her keys. She didn't bother with a sideways glance into her office at the jumble the cops had made of her files as she pushed through the front door.

Once in her Jeep, she cranked the engine and backed out. As she drove home the surge of adrenaline from her interview began to fade.

Lindsay felt weary and so alone. She couldn't tell the cops about Nicole. The woman was just getting her life back. She prayed the real killer would be found soon so the spotlight would leave her.

Fifteen minutes later, she pulled in front of her town house. She moved up her walkway and shoved her key in the lock. God, all she wanted now was a hot bath and a cup of tea.

"Lindsay!"

Sam's cheerful voice had Lindsay turning. He wore khakis, a white button-down shirt, and loafers without socks. The late afternoon light pulled red highlights in his thick sandy blond hair.

In a flash she remembered her promise to have dinner with him tonight. "Sam."

"Sorry I'm late," he said.

She glanced forlornly at her home. God, but she wanted to get into bed and pull the covers over her head. "Oh, no problem."

Creases formed around his blue eyes. "You forgot, didn't you?"

She glanced down at her keys in the door and grinned. "Or maybe I saw you drive up and was headed out to meet you?"

He laughed. "We can go with that story, if you like."

She could feel her blood pressure dropping. "Works for me."

Sam's eyes grew serious. "If you want to bag tonight, it's fine. You look like you've had a tough day."

Her hand went to her ponytail, which had sunk low on her head. "I'm good. I need a night out or I'll sit at home and stew."

He grinned. "Good. There's a new French restaurant out on Patterson."

"I should change."

"Naw, you look good. Besides, it's casual."

She wasn't hungry. Lunch had been filling. Still, an evening out that wasn't emotionally draining would be welcome.

Sam guided her to a sleek Audi and opened the door for her.

Lindsay couldn't help but smile. "You're spoiling me."

"You could use that once in a while." He closed her door and came around the front. The car's interior smelled new.

He slid behind the wheel and started the engine. The soft scent of his aftershave reminded her that this was a *date*.

Crap. Didn't she have enough on her plate?

They'd not driven a block when his cell rang. He glanced down at the number and sent the call to voice mail.

"Why don't you answer that?" Lindsay said. Zack always took his calls.

"It's not important. You are."

Not all men were like Zack.

And that was a good thing. Right?

Alone in the car, this close to Sam, she felt a bit awkward. If he'd been Sam the *friend*, she'd have had no trouble talking to him. But Sam the *date* felt like an entirely different person. Suddenly pressure existed where there'd been none before.

"So how was the hospital today?" she said.

He kept his gaze on the road. "Same old, same old."

Normally, Sam had half a dozen stories to tell about his day in the ER. And his unexpected silence had her scraping for something else to say that would keep the conversation going. "No war stories?"

"None. Ever notice we always talk about work?"

"Yeah."

His expression turned serious. "Let's do our best not to talk shop tonight."

Suddenly she was tongue-tied. What would they talk about? First Zack and now Sam. Why couldn't she carry on a conversation with an adult male? "That doesn't leave much."

He grinned. "There's the weather."

She laughed but realized seeing Sam like this felt dishonest somehow. She was legally separated from Zack and a signature away from finalizing the divorce. She was rebuilding her life without him. Dating was *okay*.

Sam pulled into the restaurant's parking lot and parked in a spot close to the door. She got out and met him at the front of the car. He placed his hand into the small of her back and guided her into the restaurant.

It was a quiet, small bistro that had only opened a couple of months ago. Most weekends the place attracted large crowds. Tuesdays offered a slower pace.

The hostess led them to an intimate table in the back

near a fireplace filled with votive candles that flickered in the dimly lit room. "Stop indulging me."

He chuckled and took his seat. "You deserve to be spoiled once in a while."

Lindsay spread her napkin over her lap. "I'm so used to taking care of everything. Being spoiled makes me feel uncomfortable."

The waitress arrived and Sam ordered a bottle of wine as well as a sampling of appetizers. Within minutes they arrived. The wine was excellent, as was the display of cheeses.

As he swirled the Merlot in a glass, his gold signet ring winked in the candlelight. "So why are you so used to taking care of yourself?"

She shrugged. "Long, long story, Sam."

Sam laid his hand on hers. It was warm, soft. "Is there anything I can do to make this day better?"

Her hand felt steadier as she raised her glass to her lips. "Know any good defense lawyers?"

The Guardian watched a drunken Burt Saunders stagger out of the bar on Third Street. In less than twelve hours the bastard had made bail. No wonder people said the American justice system was in the toilet.

Anger roiled inside the Guardian as Saunders lumbered down the sidewalk toward a red Lincoln with a white convertible top. A pink parking ticket lay flat under the windshield wiper. Saunders tossed the ticket in the gutter and fumbled in his pockets for his keys.

He didn't realize that Death stalked him.

Saunders dropped his keys on the street by his car door. He wobbled forward and patted the ground for the set. He lost his balance and hit his shoulder hard against the car door. He swore.

The Guardian moved closer until inches separated them. "Looks like you're having a bit of trouble tonight."

Saunders's bloodshot eyes narrowed. "Fuck off."

No manners. Typical. "You look like you could use a score."

Saunders found his keys and snatched them up. "Like I said, fuck off, bitch."

Killing this fool was going to be a true pleasure, one destined to be savored. "I've got some coke if you're interested. It would go a long way to taking the edge off."

Licking his lips, Saunders glanced around to make sure no one watched. "I don't know what you're talking about."

The fish had taken the bait. "I can make all the pain go away."

"You look like a cop."

"Follow me and I'll show you what I've got."

"I don't need you." To punctuate his statement, he tried to put his key in the car door lock. His hands trembled so badly that he couldn't manage the task.

"Suit yourself." To be too eager would spook the prey. Saunders was a mean son of a bitch but he wasn't stupid.

The Guardian started to walk back toward an alley.

Saunders hesitated and then staggered forward. "How much?"

"Fifty."

"Thirty is all I've got."

"Make it forty."

Saunders considered the counteroffer and then nodded. "Fine."

Gotcha. "In the van in the alley over there."

The drunk nodded and followed. In the moonlight the shadows were long and narrow, shrouding the alley in the darkness. The scent of garbage and urine clung to humid air.

Saunders's large feet shuffled as he moved away from

the street. He pulled two crumpled twenties out of his pocket.

The Guardian thought about Saunders's wife, Gail. The woman had been broken and afraid when she'd run from the hospital yesterday. She'd tried so hard not to cry when she'd fumbled with her keys in the hospital parking lot. So brave. So much like Debra. "In the van."

Saunders climbed in, the hunger bright in his eyes.

From a jacket pocket, the Guardian pulled out a baggy filled halfway with white powder. Saunders tossed his money on the seat and snatched the bag.

As he turned to leave the van, the Guardian pressed a Taser to Saunders's neck. The tall man's body jerked and convulsed and he fell back against the seat.

Fear sharpened the haze in Saunders's eyes. "What the fuck?"

The Guardian jabbed the Taser to the soft flesh of Saunders's neck again. The man convulsed painfully. His eyes rolled back in his head and his chest rose and fell as he struggled to suck air into his lungs.

"*Retribution is mine,*" the Guardian whispered, uncapping a syringe and shoving it into Saunders's arm.

Within seconds Saunders's eyes glazed over. The Guardian started the van and eased into the street. There was no hurry tonight. No nervous fear either, like the other night with Turner.

Lindsay couldn't fall asleep. Today had started off as a good day. She had finished her first week in kindergarten and was excited about the day she'd just spent in school. Her teacher had shown the class how to make paper butterflies. Lindsay had loved the colors and the way the crepe paper folded and made delicate wings.

But the joy she'd felt at school had quickly faded when she'd re-

turned home. Her mother had been edgy and worried. When Lindsay's father came home the tension had gotten worse. Her father didn't like the dinner her mother had prepared and he seemed determined to find fault with everything.

Now Lindsay lay curled on her side in her bed with the covers pulled over her head. Her father was shouting at her mother and her mother was crying.

"Who gives you the damn right to talk to him about our problems? I'm your family."

"He's my brother."

"A brother who's not been around for years. I've been here all along. I've been the one putting food in your mouth and clothes on your back. He hasn't."

"He was just worried about me. And I missed seeing him."

"Well, if you think he's so damn great, you go and live with him. But Lindsay stays with me."

"I'll never leave her."

"She's mine. Just like everything else in this house. So if you want to leave, you leave with the shirt on your back."

Footsteps sounded down the hallway toward Lindsay's room. Her mother was crying louder and her father was shouting more. Lindsay's door opened and light from the hallway shone into her room.

"Don't touch my daughter!" her mother shouted.

Flesh smacked against flesh and someone stumbled back. Lindsay peeked out from under the covers and saw her mother fall.

Lindsay started to cry.

Lindsay's cell phone, perched on her nightstand, rang just after midnight and jerked her awake. Accustomed to being awakened in the middle of the night, she sat up and answered it. "Hello?"

No answer.

She shoved back her hair and glanced at the clock on the bedside table. Sam had dropped her off over three hours ago and she'd fallen into bed exhausted. "Hello?"

There was breathing on the other end. Normally, when she got late-night calls, it was a frightened woman hiding out from her abuser, too afraid to talk. Often she had to coax the woman into speaking.

But tonight, she didn't sense someone in trouble. She sensed danger. Her voice harsh, she demanded, "Who is this?"

There was a moment's pause. And then the line went dead.

Lindsay checked the incoming number and discovered it was blocked. She closed the phone. Fully awake, she swung her legs over the side of the bed and clicked on the bedside lamp.

A chill slithered through her.

It wasn't like her to be so easily spooked. She got out of bed, clad only in an oversized T-shirt. The air-conditioning chilled her skin.

Careful not to wake Nicole, Lindsay hurried past her roommate's closed door and went down the carpeted stairs to check the lock on the front door. She peered out the peephole. Nothing. Then she went to the back sliding glass door. Locked. She moved from window to window checking them. All locked.

She flipped on the floodlight and it shone over her backyard garden. She stared into the yard looking for any sign of movement.

Nothing moved.

And yet she had the feeling that someone was watching. Hugging her arms, she stared into the darkness inside her home. There was no one there.

She shoved stiff fingers through her hair. This was insane. She was driving herself nuts over what was likely a wrong number. She shut off the backyard light. "Too much caffeine."

She opened the refrigerator and peered inside at the carton full of leftovers from the bistro. She opened the container of chocolate cake and sampled a piece. It melted in her mouth. After closing the door, she moved into the living room, switched on a light, and sat down. In the silence, she ate the cake, savoring every bite.

As she rose to pitch the takeout container in the the kitchen trash bin, she spotted the door under the stairs. Behind it was a small storage place where she kept a box of old pictures. She tossed the carton, wiped her hands, opened the door, and removed the worn box. She carried it to the couch, sat, and dug among the photos, careful to avoid the ones with Zack. She'd never organized or put the photos in an album, but she'd written dates and notes on the back of each.

There were pictures of Lindsay with her friend Joel. They were at the pool, smiling. Joel had his arm wrapped casually around her shoulder. She smiled as she traced Joel's face. Joel and his dad had been the ones who'd gone back to the house after her mom died and gotten these photos and her clothes.

Going deeper in the photo box, she found a picture of herself as a baby. Other pictures of herself at swim and tennis meets with her father and mother smiling proudly behind her. They looked so happy. Picture perfect.

And yet, behind the smiles, there was tension in her parents' eyes. Most wouldn't have noticed it, but she did.

She found deeper in the box black and whites of her mother as a young girl before she'd married her father. Her mother had had a bright smile, dark wavy hair that set off her hazel eyes and peaches-and-cream complexion. In one photo, Lindsay's mother stood with her older brother, who was fifteen years older than her mother. He looked to be about twenty-five in this photo. His arm was slung casually around her mother's shoulders, and he wore a sailor's uniform that accentuated his trim waist and broad shoulders. She had no memories of her uncle except for the rare story her mother told.

Buried at the bottom of the box were pictures of three-year-old Lindsay holding a baby boy. The child had been her younger brother; he had died of crib death when he was just seven months old. Her mother had rarely spoken about her brother, Bobby, but Lindsay knew the boy's death had left a hole in both her parents' hearts that had never healed.

Maybe if Bobby hadn't died. Maybe if . . .

These stupid mind games weren't going to change her past. It was what it was. A mess.

She dropped the pictures back in the box, unable to bear the sadness. She replaced the lid and put the box back in the closet under the stairs.

Suddenly very tired, she climbed the stairs and got into bed. The sheets felt cold against her skin. Despite her fatigue, her mind was restless.

She reached for the light. She'd searched the house and assured herself that she and Nicole were alone. And yet, she still felt as if someone stood over her.

Watching.

The Guardian checked Saunders's bindings. Secure. The man lay unconscious, his arms and legs stretched wide and tied to stakes driven in the concrete floor.

After turning on the three TVs, the Guardian flipped on the evening news reports. He wanted to see what the press was saying about him.

The first two stations had nothing to report beyond police

were still trying to unravel the murder of a local attorney. He flipped to Channel 10 to see Kendall Shaw reporting.

. . . a troubled past marred by the violent murder of her mother. When I spoke with Lindsay O'Neil earlier this spring, she talked about her passion for saving women in abusive relationships. But Lindsay O'Neil harbored a dark secret. Her father, Frank Hines, a garage owner in Hanover, a church leader and well known in his community, routinely beat his wife—Lindsay's mother.

Two days before Lindsay's seventeenth birthday, Hines killed his wife and then shot himself.

Now exactly twelve years after the Hines murder/suicide, the body of a murdered man has been found behind the women's shelter O'Neil created. The victim, Harold Turner, a local attorney, was seen just weeks ago arguing with O'Neil at a local fund-raiser.

Tension rippled through the Guardian's body.

Kendall Shaw's news report bordered on hateful. She'd all but called Lindsay a murderer.

Facts could suggest that O'Neil could have embarked on her own plan of revenge.

Kendall Shaw's raw ambition had driven her too far. She was twisting facts to suit her own purposes. She was a liar and a manipulator and very much like the men who abused their wives. She abused the public trust with her half-truths and innuendo.

The Guardian turned back toward Saunders. He was out cold. No good. He needed to be awake.

He needed to feel pain.

A broken ammonia capsule waved under his nose woke Saunders instantly. Wide-eyed, the man stared around the room, trying to take in his surroundings. He muttered several foul words through his gag and tested the ropes that held him.

"We're in a basement, Mr. Saunders. It's very secluded. Very private."

Bloodshot eyes focused on the Guardian. Confusion gave way to anger. Saunders jerked at his restraints.

The Guardian was pleased. "You're not going any-where. Not until you've learned a few lessons."

Saunders kicked his legs, trying to loosen the ropes. They didn't budge. He screamed into his gag.

"You're a fighter. I like that." The Guardian grabbed a black bag. "Harold Turner caved when I cornered him. He cried like a baby. You aren't going to cry are you, Mr. Saunders?"

Saunders's eyes narrowed.

"Good. I don't like criers."

From the black bag came the machete. The shiny blade reflected the dim lamplight. "You know what this is? It's the blade I used to cut Harold's hand off."

Saunders swallowed. His fingers clenched into tight fists.

The Guardian traced the flat side of the blade over the man's left wrist. "Are you afraid?"

Defiant, Saunders clamped down on his gag. But the Guardian saw the sweat beading on his upper lip.

"Fear is an uncomfortable feeling, isn't it, Mr. Saunders?"

When he didn't budge, the Guardian traced the sharp blade over Saunders's wrist. This time bravado gave way to terror.

"Fear is what Gail lives with every day. You put that fear inside her. Didn't you?"

Saunders stared, his eyes wide as he shook his head "no."

"You enjoyed seeing her afraid. You enjoyed knowing you had total power over her life." When Saunders didn't answer, the Guardian drew the blade over the inside of his arm, splitting the skin and spilling blood.

Saunders groaned as the pain burned.

"Did you enjoy hurting your wife?"

He nodded.

"And now you will be punished."

Saunders strained at his bindings. He screamed, the sound swallowed by the gag.

"I shot Harold first and then took my trophy. But this time . . ."

Saunders's muffled screams filled the room as the Guardian raised the machete high. In one clean chop, he brought it down and severed Saunders's left hand from his wrist. Blood splattered.

Saunders's eyes rolled back in his head and he pissed on himself. He screamed through the gag. The thick scent of urine filled the air as the coppery blood drained out of the stump on his left arm and pooled on the basement floor.

Energy surged through the Guardian as life seeped from Saunders's body. Nothing had ever felt sweeter.

"You should be feeling some relief now. Your sins have been cleansed with your own blood."

Saunders's body began to shake. He was going into shock.

The Guardian watched, anticipating a river of blood. He expected Saunders to bleed out in minutes, but as the minutes ticked by, the blood flow began to slow. Ten minutes later the blood flow was little more than a trickle. Saunders was still breathing.

"Damn." The arteries had sealed. "You're a tough old bastard. Foolish to think I could destroy evil so easily."

Undeterred, the Guardian grabbed a knife from the workbench and sliced through the femoral artery in Saunders's leg. Saunders screamed. And this time the blood did flow. Saunders was dead in five minutes.

The Guardian hovered, mesmerized by the sight of Death, and with trembling hands combed Saunders's hair until it was smooth. "There are so many more to kill."

Chapter Nineteen

Wednesday, July 9, 5:30 A.M.

Lindsay woke with a stiff neck and a dull headache throbbing behind her eyes. She'd spent the better part of the night tossing, turning, until finally around three A.M. she'd fallen into a fitful sleep. She dreamt of eyes watching her.

She swung her legs over the side of the bed, shoved her hands through her tangled hair, and glanced at the clock. With a groan, she pushed out of bed and walked to the pile of running clothes by her door. Most mornings, she ran or did yoga. Physical exertion had a way of resetting the barometer in her body no matter how messed up life felt.

Today, she didn't need quiet meditation. She needed to sweat, to push her muscles until they burned, and to have endorphins flooding her brain.

She dressed in jogging shorts and a tank and slipped on running shoes. Combing her fingers through her hair, she swept her thick blond strands into a high ponytail and moved quietly into the kitchen. She didn't want to wake Nicole, who was an extremely light sleeper.

The coffeepot, always set for 5:45 A.M., was full of hot coffee. She poured a cup and sipped as she moved to the small table by the bed, where she kept her cell phone on a charger next to her house key. She glanced out the front window and searched for the morning paper. It hadn't arrived. Frustrated, she took a few more sips of coffee and then hooked the phone to her waistband. She did a few stretches to loosen up her muscles.

Lindsay had a running buddy, Tasha Winters, and the two met near the University of Richmond on Wednesdays at Bandy Field, a small park inside the city limits. They started their workout with a few laps around the park's large open sports field, and then they cut through either surrounding neighborhoods or the university campus.

She arrived at the park a couple of minutes past six and found Tasha stretching. Tasha was in her late twenties, petite, and had a tight muscular build. She reminded Lindsay of a pixie—a term Tasha hated. Too many people underestimated Tasha because of her small size, and all were surprised to learn she was a cop and a member of Henrico County's canine unit.

Rex, Tasha's Belgian shepherd, sat next to her, quietly waiting, watching, and ready to spring if she gave the command. The two had passed their twelve-week training course just six months ago and already they were inseparable. Rex was trained to find explosives.

Tasha saw Lindsay and waved. "Happy birthday."

She'd forgotten her own birthday. "Thanks."

"You look like hell."

Lindsay shrugged. "It's been one of those years."

"Tell me on the trail. We've got to get cracking. I've got to be at headquarters by nine."

"Right." The two started off at a slow jog moving around the dirt path that circled the mile-long trail that cut through the park. Even after a mile Lindsay's muscles didn't relax. Normally during a run, this was when she hit her stride.

Tasha picked up her pace a notch, knowing Rex liked the workout. "So, what's up?"

Lindsay struggled to match Tasha's gait. "Do you want the long version or the short?"

"We've got five miles to go. How about the long?"

"Zack."

"Ah." Tasha had worked with both Lindsay and Zack and knew their history. "Is he investigating the homicide at the shelter?"

"He's one of the detectives on the case."

"So how did it go seeing him?"

"Very weird. I don't see him for a year and now he's everywhere I turn."

Tasha frowned. "This can't be good."

"We went out to lunch yesterday. He took me to his parents' restaurant."

"And?" Tasha didn't sound happy. She'd consoled Lindsay after the separation. She'd watched Lindsay cry until she was nearly sick.

"It felt very odd."

"Sounds like you're having doubts about the divorce. *Again.*"

"No, I'm not. I need to finalize this."

"Then why haven't you?" The tension in her voice had Rex perking up his ears. Tasha smiled at the dog to reassure him.

"I don't know." She was having trouble finding a comfortable rhythm today.

Tasha wiped sweat from her brow, jumped over a pothole. "You know his work always—*always*—comes first. And don't forget that little thing called his drinking problem. Or the little detour into that little cheesecake's bed."

The recap of Zack's faults made Lindsay cringe. "I haven't forgotten any of it. There were times I wished I could forget, but I haven't forgotten."

"Good."

Too many nights she longed for the old Zack. He'd been strong. With him she'd felt safe, a feeling she'd not had in more years than she cared to count. "He seemed different yesterday."

Tasha shot her a you've-got-to-be kidding look. "Different how?"

Her heart raced and she found it harder to breathe evenly. "Different in the way he used to be, before the drinking."

Tasha stopped and Rex halted. "You're joking."

Lindsay stopped. Sweat dripped from her forehead, stung her eyes. "What? I'm just saying he seems different."

Tasha placed her hands on her hips. Her blue eyes looked as if they could breathe fire. "Do you know what you sound like?"

Lindsay wiped her brow. "I know, I know. One of my clients."

"That's right. You sound like every woman whom you've ever counseled. How many times have you wanted to pull your hair out because one of *your* clients couldn't see the bad in the man in her life?"

Lindsay's defenses went up. "Zack is far from perfect, but he *is* a good man. He's not like the others."

"Hey, don't get me wrong. Zack isn't a bad man. He's flawed but he's good at heart. And I like Zack. He's one of the best cops on the force and I wish him the best. But he's not husband material."

Unshed tears stung Lindsay's throat, forcing her to swallow hard. "I know."

"Look," Tasha said more softly, "my job here is not to rip out your heart, stomp on it, and make you suffer. But

I don't want you to forget that you and Zack separated for very good reasons."

"You're right. You're right." Maybe if she said it over and over it would sink into her own brain.

Tasha patted Lindsay on the shoulder. "There are a lot of really nice fish in the sea, kiddo. And a lot of them don't come with the kind of baggage Detective Kier has. Don't you have that nice doctor who's interested?"

"Yes."

"Well?"

"Got it." Only she wasn't interested in the other fish. She wanted Zack. Wanted what they'd had in the beginning.

They finished their loop around the park and it came time to cross Three Chopt Road and extend their run through the neighborhoods. Tasha went first and as Lindsay followed a van unexpectedly rounded the sharp curve. The driver hit the brakes and blared the horn.

Lindsay bolted the rest of the distance but paused on the side of the road, her heart pounding in her chest. "Damn."

Tasha stopped. "Are you all right?"

Lindsay glanced at the van as it sped through the light a block away. "Yes."

They started running through the neighborhood. The houses were small, one story, and most were built in the 1940s. The lots were large and most of the lawns were well manicured. Lindsay had always liked this neighborhood. She loved the feeling she got when she drove through. If she lived in this area, she could walk to get coffee or jog over to the university.

There was a house on Morgan Street that she had always loved. It was one of the simpler houses and needed a lot of work. But there was a large bay window in the front, and the backyard was huge and got at least five hours of sun a day. She'd always been able to imagine herself filling the barren yard with loads of flowers.

"Let's go by my house and see if it's still for sale." She'd been ecstatic to learn that last month it had gone on the market. She'd thought maybe she could put together some kind of creative financing plan and swing the asking price—that is, until she pulled the listing up on the Realtor's Web site and saw the actual cost.

Tasha grimaced. "Why do you torture yourself? It's too expensive."

"A girl can dream." She grinned. "Besides, it's my birthday, remember? You have to humor me."

"I'm going to humor you *only* because it's your birthday."

They rounded the corner and turned down her street. She'd loved this street since the first time she'd jogged down here with Tasha a couple of years ago. They came almost weekly, though in the last few weeks, she'd been so absorbed with work that they'd had to cut their runs short before they reached this neighborhood.

As Lindsay approached her house, she noticed the FOR SALE sign was gone. For a moment she stopped. Her house had been sold. She didn't realize until this moment how many dreams she'd pinned on this house. "Somebody bought my house."

Tasha jogged in place. "Maybe it's for the best."

It didn't feel like it was for the best. "I guess."

Lindsay started to turn but spotted a Jeep in the driveway. The vehicle was black, had a soft top and a dented back right fender. It looked like Zack's Jeep. And then she noticed the unmarked police Impala parked in front of it.

Zack.

"What the devil are Zack's cars doing in the driveway of *my* house?" Lindsay said.

Tasha groaned when she saw the cars. "It's not your house, Lindsay."

Angrily, she swiped sweat from her brow. "Yeah, I know, but it's not *his* either."

"He could be the person who bought it."

Lindsay couldn't imagine why Zack would have bought the house. He'd never really liked it. When they'd driven by it a few times, he'd always complained that the place would be a money pit for whoever bought it.

She clenched her fists. "He can't buy *my* house. He knows how much I love this place."

"Lindsay, you're sounding a little crazed and you're getting worked up over a house that never belonged to you. Who cares what house Zack buys?"

"Logically, I understand that what he chooses to do with his life now is none of my business. I should just walk away." Instead she marched up the driveway.

"Where are you going?" Tasha demanded.

"To find out why Zack bought my house." Lindsay stomped up the front steps and knocked on the door. When there was no answer, she pounded on it.

Tasha hovered in the driveway, not sure if she should run or drag Lindsay off the porch. "This is insane. We don't even know if that's Zack's car."

"It's Zack's." Footsteps sounded in the hallway inside. Just to irritate him more, she banged on the door again.

"I'm coming!" Zack's voice boomed through the closed door. There was no mistaking that he was pissed. Good. She could use a good fight now.

The front door swung open. Zack wore suit pants, a dress shirt, and a tie not yet knotted. His shirt cuffs were rolled midway up his forearms and his gun holster and cuffs hung from his belt. He smelled faintly of soap and aftershave. He held a cup of coffee in his hand.

Zack's gaze initially reflected annoyance, then confusion and then understanding. "What are you doing here, Lindsay?"

The softness in his voice caught her by surprise and for a moment she hesitated. God, she had lost her mind. Quickly, she regrouped. "Why did you buy my house?"

He didn't smile, but his eyes sparked with amusement. "It wasn't your house."

She planted her hands on her hips. "But you know I wanted to buy it."

He sipped his coffee as if savoring this moment. "As I remember, there were no other bidders on the house." He sounded so damn reasonable.

Sweat dripped into her eyes. She swiped it away. "But you knew I loved this house."

His shoulders filled the doorjamb. "What do you want me to say, Lindsay?"

She was acting like a lunatic. Unreasonable. And she didn't care. "Damn it, Zack. This is my house. You know how much it means to me. Of all the houses in Richmond, why would you buy this one?"

Her tirade didn't affect him in the least. "Care to have a look around?"

The abrupt shift caught her off guard. "What?"

"Care to look around? I'd be happy to give you a tour." And without taking his gaze off Lindsay, Zack added, "Tasha, you and Rex are welcome to come in and look around as well."

Tasha chuckled. "Front row seats to World War III? No thank you. Lindsay, let's just get going. The house is gone."

A bit of the fight drained from her. Tasha was right. The house and her dreams were gone.

Zack seemed to sense her shift in mood, but instead of encouraging her to leave, he challenged her with his darkened gaze. "Are you leaving or staying, Lindsay?"

Lindsay fumed. He knew she'd always wanted to look inside the house. He was using the house to get to her. Well, he was mistaken if he thought he could get under her skin again. "Tasha, I'm going to have a look around."

Tasha shook her head. "Why?"

"I want to see the place," Lindsay said defensively.

Zack sipped his coffee as if to hide a smile.

Tasha shook her head. "Well, I'll take a pass. I'll call you later."

"Thanks." She watched as Tasha and Rex jogged down the street back toward her parked car, just a few blocks away.

"Are you coming in? I've got to be at work in an hour," Zack said.

Now very aware that she and Zack were alone and that she wore only her jogging top, thin shorts, and running shoes, Lindsay felt her resolve fade a fraction. But pride goaded her forward as she moved around him, careful not to touch him.

The house was a disaster. Piles of construction supplies were stacked high in the living room alongside unpacked moving boxes. Dust covered scuffed hardwood floors and the paint on the walls was an obnoxious shade of avocado green. She doubted the interior had been updated since the sixties.

But Lindsay could see beyond all that. The bones of this house were excellent. Plaster walls under the green paint were sure and strong, the doors were solid wood, and the hardwood floors would glisten once they were sanded and refinished. The large bay window in the living room looked even better from the inside and once it was cleaned would allow sunlight to fill the room.

She moved down the center hallway to a kitchen in the back. Zack had furnished the room with a retro Formica kitchen table that had a funky appealing style to it. Knowing Zack, he'd chosen it more for utility than style, but it fit the kitchen perfectly. On the kitchen counter, a modern coffeepot simmered fresh coffee.

Except for the refrigerator, which she'd bet was empty, the appliances were outdated and would need replacing sooner than later, but morning sunlight streamed into the room through the large picture window. It would be a bright cheery room once it was updated.

Seeing this place stirred dreams of children and laughter. For a moment, emotion tightened her throat. "You've got yourself a winner here."

"That's what I thought." The deep timber of his voice sunk into her bones. "By the way, happy birthday."

It surprised her he'd remembered. "Thanks."

"Are you doing anything special?"

"No. This week's a little out of control."

"An understatement."

She moved to the window over the sink and studied the backyard. It was a patch of weeds, and the oak tree way in the back needed serious trimming, but already she could picture marigolds and geraniums brightening up the darkness.

"Any suggestions for remodeling?" He stood so close she could smell the scent of his soap.

She had tons. Mentally, she'd already painted the living room a pale yellow and arranged her furniture to catch the light. She stopped her train of thought.

This house and the dreams that came with it were from a life she'd had to let go. "No, this is your gig. I'm going to have to find another dream house." And that thought triggered a swell of emotion. She hadn't realized how often she'd dreamed about this house—about turning it into a real home. *With Zack.*

He brushed against her as he reached around her and set his coffee cup on the counter. The electricity from his touch startled her. It had been so long since he'd touched her and she felt half starved for contact. Sexual energy burned inside her.

"Part of the reason I bought this house was that you loved it so much. I remember how you used to talk about the yard, the gardens."

"I'm not sure what to make of that comment, Zack." Her voice sounded husky. And she wanted to touch him.

"I've dreamed of us living in this house too." His voice was raspy with emotion.

She met his gaze and, in a rare moment, saw the strong emotions he held on to so tightly. She nearly went to him.

And then she caught herself.

Tasha was right. This was a mistake. "I'd better go."

Lindsay pushed past Zack and headed toward the front door. She had her hand on the doorknob.

"Lindsay, don't go."

She hesitated, realizing how much she wanted to stay. She turned and took a step toward him.

He moved with purposeful steps down the hallway, closing the distance between them. Their faces were only inches apart.

Her heart pounded hard against her chest, its beat filling her ears. She was certain he could hear it.

As their gazes held, she felt a change in the atmosphere. He wanted to kiss her. And she wanted to kiss him.

This is stupid, she thought, yet she didn't move away.

Leaning forward, he kissed her. The kiss was soft, gentle, a testing of the waters, but it was enough to set her on fire. She wrapped her arms around his neck and kissed him back. Warm lips molded against hers.

Zack pressed her back against the door, deepening the kiss. A calloused hand slid up under her tank top and cupped her breast and teased her nipple into a hard peak. Sexual desire exploded. She moaned her pleasure and pushed her tongue into his mouth.

This doesn't mean anything. This isn't reconciliation. This is purely about sexual release.

And the need for sexual fulfillment overrode everything. Lindsay refused to think about tomorrow, this damn house, or her messed-up childhood. She just wanted sex and the temporary ecstasy it promised.

Zack moved his mouth to the base of her neck as he pressed his body against her. His hand slid from her breast down to her flat stomach. His fingers moved under the waistband of her shorts to the nest of hair. He explored her moist, tender flesh and she thought she'd explode.

She cupped his buttocks with her hands and then slid her hands over his hard, flat stomach. It felt so good to touch him, as if she had come home.

She reached for the buckle of his belt and unfastened it, then unhooked the button on his pants. She pushed the fabric away and wrapped her hands around the smooth hardness of his erection.

Zack kissed her harder, driving his tongue deep into her mouth. A deep primal groan rumbled in his throat. "I've dreamed about this," he murmured.

So had she but she couldn't speak the words out loud. Her hesitation had him pulling back to study her face. Rigid control held his lovemaking at bay. "Do you want this, Lindsay?"

She didn't want to think. She just wanted to feel.

But he seemed to need to hear the words. "Do you want this?"

She moistened her lips, which now tasted of him. "Yes. I want this."

Those words were all Zack needed to hear. He yanked

her shorts and panties down, exposing her. She was moist, ready. He pressed his erection against her and kissed her on the lips. His kisses trailed down her neck to her cleavage. He licked the top of her breasts. This was strictly about sexual need, she told herself.

"God, I've missed you." His warm breath brushed against her cheek as he spoke.

The need in her had built to a fever pitch. The pulse in her loins had robbed her of everything other than the desire for fulfillment. She stepped out of her shorts and panties and pressed her body against his. "Don't make me wait any more."

His kiss devoured her lips, and then in one swift move he lifted her off the floor as if she weighed nothing. He pressed her back against the door and she wrapped her legs around his waist and guided his erection to her. He drove into her. For a moment, she was overwhelmed by the sensation of him stretching inside her. Seeming to sense this, he went still and waited for her to become accustomed to him.

She dug her fingers into his back as he started to slowly move inside her.

Desire built and then she dropped her head against the door as the first spasms rolled over her and rocketed through her body. Within seconds a violent orgasm washed over her.

Zack pushed harder into her. Faster and faster. Tension racked every muscle in his body and he pushed in to the hilt. And then he stiffened and came inside her.

He collapsed against her and rested his face in the crook of her neck. Neither moved. Their hearts hammered in their chests. His breath felt warm and soothing against her skin.

For a brief moment, she felt at peace, as if everything in the world made sense.

But as the seconds clicked away, the passion faded. And as quickly as it had risen, it vanished. Even with him close against her, she felt a chill as the full emotional impact of what they'd done sank in. They'd had sex.

Unprotected sex. No birth control. Jesus, she'd lost her mind.

Lindsay shifted under his weight. "Zack."

His breathing had slowed to a lazy pace. "Yes."

She tried to wriggle out from under his weight. "This was a mistake, Zack. It shouldn't have happened."

He nuzzled her neck. "It didn't feel like a mistake. It felt pretty damn incredible."

God, she'd been so stupid. Tasha had just warned her not to come into the house but she didn't listen. "Zack, I need to go."

He raised his head and held her gaze. He looked confused. "Why?"

"I just need to go."

"Stay."

She pushed him away and yanked up her panties and shorts. "I've got to go."

He stepped back and jerked up his undershorts and trousers. "Don't just run away, Lindsay. I want to talk about this. There's too much between us that needs to be dealt with."

Panic rumbled inside her. "I don't want to talk."

"We have to talk."

"I can't. I can't love you again. I can't."

"Lindsay, please stay."

"No." She fumbled for the doorknob, turned it, and rushed outside. The heat and humidity had already burned through the crisp morning air.

She hurried down the three steps. Her legs felt like rubber, and she needed to keep her gaze trained ahead. And still, she turned to look at him again.

Zack stood in the doorway. His shirt was untucked as he ran fingers through his dark hair. He expression looked stricken.

"Let me drive you to your car," Zack said.

She needed to get as far away from Zack as she could. She would not allow herself to trust him again. He would never hurt her again. "No. Thanks."

He came out onto the front porch and halfway across the yard. "Lindsay, use some common sense."

Hysterical laughter bubbled in her chest. She'd lost all her common sense. She felt like she was losing her mind.

She turned and started to run, picking up her pace as if her life depended on it.

God help her.

She still loved Zack.

But this time, she didn't look back.

Chapter Twenty

As Zack drove in to work, he was in a foul mood when his cell phone rang. Sex with Lindsay had been better than he could have imagined. And for a moment he'd thought their troubles were behind them and they would find a way back together. And then she'd panicked and bolted.

He took the Parham North exit off I-64 toward police headquarters. He unhooked the phone from his belt and snapped, "Detective Kier."

"It's Warwick. We've got another mutilated body."

Zack's fingers tightened on the steering wheel. "Where?"

"At Meadow Farm Park."

Zack glanced at the dashboard clock. "I'll be there in fifteen minutes."

He did a U-turn at the intersection, merged onto I-64 east, and followed the interstate to the Mountain Road exit. He pulled into the graveled parking lot. A dozen cruisers, blue lights flashing, filled the lot. It looked like a three-ring circus.

Zack got out of the car. Already the heat of the day was oppressive. Sweat trickled down his back. He removed his coat, tossed it in the backseat, and rolled up his sleeves. He headed toward Warwick, who stood outside the yellow tape that roped off a colorful playground play set. "What do we have?"

Warwick wore khakis and a black T-shirt. His gold badge hung around his neck. "The call came in about a half hour ago. A jogger found the body."

Both donned rubber gloves and put paper booties on their shoes.

"Ayden will be along soon," Warwick said. "The chief is chewing his ass out. The county manager is going nuts. The area hasn't seen a stranger murder in years and now we've had two in three days. It looks like no one is sleeping until this guy is caught."

Zack followed Warwick under the yellow tape into the wooded area. The body was propped against a thick oak tree. The victim was a white male in his midforties with a shock of black hair on his head and dark stubble covering his square jaw. His jeans and burgundy sports shirt were covered in dirt, blood, and the thick scent of urine. His left hand had been cut off.

"I know this guy," Zack said.

"Burt Saunders," Warwick said. "He attacked Lindsay yesterday as she left work for lunch."

Zack shoved out a breath. He hoped Lindsay had an alibi.

"He wasn't shot," Warwick said. His expression was grim. "It looks like Saunders bled out from his wrist and a sliced femoral."

"Jesus," Zack said.

Warwick pointed to the body. "He has pronounced bruising on his right hand and around his ankles. He fought against his restraints."

Zack squatted, studied the body. "There's not much blood here. He was killed somewhere else."

"Wherever he died has to be soaked in blood."

Humid heat clung to Zack's skin as he stared at the stump that had been Saunders's left hand. "Look at the cuts. The killer wasn't in a rush. He worked the guy over pretty well."

Warwick frowned. "And the victim is another connection to Lindsay."

Zack was loyal to his wife. "Lindsay is no murderer."

Warwick's silence telegraphed his uncertainty. "Do you know where she was last night?"

"No." He sighed. "Where is the guy's wife?"

Warwick checked his notebook. "His wife, Gail, has a sister in Blacksburg. I called there a half hour ago and spoke to Gail. And her sister will verify that Gail hasn't left her sight since she arrived thirty-six hours ago."

Two men who both were accused of beating their wives were dead. Both wives had an alibi. Jesus. He didn't want to consider that they had a serial killer on their hands.

"Is there a note?"

"No."

"Any sign of the hand?"

"Not yet." Warwick shoved the notebook in his back pocket. "I reviewed the Channel 10 news tape from Monday. The cameraman caught the edge of a vehicle arriving at Sanctuary and a delivery man sprinting to the door with a flower box. The tape shuts off before he turns. I can't tell what kind of vehicle it was and the driver is unrecognizable."

"You think it was the Guardian?"

Warwick nodded as he stared at Saunders's body.

The rumble of a truck had them both turning. The Channel 10 news van rolled to a stop.

Kendall Shaw got out. She looked cool and sophisticated as her gaze scanned the scene. A faint smile
danced behind her eyes.

"Speak of the devil," Warwick said, staring at her.
"She's eating this up with a spoon."

"This story will be national by tomorrow."

Zack watched the reporter approach the yellow tape.
The uniforms blocked her advance. The patrolman
would keep her out of their hair for the time being.

"Where is Lindsay now?" Warwick said.

The image of her fleeing his house an hour ago dug
at him. "I'm guessing she's at home."

"We'd better head over there."

"You're right. If the Guardian repeats his last perform-
ance, she's going to get another hand."

"She also has questions to answer," Warwick said.

"Let's go."

The forensics van arrived. Sara got out and Kendall
Shaw was forgotten. The tedious process of data collection began.

As Kendall Shaw watched Kier and Warwick leave the
murder scene, she tapped a manicured finger against
the side of her microphone. "Now why are they leaving?"

Her cameraman, Mike, a tall burly man with a walrus
mustache, hoisted a camera on his shoulder. "Is it important?"

"He's investigating a murder and he leaves five minutes after arriving with the other lead detective. You
know he's married to Lindsay O'Neil?"

"No shit?"

"Yeah. I searched her name at the Department of Vital
Statistics. Their marriage license popped up."

"They don't act like they're married."

"Separated."

Where was Lindsay's husband going? She'd bet money that he was headed out to find Lindsay.

"Hurry up and shoot as much as you can."

"I'm not going to get much. The cops have us too far back and they've parked their vans right in front of the body."

"Can we get enough if I need to fall back and write a report?"

"Give me twenty minutes."

"Good. After you're finished we're leaving."

"Where, dare I ask?"

"I want to go to Lindsay O'Neil's town house."

Mike lowered the camera, giving her a "you're a diva" look. "And why is that?"

God, he could be so shortsighted. "Because," she said, lowering her voice, "Lindsay O'Neil's husband just left the crime scene and he'd only do that if it were really important. He's worried about his wife."

Mike shrugged. "Okay. Whatever."

"Let's shoot those scenes and get over to Lindsay's."

Lindsay lingered in the shower longer than she should have. But the hot water felt good against her skin. And she hoped if she stayed under the cleansing spray long enough she'd erase the memory of this morning from her mind. She had soaped up her entire body and washed and applied conditioner to her hair. Now, as she rinsed the conditioner from her hair, the hot water started to cool. She'd drained the hot water heater.

After shutting off the water spray, she toweled off. Through the fog on the bathroom mirror she stared at herself. "What insanity possessed you today?"

She turned away, then dressed in a simple black skirt and a white collared shirt. Normally, she didn't wear a skirt to work, but normally she didn't have to cancel morning appointments to make time for a meeting with Dana. She dried her hair and put on lipstick and mascara before sweeping her hair into a ponytail, then headed downstairs.

Lindsay made a fresh pot of coffee. As the machine spit and hissed, she stared out the back window into her garden. Normally, just staring at the lush plants calmed her. But not today. Today she was filled with a restlessness that made her feel as if she could jump out of her skin.

Sex with Zack. It was the dumbest thing she could have done.

Lindsay had sworn she'd never be like her mother. In college she'd been labeled "ice queen" by the men she'd dated on campus. She'd refused to get close to anyone, because no man was going to ruin her life. Or make her repeat her mother's mistakes.

But the moment she'd met Zack, all her vows to keep men at arm's distance had vanished. When she'd met him, he'd had long hair and worn a small gold hoop in his left ear. He'd had a two-day growth of beard on his chin and he'd reminded her of a pirate.

From the very beginning, she'd been drawn to him. She hated the terms *soul mates* and *We were meant to be,* but both described how she'd felt about Zack in the early days. The ice had melted, and for the first time life was filled with brilliant color and hope.

He was dedicated to his work. He loved catching the bad guys, as he liked to say. In her mind, he was the warrior-protector. With him, she felt safe.

Their third date had been a charity fund-raiser for the yet to be opened Sanctuary. It was a pancake breakfast and she'd vowed to make and sell a thousand hotcakes to raise money for the shelter. She'd had five volunteers on board to help, and when two hadn't shown up, she'd panicked. Zack had chosen that moment to stop by, and when she'd told him of her dilemma, he'd rolled up his sleeves and started making pancakes. He'd dazzled the crowds and was a better cook than she was.

They'd made love for the first time that night. And Zack had been touched and humbled when she'd shyly confessed that she was a virgin.

After that their courtship had been quick, hot, and intense. They'd met in March and by mid-April they were on a plane bound for Las Vegas. They'd driven straight from the airport in a rented Jeep with the top down. The sky had been a brilliant blue and the air warm.

Lindsay had been nervous but Zack had been steady as a rock. They'd bypassed the hotel and gone to the Little White Chapel, ending up in the Chapel of Promises in front of a justice of the peace. They'd both worn jeans and she'd carried a bouquet of white roses that Zack had purchased at the chapel. They'd exchanged traditional vows and in that moment Lindsay had believed in happy endings.

But once they had returned home the tide had quickly turned against them. Lindsay had thrown herself into the creation of Sanctuary and Zack had returned to undercover work almost immediately. His case, which had involved child trafficking, had required that he be gone for days at a time. When he had been home, he had drank more than she had thought was good for him. When she'd mentioned his drinking to him, he'd told her to back off. His anger had felt like a betrayal and she'd fallen into her old habit—she'd retreated into herself.

Zack had apologized. She'd accepted his apology. He'd confessed that the case wasn't going well—that he'd seen things that could never be erased from his mind. She'd tried to understand. They'd made love and she'd thought that was the end of it. But within days he had been drinking again and they had been fighting again.

As quickly as they'd fallen in love, they'd seemed to have fallen out of love. The wall that had risen between them felt unbreakable.

And then this morning Zack had touched her, and her vows to guard her heart had evaporated. In those explosive moments, there'd only been the heat of his touch and the pulse of desire in her body.

"Stupid, stupid, stupid."

Yesterday, she'd spoken to Nicole about options regarding pregnancy. She'd sounded so reasonable and so calm. But now that she faced the same problem, black and white faded to gray. Her hands slid protectively to her stomach. What if she was pregnant?

Lindsay halted her dangerous train of thought. "Don't borrow trouble."

After clicking off the coffee machine, she got her purse. She had no time to spare if she was going to get downtown for her nine o'clock meeting with Dana.

She headed outside, closed the door behind her, and clicked the dead bolt into place. This time she pocketed the key, instead of putting it under the flower pot.

Dashing down the walk, she spotted the morning paper. "Finally." She reached down and scooped it up.

The instant she touched the newsprint, she knew something was terribly wrong. The paper was too heavy and bulky, and it was wet.

She glanced down and saw the red stain of blood seeping through the newsprint and onto her hand. Terrified, she screamed and dropped the paper.

Her hand was covered in blood.

And at her feet lay a severed hand.

* * *

Warwick's cell phone rang as Zack pulled the Impala into Lindsay's neighborhood. "Warwick."

The cop's face tightened as he listened. "Right. We're minutes away."

Zack sensed the shift in Warwick's tone instantly. Warwick hung up. "What happened?"

"You were right. Lindsay O'Neil just got another delivery. A hand wrapped in her morning newspaper."

A protective urge exploded in Zack. "Is she all right?"

"Yeah, she's fine, but the patrolman says she looks like she's about to freak."

Zack maneuvered the Impala down the side streets. As he rounded the final corner to Lindsay's cul-de-sac, he saw the blue and white patrol cars and their flashing blue lights. He parked the car and he and Warwick got out.

Yellow tape looped around bushes and a light post and blocked the sidewalk leading to Lindsay's town house. A crowd had gathered.

Lindsay sat in the backseat of a patrol car. The door was open and her head rested in her hands. Even from fifty feet away, she looked rattled.

He strode to Lindsay and crouched by the open door. He wanted to touch her but was careful not to. He was mindful that Warwick's gaze was trained on him. "Are you all right?"

Lindsay lifted her head. Her eyes were red as if she'd been crying. "No, I'm *not* all right. I'm completely freaked out."

"What happened?"

"I was on my way to a meeting with my boss. I spotted the paper and picked it up. Immediately, it felt wrong. Then I saw the blood. I dropped it, and then I saw the hand and screamed. The maintenance man heard me and called the police."

"Did you notice anyone different standing around?"

The question came from Warwick, who now stood behind Zack.

"No. But I was running late and I was distracted. And then after I saw the hand, I didn't see anything else."

"When's the last time you saw Burt Saunders?" Warwick asked.

Her lips flattened. "You were there yesterday. He attacked me in the parking lot at Mental Health Services."

"You haven't seen him since?" Warwick said.

She glared up at him. "No." She paled. "Is that his hand?"

Zack rose and faced Warwick. "Did anyone call the EMTs? Lindsay should be checked out."

Warwick frowned. "She looks fine to me."

Lindsay got out of the car. "I *am* fine. Do you know whom that hand belongs to?"

"Do you have an alibi for last night?" Warwick said.

"I was out with a friend." She sighed. "Dr. Sam Begley."

Zack frowned but said nothing.

"He's at Mercy Hospital?" Warwick said.

"Yes." She kept her gaze on Warwick. "He's the one who called me about Gail Saunders. We went out for dinner."

"He's also the doctor who treated Jordan Turner and Gail Saunders," Zack said.

"He didn't have anything to do with this," Lindsay said.

Zack's brow lifted, surprised by her defense of the man.

She shook her head. "I know how cops think. Everyone is a suspect."

Warwick studied her. "The doctor has a connection to both victims."

"Dr. Begley is one of the good guys."

"How long have you known him?" Zack said.

"Seven months."

"Are you dating?" Zack challenged.

"That's my business."

Zack muttered an oath as the forensics van arrived. Warwick excused himself and went over to the technician as he unpacked his equipment. Zack caught Lindsay glancing toward her town house. "Is something wrong?"

"No."

"Is someone in the town house? Maybe your Dr. Begley?"

She met his gaze. "Sam is not in my town house."

Two hours ago, Zack had been inside her. In those moments they'd been so close, the world had felt right, balanced. Now, she was doing her best to keep space between them. They were back to being near strangers. "Is there anything else I should know?"

She shook her head. "You have all my shelter records. I don't have any more secrets to hide."

"You're protecting someone. I know it. Is it Dr. Begley?" Zack challenged.

Her face flushed. "I told you, Sam has nothing to do with this."

He lowered his voice so that only she could hear him. "You're holding back on me."

"I've done nothing wrong."

"Warwick is running this investigation now. He's got a reputation for being tenacious as hell. He won't give up until he has answers. Tell me what you're hiding."

The slight shift in her gaze spoke volumes. "I'm not hiding anything."

He'd felt nothing but frustration from the moment he'd laid eyes on her two days ago. "Don't make this harder than it has to be."

She almost smiled. "It was never easy for us, Zack. So why start now?"

Zack cursed and strode away.

Vega and Ricker pulled into the parking lot in front of the church. Vega shut off the engine. His phone rang and it was Warwick who updated him on the latest murder.

"Thanks," Vega said. He gave Ricker the rundown.

She shoved out a breath. "This gets nastier by the minute."

"Yeah."

Ricker checked her notes. "Pam Rogers has a brother and a half brother. She and the accountant shared both parents. She and the minister share only a mother. The accountant checked out, so now let's have a chat with the minister."

They got out of the car and crossed the graveled lot toward the modern church. "The church was built last year," Ricker said. "It already boasts three hundred families on its Web site."

Vega shrugged. "Business is booming."

They entered the side door and followed the signs to the office. At this early hour, the place was quiet. It felt deserted and kind of creepy as far as Vega was concerned. And the new-carpet smell didn't sit well with him either.

There was no one sitting at the reception area, so Ricker pushed past it to the door to an inner office. She knocked on the door.

"Yes?" The voice was male, cultured, and sounded a little annoyed.

Ricker pushed open the door. "Pastor Richards?"

The young minister looked up from his computer. He

sat behind a large modern desk. Behind him were rows of shelves filled with books. A large wooden cross hung on the wall across from him. "Yes?"

"We're detectives with Henrico police. We have a few questions."

The minister was dressed in a golf shirt and light-colored pants. He rose. "What is this about?"

"Lindsay O'Neil," Vega said.

Recognition flashed in the minister's eyes. "Come in and have a seat."

They each took one of the seats in front of the desk.

Vega didn't feel like beating around the bush. "You know Ms. O'Neil?"

"I do. Our church has kind of adopted her shelter in the last couple of months."

Vega didn't like the guy. He was too polished. "Does she know that your sister was a resident at Sanctuary?"

The minister's brows knitted. "No. I never told her that Pam was my sister."

"Why not?"

He steepled his fingers. "I've wanted to. In fact, I almost did the other night. She was here speaking to a group of parishioners about domestic violence and she used Pam's story as a case study. It nearly broke my heart."

"Why didn't you tell her?"

"I like her. I know Pam's death hurt her. I didn't want to cause Lindsay any more pain. The woman is practically a saint."

"How did you two hook up?" Ricker said.

"A couple of months ago, I was looking for an out-reach project for the church and I saw the article about her in *Inside Richmond*. It felt like a sign from God, so I called Lindsay."

Ricker's eyes narrowed. "*Lindsay*. You've called her Lindsay twice."

"That a problem?" Richards asked.

"It's the way you say her name. You really like Ms. O'Neil, don't you?"

He swallowed. "There's a lot to admire about her."

Vega picked up Ricker's vibe. "Feels like a little more than admiration."

Richards stiffened as if he'd been caught doing something illicit. "Does this have to do with the murder at the shelter? Because if it does, I can tell you I had nothing to do with it."

Rickard leaned forward. "Where were you early Monday morning and early this morning?"

"Here, working at the church on sermons and budgets."

"Any witnesses?" Vega asked.

The minister shrugged. "No."

Chapter Twenty-One

Wednesday, July 9, 10:10 A.M.

Lindsay worried about Nicole as she numbly sat in the back of the police car watching the forensics team do its job of collecting evidence. Warwick interviewed the complex's worried-looking maintenance man, Steve, while Zack talked to neighbors. No doubt they'd check Steve's past and also look into Sam's background. Everyone she knew was being pulled into this mess.

One killing had been sensational enough. Two equated a pattern—and major headlines, a fact that was driven home to her when Kendall Shaw arrived with her cameraman.

The last thing Nicole needed was for Lindsay to be the center of a major news story.

Across the street, a black Mercedes pulled up and Dana Miller got out. She was dressed in white Armani and carried a thick, efficiently designed purse. She frowned as she surveyed the scene from behind large white-framed sunglasses.

Lindsay rose and moved toward her boss. "Dana."

Dana offered a curt smile. Her expensive perfume

swirled around her. "I got your voice mail. When you said there was trouble I decided to see what was happening for myself. What's going on?"

The story was so outlandish, she felt foolish telling it. "Another man was murdered. And another hand was sent to me."

Dana's rouge-painted lips flattened. She reached in her purse and pulled out a long, slim cigarette case. "Is the murder victim connected to the shelter?"

"Not to the shelter, but to me. I think the victim's name is—was—Burt Saunders." She recapped the highlights of the last few days.

Dana removed a cigarette from the case and lit it with a monogrammed lighter. She inhaled deeply and exhaled slowly. "This is not good, Lindsay."

Lindsay's worried expression reflected in Dana's sunglasses. "I know."

Dana glanced toward the camera crews. "Do you have any idea who's behind this?"

The question almost made her laugh. "If I knew I'd be sharing it with the cops."

Dana studied the scene. Her frown deepened when Kendall Shaw started her report. Neither could hear what the reporter was saying, but they got the gist of it. "Lindsay, I've always believed you were Sanctuary's best asset. You're a big part of our success. You have a passion for your work that few possess."

Her boss rarely tossed out compliments. "But . . ."

"But right now, you are our biggest liability. The press is on your doorstep because some crazy person is fixated on you. By tomorrow, you won't be able to move without someone spotting you."

"Dana, I've worked under pressure before. I can handle the media."

"That's yet to be proven."

An uneasy helplessness tightened Lindsay's belly. "Then let me prove myself. I don't want to abandon Sanctuary."

Dana puffed on her cigarette. "I'd like to. I really would. But none of us can afford the bad press."

Us. Dana didn't want the bad press.

"I've called in every favor to keep this story as quiet as possible, but nothing is going to keep the media away from this."

"Dana, let's just give this another day or two. The police might find the killer and then all the questions will be answered."

Dana dropped her half-smoked cigarette to the concrete sidewalk and ground it with the tip of her high heel. "I wish it were that easy, but it's not. I've no choice but to suspend you."

Lindsay couldn't swallow her outrage. "You're firing me?"

Dana looked away. "Not firing, but suspending you until this mess is cleared up. I don't want you associated with the shelter."

Lindsay curled her fingers into fists at her sides. "I didn't do anything wrong."

Dana lifted her chin. "No one said you did. You're a victim."

"I am not a *victim.*" How many times had the social workers said that Lindsay was a *victim?* A *victim* of a bad family. A victim of domestic violence. A victim of fate. "I can overcome this."

The force behind Lindsay's tone had Dana softening. "I've no doubt that in time you will. You're smart and bright. However, in the short term you are a liability to the shelter and me. Don't take it personally, Lindsay. This is business."

Aware that Kendall was watching, Lindsay kept her

voice low. "Dana, how can I not take it *personally*? You're canning me."

"I'm not firing you. This is a paid leave."

"Sanctuary is more than a business to me. It's more than a paycheck."

Dana pulled her Blackberry out of her slim purse. Consciously or not, Dana was shifting her mind to the day's next problem. "I've got to go."

Lindsay once again clenched her fists at her sides. "That's it? I'm out?"

Dana checked her watch. "Call my secretary. We'll set up a meeting. Hopefully, this will all be behind us in a week or so." She hurried toward her car and vanished behind tinted windows.

Lindsay had the sick feeling that *this* was going to be with them for a long, long time.

She stood alone, her fists still clenched, her stomach churning.

Zack walked up to her as Dana drove off. "What was that all about?"

Unshed tears tightened her throat. She wanted to bury her face in his chest. "I've just been canned."

His hands slid to his waist below the black handle of his shoulder holster. "She fired you?"

"I'm on 'paid leave.' But I know that look. I'm done with Sanctuary." A wave of helplessness washed over her, reminding her of the months following her mother's death. No matter what she'd done then, she hadn't been able to regain control of her life.

Zack frowned. "Your boss is an idiot."

She was grateful he didn't toss any pity her way. That would have been her undoing. "She's very savvy. And very image conscious. I'm now a liability."

"Like I said, an idiot."

Silver bracelets jangled as she ran her hands through her hair. "I want this guy caught, Zack."

His eyes narrowed. "We all do."

"I'll do whatever I can to help."

He lifted a brow. "That's a change."

"This guy, the Guardian, is tearing at my life. I won't be able to help anyone if he keeps at it. I want him stopped. I want my life back."

"The detective going through your shelter records would appreciate your help. She was having trouble deciphering your handwriting in some of the files."

She was eager to get started. "I can go by headquarters now."

"First, I want you to see something."

The delay frustrated Lindsay and it showed in her voice. "What?"

Zack disregarded the snap in her tone. "The Guardian left another note."

"Where?"

"It was wrapped in the newspaper."

"What does it say?"

"I'll let Warwick tell you." Tension laced the words but she was too worried to question them.

Zack guided Lindsay over to the edge of the yellow tape roping off the front of her town house. She'd been shut out of Sanctuary and wondered now if she would be barred from her home.

Warwick approached her. "Ms. O'Neil."

Lindsay braced. "Detective. What does the note say?"

Warwick glanced at his notebook. "'*One less demon to battle, Lindsay. P.S. Be careful of cars when you jog. The Guardian.*'"

Despite the heat, a chill shot down her back. "He's watching me."

"When's the last time you went running?" Warwick said.

"This morning. I ran near Bandy Field. I was nearly hit by a van when I crossed Three Chopt." Anger rose up in her. "The bastard is watching me."

Zack's jaw tightened. "Did you see anyone this morning?"

She couldn't look at him as the memories of this morning returned. "No. But I wasn't running alone. I was with my friend Tasha Winters. She works with the canine unit. I can call her. She might have seen something."

Warwick shook his head. "I'll take care of it. What time were you running?"

"Between six and seven."

"Winters was with you the whole way?" Warwick said.

Color flooded her cheeks. "No. She had to get to work. I ran longer."

Zack straightened at the simple lie that masked their complicated meeting. "You might as well hear this from me, Warwick. Lindsay was at my house this morning."

Warwick lifted a brow. "Your house?"

Lindsay wanted to melt into the ground. "That has nothing to do with *this*."

Zack held up his hand to silence her. "When Lindsay and I were together, she admired a house near her jogging route. I recently bought the house. She asked for a tour."

Warwick frowned. "How long was she at your house?"

Zack didn't flinch. "About a half hour."

A half hour? Is that all it had been?

"What did you two talk about?" Warwick said.

"Personal things," Lindsay interjected.

"Nothing related to the murders," Zack said.

Warwick didn't look pleased. "All right."

"Lindsay privately offered to go through her case files with Ricker and see if any suspects come to mind."

Warwick nodded. "All right."

"Hey, Lindsay, what was that in the newspaper? It looked like a severed hand." The voice belonged to Kendall Shaw. She stood at the edge of the yellow tape with her cameraman. "Your friend sending you tokens of his affection?" Lindsay ignored the question and turned from the camera. Zack and Warwick refused to comment.

Kendall was patient as she watched the maintenance man move away from the cops. The guy looked pale and upset. He'd seen something. She turned to Mike. "Stay put. I want to talk to the maintenance man."

"Whatever."

Kendall cut through the growing crowd of curiosity seekers and made her way up to the guy. She thought about tossing him one of her smiles but decided she needed to be more subtle with this guy. She'd play it concerned. "Hey, are you all right?"

"Not by a long shot." With a shaky hand, the guy reached into his breast pocket and pulled out a pack of Camels. He pulled one out and lit the tip. Smoke billowed around his lean face as he puffed.

"What's got you so spooked?"

His eyes narrowed as he stared at her through the haze. "You're a reporter."

She smiled. "Yeah."

"You're with Channel Ten?"

"I am." She moved closer to him and gently laid her hand on his shoulder. "Can I get you anything?"

"A six-pack of beer?"

She lifted a brow. "It can be arranged."

He shook his head as he took anther drag. "God

knows I deserve a drink. But the property management firm will fire my ass if I drink on the job."

She held out her hand. "I'm Kendall Shaw."

He took her hand and held it gently. "I know. And I'm Steve Hess."

"Nice to meet you, Steve."

He moistened his lips. "I watch you on TV a lot. You're good."

"Thanks."

"Every time I see you, I wonder why you're not in a bigger city."

She grinned. "From your lips to God's ears."

He chuckled, and with a hand that still shook a little, he took another drag off his cigarette.

"You see my piece last night?"

"Naw. I ended up working overtime in a flooded unit. Fucking pipes burst."

If he was a Lindsay devotee it was better he hadn't seen the piece. It had stirred quite a buzz. And she'd gotten just as many negative e-mails as positive. "I hear you're the one who called the police for Lindsay."

"I was in my truck across the street when I heard her scream. She was so freaked out."

Kendall decided to play a hunch. "It was bad for you too, wasn't it?"

"Yeah."

"I still think you could use a drink. After what you saw, I can't imagine any boss would deny you a stiff one. They don't pay you enough to see what you saw."

A sigh shuddered through him. "Jesus, it was a mess."

He was a volcano ready to erupt. He just needed a nudge and someone to listen.

"I saw the body at the park."

Steve looked at her, his eyes alit as if he'd found someone who understood. "Was he missing a hand?"

That caught her up short. "Yes," she lied.

"Jesus, whoever this nutcase is, he's sending the hands of his victims to Lindsay. She said he sent her a hand on Monday as well."

Kendall hid her smile. "Does she know who's doing this?"

"She doesn't have a clue. But it's starting to mess with her."

She leaned forward, and in a low tone said, "I can't imagine what she's going through."

Chapter Twenty-Two

San Francisco, Wednesday, July 9, 10:00 A.M. PST

   Detectives Dominic Rio and Monica Perry arrived at the burned-out New Age bookstore, which was still hissing with charred timbers. Lights on three fire trucks flashed as firemen sprayed a stream of water on the coals. A collection of people stood behind the barriers looking stunned and frightened.

   Rio put the car in park and set the emergency brake. Perry grabbed her notebook. Perry was in her early thirties, divorced, and originally from Minnesota. She was brutally efficient, detail oriented, and cool to most. Rio was a bachelor, a Texan by birth, dark skinned, and had hair so black it looked blue in sharp sunlight. At first glance, he seemed outgoing and laid-back but he was just as detached as Perry.

   The two had worked together for two years. They'd fallen into an easy relationship, each able to anticipate the other's thoughts. Other cops in the division jokingly called them an old married couple, though romance had never sparked between the two.

   A lazy mist had settled over the city, sending temps

into the sixties. Rio got out of the car and pulled off his sunglasses. He paused at the front of the car and waited for Perry. She wasn't fond of the chivalry but had long ago accepted that it came with his Southern roots.

They walked side by side up to Fire Battalion Chief Stanley. Stanley had thick silver hair and mustache and a booming voice that could be heard over any siren.

Rio stuck out his hand. "Stanley."

Stanley shook both their hands. "Thanks for coming."

"You have a body?" Perry asked.

Soot deepened the lines on Stanley's face, making his grim face sterner than usual. "Yeah. She wasn't killed by the fire. She was murdered."

Rio hooked his thumb in his belt loop. "You know this how?"

"The fire was pretty hot and would've completely obliterated the body if a metal shelf hadn't fallen on it. It acted as a shield against the flames." He released a breath. "Her body was in the back, out of sight of the street."

Perry scratched down a few notes. "Is it safe for us to take a look?"

"Yeah, but I've got helmets for you both, just to play it safe." Stanley handed each a helmet and glanced at Perry's steel-tipped boots and Rio's loafers. "Rio, your shoes are pretty but not practical. Take a page from your partner's book and wear a more substantial shoe."

Rio raised an eyebrow as he stared at her practical, but ugly boots. "Naw."

Perry smiled crookedly at her partner. "Rio's got a thing about his image. Likes to look good."

Rio shrugged. "And you're a Girl Scout."

They made their way into the charred building. The smell of smoke blended with the scent of Perry's perfume. Carefully, the trio picked their way through the rubble of incinerated books and collapsed shelves and beams toward the back of the shop.

Perry's stomach tumbled when she saw the body. The dead woman lay on her back, her hands stretched out in a T-shape. The heat of the flames had all but incinerated or melted the bottom half of her body. But her torso and head had remained untouched by the flames. "Jesus."

The victim's face had been systematically cut with diamond-shaped patterns. By the looks of it, the killer had used a scalpel.

Stanley's jaw tightened. "Like I said, that metal shelf shielded her face from the worst of the blaze; otherwise, there wouldn't be anything left of her."

Perry leaned forward and studied the position of the shoulders. "This some kind of ritual killing?"

Rio squatted down, his long tanned hands draped over his knees. "The guy who did this enjoyed himself."

Perry checked the name of the store owner in her notes. "If this is the store owner, then her name is Claire Carmichael. She's clean, just a speeding ticket in ninety-nine."

Rio rubbed his chin. "Let's have a look at the crowd. Maybe someone saw something. Stanley, the forensics van should be here any minute."

Stanley spoke matter-of-factly. "What the fire didn't destroy, we did when we put it out."

Rio scowled. "Something our killer was banking on."

Richmond, Virginia, 11:00 A.M. EST

Nicole couldn't take it any longer. She had stayed inside, out of sight of the police, because Lindsay had asked her to. Lindsay was trying to protect her. But Nicole had had enough of running scared. And hiding.

Richard be damned.

She'd not cower anymore. Especially now that Lindsay needed her.

Nerves jumping, she opened the back patio door, cut through the backyard garden, and pushed open the privacy fence door. She moved around the side of the town house to the edge of the yellow tape. Reporters started to swarm toward Lindsay.

Two men already stood beside Lindsay. The first had his hand raised to block a cameraman's lens. He was dark. Brooding. Zack, she guessed. Lindsay had only spoken about him a little.

The second man was just as tall as Zack but he had hard eyes, a nose that looked as if it had been broken once. This man caught sight of Nicole almost immediately. His gaze bore into her with an intensity that made her want to run.

Nicole held her ground as he excused himself and moved toward her. He moved like an athlete, sleek and graceful, yet powerful. He stopped just feet from her. "Where did you come from?"

The suspicion in his raspy voice had her straightening. "I'm Nicole. I'm Lindsay's roommate."

Warwick frowned. "She never said anything about a roommate."

"She's trying to protect me."

"From whom?"

"My husband."

Warwick signaled for Zack and Lindsay to come over. When Lindsay saw Nicole, she immediately glanced behind her to make sure the camera crews weren't filming. "Zack, can we have this conversation inside?"

Zack nodded toward the door. "Sure."

The four stepped into Lindsay's town house.

Lindsay closed the door. "Nicole, you should have stayed inside."

Nicole shook her head, aware of Warwick's gaze. "No more hiding, Lindsay."

"I could have handled this."

"Thanks, but I don't want you to protect me anymore."

Zack pulled a piece of gum from his coat pocket and popped it into his mouth. "Mind introducing us, Lindsay?"

Lindsay glared at him and then at Nicole. "I wanted to tell you."

Zack folded his arms over his chest. "I'm all ears now."

"This is Nicole Piper," Lindsay said.

Nicole felt awkward but held her ground. "I've been living with Lindsay. She's been helping me hide from my husband. He could be quite violent."

"Who is your husband?" Zack said.

She hated thinking about him, let alone saying his name. "Richard Braxton. He's a businessman based in San Francisco."

"Did you ever file charges against him?" Warwick asked.

A sad smile lifted the corner of her mouth. "No. I was too afraid of him. Two and a half months ago, while he was on a business trip, I fled with the clothes on my back and two hundred dollars cash. If not for Lindsay, I don't know what I would've done."

"How do you know Lindsay?" Doubt clouded Zack's eyes.

Lindsay cleared her throat. "We went to college together at USC."

"Were you here on the night Harold Turner died?" Zack asked.

"Yes," Nicole said.

"Can you verify Lindsay was here?" Warwick said.

Nicole glanced at Lindsay. "I wish that I could. But

we both slept very hard that night, as if we were drugged."

"Why do you say drugged?" Warwick said.

"Every night since I left my husband, I've had nightmares. I didn't dream at all that night."

"Would you be willing to submit to a drug test?" Zack asked.

"Certainly."

"Do you think there'd be any traces left in our systems?" Lindsay said. "It's been forty-eight hours."

Nicole shrugged. "We can try."

Warwick looked around the apartment. "Have you noticed anyone strange around here lately?"

"No. But I started working at a photography studio last week, so I've stayed busy."

"A job? A job would expose you to your husband," Warwick said. "Your Social Security number can be traced."

Lindsay cleared her throat. "She's changed her name. Her real name is Christina Braxton. And I encouraged the name change and a new hair color and cut. I also got her a new Social Security number."

"How?" Zack challenged.

Lindsay wasn't apologetic. "I have contacts."

Zack muttered an oath. "There are legal channels she could've gone through. Social Security can change numbers in domestic-abuse cases."

"I was afraid Richard would find out," Nicole said.

Zack kept his gaze on Lindsay. "Have you gotten new IDs for others before?"

"Sometimes the only solution is to vanish and then create a new identity."

Zack stared at her long and hard. "That's what you did after your mother died."

Lindsay swallowed. "Yes. Look, if you need to file

charges against me for buying the ID of a dead person, go ahead. But Nicole had nothing to do with it."

Nicole shook her head. "I knew what I was doing, Lindsay. I take full responsibility." Nicole felt sick. "What do we do now?"

"First things first," Warwick said. "Let's get those blood tests."

"And after that, where does Nicole go?" Lindsay said. "She can't stay here. It's only a matter of time before the press will spot her and word will get back to her husband."

"I know a place," Zack said.

"Where?" Lindsay said.

"My folks' house."

Lindsay could see that Sam was upset as he drew her blood. Outside the curtained examination room Zack stood like a modern-day centurion. "I've never seen you frown so much."

Sam took the vial of blood and laid it on the metal tray by the exam table. "Lindsay, the cops want me to do a full toxicology screen. What happened?"

The concern in his eyes touched her heart. "They think that whoever killed Harold on early Monday morning might also have drugged Nicole and me. My sleeping in put me about three hours behind; otherwise I'd have been at the shelter at the same time the murderer was."

His jaw tightened. "I don't like this. I'm worried about you."

"Hey, I'm okay. I'm always okay."

He shook his head. "Don't kid yourself. I saw the news reports. All this has to have churned up stuff from your past."

"I'll muscle through it, just like always." That was a lie. She honestly didn't know how she was going to see her way clear of this mess. "Look, I've got to go. I need to get Nicole settled."

"Right."

"Make sure you also run a pregnancy test on her." In two weeks Lindsay could very well be doing the same for herself.

"Sure."

Lindsay kissed him on the lips. Unexpectedly, he wrapped his arm around her waist and pulled her close. The move was possessive, as if he was staking a claim. She let him hold her until she ended the kiss.

"See you soon." She pushed back the curtain.

Zack shot Sam a hard glance and then escorted her to the elevators, where Warwick and Nicole waited. Next to the cop, her friend looked so pale and fragile. And if not for Nicole, she'd never had agreed to go to the Kiers' house.

As Zack began the drive to Hanover, Lindsay stared out the backseat window, knowing she was about to face her in-laws after nearly a year of silence. She felt as if she were venturing into a lion's den.

Zack slowed the car and pulled into a gravel drive-way. The Kiers' farm was located off a rural road in Hanover County about thirty minutes north of the city. Dust kicked up around the car and gravel popped under the tires as Zack continued down the driveway. At the end stood an old white farmhouse that her in-laws had purchased about ten years ago and were still renovating. Audrey had often joked that she'd be in her nineties before her husband would be finished working on all his projects.

Zack parked the car in front of the wide front porch and got out. He opened the door for Lindsay. Under better circumstances, she'd have kidded him about such chivalry. Today she wasn't interested in any sort of humor.

Warwick opened Nicole's door. She looked so small

and delicate next to the detective, who stood a good ten inches taller. Nicole held her shoulders back. If she was afraid, she was doing her best to hide it.

The screened door opened and out stepped Mr. and Mrs. Kier. They were smiling, but Lindsay saw the strain in their eyes.

Audrey Kier was a tall woman with silver hair, which she'd swept into a ponytail. Mr. Kier's dark hair had turned salt and pepper and the sun had left deep wrinkles around his blue eyes.

Audrey came straight up to Lindsay and gave her a hug. "It's so good to see you, dear."

Lindsay tried to relax but the unexpected contact felt awkward. "Thank you for having us, Audrey. I really do appreciate it."

The older woman stepped away and let her gaze drift over Lindsay. "Ellie said you were too thin."

Lindsay pretended she didn't hear the comment or the genuine concern in Audrey's voice. The less attached she remained, the better.

Audrey's vivid gray eyes, so like her son's, shifted to Nicole. Her assessing gaze took in a dozen different details in a split second. "Welcome."

Nicole seemed stiff and nervous. "Thank you for having us, Mrs. Kier."

Audrey smiled. "Please call me Audrey. Mrs. Kier always sounded so formal to me."

Mr. Kier cleared his throat. He was as tall as Zack and his shoulders as broad. His body remained fit. Only the deep wrinkles around his eyes and the calloused palms from working his hands gave his age away. "She's been Mrs. Kier for almost forty years and she's never gotten used to it."

Audrey tossed her husband a bemused look. "Why

don't you girls come inside and I'll make you something to eat."

Lindsay's mother-in-law had always fretted over Lindsay's eating habits. "Thanks, Audrey. It's very generous of you to open your home."

"Nonsense, honey. You're family."

Family. Lindsay's throat tightened. Fearful her voice would crack, she simply nodded.

The older woman hooked her arm around Nicole's shoulder and led her into the house.

Warwick looked to Mr. Kier. "I've numbers for you in case of an emergency."

Mr. Kier tossed a curious look at Lindsay and Zack. "Come inside. I'll write them down."

Warwick nodded. "Sure." Mr. Kier and the detective disappeared inside the house.

Lindsay hesitated on the second step. For better or worse she owed Zack. "I'd forgotten how nice your mom is."

He stopped at the bottom stair. They were almost eye to eye. "She was glad to do it."

It was hard to hold his piercing gaze. "I know I'm not her favorite person these days."

He took her hand in his. "Lindsay . . ."

She pulled away. "Please, don't."

Zack shoved his hands in his pockets. "She loves you, Lindsay, like a daughter. Nothing has changed that."

The loss of the Kier family stung. "She's a nice woman. It's in her DNA to be kind."

"Oh, Mom has her dark side. She's let me have it more than a few times this past year. She knows why we split up."

Zack's infidelity and drinking had humiliated her. And now his mother, a woman she'd always respected and liked, knew. "Why did you tell her?"

He didn't look away. "I wanted her to understand why you were so angry."

Frustration spilled from her. "What I don't understand is why you did it. I know that that last night we fought bitterly, but to just run to another woman's bed?"

His face was rock hard, expressionless. "The booze was a big part of it. It clouded my mind. You'd tossed me out. That hurt like hell. You were the savior for so many wounded souls and when I hit trouble you ditched me."

Guilt mingled with anger. "You were addicted to alcohol. Throwing you out was the only thing I could think of to get your attention."

His jaw tightened and released. "I see that now. Hell, I'd have done the same thing to me if I were you. But then I was angry as hell. And I wanted to hurt you back."

Tears burned the back of her eyes. "You couldn't have done a better job if you'd planned it."

He sighed. "I know and for that I will always be sorry. I'd never cheat on you again, Lindsay."

As much as she wanted to believe, she refused to allow herself. "I know you believe that."

Zack raked his hands through his hair. "I've waited a year to talk to you, for us to be clearheaded enough so we could say what needed to be said. I want to fix this."

Pain pierced her heart. "Some things can't be put back the way they were."

He spoke slowly, patiently, as if he'd practiced a thousand times. "So we build something different and stronger this time. Different doesn't mean it won't be better. We're stronger together."

His words tempted. She wanted to give herself to Zack and love him like she once had. "Forgiveness leads to terrible things."

"I'm not your father, Lindsay. We're not like your parents."

Lindsay shook her head. "I saw my mother return to him too many times. Each time he hurt her. I can't do it."

"Lindsay, we can work through this."

Her chest tightened and her breathing felt labored. "I've got to get out of here."

"You don't have a car and you have nowhere to go. Your apartment isn't safe. The Guardian knows where you live."

She couldn't stay here. This place reminded her of what she wanted most and what she'd never have again—a family. "I work the hotline tonight at Mental Health Services. It's not my regular night but they always can use the help. I'll be in a lockdown facility with security guards."

"Lindsay, stay with my folks." He enunciated each word carefully.

"I need to work."

"You need to worry about yourself. The world can survive a night without you working."

Lindsay felt anxious. "I don't know how to be still."

Zack laid his hand on her shoulder. "For your own well-being, figure it out. You need the night off."

The front door opened and Warwick appeared. He glanced between the two and then said, "I just got a call from Ayden. We need to head back to the office."

Lindsay looked at Warwick. "Can I snag a ride back? I've got to get my car."

Warwick lifted a brow. "Sure."

Zack glared at him. "She's staying put. End of story. Call the office and tell them to get someone else."

"But . . ."

"No," Zack said. "It's too dangerous now."

They left Lindsay standing in the front drive, looking as if she could kill.

Chapter Twenty-Three

Wednesday, July 9, 3:00 P.M.

When Zack arrived at headquarters, the rest of the homicide division was in the conference room. Ricker, Warwick, Vega, and Ayden had the television on and were watching Kendall Shaw's latest report.

According to my contacts on the scene, the killer is mutilating his victims by cutting off their left hands and delivering the hands to Lindsay O'Neil. Police won't confirm these reports but . . .

Shaw's report continued.

Zack turned away, disgusted. "Jesus, that woman is determined to blow our case."

"How did she find out about the hands?" Ayden asked. His words were laced with restrained fury.

A headache pounded behind Zack's eyes. "Shaw arrived at Lindsay's just after I did. She might have caught a glimpse of the hand on the sidewalk before I covered it. And I saw her talking to the maintenance man."

Grim faced, Ayden sat across from Zack. Vega sat down on Zack's right and Warwick on his left. Ricker took a seat next to Ayden.

"So what do we have?" Ayden said. "And tell me we have something. Two murders in three days and the chief and county manager are breathing down my neck. Ricker, you lead off."

"I've been through Turner's phone records," C.C. said. "All his calls pan out expect one. The questionable call was placed at one A.M. Monday morning to Turner's cell. The call came from a prepaid phone purchased at a local store. I'm trying to trace the phone to the store. Once I have the store, I'll start sifting through register receipts and if we're lucky surveillance cameras."

A long and tedious process that was necessary. "Okay," Ayden said. "What about Turner's car?"

"Found at the mall near the shelter. Forensics is going over it now, but so far it looks clean," Vega said.

Ricker shifted the papers in front of her. "Lindsay and I spoke a half hour ago. She did help me with deciphering her files. We discussed her twelve hottest cases. Six of the abusers are in prison now, five have rock-solid alibis, and one is unaccounted for. We're looking for him now. But it's not likely he'd go to Lindsay's aid. She has a restraining order against him."

"What about Sam Begley?" Zack asked.

C.C. checked her notes. "Been at Mercy about eight months. No record. Liked by his coworkers. Last random drug test at Mercy was negative." She flipped a page and lifted a brow. "I did discover the guy likes to gamble. He owes over ten grand to a local bookie."

Ayden rubbed the back of his neck. "That doesn't make him a killer."

Zack was sorry they couldn't pin more on the guy. He didn't like or trust him. "I'd still like to talk to him."

Warwick's cell vibrated. He checked the number and rose to take the call in the hallway.

Ayden shifted his gaze to Warwick. "Neighbors? Her assistant, Ruby?"

Vega shook his head. "Ruby and the neighbors have nothing new to offer." He flipped through his notes. "Also, Saunders was last seen in Byrd's Bar. The bartender stopped serving the guy around eleven and sent him on his way. No one saw him after that and he didn't appear at work in the morning." He raised an eyebrow. "Here's an interesting note. Remember Pam Rogers? She has two brothers and one is a minister close to Sanctuary. And his church has taken the shelter under its wing."

Warwick returned to the room. "That was the medical examiner. It appears Saunders's hand was cut off before he died. But the veins and arteries collapsed and blood flow slowed to a trickle. That explains why the killer cut the femoral artery. He wanted his victim to bleed to death."

A heavy silence settled in the room.

"The killer is getting more violent," Zack said.

Ayden pinched the bridge of his nose. "Let's dig a little deeper into the minister's comings and goings. What do we have on Lindsay's roommate?"

Vega scanned his notes. "Nicole Piper's prints do match Christina Braxton's, which were on file, because she was arrested at an animal rights rally when she was in college. No missing person reports have been filed on Ms. Braxton. However, the phone number for her photography studio has been disconnected and her Web site is off-line. She was building quite a name for herself on the West Coast as a photographer. But she stopped taking clients and showing her work about a year ago."

"That fits with a domestic-abuse situation," Ayden said. "Her husband was isolating her."

Vega nodded. "She appeared out here as Nicole Piper two weeks ago and started working at a mall portrait studio ten days ago. I spoke to her current boss. Nicole is already very popular with his customers. Basically, her story checks out."

"Still," Ayden said, "she came out of nowhere, moved in with Lindsay just two weeks before the Guardian started killing people."

Warwick shook his head. "She's just over five feet and weighs a hundred and ten pounds soaking wet. Maybe she could have gotten the jump on Turner, but there's no way she could have subdued a man like Saunders. The guy outweighs her by a hundred pounds."

"She could have drugged him," Ricker offered. "Just because she's small doesn't mean she's not cunning. Do we have the toxicology reports on Lindsay and Nicole?"

"They were negative," Zack replied.

Vega said, "I spoke to Sara. She has nothing to report on the second note. It's as clean as the first. No prints. No hair fibers. Standard paper. Standard printer."

Ayden again rubbed the back of his neck with his hand. He looked like he hadn't slept last night. "So the only link we have to this guy is Lindsay O'Neil. '*Be careful of cars when you jog.*' The tone of the note sounds paternal. It's something I'd say to my own boys. He was worried about her." His gaze flicked to the television screen. "Shaw could be right. This killer could be from her past."

"What do you know about her extended family?" Vega asked Zack.

"When her folks died she ran away. She was seventeen and Social Services didn't make an effort to track her down. She said something about family in California. I'll ask."

Ayden nodded. "Every family tree has its nuts. Let's shake hers and see what falls out."

* * *

"Gin!" Eleanor laid down her cards on the kitchen table.

Lindsay laid down hers. She'd not been able to make a single match or straight during this round. "You got me again."

Eleanor frowned. "You used to play better, Lindsay. Today you're awful."

Audrey, who stood at the kitchen sink, frowned. "Eleanor."

Eleanor shrugged. "Sorry, but she *is* an awful player today."

Lindsay rose and watched Eleanor gather the cards to shuffle again. "My mind is distracted. I'm just worried about work."

Eleanor started to deal the cards. "It's okay, Lindsay. We can try another game."

Lindsay thought she was going to go mad. She'd had to call in and get a replacement for tonight. Her boss had been happy to accommodate her and, in fact, had sounded a little relieved. But she felt as if she was letting everyone down.

Still, Lindsay smiled. "Eleanor, let's take a break. I'd like to go outside for a minute."

Eleanor rolled her eyes. "It's a thousand degrees out there."

"I love the heat," she lied. "I'll be back."

Before anyone could disagree, she bolted outside. The afternoon sun bore through the trees and the humidity hit her like a brick. Sweat started to bead on her forehead. At least outside, she could breathe.

She stared at the line of trees wondering why the Guardian had chosen her. Had they randomly crossed paths? Had she done something inadvertently to trigger this chain of events? She dug her hands through her hair and paced back and forth.

The screened door squeaked open. Lindsay turned and saw Audrey standing outside with a pitcher of iced tea and a plate with a sandwich. Nervously, Lindsay rubbed damp palms on her skirt.

"You've got to be thirsty and hungry," Audrey said.

Lindsay folded her arms over her chest. "You don't have to worry over me."

Audrey frowned as she set down her tray on a small table. "Of course I do."

Lindsay didn't want the Kiers to be kind. She'd bonded with them once and she'd lost them once. She couldn't go through that a second time. "Thanks, but I've been thinking that I'll call a cab and head back to town."

Audrey didn't hide her shock and disappointment. "A cab? You can't leave now. It's not safe."

"I'll go straight to the Mental Health Services building. It's got locks and guards and I have tons of work."

Challenge had Audrey's back stiffening a little. "I'm not going to argue with you, Lindsay. If you want to call a cab, then call one. But for just five minutes, sit, relax, and eat something. At the rate you're going you're going to collapse."

To appease Audrey, Lindsay took half the sandwich. She bit into it and discovered it tasted good. "Thanks."

Audrey looked satisfied. "I saw the noon news report."

She felt so weary. "I missed it. What did it say?"

Disgust darkened her eyes. "Kendall Shaw talked about your past."

An odd sense of acceptance rolled over her. How the reporter had found out didn't matter at this point. "It was inevitable that it would all come out. Frankly, I'm even a little relieved."

Audrey hesitated as if she wasn't sure she should speak. "I knew you'd lost your parents, honey, but I had no idea that you'd suffered such a tragedy. Zack never told me."

"I asked him not to tell you."

"Why?"

"I guess I was embarrassed. My home life wasn't exactly *Leave It to Beaver*. And your family life just seemed so perfect." Her reasons for keeping silent sounded silly when she voiced them. "I didn't want you to think less of me."

Audrey shook her head. "Perfect families don't exist, Lindsay."

She pinched a corner of the sandwich off. "Yours seems pretty close to perfect."

A sad smile tipped the edge of Audrey's lips. "Don't be fooled. Robert and I have had our share of hard times. Things were particularly bad after Eleanor was born. She was our first child and we had such hopes. And then the doctor's told us she had Down's."

That surprised Lindsay. "You all adore her."

"Of course we do. But in the beginning, it was so hard to deal with the fact that our firstborn wasn't perfect. All those dreams we'd harbored when I was expecting her vanished. It was especially hard on Robert." She slid her hands into the pockets of her khaki pants as if the memory made her uncomfortable. "She was so sick in the beginning. Not only did she have Down's but her heart was defective. A couple of times we almost lost her. Robert and I were so tired, so scared, and we fought a lot then. We even separated for a few months, because he simply couldn't handle the stress."

"From what Zack said, Robert is Eleanor's staunchest ally. He lobbied the schools, Girl Scouts, and the local soccer teams to make sure she'd have a chance to do everything she wanted to do."

"Yes, he's great. But after Ellie was born, it was just too

hard for him. So he left." A shadow crossed her face as the memories returned, and then she caught herself. "He learned that living without us was unbearable. So he asked for a second chance. I wasn't going to give it to him. I remember telling my mom we weren't meant to be. Boy, did that ruffle Mom's feathers. She said, 'Love may happen by chance but a good marriage is just plain hard work.' I gave him—us—that second chance. And I thank God every day I did."

Lindsay had fallen in love with Zack because he'd seemed so strong. She'd felt safe with him. And when he'd failed to measure up and showed weakness, she'd been devastated. And she'd run.

Now he wanted a second chance.

Was she ready to give him one?

Lindsay pinched a piece of crust off her sandwich. The question was too huge for her to consider right now. "The gardens look great."

Audrey accepted the change in topic with grace. "It's finally coming back after the hurricane last year."

The place looked perfect. "You had a lot of damage?"

"Thirty-three trees down. And we lost all the azaleas. But on the bright side, the house didn't see any damage."

"That's good." She shoved her hands in her pockets. "My mother used to take such pride in her gardens."

"I've never heard you talk about your mother."

Lindsay set her sandwich down. "I guess it just hurts too much."

Audrey folded her arms and stared at her with interest. "What was she like? What did she enjoy?"

The questions surprised Lindsay. No one had ever asked them before. The people had always focused on the pain and sadness. Normally, she kept her emotions bottled tight, but sometimes, they bubbled over, and now hot tears burned her eyes. She swallowed. "She loved her gardens. And she loved music."

Audrey moved beside her. "What's your favorite memory of her?"

Lindsay cleared her throat. "There are a lot. She was at every one of my swim meets cheering me on. She baked the best chocolate cakes for my birthday. And she gardened for hours. When I was ten she won a blue ribbon for her tomatoes at some fair."

Audrey touched Lindsay's shoulder. "I'm sorry you lost her. I know she'd be very proud of you."

Stunned, Lindsay's hands hung stiffly by her side. "Thanks."

Audrey squeezed Lindsay's arm. "I'd love to see a picture of her."

"I have a box at home."

"Sometime you'll show it to me?"

"Sure." It was a promise Lindsay doubted she'd ever keep.

Talking about her mother stirred a deep restlessness inside her. Work usually kept the old issue at bay, but without it she felt backed into a corner.

She needed space. She needed time alone. "Audrey, can I borrow your car? I'd like to go visit my mother's grave. It's only about five miles from here."

Audrey planted a hand on her hip. "I will if you stay in Hanover and promise not to go home until Zack gives the all clear."

The mother was as shrewd as the son. "Deal."

"Promise?"

"I swear."

"All right."

Ten minutes later, Lindsay was headed north into Hanover County. After several miles she turned off of Route 360 and headed down a smaller road that cut through rolling cornfields. A few more twists and turns of the road and she arrived at the quiet cemetery where her mother was buried.

She passed through the twin brick pillars at the entrance; waved to the groundskeeper, who smiled back at her; and drove to her mother's grave. Located in a treeless grassy part of the park, the grave site was set apart from the others. She parked Audrey's car on the access road and walked through the wet grass to the grave site.

She'd come empty-handed. No flowers, no greens to fill the urn that was usually set upside down and empty. Guilt washed over her. She'd not done such a good job of tending her mother's grave in the last year.

Thick, hot air and afternoon sun made her sweat, but she savored the gentle sound of the leaves being rustled by the breeze. She'd forgotten how quiet the country could be.

When she reached her mother's spot, she was surprised to discover that the brass urn was turned right-side up and filled with freshly cut white roses.

Lindsay knelt by the bronze plate, unable to take her eyes off the roses. Gingerly, she touched a silky petal. "Who put the roses here?"

She glanced around at the headstones, still decorated with Independence Day reds, whites, and blues.

There was no one around.

She frowned. "Roses were your favorite."

It touched her heart that someone had remembered her mother.

She picked up a stray leaf and tossed it aside. "I saw Zack. He looked good and had clear eyes and a steady hand. It's as if he never drank." She shook her head. "All the crap that guy put me through and he still makes me weak in the knees."

Until this week, she'd thought her feelings for Zack were dead and buried. But after seeing him again, she realized he was still under her skin.

"I have no idea what I'm going to do about him."

Closing her eyes, she tried to imagine her mother's bright smile and the advice that would follow. But in the silence, there were no answers.

She dusted the dirt from her palms. Sweat damped her shirt and plastered her bangs to her head.

The crunch of gravel had her turning. A tall, lean man stood ten feet from her. The sun behind his back shadowed his face. "Afternoon."

Rising, she shadowed her eyes with her hand. She recognized the cemetery caretaker. They'd never spoken before but she'd seen him out here before. "Hey, how's it going?"

The caretaker smiled. He had rawboned features, tanned skin, and rough hands that looked used to manual labor. "Going well, thanks." He glanced at the headstone. "Who are you here to visit today?"

"My mom."

"I've never seen you here before."

The simple comment stirred guilt. "Yeah, I've been busy. I haven't been such a good daughter. But I was here at Easter. I think I saw you then."

He nodded. "Sorry, don't remember."

"I was leaving and you were coming."

He glanced at the headstone. "You couldn't have been more than a kid when she died."

"Yeah."

"I bet you were a fine daughter when she was alive."

"I always felt like I should have done more."

"We all do the best we can at any given time."

Emotion tightened her throat. "Sure is a hot day, isn't it?"

He stared at her for a long moment and then pulled the bill of his hat forward. "Supposed to top a hundred, I hear."

"I can believe it. Hey, do you know who put these flowers in this urn?"

He frowned. "No, don't believe I do. Are they a problem?"

She squinted into the sun. "No. No. I just thought it might be some mistake. Mom didn't have many relatives except me."

"Well, the ladies at the church down the road put flowers on graves from time to time. Especially around a holiday."

"That's kind. Is there anyone at the church I can thank?"

"Oh, they're not looking for thanks. Just happy to do it." He touched the bill of his hat. "Well, I've leaves to rake and flowers to plant. You have a good day. I've got to get back to work."

"Thanks."

He turned and walked back to his pickup truck. Lindsay captured another petal between her fingertips. Soft. Delicate. As she pulled her hand away, she saw a white slip of paper. She removed it from the tangle of stems and unfolded it. Written in bold Times Roman print was the statement, *You are stronger than her.*

The Guardian. For a moment she felt dizzy as she stared at the words. She glanced around the cemetery. The caretaker was gone.

Her hands trembled as she laid the note on the grass. He'd been *here.* He'd left flowers at her mother's grave. She dug her cell out of her purse and dialed Zack's number.

Zack answered on the second ring. "Hello."

"Zack, it's Lindsay. He was here. The Guardian was here." She couldn't hide the fear in her voice.

"Where are you?" His voice was razor sharp.

"I'm at my mother's grave." She gave him the directions.

He swore. "I'll be there in twenty minutes. Get in your car and lock the doors."

Lindsay hugged her arms around her chest. She didn't want to be afraid. She didn't want to be intimidated. But she was. She went to Audrey's car, got in, and locked the doors. Despite the heat of the day, she felt cold.

Less than five minutes later two Hanover deputies appeared. They inspected the flowers, careful not to touch the note or the urn. They searched for the caretaker but couldn't find him. All three waited until Zack and Warwick arrived fifteen minutes later, lights flashing. Lindsay got out of her car as Zack got out of his. He strode toward her, closing the gap in seconds. He laid a hand on her shoulder. "Are you all right?"

She wanted him to hold her. "Yes."

"Where's the note?" The question came from Warwick.

She didn't pull away from Zack's touch. "I left it by the grave."

Warwick snapped on rubber gloves. "What did it say?"

"'*You are stronger than her.*' I think he's talking about my mother." When Warwick only stared, she added, "She forgave my father over and over again. She was too afraid or too in love to ever stay away from him too long."

Warwick's gaze darted between Lindsay and Zack. "Is he referring to your relationship with Zack?"

Zack stood stock straight, his jaw tight. "I think so."

Lindsay pushed her hand through her hair. "It's no secret that I haven't signed the divorce papers. And if he was watching me this morning he knew we visited."

"Visited," Warwick said. The word had a volume of meaning.

"Was anyone else out here?" Zack said.

"Just the caretaker."

"Where is he now?" Zack asked, glancing around.

"I don't know. He walked away before I found the note."

"How do you know he's the caretaker?" By the brick front gate, Zack spotted a set of surveillance cameras. He pulled out his notebook and made a notation.

Lindsay thought Zack was being overly paranoid. "I've seen him here before."

"When did you first notice him?"

"Easter. He was headed toward this direction with a rake as I was pulling out of the cemetery. I caught a glimpse of him in the rearview mirror."

"Have you two spoken before?"

"Not before today."

Zack's expression was grim. "Did he see *you* at Easter?"

"No."

His jaw tightened as he surveyed the deserted grounds. "You shouldn't have been out here alone."

"I never figured that the Guardian would know about this place."

"I don't think it's a coincidence that Harold was killed on Monday, which was the anniversary of your mother's death, and Saunders was killed on your birthday."

"The Guardian is from my past?"

"I think so."

"Well, it can't be the caretaker. I've never seen him before."

He tried to smile but failed. "Don't worry. We'll figure this out."

"Sure." Her knees felt weak. She watched as Warwick

and Zack strode toward the headstone. They knelt by the grave, studied the flowers and the note.

Another deputy's car arrived as Warwick pulled a pen from his pocket and gingerly lifted the flap of the note. He read it. His frown deepened. He spoke to Zack but she couldn't hear what was said. They both glanced toward the front gate and the cameras.

Zack rose and approached her. "Is that Mom's car?"

"She let me borrow it."

His annoyance seemed to be growing. "I'm taking you back to my parents' house. And as soon as I can get a sketch artist scheduled you'll talk to her."

She shook her head. "I didn't see his face. The sun was to his back."

"Can't hurt to try."

Unconvinced, she got into Audrey's car and, with Zack following, drove the five miles back to the Kiers'.

When she parked the car, Zack was waiting. He placed his hand in the small of her back. "Do you remember the first time we met?"

Confused, she tried to follow his train of thought. "It was at the triathlon in Charlottesville. The awards ceremony."

"I saw you before that. I was on my second loop of the bike portion of the race when I came around a corner. You were about a hundred yards ahead of me. On the side of the road there was a kid, not more than fifteen. He'd dropped his bike and was holding his stomach. Five racers in front of you had just passed the kid. You stopped."

She'd never noticed Zack. "He had stomach cramps."

"I rode ahead to the aid station and sent back a medic."

"What does this have to do with us and now?"

"I fell in love with you that day, L. I knew you were the one for me. The problem is I forgot that along the way. I blew it. But I'm going to fix this between us."

"You can't fix what I don't want fixed."

He didn't move toward her. "It took me months to screw things up between us. It'll take at least that long to fix it, but I will." He moved toward the front door. So arrogant.

She stood her ground. "Let it go, Zack. Let *us* go."

He opened the front door. "No."

He strode inside.

Numb, she followed and found him lecturing his mother about lending out her car. Audrey got the message loud and clear. Lindsay was to stay put.

Zack kissed his mother. "I'll be back later tonight."

"Don't strand me here," Lindsay said.

"You're safe with my folks."

Eleanor came around the corner with the games *Operation* and *Monopoly* in hand. "Lindsay, don't be worried. Nicole's awake and ready to play a game. This is going to be fun family time."

There was no escaping the Kiers.

Richard Braxton sat in the back of his Gulf Stream plane. The pilot he'd hired was waiting for clearance from the San Francisco tower.

He picked up the morning edition of the *San Francisco Chronicler* and reread the article on page A3. He smiled. According to the article, the fire had destroyed most of the evidence and the lone victim's identity had yet to be confirmed.

He licked his bottom lip, remembering the way the woman had whimpered as he'd sliced the flesh on her face. The killing had been thrilling, more exciting than anything he'd ever done. Already he wanted to kill again.

Beyond the pure entertainment value, though, torturing the woman had not gotten him what he'd wanted.

She had been a stubborn bitch and had refused to tell him anything about Christina.

However, Carmichael's cell phone had told him quite a bit. Her "address book" hadn't panned out, nor had "recent calls." But under "missed calls," there had been a call from a number in Richmond, Virginia.

Richard had been unable to resist and had called the number as a dying Claire had watched. There had been no answer. He'd then called Vincent and had given him the number. Twenty minutes later, Vincent had a name. The number, along with another number, belonged to Lindsay O'Neil. Richard had called her, half expecting to hear Christina's voice. When he hadn't recognized the voice, he'd hung up.

Three hours later, Vincent had called him with a great deal of information about Lindsay O'Neil, including the fact that she'd gone to USC with Christina and was now the suspect in two local murders. Vincent believed Christina was staying with Lindsay.

Richard tapped his finger on the morning paper. Soon he'd be in Richmond. Soon he'd find Lindsay O'Neil and his wife. Soon both women would curse the day they'd crossed him.

Chapter Twenty-Four

Wednesday, July 9, 8:15 P.M.

Marcus Greenland came out of the convenience store with a six-pack of beer and a bag of chips tucked under his arm. He had seen the evening news. That reporter had talked about that bitch O'Neil—the one who had hid his wife and kids from him. It figured the cunt had some kind of screwed-up past that made her hate men. *Bitch.*

But he'd be damned if he'd end up one of her victims. She'd not get her hooks into him.

"Hey, are you looking to make some money?" The raspy voice had Greenland whirling around. An old white guy stood directly behind him. The stranger had come up behind him without making a sound.

Shit. There was a time when no one snuck up on Marcus Greenland. His heart hammering, he said, "What the hell do you want?"

The guy flashed a lopsided grin that was almost apologetic. "I'm looking for a strong man who can do some heavy lifting. I've got a piano to move."

Greenland glared at the old man. He had stooped

shoulders, gray hair, and horn-rimmed glasses. The son of a bitch didn't look like he could lift a bag of sugar. "It's after eight o'clock at night. Who the hell moves a piano late at night?"

The old man shrugged and smiled sheepishly as if he was embarrassed. "Hey, it's not me. It's my wife. She wants the damn thing moved before a party she's having this weekend. Personally, I think it looks fine where it is, but she wants it moved. Just between you and me, my wife can be a pain in the ass when she doesn't get what she wants, so I'm not arguing with her."

"Can't live with 'em, can't shoot 'em." Greenland laughed at his own joke.

The stranger hesitated before he laughed. He reached in his pocket and pulled out a hundred-dollar bill. "It won't take more than an hour of your time."

Greenland relaxed when he saw the bill. He sure as hell could use the money. "Sure, why not?"

Behind the horn-rimmed glasses, blue eyes glistened. "Great. My van is over here."

Greenland snagged a beer from the six-pack and popped it open. He took a long drink, savoring the cool liquid on his throat. It would take at least the six-pack to get even a mild buzz. "You'll bring me back to my car?"

"Absolutely. I'll have you back in less than an hour."

Greenland followed the man to a simple white van. The vehicle looked nicked up and well used. "I figured you for a Volvo or a minivan kind of guy."

The man pulled keys from his pocket. "This is a rental. The trunk of my Audi is big but not big enough for a piano."

Greenland was impressed. He liked nice cars. "An Audi. A-6?"

"Yeah."

"Good car. It hugs the corners real well." He sipped his beer. "I used to sell cars."

"That so? What kind?"

They'd been used cars. "Lexuses mostly."

"Nice."

The stranger slid behind the wheel as Greenland climbed in the passenger side. With a hundred bucks, he could buy his boys that new video game and maybe a nice bottle of bourbon.

Thinking about the boys made him sad. The last time he'd seen the kids, he'd hit Jamal, because the kid wouldn't stop talking. The boy had fallen to the ground hard. Damien had cried and cowered. He had tried to console Damien, but the child had only wailed. That had pissed Greenland off. He'd smacked the kid until he'd shut up.

Now, guilt gnawed at him. As their father, he wanted the boys to respect him, but he also wanted them to love him. That video game would make it up to them.

The stranger fired the ignition. Greenland settled back in his seat. "Want a beer?"

"No thanks. The wife doesn't like it when I drink."

No matter how rich you were a wife could bring you down. "Is she a real ballbuster?"

The stranger's hands tightened on the steering wheel as he smiled. "You could say that." He pulled out onto the main road and quickly merged onto the interstate. They headed west toward farmland bathed in the setting sun's amber light.

Greenland took a long draft from the beer. The alcohol loosened him up. "My old lady busted my chops every time I had a drink too many." Just thinking about Aisha pissed him off. He killed the first beer and opened a second. "My wife is a bitch. And full of lip. And now she's taken my kids—*my sons*—and run off. It isn't right that a man can't see his own flesh and blood. I have a right to them."

The man frowned. "Family is about the most important thing there is."

"Damn straight. Once I get me a real job, I intend on getting mine back."

"You said you sold cars?"

"Did. Now it's construction mostly. I'm also licensed to drive trucks."

"Well, then you should have no trouble getting work. Construction is booming."

He couldn't seem to hold a job. "Not so easy. All the outfits are run by pricks. That's what I say."

The stranger kept his gaze on the road. "Hey, don't I know you from somewhere?" He snapped his fingers. "You played college football for Tech."

Greenland grinned. "That's right."

"Heard you went to the pros."

"Did for a while. Then I busted my right knee."

"Damn."

Greenland took a long drink of beer. It still pissed him off the way that coach had cut him loose as if he were nothing.

"That was one hell of a catch in the Sugar Bowl."

"Yeah." The memory of that one night made him proud. "I was a damn superstar that night."

"And rightly so."

The stranger pulled off the highway and skirted down a rural road. Soon the lights of the interstate vanished. Only the headlights of the van lit the way.

"Is it going to be much farther?" Greenland asked. He had to pee.

"Just another mile or two."

"Okay." Greenland didn't like the country. Full of wild animals, snakes and shit.

They pulled off the side road down a gravel driveway. Tall trees hovered over the road. Gravel popped under the tires. It felt as if they'd driven off the face of the earth.

At the end of the road was a clearing. No house.

Greenland leaned forward. "Where the hell are we?"

The stranger put the car in park and shut off the engine. He pulled out a gun and pointed it at Greenland's head. "The end of the line. Get out."

"Hey, man, if this is about robbery, then you've got the wrong guy. I don't have two damn nickels to rub together."

He cocked the gun. "Get out."

"Like hell I will."

Behind the horn-rims, the eyes that had looked old and weary hardened. The stranger fired past Greenland's head and the cab exploded with sound as the bullet shattered the passenger window. Broken glass nicked the back of Greenland's skull. He dropped his beer on the floor. "Shit!"

Fumbling for the handle, Greenland opened the door and lunged toward the ground. He didn't know who the hell this freak was, but he wasn't going to stick around and find out.

The hard rains from Monday had left the normally marshy ground even softer and he slipped in the mud. He struggled to stand. He slipped again. The freak got out and walked around the side of the van.

Greenland pulled himself upright. He held up his hands in defense. "Hey, man, I don't want no damn trouble. Just let me go and we'll call it even."

The stranger looked taller, stronger now that he held his shoulders upright. "We are far from even."

Panic knifed Greenland. "Who the hell are you?"

"The Guardian." He said it with pride.

"What the fuck does that mean?"

"It means, I kill men like you."

Greenland felt sick. "Hey, man, I ain't never done anything to you."

Moonlight glinted on the gun barrel. "You should have treated your wife with more respect." He fired. The bullet sliced into Greenland's left knee. Pain scorched through his body and he dropped to the cold, soft ground. He clutched his knee.

"What the fuck!" Greenland howled. Blood oozed out from under his fingers. "Did that bitch wife of mine send you to kill me?"

The Guardian loomed over him. "Don't talk about the mother of your children like that."

Greenland's entire body burned. He tried to breathe through the pain like his coaches had taught him in college. *Suck it up.* But this pain was worse than any lineman's tackle. He could barely think as he rolled on his side into a fetal position.

The Guardian stepped closer. Greenland's hands were inches from his feet. This son of a bitch was going down. Moving quickly, he grabbed the Guardian's ankle and yanked as hard as he could. The Guardian fell backward and hit the ground hard, grunting in pain as his ribs connected with a stump. The gun flew off into the darkness.

The Guardian's pain gave Greenland satisfaction and hope. He started to crawl away. If he could get to the thick of the woods around them, he could hide.

The Guardian wrestled his body to a sitting position. His breathing was ragged and labored. With a grunt, he started to crawl around and look for the gun. He couldn't find it.

Greenland clawed at the dirt and dragged his useless leg behind him. "Jesus, save me."

Get to the woods. Get to the woods.

Greenland looked back and saw the Guardian chasing him. Determination had hardened the set of his jaw.

"Oh, Jesus," Greenland muttered. His knee burned. His lungs ached with the effort of breathing.

The Guardian's gait was uneven, but his two good legs easily overtook Greenland.

The Guardian kicked Greenland in the head. The blow cracked teeth and robbed him of the air in his lungs. Greenland rolled on his back. He tasted blood and spit out a tooth.

Every nerve in his body screamed.

"You're not getting away from me," the Guardian growled. He went back to the van, retrieved a machete, then hurried back to again kick Greenland, this time in the side. Ribs shattered. Greenland was near passing out when the Guardian planted his booted foot on his left forearm.

The Guardian ground the bottom of his boot into the tender flesh of Greenland's arm. "Retribution is mine."

"Why?!" Greenland shouted.

The Guardian didn't answer. Instead, he raised the machete high over his head. The blade caught the moonlight before it came down and sliced through the wrist's flesh and narrow bone.

Greenland screamed until his throat felt raw. He pissed on himself. His own blood pooled around his body, dampening the ground under him.

The Guardian held up the severed hand and howled with satisfaction.

That was Greenland's last image before he passed out.

Chapter Twenty-Five

Thursday, July 10, 5:30 A.M.

Warwick was operating on next to no sleep. Zack had been up half the night running down leads on the Turner/Saunders murders. He'd been going over Saunders's phone record and studying Kendall Shaw's news tape from Monday. So far, he'd come up empty-handed. And the brass was getting very antsy. If an arrest wasn't made soon, jobs were going to be lost.

They'd left the office at four A.M. Warwick had headed to the gym for a quick forty-five-minute workout that he hoped would at least get his blood flowing and sustain him through the day.

The gym had been dark when he had arrived, so he had used his key and let himself in. Now he pounded the punching bag, driving the full weight of his frustration into it. Kendall Shaw had called him four times yesterday, trying to get a quote for her next report. He had refused her once and had told her not to call again. But she had.

The woman didn't understand the word *no*. She was a pain in the ass. And still he'd imagined Kendall Shaw walking toward him with her hair flowing around her shoulders and wearing only a red silk robe. He'd pictured her dropping the robe in a puddle around her feet and in the soft moonlight lying down for him and opening her legs. Moaning with pleasure, he had straddled her and cupped her full white breasts. She had smiled up at him, begged him to take her, and he'd driven his hard cock into her.

The fantasy had left him hard and restless.

"Shit," Warwick grumbled before he smacked the bag one last time.

He finished his workout and hit the showers. After a quick shower, he dressed in jeans and a T-shirt and slicked back his still-wet hair. Gym bag in hand, he headed into Pete's office. He'd promised to spar with one of Pete's fighters on Saturday, but at the rate things were going, he wasn't going to make it. Everyone would be living at the station until the killer was found.

He moved down the dim hallway past the dozens of black-and-white photos that spanned two decades. The images were of Pete's fighters. Some were taken during fight matches, others were publicity head shots, but all of Pete's fighters were on the wall. Pete took pride in his fighters—his family, as he'd often called them. Warwick glanced at his own picture taken when he was eighteen. He grimaced, amazed he'd ever been that young.

He knocked on the office door, which was ajar, thinking maybe Pete had slipped in while he was working out. "Pete?"

The door swung open. The lights were off in the office. Warwick flipped them on.

Like always, Pete's dark wooden swivel chair sat in front of a large desk that butted against the wall. The desk was a mess, covered with papers, newspapers, books, and, in the center, a state-of-the-art computer, his only concession to the modern world. Pete updated his computer every year and had the latest software on it. Above the desk on the wall hung a bulletin board covered with news clips covering the charity events Pete had hosted in the last few years. And there were more photos.

Warwick found a pencil and a Post-it pad. Quickly he scratched out a note begging out of the bout scheduled for Saturday. As he pressed the note to the computer screen, he caught sight of a framed picture nestled on the far-right corner of the desk. He never remembered seeing the picture before. Curious, he picked it up.

Unlike the others, this picture was of a twentysomething Pete holding a young girl not more than five. She had yellow hair, fair eyes, and a big gap-toothed grin. Pete stared down at the girl, his gaze tender and full of love.

Did Pete have a kid? In all the years Warwick had known Pete, he'd never talked about having any other family. He'd always said Warwick was all the family he'd needed.

But who was Warwick to criticize the old guy for having a few secrets.

God knows, Warwick had his share.

Richard Braxton arrived at the posh Richmond Hotel suite just after seven. His back was stiff and his head pounded as he watched the bellboy set his overnight bag on a luggage rack at the foot of the bed. Richard set his computer bag on the bed, pulled a fifty from his pocket, and handed it to the bellboy. "Thanks."

The kid glanced at the fifty and his eyes brightened. "Anything else I can do for you?"

"Where can I set my computer up?"

The bellboy pointed to a table by the large window that looked out toward the river. "Just call down to the front desk and they'll give you the password for the wireless hookup."

Richard handed the kid another twenty. "Do me a favor and get the password for me. There should also be a package for me at the front desk. Deliver both back to my room in thirty minutes along with an egg-white omelet, orange juice, and whole-wheat toast dry.

The bellboy pocketed the bill. "The package arrived before you did." He walked into the sitting room. "Here it is."

Richard took the twelve-by-twelve-inch box. "Thanks."

"I'll take care of the password and omelet right away."

"Good."

The kid was annoyingly bright eyed but useful. "Is this your first time in Richmond?"

Richard managed a smile. "Yes."

"Business or pleasure?"

"A little of both." He hated travel. It threw off his routine and generally put him in a foul mood.

"If there is anything else I can do for you, just ring. Ask for Johnny."

"Thanks, Johnny. I'll do that."

When Johnny closed the door behind him, Richard turned to the window and loosened his tie. This city was as hot as blazes and the humidity was so thick he could cut it with a knife. He missed California, his views of the Pacific Ocean, and he couldn't wait to return.

But he was willing to put up with all the inconveniences if it meant finding his Christina. His home hadn't felt right without her.

He opened the box. Inside was a strand of nylon rope, a .38 pistol, a switchblade, vials of sedatives, and syringes. Lessons would have to be taught to Christina. She would have to understand that running from him was wrong.

"Soon, Christina, soon I will find you and soon you will come home with me, where you belong."

Greenland's body, now wrapped in tarp, was heavier than the Guardian had anticipated. Add to that the pain of his cracked rib and it was a struggle to haul the body out of the white van as the sun rose.

The Guardian grabbed the rope around the tarp and jerked hard. Pain scorched through his midsection and shot up and down his spine. For a moment he had to pause and catch his breath.

Sweat beaded on his forehead. He'd gotten sloppy last night. He'd underestimated his enemy and he'd nearly screwed everything up. He rubbed the sweat from his brow. He'd not slept in four or five days and his reflexes were off. But to sleep would mean a break from the killing and he wouldn't stop. *Couldn't* stop.

He could have left the body in the woods but it was important to display his work. People needed to know that monsters like Greenland weren't safe from *him*.

After wiping more sweat from his forehead, he gritted his teeth and pulled the body to the ground. He dragged it across the dry earth toward a tall oak by the mountain biker's trail in Deep Run Park. Few traveled the path this early, but by midday it would see enough traffic that someone would find the body.

With a grunt he pulled the body upright. Quickly, he unwrapped the tarp, uncovering Greenland's head and torso. He'd position the body and then deliver the hand—the trophy—to Lindsay.

The cracking of twigs had him stiffening. Damn. Who the hell was out this early?

"Holy shit!"

The strained voice had the Guardian whirling around.

Two teenage mountain bikers paused on the trail as they straddled their bikes. The taller one was a male, no more than seventeen. Long stringy hair accentuated oily skin and acne. The shorter one, also male, had blond hair and a KISS T-shirt. Each wore bike helmets and gloves.

The Guardian's heart hammered. Jesus, why did they have to find him? He released Greenland's body and reached for the gun tucked in his belt at the small of his back. "Hey, guys, it's not what it looks like. I'm a cop." To prove his claim, he flashed a badge.

The taller teen's eyes narrowed. "What the hell is that?"

"A dead body." There was no hiding what they'd seen and there was no disguising his own face as he tucked the badge back in his pocket. They had seen him. Damage control was his sole option. He didn't want to sacrifice them. Shit. They didn't deserve to die. But the Greater Good was at stake here. Hadn't God tested Abraham by asking him to kill his only son?

He smiled. "I've just called for backup. More cops are going to be here soon."

The shorter teen laid his bike down and took a step closer. "What happened to that guy?"

"Shot, by the looks of it. We won't know until the medical examiner gets here." Hand still behind his back, he pulled the hammer back on the gun.

"Damn," the teen said. "I've never seen a dead body before."

"It's rough."

The other teen had made no move toward him. "Hey, Mark, come on back. You shouldn't get that close."

Mark shrugged. "He's dead, Jeff. He can't hurt me."

The Guardian smiled. "Naw, he can't hurt you. Have a good long look." As Mark moved even closer, the

Guardian jerked the gun free but his ribs pinched hard and slowed what should have been a fluid motion.

Mark saw the gun and immediately started running toward his friend.

He fired. The first bullet went wide and missed Mark. He fired again and this time hit him in the leg. Mark fell to the ground, screamed, and clawed at the dirt. He cried for his mother.

For a split second, the Guardian froze like a deer caught in the beam of headlights. "Jesus, please forgive me. Forgive my sins."

Jeff stared in horror at the Guardian and his wounded friend. Fear turned to shock and then anger. He dropped his bike and scooped up a branch. Screaming, he rushed toward the Guardian.

The branch tip caught the Guardian on the shoulder and drew blood. Pain jerked him out of his own funk. Instinct took over and he fired.

The bullet hit Jeff in the chest. He stood stunned for a moment as if not quite sure what had happened. And then a plume of blood began to stain his shirt and he dropped to his knees. Air gurgled from the hole in his chest.

The Guardian's ribs ached and his shoulder burned as he staggered over to Mark, who was crying and calling even louder for his mother.

The Guardian stared at him. "Damn it, kid. Why did you have to be here?"

Tears streaked Mark's freckled face. "Why are you doing this to me? Me and Jeff never would have told."

"I'm sorry. I couldn't take that chance." Tears filled the Guardian's eyes. "Dumb, damn kids. You shouldn't have been here."

He raised his gun and shot Mark in the head.

* * *

Frank Hines's angry voice echoed through the house. His wife, Deb, was crying. He'd been drinking again, and judging by the sounds, he'd been hitting Deb again.

"I told you I don't want that worthless brother of yours coming around here!" Frank said.

"Why, Frank? He's my brother. He's family."

"I am your only family!"

Lindsay was ten. And she was hiding in the darkened closet of her bedroom. She was too old for teddy bears and yet she clutched the threadbare one she'd had since she was a baby.

Her father began to yell again. She had grown to hate her father, and though her mother had told her to hide, she could no longer stay cowered in the dark closet in her room. The shouting and the crying was driving her insane.

She wiped the tears from her face and stood. Slowly she opened the closet door and moved through her room down the hallway to her parents' bedroom. She opened the door and peered inside. Her father stood over her mother, his arm raised in the air. He brought the back of his hand down. The blow connected with her mother's jaw and it sounded as if it had shattered some of her mother's teeth. Her mother cried and ducked her head low.

Rage filled Lindsay. She pushed open the door and ran toward her father. She wanted to make him stop. "Leave her alone!"

He turned and glared down at her. "Brat!"

The ferocity in his gaze made her hesitate with fear. He was so tall.

Her mother raised her head. "Lindsay, go away. Run."

She fisted her fingers. "Leave my mother alone!"

Her father grabbed her and twisted her arm so hard she felt flesh and bone tear and break. She dropped to her knees. Anger collided with a deep feeling of helplessness that seared her soul.

Lindsay awoke with a start. Her body was covered in sweat and she could barely breathe. She glanced around the dark room trying to get her bearings. For several sec-

onds she didn't know where she was. And then she saw
the sewing machine in the corner, the flowered wallpa-
per, and the chair with her purse slung across it. She was
at the Kiers' house.

"I can't hide. I've got to get out of here."

Zack walked into Warwick's office just after seven.
Warwick gently set the telephone down in its cradle. He
wore a deep, pensive frown.

"What's happening?" Zack asked.

"That was a Detective Rio from the San Francisco
Police Department. I was returning a call in response to
a teletype he sent me late last night."

"About?"

"Your wife."

Zack tensed. "What does San Francisco PD have to
do with Lindsay?"

"Rio is investigating the death of a Claire Carmichael.
She was killed two days ago in San Francisco. She owned
a New Age bookstore. The murder was grisly and the
killer burned her place to the ground."

"I don't see the connection."

"Claire placed a phone call from her store to Lindsay
the night she was murdered. The call was logged in at
eleven P.M. pacific coast time, or two A.M. eastern standard."

Zack's mind turned. "Lindsay knows a lot of women in
high-risk relationships."

"Claire wasn't involved with anyone. And witnesses
report that she closed her shop early on Tuesday.
Around lunch. Friends say Claire never closed early. And
she also volunteered at a local women's shelter from
time to time."

Zack's stomach clenched. "Richard Braxton is from
San Francisco."

"Yeah."

Warwick's phone rang and he snapped up the receiver. Immediately he cradled the phone under his chin and started to write notes on a pad. "We'll be right there. And keep a tight clamp on the entire area. I don't want the media to even get a whiff of this."

"What is it?"

Warwick hung up and grabbed his coat off the back of his chair. "Marcus Greenland's body was found in Deep Run Park. He was at the top of that list Lindsay reviewed with C.C. He's one violent SOB."

"Lindsay was at my folks' place last night."

"There's no pinning this one on her."

"Why?"

"Two teenagers came upon the killer as he was dumping the body. He shot them both."

Zack felt sick. Damn it. "How are they?"

"One is dead and the other is in critical condition at Mercy Hospital. He's the one who called in the shooting from his cell phone."

"Can he give us a description?"

Warwick shook his head. "He's in surgery right now. It'll be a couple of hours."

Tension tightened the muscles in Zack's back. "I'll drive us to the park."

"Fine."

Zack tried to call Lindsay several times on her cell but she didn't pick up. He called his parents' house and got Eleanor, who told him Lindsay had just left in a cab. "Damn it. Can't the woman listen just once?" he muttered.

He covered the ten-plus miles to Deep Run Park in rush-hour traffic in less than twenty minutes. He wove in and out of traffic, one hand on the steering wheel and a cell under his ear as he called Ayden.

He pulled into the park entrance and rolled down the hill to the back parking lot near the soccer fields, where ten police cruisers were parked.

Zack got out of the car. He shrugged off his jacket and tossed it on the front seat. Rolling up his sleeves, he moved toward Sara, who was squatting by Greenland's body as she photographed it. She stood and moved to the edge of the yellow crime scene tape.

Sara looked pale and grim. Any death involving a kid shook everyone to the core. She pulled rubber gloves and booties from the pocket of her white jumpsuit and handed them to Zack and Warwick. They put them on and ducked under the yellow tape.

Zack yanked off his sunglasses and squatted by Greenland's body. Greenland's dark skin had turned a pasty gray and his lips blue. His eyes were half open. The tarp had been partially removed and he could see that Greenland's right hand had been chopped off.

"He didn't finish his job," Zack said.

"The boys interrupted him." Warwick muttered an oath as he glanced at the covered body of the teenager. "Sara, did he leave anything else behind?"

Sara pointed to an orange flag sticking from the ground. "A forty-five shell casing. And I found traces of blood on the tip of a stick the dead boy was holding. I've already bagged it and sent it to the lab."

Zack rubbed the back of his neck with his hand. "Let's hope he's in our DNA database."

"Any sign of the hand?" Zack said.

"None."

Zack glanced at Warwick. "The last two hands were delivered to Lindsay. We need to find her."

Warwick nodded. "Right."

* * *

Dressed in yoga pants and a tank top, Kendall had been up half the night listening to the police scanners. There'd been nothing out of the ordinary. The piece she'd done on the killer had been priceless. The fact that he was mutilating his victims and sending the hands to Lindsay was more than she could have hoped for.

She'd received five times the usual number of e-mails from viewers. But there'd been no response from the killer or the network producers to whom she'd overnighted tapes.

Exhausted and hungry, she'd reached her limit of listening to the routine police calls: loud music, drunk teenagers, an overdose in a convenience store parking lot, and a speeder on the interstate.

She rose from the varnished kitchen table and opened the refrigerator. Eggs, a half carton of milk, and a salad left over from the salad bar at the grocery store. When she'd been a kid, her mother had kept this refrigerator stocked.

Crap. She needed to get out of this house and start fresh away from Richmond.

She set a pan on the stove, clicked the burner dial to medium high, and cracked a couple of eggs in the pan. *Eat first and then catch an hour or two of sleep.* She and Mike needed to be at the station by noon.

"Dispatch, this is 8021."

Kendall was only half listening now. "Dispatch, over."

"Dispatch, the mutilated body found in Deep Run Park—"

"8021, Homicide has requested this communication be handled on a secure channel. Switch to . . ."

"Shit." Kendall's mind reeled. Mutilated body. The eighties were the western end of the county, which was near her and the shelter. She ran to the avocado green wall phone and dialed her cameraman's phone number.

On the fourth ring, a gravelly voice heavy with sleep answered. "What?"

"How soon can you pick me up?" She paced the kitchen, frustrated that a phone cord tethered her to the wall.

"Kendall?" He swore. "Why?"

"Body at Deep Run Park. I think it's our guy."

He cleared his throat. "Give me twenty minutes."

"Make it fifteen and I'll be out front waiting."

"Right."

Fourteen minutes later, she stood outside, briefcase in hand. She didn't have the time to shower, so she'd swept her hair up with a French twist comb, quickly applied her makeup, and slipped on a simple blue sheath and heeled sandals.

"So where we going?" Mike said when he pulled up. Thick stubble covered his square jaw, and his thinning shoulder-length black hair was loosely bound at the nape of his neck. His Hawaiian shirt flapped in the air from the AC vent.

She flipped through her notes. "To Lindsay O'Neil's house."

Mike sipped the last of yesterday's Big Gulp as he put the van in reverse and backed out of the driveway. The faint smell of cigarette smoke hung in the air. "I thought the body was at some park. I know the other news teams will be there."

"And I know the cops are going to have the area locked up tight."

"So why Lindsay's again?"

"Because after the last two murders, there was a disturbance just a few hours later near Lindsay. If our friend Steve is correct, the killer is sending hands to Lindsay. My guess is, the killer is going to send her something now and I want to be there when he does."

"Why send her a hand?"

"Who knows? Who cares really? He's like a cat that dumps a mouse at its master's feet."

He considered what she'd said. "The killer thinks of Lindsay as his master?"

"Maybe. Or maybe he's fixated on her. Whatever his motivations, we've got three murders now. Richmond has a serial killer." She tapped her foot. "If I could find a way to draw this guy out, I could write my own ticket."

Mike looked at Kendall as if she'd lost her mind. "You want to draw out a serial killer."

"I sure do."

"How are you going to do that?"

"Go after Lindsay. If I can make her miserable enough, hound her with the cameras, I'm willing to bet our guy gets pissed and shows himself."

"Or he just kills you."

The thought didn't frighten her enough to change her mind. "I'll be fine."

This story was going to take her places. She dug her cell out of her purse and punched in her news director's number. She relayed the information and told him to call the network. This was the stuff of national news.

Mike drove by Lindsay's town house. "I don't see her Jeep."

"Park the van down the street out of sight."

"And?"

"Get your camera and come with me. We'll wait out of sight. Five'll get you ten the fireworks explode sooner than later."

Lindsay wasn't going to hide anymore, from anyone. She needed to reclaim her home, her life, and she needed to prove that she was in control.

It had been easy to be brave on the cab ride over. But now as she stood alone and stared at the yellow crime scene tape by her front door, she found herself searching the bushes and the surrounding terrain. He could be out there watching her.

No one lurked nearby and there were no grisly packages waiting for her. And still her nerves danced with tension. She had hoped the worry that had kept her up most of the night would vanish once she was back at her own place. But it didn't.

Digging her keys out of her purse, she moved up the sidewalk, careful to step around the spot where she'd dropped the bloody hand wrapped in the newspaper. Sucking in a breath, she moved toward the front door. As she shoved her key in the lock, she realized the door wasn't locked.

Immediately, she backed away, leaving her keys to dangle in the lock. Heart hammering, she dug in her purse for her cell phone.

Her hands trembled as she punched in Zack's cell phone number. Her front door opened.

Steve, her maintenance man, came out. He was frowning.

Her thumb on the "send" buttons, she paused. "Steve, what's going on?"

He held a screwdriver in his hand. "I thought I'd check the place out for you. After what that creep left you yesterday, I wanted to make sure your place was secure. And then I figured I'd go ahead and fix your AC."

She noticed his white van across the street and felt foolish. She closed her phone and dropped it in her purse. "Oh. Sorry, I'm just a little on edge."

"Understandable." He smiled. "I was just on my way to the van to get a different screwdriver."

"Right." Lindsay waited as he retrieved a large flathead screwdriver. "What do you think caused the AC to go?"

He shrugged. "Part blew. Looked like an overload. And the power outage the other day sure couldn't have helped."

She followed him inside to the living room. The house was quiet and the drawn shades blocked out almost all of the morning sun. She moved into the kitchen to brew a pot of coffee. She'd left so early from the Kiers' that she'd not had any. And now she felt so exhausted. She needed something to get her moving.

Steve went to the AC utility closet sandwiched between the living room and the kitchen. "Sorry it's taken me so long to get to this."

"Believe me, I've got bigger problems than no AC."

Steve unscrewed the front panel of the unit and then pulled out the filter. He clicked on his flashlight and stared into the comb of wires. He frowned. "Have a look at this."

"What?"

He reached inside the air conditioner and pulled out an electronic box with an antenna on top. "I didn't see it before because it was tucked in the back."

She frowned. "It looks like a transmitter."

"Why would there be a transmitter in your place?"

"I've seen pieces like that before, at a security conference I attended last year. It can be used to boost the signal of a camera."

He looked puzzled. "I service every unit in this complex and I've never seen this."

"Is there a wire attached to it?"

"Yeah."

"Where does it go?"

He shined the flashlight into the unit. "The wire

snakes out a small hole in the back of the unit and crosses to another hole drilled in the wall."

Lindsay glanced behind the unit and saw the wire. "It vanishes into the wall between the closet and living room."

Steve shined the flashlight into the hole in the wall. The wire rose up and vanished into the darkness. He moved out of the utility closet and into the living room. Above their heads was a grate. "That's odd."

Lindsay didn't like the concern in his voice. "What?"

"That grate on your living room ceiling shouldn't be there."

She stared at it. She'd never noticed it before.

"Let me get a ladder."

Lindsay folded her arms around her chest. "Sure."

He was back in less than a minute and on the ladder. He undid the screws and popped off the grate. Drywall and paint tore. He peered into the hole.

Lindsay stood on tiptoe. "What do you see?"

He removed a small electronic device. "A camera."

She felt sick inside. She'd heard about cameras like this. They were easily found on the Internet and were used by people to spy on other people.

Someone was spying on her.

Someone was watching her.

Steve climbed down from the ladder. He handed her the camera. It was small, compact, and state-of-the-art. She knew this model could send a signal up to seven miles away.

Lindsay rolled the device between her fingers as she glanced behind her trying to imagine the angle of the camera. "It would have recorded everything happening in the living room."

The Guardian. He'd been watching her.

Steve shook his head. He looked worried. He had full

access to the units and he'd be the first questioned by the police.

A deep sense of shame washed over her. She felt violated. The Guardian had been spying on her during her most private moments. She remembered the other night when she'd been awakened by the phone. She'd had the creeps then and sensed she was being watched. Had he been watching her then? Had he been the one to call her?

Lindsay dug her cell out of her purse and dialed Zack's number. He answered on the first ring. "Where are you?" He sounded terse, and in the background she thought she heard tense voices.

Her hand shook as she shoved it through her hair. "I'm okay. I'm at my town house. My maintenance man found a camera in my AC vent."

A heavy silence followed. "Don't move, I'm only five minutes out."

"Thanks." She wanted him close, wanted his protection. She could have listed seven reasons off the top of her head why it was wrong to depend on him, but right now she didn't care about reason. She needed Zack. And she knew he would be there for her.

Steve held the screwdriver in his hand in a tight grip. "I didn't have anything to do with this."

"It's going to be okay," she told Steve. "The police are coming."

Steve looked worried and he started to pace. "I didn't do this."

His agitation caught her off guard. He'd always been so easygoing and quick with a joke. "No one said you did."

He shook his head. "They might think I'm guilty when they discover that I have a police record."

Lindsay stared at him and her concern grew. Truthfully, she knew nothing about him. Steve could be the Guardian. "What were you in jail for?"

He shoved out a breath. "It doesn't matter. I have a record."

Lindsay glanced toward the open door of the town house. "I'm going to wait outside."

He nodded. "Me too."

Hugging her arms, she ran out into the sunshine and moved away from Steve.

Instead of waiting with her, he moved quickly toward his van.

"Where are you going?!" she shouted.

"Away. I've seen those tabloid news shows. I'll be tried and convicted on the news before I even get to court."

"The police are coming to talk to you."

"Screw the police." He got in the van and fired it up. Gravel kicked up as he punched the gas and drove off.

Lindsay stood on the corner, counting the seconds until Zack arrived.

Minutes later, the white Impala pulled around her street corner. The wheels had barely came to a stop when Zack hopped out of the vehicle. He strode directly toward her. He stared at her for a long moment before asking, "What did you find?"

"My maintenance man found a camera in an AC vent. He swears he didn't put it there."

"Where is he?"

"He drove off. Said he had a police record."

Zack's jaw tensed. Warwick got out of the police car as Zack moved toward him. He relayed what she'd said and Warwick grabbed the radio. He called in a description of the van and Steve.

The sound of sirens echoed in the distance. More cops were coming.

Zack moved toward her. "Lindsay, there's been another murder. Marcus Greenland."

Her brows knitted as she stared back at her house. "I was on the phone with Aisha Greenland the other night. I sat right in my living room and talked to her about her divorce. She was scared. The Guardian must have been watching and listening." She felt sick. "He calls himself the Guardian. Does he think he's helping me?"

"In his mind, it might have started out that way, but its grown way beyond that."

"What's happened?"

"While the Guardian was dumping Greenland's body early this morning, two teenagers came upon him. He shot at them. One is dead and the other is at Mercy undergoing surgery."

"My God." Her voice hitched with sadness and tears pooled in her eyes.

Zack worked his jaw. "He's not helping anyone."

Two teenagers—*children*—shot.

"Did you find any other cameras?" Zack asked.

"We haven't looked yet."

Warwick strode up to them. "I've called for the cavalry. They'll be here in the next few minutes to sweep the place. With any luck, we can link this system to the guy who installed it."

Her skin felt clammy. "The Guardian is taking over my life."

"Who's the Guardian?" Kendall Shaw's voice caught them all off guard.

They turned, stunned.

"Where did you come from?" Zack demanded.

Kendall ignored him. The light on the cameraman's camera clicked on, and like a lioness looking for prey, Kendall shoved a microphone toward Lindsay's face. "Is the Guardian the guy who's been killing those men? Has he been secretly videotaping you as well?"

Lindsay stared, stunned. Warwick frowned.

Zack raised his hand and blocked the lens of the camera. "This is not the time or place for this."

Kendall didn't flinch. "Come on, Lindsay, Detective Kier. I know this killer has been on a rampage since Monday. And it's the anniversary week of Lindsay's mother's death. Lindsay lost her job because of him. He's killed four, maybe five people."

"No comment," Zack said.

But Lindsay's temper roiled. Not at the reporter, but at the Guardian. He had invaded her life, ruined her job, and watched her while she moved around her home. She'd promised herself this morning she'd not hide anymore. If the Guardian wanted her, he could come and get her.

Lindsay said in a loud voice, "I don't know who the Guardian is."

"Lindsay," Zack warned.

Mike stepped sideways so that he had a clear shot of Lindsay. Kendall moved closer. Her eyes gleamed with hunger.

"I can tell you this," Lindsay said. Zack grabbed her arm, squeezing a gentle warning for her to be silent. But she wouldn't stay silent. This creep wasn't going to hurt anyone else if she could stop him. "I've grown to hate and resent whoever is doing this to me."

"Why is he sending you the severed hands of his victims?" Kendall asked.

"I don't know. He's got a twisted form of justice that I want no part of. If the Guardian is watching, back off. Leave me alone. I don't want your help or anything else to do with you."

Zack slapped his palm over the camera lens. "Enough."

Kendall smiled. "That was excellent, Lindsay. Really excellent." She'd gotten the quote she wanted. "We're going. I've got to hurry if we're going to get this edited for the noon news."

Zack's expression was harsh as he watched Kendall and Mike leave. "Get them out of here." He shook his head. "You could very well have turned yourself into a target, Lindsay."

She dug her hands through her hair. For the first time since she was a child she felt oddly in control. "Good. Better me than another child."

Richard Braxton sat in his rented Mercedes down the street from Lindsay O'Neil's town house. The place was swarming with cops. There was no sign of Christina, but in the center of the cops stood two women. He glanced at the photo of Lindsay O'Neil and then back at the two women. The shorter one was O'Neil.

He twisted his wedding band around his finger. "Where are you hiding my wife, Ms. O'Neil?"

The cops wouldn't surround her forever. Soon there'd be an opportunity to get her alone. And when he did, he would make her regret that she'd ever interfered with his marriage.

Patience.

Chapter Twenty-Six

Thursday, July 10, 11:00 A.M.

Lindsay felt dirty and violated as she watched the cops go through her house searching for electronic bugs. So far they'd found five: one in the kitchen, one in the back patio, one in the front entryway, and two in the living room.

Zack came down the stairs and moved within inches of her. "We didn't find any bugs in your bedroom or the bathrooms upstairs."

She didn't feel any relief. "I guess that's the Guardian's way of protecting my privacy."

Zack nodded. "I think you're right. In his own way, he seems to be looking out for you."

She glanced around the room at each of the vents. She hugged her body, warding off a sudden chill. "Nicole said this place gave her the creeps. I even felt it once or twice. But I shrugged it off to fatigue. Do you have any idea how long the bugs have been there?"

"No. But if I had to guess I'd say all this started around the time that article came out in the paper about you."

"I agreed to that damn piece because Dana had said it

would boost fund-raising. Now I wish I'd never met Kendall Shaw."

"That article landed you on someone's radar," Zack said. "Anyone different you've noticed lurking around lately?"

She lifted an amused brow. "Zack, you know me. I'm so busy on any given day I couldn't tell you if it's raining or not."

Zack offered her a half smile as if a memory played in his head. "Can you think of anyone who might have come into your home?"

"Just Steve the maintenance guy as far as I know. But I don't own this place. The property management firm has the right to send in anyone they want if there are maintenance problems."

"What about Nicole? Did she bring anyone in here?"

"No. She's barely getting used to the place herself."

He considered what she'd said. "Does the property manager have to notify you when they come in?"

"They're supposed to. But the girls in the rental office are young and not so focused on their jobs."

Zack's face looked as if it had been carved from stone. "I'll talk to the rental office. How many people know you legally changed your name when you turned eighteen?"

"Since I returned to Richmond, I've told no one about my past except you. But I grew up in Ashland, and any one of the people there could have seen the article and recognized me."

"Have you had contact with anyone from the old days? Like Joel, maybe?"

"How do you know about him?"

"Warwick and I spoke to him the other day."

She couldn't be angry. He was being thorough. "I haven't seen him since high school."

"He was worried about you."

"He was a good guy."

He didn't confirm or dispute the comment. "What about family?"

"There wasn't much family. My dad was an only child and his parents were gone by the time I was born. My mom's parents were dead too. And her brother only saw her rarely." She stopped, remembering the dream she'd had last night. "I remember my uncle called my mom when I was about ten. Mom had lunch with him. My father was furious."

"Any pictures of your uncle or your parents?"

"As a matter of fact, I found a few pictures the other night." She went to the closet below the stairs and pulled out the box of photos. She had to dig deep to find what she wanted. She handed Zack the grainy color photo. "It was taken on my parents' back porch. That's my mom and dad, me in the center, and my uncle on the end."

Zack studied the picture. "He's in a Navy uniform."

"Yes. That's why he was away so much."

"What was your uncle's name?"

"Henry is all I remember."

"O'Neil?"

"No. He and Mom were half brother and sister. They had different fathers. There was a fifteen-year age difference between them. I don't remember his last name."

"Which would make him how old?"

"Sixty-nine. Mom would have been fifty-four this year."

As thirty loomed for her, she realized just how young her mother had been when she'd died.

He tucked the photo in his pocket. "Who is Claire Carmichael?"

The out-of-the-blue comment stunned her. "Claire? She runs a bookstore in San Francisco but also does a lot of volunteer work with battered women. She gave Nicole money so she could leave the city. Why?"

"She was murdered on Tuesday."

Grief washed over her. Claire and she had been good friends. They'd lost touch but she'd liked the woman immensely. "My God."

"Someone placed a call from her cell to your phone on the night she died. Tuesday night."

"I got a late-night call on Tuesday on my cell phone. It woke me out of a sound sleep. It really rattled me. The call came from outside the calling area, so I just figured it was a misdial. Was it Claire who called me?"

"We don't know."

An unthinkable thought crossed her mind. "Richard Braxton got to her."

"Whoever killed Claire was a sadist."

"Nicole said Richard could be quite violent. We've got to warn her."

"I'll have a sheriff's deputy posted outside my folks' place so we can keep an eye on her. I want you back there."

"No." When he frowned she added, "I appreciate what you're doing, Zack, but I can't let the Guardian or Richard ruin my life."

"You can't stay here."

"I know. I'll bunk with Ruby. No one will ever find me there."

The elevator doors opened to Mercy Hospital's fifth floor and out stepped a grim-faced Captain Ayden. Anger overrode fatigue and fueled him as he approached the intercom by the locked metal doors of the surgical recovery floor. He'd not slept in forty-eight hours. He had arranged for his boys to stay with the neighbors and had called them a couple of times just to hear the sound of their voices. He missed them now more than ever.

This latest shooting of the teenage boys had hit too close to home for him. His own sons, fourteen-year-old Zane and sixteen-year-old Caleb, were athletic and active in local mountain bike clubs. Each could have been on that trail this morning and stumbled upon the Guardian.

Ayden pressed the buzzer that sounded at the ICU nurses station.

"Yes," a woman said.

"I'm Captain Ayden and I'm here to see Dr. Moore."

"Sure, just a moment." Another buzzer sounded and this time a lock on the door clicked and the doors swung open.

Ayden strode into the ICU ward toward the nurses station, where a woman stood reading a chart. She was in her early fifties and wore her shoulder-length dark hair tied back with a rubber band. Wisps of hair stuck out, framing her angled face. Dark shadows hung under vivid blue eyes.

He pulled out his badge. "I'm Captain Ayden."

The woman closed the chart and set it down. "My name is Dr. Moore. I'm Mr. Langford's surgeon."

"*Mr.* Langford." Ayden swallowed an oath. He was doing his best to keep his voice calm. "The kid isn't old enough to shave and we're talking about him like he's an adult."

Dr. Moore kept her expression neutral, unapologetic. "The less attached I am the better, detective. I can't do my job if I'm emotionally involved. A cop should understand that."

Ayden frowned. "I understand but I still don't like it." He turned his back to the curtain separating them from patients. Unseen monitors beeped. "How's the kid doing?"

"The bullet tore into his chest."

"But he will live," Ayden said.

Dr. Moore met his direct gaze head-on. "I'm going to do everything I can to save him. Either way he's got a long road ahead of him."

He shoved out a breath. "Does he know his friend died?"

"No."

"Can I talk to him?"

"You can only if you promise to keep your conversation very short. The boy's only been out of surgery for an hour."

"Understood," Ayden said. "I won't do anything to jeopardize his health."

Dr. Moore led Ayden to a corner cubical curtained off from the rest of the floor. She pushed back the curtain. The boy in the bed was deathly pale and shirtless. IVs stuck in each arm. Sensors were pasted to his bare chest. Blood dripped from a bag into his arm.

"Mr. Langford," Dr. Moore said.

The boy laid open-mouthed, his eyes shut.

Ayden shifted. "What does his mom call him?"

Dr. Moore checked her chart. "Jeff."

Ayden leaned close to the bed, careful not to disrupt the wires. "Jeff."

The boy's eyelids fluttered.

"Jeff," Ayden said louder.

A monitor indicated that the boy's heart rate rose from sixty beats a minute to seventy. He was waking up.

"Jeff, I'm a cop. I'm trying to figure out who shot you. Can you tell me anything about the person who did this to you?"

Jeff moistened his dry lips. In a bare whisper, he said, "Never saw him before."

"What did he look like?"

"Gray hair." He ran his tongue over his dry lips again.

Ayden laid his hand gently on Jeff's. It felt cold. "Can you tell me anything else, Jeff?"

"He limped, like he'd been hurt." The boy shut his eyes.

Dr. Moore glanced at the monitors. The boys heart rate was dropping again. "He's not going to be able to give you much more. Not until tomorrow."

"Where's Mark?" the boy whispered.

Ayden squeezed the boy's hand. "Don't worry about him now."

Jeff's eyes fluttered closed.

Frustration dogged Ayden. This boy was the key to catching the psycho. "I have just one more question."

The doctor looked annoyed. "You can ask all the questions you want but the boy isn't going to talk. He's heavily sedated and his mind isn't going to clear for at least twenty-four hours."

Ayden handed his card to the doctor. "Call me when he can talk again. I don't care if it's day or night."

She tucked the card in her white coat pocket. "I'll do that."

He was grateful to leave the room and the hospital with its antiseptic smells and dull green colors. It was time to turn his attention to what he did best—catching killers.

Kendall Shaw had filed an updated news report on the Guardian just barely in time for the news at noon. It was a good piece. No, it was a *great* piece. Her best.

She'd known when she'd stuck the microphone in Lindsay's face that she was going to get a hell of a quote. Lindsay was a powder keg. And it hadn't taken much to set her off and get her talking.

And then Kendall had looked directly into the camera

and challenged the Guardian. She'd called him a coward who hid behind Lindsay O'Neil.

If this wasn't going to be *the* tape that got her noticed she'd be shocked. Success was so close she could almost taste it.

Kendall's heels clicked on pavement as she crossed Channel 10's small city parking lot to the side street where she'd parked her car. The sun was low in the sky and the day's heat waning. She was headed to her hair dresser to treat herself to a wash and blow-dry. There hadn't been much time to doll up before the noon news report, but when she rebroadcast at six she wanted to look her best.

Kendall reached her red sports car and clicked the lock open with the keyless remote.

"Ms. Shaw?"

The raspy voice had Kendall turning toward a pleasant looking man dressed in khakis and a white collared polo shirt. His graying hair was brushed off his face. Deep lines around his eyes made him looked distinguished more than old.

"Yes?"

"I saw your news report today. It was something else."

She opened her car door, aware she had no time to spare if she was going to get her hair done and be back at the station in forty-five minutes. "Thank you for noticing."

A smile tipped the edge of his mouth. "You're one great reporter. Not many would have the spine to call this killer out."

She was accustomed to being recognized. It was part of the job. She'd learned long ago to be nice to viewers while not getting pulled into lengthy conversations. Still, the clock was ticking. "Thanks. I'd chat but I'm really late for an appointment."

He held up calloused hands. "Oh, no problem."

She tossed her purse in the car, grateful that this guy, whoever he was, wasn't going to ask a thousand questions. "You have a good afternoon."

"You too."

Kendall had all but put the man out of her mind when she felt the first sharp electric bolt rip through her body. Every one of her muscles convulsed and gave way. Her knees buckled. She'd have hit the ground hard if the guy hadn't grabbed her.

He smiled down at her, no hint of surprise in his warm brown eyes. "You all right there, Ms. Shaw?"

She couldn't speak.

"Cat got your tongue?" He pulled her up and half walked, half carried her toward a van parked next to her car.

Oh, God. Oh, God.

"I wasn't real happy about your report today. You baited Lindsay and made her say things she wouldn't normally have said. You called me a coward. I didn't like that either."

Her blurred senses started to scream. This man was the Guardian.

A deep moan formed in her chest. She wanted to scream, to run, but her body refused to work. As if he read her thoughts, the Guardian touched her with the Taser again. Her knees buckled and he now supported her weight completely. He had surprising strength.

The Guardian opened the back door to the van. He laid her on the metal bed of the van, climbing in, and closed the doors behind them. He clicked on a dome light, whose light was contained by the blackened windows.

Kendall knew the grim statistics. Once a victim was trapped in a vehicle her chances of survival drastically diminished.

Her left hand twitched. If her body would start working, she could ball her fingers into a fist and punch him. She could still get away.

The Guardian put his lips close to her ear. "I know what you're thinking. But you're not going anywhere." He raised the Taser close to her face. The electrical current snapped and popped just inches from her eye.

He jabbed the Taser into her side. Her head jerked back as she convulsed and a silent scream clogged her throat. "You're not going anywhere. Not until you've paid like all the other abusers."

He grabbed a length of rope and tied her wrists together and then her ankles. Her fingers tingled as her too tight bindings constricted the blood flow. She forced herself to meet his gaze. She wanted to memorize every detail so that she could tell the police what this bastard looked like.

He wadded up a cloth, shoved it in her mouth, and secured it with a piece of duct tape.

She struggled to breathe and her bravado waned. Tears welled in her eyes and she hated her weakness. She needed to stay calm. If she was going to get out of this alive, she needed to think. Her cell was in her purse in her car. She had a meeting with Mike soon. Would he see her car in the side street and launch a search for her?

The Guardian stroked her hair back off her face. "So soft and so pretty. But you have a heart of stone." He sighed. "You know what I do to my victims, don't you?"

She winced as he jabbed a needle into her arm and emptied the syringe.

"I cut their left hands off," he said quietly. He ran his hand lightly down the length of her arm to the hands tied behind her back. His fingers encircled her wrists. "What you may not know is that they're alive when I take my trophy."

The matter-of-fact tone made the statement all the more frightening. Panic could easily have tipped to hysteria, but the drugs he'd put into her system had started to take effect. Her mind grew foggy.

The Guardian cupped her chin in his calloused hands and moved his lips up to her ear. "I won't have any trouble snapping your delicate wrist in two with my machete blade."

Tears ran down Kendall's face. She shook her head. This couldn't be happening.

The Guardian got behind the wheel of the van and fired up the engine. He calmly merged into traffic as if he had all the time in the world. "I never thought I'd kill a woman. It just seemed wrong in so many ways. But then I saw that broadcast of yours today and I knew you would be the exception to the rule." He chuckled. "I never have liked you. And you know, from the moment you started covering this story, I knew we'd clash. I just knew it."

Her mind tumbled and her muscles went slack.

"Look at the bright side, Kendall. You'll be headline news tomorrow when they find your body."

Lindsay sat in her car, a suitcase packed and sitting on the passenger seat. Zack was wrapping up details at the town house, and then he was going to escort her to Ruby's. She'd agreed that she couldn't stay in the town house. In fact, she doubted she could ever live there again. And Zack had understood that she felt uncomfortable at his folks' place. They'd compromised. She was staying at Ruby's.

Before she headed out she wanted to touch base with Nicole. She called her at the Kiers', and spoke to Eleanor briefly before Nicole picked up. "Nicole?"

"Hey, how are you doing?" Nicole's voice sounded stronger, as if she'd gotten some sleep.

"Been better. But I'm hanging tough. I wanted to let you know that I'm staying at Ruby's tonight. I'll drive out to see you in the morning."

"Sounds good."

"Hey, have you run that test yet?"

"No. I'll do it first thing in the morning." She sighed. "Pregnancy is a problem I don't want right now."

"One step at a time."

Nicole hesitated. "I dreamt about Richard again. I can't help but think that he's close."

Lindsay thought about Claire. She chose not to tell Nicole. "Stay close to the Kiers. They'll keep you safe."

"Thanks."

"I'll call you in the morning."

"Good."

Lindsay rung off and dialed Sam's number. He'd have the results of the bloodwork by now. His phone rang five times and then went to voice mail: "This is Dr. Sam Begley. Leave me a message unless this is an emergency. If it is, hang up and call 911."

"Sam, this is Lindsay. Where are you? Call me. I need to talk to you."

"Detective Warwick, this is Rio from San Francisco." Warwick glanced at the clock on his desk. It was ten here so it was seven in the evening on the West Coast.

"Were you able to find Braxton?"

"My partner and I went to his house. He's gone. According to his secretary, he filed a flight plan to Vancouver. He has businesses up there. Airport records show that he did file the flight plan."

Warwick closed his eyes and pinched the edge of his nose. He was bone tired. "Did you find him in Vancouver?"

"Not yet. But we're in contact with Canadian authorities. I'll let you know as soon as we find him."

"If you even get a whiff that he's headed east call me. Anytime."

"Consider it done."

"I don't know anything about Braxton. What's your gut reaction on this one?"

Rio sighed. "He's a tricky bastard. Looks clean and acts clean but it didn't take much digging to find out he came up hard. When he was seventeen he killed a man. Because he was under eighteen, he got off with time in juvenile hall. He was linked to other violent crimes but nothing ever stuck. I wouldn't put anything past him."

Chapter Twenty-Seven

Friday, July 11, 6:00 A.M.

Richard Braxton sat on the edge of his bed. The whore who'd showed up in his room late last night lay under the rumpled sheets. Her dark hair swept over her face. He imagined that in the right light, she could look like Christina.

He rose and pulled on his trousers. He handed her several hundred-dollar bills.

A sly smile lifted her lips. Now that his desire had cooled, he could see that the woman had coarse features made worse by layers of makeup. She swung her legs over the side of the bed. Her naked breasts bobbed and she pulled a tight T-shirt over them. She wriggled into her skirt and slipped manicured feet into four-inch heels. "It was fun. You in town long?"

Richard slipped on his shirt and buttoned it. "Long enough."

She slid her hands seductively down her thighs. "If you want another romp, call me."

Now that his desire had been satisfied, the whore

disgusted him. Like yesterday's trash, she needed to be dealt with. "I need for you to make a phone call."

She traced a long finger down his chest and looked directly into his eyes. "Sure, baby. You want Mama to talk dirty again?"

"No." Richard handed her a disposable cell phone and a piece of paper with a number and a message on it. "This is what I want you to say."

The whore shrugged and sat on the edge of the bed. She crossed her legs and dialed. She grinned up at him and ran her tongue over her lips suggestively. One ring. Two rings. "It's going to voice mail."

Damn. "Go ahead and leave the message."

She nodded and he heard a distant message: "*I can't take your call right now . . .*"

The whore sat straighter. She followed the script. She'd said she'd wanted to be an actress.

Richard moved to the other side of the bed and pulled a length of rope out of his back pocket. He leaned over the bed and kissed the back of her neck as she closed the phone. "That was nice."

"You want me to be anyone else? I could be her again. What was her name? Christina?"

Hearing his wife's name made him cringe. "I'd like that," he said silkily.

She started to turn, but he stopped her as he leaned forward and kissed her neck again. She tipped her head back, her long black hair falling over his hands. He fisted his fingers in the hair. He'd chosen her because of her hair.

As he continued to kiss her neck, he freed his hand from her hair and he carefully wound the ends of the rope around both hands and fisted his fingers around it.

In one swift move, he raised the rope over her head and wrapped it around her neck. He jerked hard, forcing her back. Immediately, she started to gag and her hands went up to his. She scratched his skin.

Her cheap perfume swirled around him as he tightened the noose. She tried to wriggle free as she thrashed her arms backward toward his face. Her fist connected with the side of his cheek. The pain pissed him off and he squeezed even harder. He could feel the vein in her neck pulsing wildly against his hand. Her body screamed for oxygen. His erection returned.

"Christina," he whispered in her ear. "You said you wanted to be Christina."

The fight slowly drained from her as her face turned bluer and bluer. Her hands dropped to her side, limp and lifeless, and finally her body slumped back against his.

To be extra careful, he held the rope in place several extra minutes until he was certain she was dead. Finally, he released her and she dropped to the carpeted floor in a heap.

Richard flexed his fingers. Now it was time to go to the hospital and wait.

Lindsay woke to the sound of her cell phone ringing. She sat up in bed, confused and disoriented. Her head throbbed and her body ached. She glanced at the phone number and didn't recognize it. Assuming it was another reporter, she let her voice mail take it.

She swung her legs over the side of the twin bed. Brianna Dillon slept in the other bed. Lindsay had called Ruby late yesterday and her friend had welcomed her into her home without question.

Rising, she pulled her jeans on beneath the T-shirt she'd worn last night. She combed her fingers through her hair and pulled it up with the rubber band she'd tucked in her jeans pocket.

Quietly, she slipped out of the room. A light in the kitchen and the smell of coffee lured her down the hallway.

In the kitchen, she found Ruby standing next to the gas stove scrambling eggs.

Lindsay stifled a yawn. "Good morning."

Ruby's green housecoat skimmed her dimpled knees. Pink slippers warmed her feet. "Come in and have some coffee, baby."

Her head felt like it was filled with cotton. "Bless you."

Ruby poured a cup and handed it to Lindsay. "You look exhausted."

"I didn't sleep well." She sipped the rich brew. It tasted so good. "Too many dreams."

Ruby planted a hand on her hip. "You dreaming about that crazy man or that husband of yours?"

"My husband."

"Was it a bad dream?"

"Not really. It was nice." The coffee warmed her chilled fingers.

Ruby pulled a cigarette out of her pocket, placed it between her lips, and lit it. "There have been a couple of men in my life that weren't good for me, but that didn't stop me from loving them. And I've got to say, your detective ain't so bad. I saw the way he looked at you yesterday. He really does care about you."

"I know."

Lindsay's phone beeped, reminding her of the voice mail message. She set her cup down and played back the call. She sighed. "It's a nurse at Mercy. There's a battered woman in the emergency room. Domestic."

Ruby shook her head. "Do you have to be the one to take it?"

"Yes."

"I promised Detective Kier—your husband—I'd keep

an eye on you after he told me that that Richard Braxton guy might have killed that poor Carmichael woman in San Francisco. There's no telling where he is. He could be in Richmond now."

"Last word on the street was he was in Canada. And I won't be afraid."

"If you had a lick of sense you'd be terrified."

"Don't look so worried. I'll be at the hospital. It's safe there."

Kendall Shaw woke and realized she was on a cold, damp floor. She shifted her weight and found that her hands were bound over her head and tied to a chain that linked to the wall. The rope around her wrists was so tight her fingers felt numb. How long had she been there? All night?

The gag in her mouth had left her mouth and throat dry. She could moan but not scream loud enough for anyone to hear.

Think. Think. Don't freak out. She twisted her hands against her restraints and discovered there was enough slack in the chain for her to move. Her body was stiff and weak but she managed to roll on her side and up into a sitting position. She tugged at the rope and chain. Neither budged.

She looked around the small, dimly lighted room that smelled of mold and rust. As her eyes adjusted she looked through an open door into a larger room. To the left, a rickety staircase led up to a closed door. On the far side, a workbench with multiple television screens.

Where was she? A basement? A root cellar? In a darkened corner a rat squeaked and scratched against the floor. She drew her feet up.

She wasn't sure how long she sat in the darkness, but

her mind became clear as the drugs dwindled from her system. Her back started to ache from sitting up, but she didn't dare sit close to the wall for fear of the rat.

And then she heard the steady thud of shoes on the floor above. Someone upstairs was pacing. The footsteps sounded as if they were getting closer, and then she heard what sounded like a dead bolt scraping free of a lock.

Her heart pounded in her chest. The door at the top of the stairs swung open. Light rushed down to the room. She blinked, her eyes unaccustomed to any light. At the top of the staircase a man's silhouetted figure appeared. He flipped on the overhead lights.

Immediately, she winced against the brightness and ducked her head. The footsteps moved closer to her as she opened her eyes slowly and allowed them to adjust.

She realized the dampness wasn't water. It was blood. She struggled to move free of it and couldn't.

"Good, you're awake." The familiar rusty voice had her straightening. He took a few more steps and stood over her. Then he crouched and pulled the duct tape off her mouth. She spit out the gag.

"Who are you?" she whispered. Her tongue was swollen and it was difficult to talk.

"I thought you'd figured it all out."

The man before her looked so ordinary, so regular. Kind even. "The Guardian?"

"Very good." The man seemed pleased she was awake and alert. "I've been waiting for you to wake up. I was afraid that I'd overdosed you last night in the van."

She remembered the needle pricking her arm. "What are you going to do with me?"

"You have to die, Kendall. You crossed the line."

A sob burned in her throat. But she kept her chin high. "What line?"

"You didn't know when to quit. Your reports were hurting Lindsay."

"I was just following the trail of evidence." She moistened her lips. If she could keep him talking, maybe she could delay or change what was to come. "Tell me what I did wrong."

He rose, wincing. He was injured. "There's no time for that."

It had been her experience that ego drove everyone. People loved to talk about themselves. "But I want to get the story right. Don't you want the world to know the truth?"

"They will soon enough." He moved to the workbench and studied the monitors.

Only two screens were on. They televised images of a living room. "You've been watching her."

"Watching over her. Protecting her." From the bench he lifted up a machete. The blade glinted in the light.

Half his face was in shadows, but she could see the intensity behind his gaze. He was going to kill her. The realization was so clear. She didn't want to be chopped into bits and watch the blood drain from her body, but she'd not lie there passively. She struggled against her binds.

Don't panic. Don't panic. "Why are you watching Lindsay?"

"I'm her only family. And family takes care of family."

"Who are you?"

He smiled. "It doesn't matter."

Keep him talking. "It does. I can set the record straight."

His face crinkled in disgust. "You've done enough damage."

Keep him talking. "Why did you kill the others?"

"They were evil."

The brick wall now dug into her spine. "What were their crimes?"

"They hurt the innocent." He ran his thumb along the edge of the machete blade. Blood appeared.

"How did you choose your victims?"

"They hurt Lindsay."

She pulled against her restraints. They didn't budge. "Lindsay doesn't appreciate what you're doing. She hates violence."

His face hardened. "You don't know her."

"I know her better than you think. We spent long hours talking when I interviewed her. I'll bet I've spent more time with her than you have."

A pained look darkened his eyes. "You talk too much."

Kendall had only just begun to talk. "Does it bother you to know she doesn't approve of what you do?"

"She's glad those men are off the street."

Kendall knew she was playing with fire but the longer she strung him along the better her chances of getting out of this. "You killed two boys. *Children.* She hated that."

Guilt shadowed his stony features. "Every war has collateral damage."

"Lindsay will never forgive you for hurting those boys."

He jerked a gun from his waistband and pointed it directly at her. "Shut up!"

She stared into the barrel. All she could seem to think about was that no one was going to miss her when she died. She struggled to keep her voice even and soothing. "Lindsay would hate this. She would want you to let me go."

"Liar. Lindsay despises you. Your lies and half-truths have ruined Sanctuary."

He cocked the gun.

"No!" she shouted.

He fired.

The bullet struck her in the shoulder and she fell back against the hard floor. Pain seared through her body. Her vision blurred and for a moment she couldn't breathe. She'd prayed the bullet would kill her outright but realized now death would not come quickly to her.

The Guardian moved toward her. He grabbed a handful of her hair and jerked her head back. "Take back all you said about Lindsay."

The pain dulled her mind. He had the machete in his hand. "Monster."

The Guardian raised the machete over his head. Through the pain she heard the phone ring. She nearly wept with relief as he released her and backed away toward the workbench. He snapped up the phone.

"It took you long enough to call me back," the Guardian growled. "Now, who is the woman Lindsay is going to see at Mercy?"

A slight tense pause had Kendall struggling to stay conscious.

"I don't care if you've lost your stomach for helping me. And I don't care about your gaming debts anymore. You're in too deep. Now tell me what you know."

The Guardian listened, his body tensing as he gripped the receiver tighter. "I'll be there in ten minutes. Be waiting for me in the garage at the regular place."

The Guardian slammed the phone down and whirled toward Kendall, the only one to absorb his rage. He grabbed a handful of her hair. His eyes were as black as Satan's.

Pain from her shoulder overwhelmed her. Her world went blank.

Lindsay swung her car around and brought it to a stop in a space close to the elevator. She took a moment to scan the deck to make sure there were no press or shadowy figures. Satisfied that the area was clear, she got out of the car and locked it with her keyless remote. She crossed quickly to the elevator, punched the button, and tapped her toe as she waited.

Thoughts tumbled through her mind. The Guardian. Richard. Nicole. The abused woman she was about to meet. And even Sam. Where was Sam? He hadn't called her and that wasn't like him. She was beginning to think that all this trouble with the Guardian might have scared him off.

There was a time his possible rejection might have hurt her feelings. But not now. If he couldn't accept her for who she was—the good and the bad—then so be it. She had to give Zack credit. He'd seen the dark side of her past and he hadn't been scared away.

Lindsay leaned forward to push the already lit elevator button again when she heard footsteps behind her. The sound had her nerves tightening like a bowstring. Her heart pounded wildly in her chest. She jabbed the elevator button again before she turned.

A man appeared from the shadows. He was dressed in a green jumpsuit and was pushing a canvas laundry cart. He touched the bill of his *Minton's Laundry* hat and nodded. "Morning."

Lindsay nodded stiffly, her nerves on alert. With the Guardian's identity still unknown, she wasn't taking any chances. The elevator dinged and the doors slid open.

She stepped back. "You first."

The guy shrugged. "There's room for us both."

"Thanks. I think I forgot something in my car." She backed away from the elevator.

"Suit yourself." He started inside the car and she immediately relaxed, chiding herself for being so sensitive. But still, she was going to play it safe.

She decided to get back in her car and drive around to the front entrance of the hospital. She'd pay for parking on the street.

Lindsay had taken five steps when a damp cloth clamped over her face. The sick, sweet scent of chloroform invaded her senses. Her hands rose up to the ones clamped over her mouth and nose and she tried to pry them away.

She struggled to hold her breath, and when she couldn't any longer, she inhaled a lungful of the chloroform. The drug invaded her system. She couldn't move. Was helpless to scream or fight.

She heard the rumble of male laughter. It was a frightening sound. Evil. Malevolent. He was enjoying her helplessness.

Her brain spun. Her knees buckled.

As she began to lose consciousness, she was aware that the man scooped her up and dumped her into the laundry basket.

He dropped her purse beside her and covered her with a handful of towels. "Now the fun begins, Lindsay."

She passed out completely.

Chapter Twenty-Eight

Friday, July 11, 10:30 A.M.

The cemetery's surveillance tapes for the past year had arrived around eight last night and Zack had reviewed them most of the night. Slowly he'd been able to piece together a chain of events. He rewound the footage and stopped the tape on February eleventh. The landscape on the screen was covered in a dusting of snow. Icicles hung from the trees. The sky was as dull and gray as the headstones.

The homicide team assembled in the conference room. Zack stood and ran his hand over his head.

The entire division had worked all night. No one was going to sleep until this guy had been caught. Detectives from other divisions and uniforms were now helping them run down leads.

Ayden, Ricker, and Vega sat down. "So what do you have? You said it was important."

"I spoke with the cemetery director yesterday because I noticed cameras posted in several of the trees and by the front entrance. It seems he installed surveillance equipment right after Christmas last year. He'd had trouble with someone spray painting satanic symbols on some of the headstones. His graffiti artists haven't reappeared or been caught on tape. But, he did catch us another fish," Zack said.

Ayden frowned. "Where's Warwick? I want him to see this."

"He's at the Department of Motor Vehicles," Zack said. "He'll be here soon." He hit "play." On the television screen a grainy image showed a white van rolling down a distant snowy road into the cemetery. "Pay attention to the vehicle entering the back entrance of the cemetery. As you can see, this segment was recorded on February eleventh. The vehicle enters but stops at the crest of the hill." He touched the screen where the vehicle stopped. "The driver doesn't pull up far enough for us to get a shot at the plates or a look at his face. But if you look closely, you can see that the driver is carrying roses, which he leaves on Deb Hines's grave. Lindsay O'Neil's mother's grave." Everyone in the room leaned forward and watched the driver. "He keeps his head low as he lays the flowers on the grave. He pauses for a moment of prayer and then leaves through the back entrance."

Ayden leaned forward. "He's paying his respects."

Vega folded his arms over his broad chest. "What time is this?"

"Eleven fifty-eight A.M." Zack hit the fast-forward button. "March sixth. The van appears again. It's about noontime. The driver again is careful to keep his face from the camera and the van out of close view. He leaves flowers and again leaves by the back entrance. The Guardian has already proven he's savvy with surveillance equipment, so he must realize the front entrance is covered by a camera."

Ayden muttered an oath. "How the hell are we going to catch this guy?"

Zack grinned. "Stay with me. Now we're coming to April second. Lindsay arrives at the grave. She leaves flowers and stays twenty minutes. She begins to leave. The van arrives. They almost meet this time. But she exits via the front entrance. She said she'd seen a van that day and had thought it was the caretaker."

"She never noticed the flowers before?" Ricker said.

"The cemetery has a policy stating that all live flowers are to be removed every Saturday. Cemetery maintenance always cleared away the old flowers before she arrived."

He hit the fast-forward button again. "It's May third. Again he leaves flowers."

Ricker cocked her head. Her curly hair was twisted up into a high ponytail and her face pale from too little sleep. "May third is the day the article on Lindsay appeared in the paper."

Zack nodded. "Yes. And on this day our mystery man lingers at the Hines grave for over an hour. He seems to be talking to the headstone. His body language suggests that he's agitated. He doesn't show his face, but this time he starts to leave through the front entrance. He catches himself and backs up. But before he does, he gets close enough for us to pull a partial on the plates. That's why Warwick is at the DMV."

Warwick came into the room. He had a file tucked under his arm and was breathless, as if he'd sprinted across the parking lot and up the stairs to the second floor. "Did I miss anything?"

Zack nodded. "Right on time."

Ayden didn't look amused. "What do you have?"

"The DMV ran the stats Kier supplied them. They had fifty-two possible matches. They'd printed out five copies of the list by the time I arrived. I haven't had a chance to look at them."

Ayden shoved out a sigh. "Great work."

Warwick handed copies of the list to the detectives. They each scanned it.

"This could take days to track all these down," Zack said.

C.C. sighed. "I can get the guys from robbery to help."

Warwick frowned as he glared down at the list. The deep tan of his face paled. He blinked and reread the list. "That's odd."

"What do you mean?" Ayden said.

"I recognize one of the names." He swallowed as if he were struggling now. "Pete Myers. He runs the gym where I work out." He shook his head. "This has to be a coincidence. Pete's a great guy."

Ayden frowned. "I just got a report back from Sara. Remember that white powder found at the Turner murder scene embedded in the footprint? She's identified the powder as talc."

Warwick shook his head. "It's not Pete. I know this guy. He'd give you the shirt off his back."

Zack understood Warwick's worry. He'd lived with it when Lindsay had appeared to be the killer. "Let's check him out first. We clear him and you'll concentrate better."

Warwick nodded, grateful. "Thanks. I'd appreciate that."

"C.C., divide the list between you and Vega and robbery. When Kier and Warwick return from Myers's gym give them some of the names," Ayden ordered. "I want this guy found."

The team disbanded. Within ten minutes Zack and Warwick were in Zack's car headed east. "So how long have you known Pete?"

Warwick's trademark confidence had vanished. He looked worried. "Since I was a kid. I still work out at his gym, but it's more than that. He raised me. I was a handful. He kept me in line, gave me direction."

"Do you know anything about him?"

Warwick tapped long fingers on his thigh. "Pete isn't the Guardian. This is just one of those damn coincidences."

No point in arguing. Evidence, not words, would sway Warwick. "I get it. But I still need to ask. What can you tell me about him?"

Warwick understood questions had to be asked even if he didn't like them. "He opened his boxing gym in town twenty years ago. I know because I slathered his grand-opening sign with eggs. He could've called the cops. Instead he gave me a job."

Zack merged onto I-95 south and headed downtown. "Do you have any background on him?"

"He did some time in the military police. Retired in his late forties and came back here to open his gym."

"So he's from Richmond."

Warwick frowned. "I don't know. I do know he has supported dozens of children's charities over the years. Last year he hosted a party at the gym for a bunch of kids whose folks were in prison. He even dressed up as Santa and handed out gifts."

"What do you know about his past?"

"Not much. I do know his name isn't Henry. He never talked about a sister named Debra or a niece named Lindsay."

"Names can be changed. And he plays his cards close to his vest."

Warwick looked troubled but seemed to shake the dark thoughts away. "Maybe."

"Anything else you can tell me about him?"

"He never talks about himself much. He talks about his fighters. He talks about the gym. He talks a little bit about when he boxed in the military." Warwick frowned. "This is bullshit. Let's get to the gym and clear this shit up so we can catch the real killer."

Zack took the Franklin Street exit. "Sure."

"Right." Warwick didn't like this.

Zack maneuvered a few corners and a side alley before he came up behind the gym. There were no cars in the lot.

"The place is usually deserted?"

Warwick got out of the car. "Not usually. But it's not unheard of for him to take off during the middle of the day if business is slow."

"Is summer a slow time?"

"It can be. The weather is warm and people want to get outside."

Zack quietly closed the car door behind him. They moved across the gritty alley to the front door. There was a CLOSED sign on the door.

Warwick tried the door. Locked.

Zack had a bad feeling about this. Warwick was praying Pete wasn't involved. But the whole situation didn't smell right. "Does he still train fighters?"

"He was training a couple last year but he cut them loose a few months ago. Hooked them up with a couple of good trainers. Said he was ready to slow down."

Zack peeked in the front window. The interior was dark. "That seem odd to you?"

"At first, but then I figured he was just getting old."

Zack wasn't leaving this place until he got a look inside. "Any other way inside?"

"There's a door in the back. I have a key." They moved around the side of the building down the chipped sidewalk. The area smelled of garbage. Warwick moved ahead of Zack toward a small metal door, shoved his key in the lock, and unlocked it. "I have a standing invitation to come into the gym. He knows my schedule is squirrelly."

"Myers sounds like a good guy."

Warwick pushed open the door. "He is."

The gym was dark. The only sound came from the drip-drip of a faucet in the men's bathroom.

"Pete!" Warwick shouted.

His voice echoed on the walls. No answer.

Warwick flipped on the lights. He moved down a dark hallway toward Pete's office. The desk was a disheveled mess. "Pete usually keeps his desk neat. Lately, he's let it go. I figured it was just because he's getting old."

Zack jabbed his thumb toward a door. "What's this?"

"Basement access."

"Anything down there?"

"Old equipment mostly."

Zack sighed. Something didn't feel right. He glanced around the office a second time. Myers's desk was covered with stacks of papers, a torn boxing glove, half-eaten food, forms. Being a slob wasn't a crime. And then he saw the black-and-white photo tucked in the corner of a bulletin board on his desk. It was the image of a twentysomething man and a young girl. "This Pete?"

"Yeah. I don't know who the kid is."

The five-year-old girl looked familiar. "Damn. This kid looks like Lindsay."

"Can't be. Look at the clothes. It's early nineteen sixties."

Zack flipped the picture over. Someone had scribbled *Deb and Pete, 1963* in bold handwriting. "You're right." Still, he flicked the edge of the photo with his thumb. "Lindsay showed me a picture of herself as a kid. She looked just like this child."

"I don't know who it is. I figured it was a sister or a cousin."

"A sister." Zack exhaled a breath. "This is a picture of Lindsay's mother."

Warwick's mouth hardened as the implications sunk in. "It can't be."

"Lindsay had a couple of photos in a box when we were married. I only saw them once. But hold up Lindsay's kindergarten picture next to this one and you'd see that she and this kid are the spitting image of each other."

"Oh, Jesus."

Zack scanned the row of shelves above the desk. "We know the Guardian has some connection to Lindsay."

"That doesn't mean Pete does. Likeness or not, this kid could be anyone."

Zack glared at Warwick. "For now we have to assume that that child pictured with Pete is Lindsay's mother."

"Pete can't be her uncle." He sounded as if he were grasping at straws.

"He sure as hell can be." There was a small television set on the file cabinet behind Pete's desk. Built into the set was a VCR. "What did Pete do in the military?"

"Something with radios and the military police."

"Electronics?"

Tension radiated from Warwick. "Maybe."

"The Guardian has been watching Lindsay. And the cameras were positioned in the living room and kitchen. Nothing in the bathrooms or the bedrooms. Private places where a good uncle wouldn't venture." Zack pushed back the VCR tape flap on the television. Inside was a tape dated *July 11*. He turned on the television and hit "Play." Instantly, a black-and-white image of Lindsay appeared. She was standing in Ruby's living room. The time stamp was less than an hour ago.

"Shit," Zack said. "She spent last night with Ruby."

Warwick paled. "Jesus."

"Vega said Ruby had a break-in last week. But nothing was taken. Something was added, though." Zack flipped open his cell and called Ayden. "We have a hit." He explained what they'd found. "Send backup."

Warwick shoved out a breath. He was struggling to hold it together. And if they'd had time, Zack would have pulled him out of there immediately. But he sensed that time was running out.

"I want a look in that basement but I don't want a defense attorney crapping on my case because I don't have a warrant."

Warwick dug in his pocket and pulled out a set of keys. "I have access to the gym with no restrictions." He rubbed the back of his neck with his hand. "If I needed a new set of gloves and couldn't find them upstairs, I'd look in the basement. It's where Pete kept extra equipment when I was here last year."

Zack smiled but there was no pleasure. "I was hoping you'd say something like that."

Warwick opened the basement door lock and flipped the light switch at the top of the stairs. Both cops drew their guns. Slowly they made their way down the rickety steps, their bodies crouched.

Halfway down, Zack moved past Warwick and peered around a blind corner. He saw the computer table. The monitors. And the rows and rows of tapes, each meticulously dated and arranged in chronological order.

Warwick stared at the room in horror and disbelief. His world was shattering. But he was holding it together. Later the problems would come as the enormity of it all hit him.

The heavy coppery scent of blood rose up as they moved toward the computer. Zack glanced toward a second door. He motioned to Warwick.

Warwick nodded. Guns raised, they moved to either

side of the door. Zack counted to three. On three he shoved open the door. "Police, come out with your hands up."

A faint moan echoed from the corner. It sounded as if someone was injured. Still, he didn't rush the room.

Careful to keep his body out of a shooter's line of fire, Zack slid his hand into the room and felt around for a light switch. He found one and clicked it on.

The first thing they saw was the blood. The entire floor was covered with it. This had been the Guardian's killing room. No doubt Saunders's DNA would be all over the place.

Warwick's gaze settled in a shadowed corner. "Oh my God."

Zack tightened his grip on his gun. "What?"

"Kendall Shaw."

While Zack covered him, Warwick holstered his gun and hurried toward the reporter. She lay on the floor curled in a fetal position. Fresh blood pooled around her and stained her clothes.

Zack still didn't trust that this wasn't some kind of trap. "Is she alive?"

Warwick touched his fingers to her neck. "A faint pulse. She's been shot in the shoulder." He flipped open his cell phone and dialed Dispatch. "All this blood. It's a miracle she's alive."

"Check her hands. Does she have both her hands?"

The doors to the hospital's garage elevator opened and Dr. Sam Begley walked out. The Guardian got out of the van and glanced at the clock above the elevator. "About damn time."

The doctor frowned and kept moving toward his shiny BMW. "I couldn't get away. We had an emergency."

"I have an emergency. I need to know where Lindsay is."

"She's not in the hospital. I looked everywhere."

"Who was the battered woman brought in? You know never to call Lindsay without calling me first."

Sam's forehead perspired. "I didn't treat a battered woman today. No one from the hospital called Lindsay."

"Damn it."

"The cops were here. They brought Lindsay and her roommate in for blood tests Wednesday. Did you drug them?"

The Guardian was running over an image of Lindsay standing in Ruby's kitchen. She'd been called by the hospital. He was certain. "Yes. It was the only way to keep them safe while I worked."

"Jesus. You never said anything about hurting Lindsay."

He didn't like the doctor's tone. "I would never hurt her."

Begley shook his head. "You shot those kids today. Christ, one is dead and the other is fighting to stay alive."

Guilt gnawed at him. "They could ID me. They had to go."

"This has gone too far. I'm out. It's just a matter of time before the cops connect us."

The doctor didn't have the conviction to honor agreements. Spoiled rich boy had had everything handed to him on a silver platter. He didn't understand commitment. "You promised me you'd help whenever I asked."

Begley lowered his voice. "I'd never have gotten into this if not for my debts. I've more than satisfied my gambling debts to you. I never want to see you again."

The Guardian slid his hand into his pocket. His fingers brushed the cool metal of his gun and silencer. "You're done when I say you're done."

Begley pulled off his glasses and cleaned the lenses on his shirt. The man actually looked defiant. "I'm finished."

The shrill tone in the doctor's voice grated. The Guardian could see the man was nervous. It wouldn't take much squeezing from the cops to make him talk. He'd like to use the doctor longer, but now he realized the time had come for them to part ways. "If that's the way you want it."

"Good."

The Guardian pulled the gun and silencer from his pocket and before the doctor realized what was happening, he fired three times. Each bullet struck Begley in the heart. For just a split second, surprise marred the doctor's face as he glanced down at the plume of blood growing on his chest. He staggered and would have fallen if the Guardian hadn't caught him.

The thrill of taking life sent a tingle through the Guardian's body. "You were part of a noble cause and I won't forget what you did for me."

Begley's eyes rolled back in his head. He was dead.

The Guardian opened the back of his van and dumped Begley's body in. He'd deal with him later. Now, he needed to find Lindsay.

He got in the front seat of the van and turned on a GPS system. The system tracked a bug he'd put under the back bumper of Lindsay's car. Since he'd seen the article about her in May and realized who she was he'd been determined never to lose sight of her again. At any given moment, he could find her.

The GPS beeped and at first he thought it was broken. Then he realized she was parked in the hospital deck. He turned on the engine and started to patrol the decks. He found her car on the bottom level. With the van still running, he got out and checked her car. It was locked. He scanned the deck but there was no sign of her.

Something was wrong.

The feeling was as intense as it had been those years

Debra had lived with her husband. He'd known she was in danger then but he'd bowed to her will and left them alone as she'd begged him to.

He got back in the van and pulled a disposable cell from his pocket and he dialed Lindsay's number. It rang six times and then went to voice mail. Something was very wrong. She always answered her cell.

He closed his eyes. *Think. Where could she be? Think.*

The Guardian's mind raced. This morning when Lindsay had been in Ruby's kitchen, Ruby had spoken of the San Francisco murder. The Carmichael woman. She'd also mentioned that Nicole's husband, Richard Braxton, was from San Francisco.

It made sense that Richard would eventually find Nicole. But he hadn't thought it would be so soon. If Richard was in the area, he'd not likely find her, because she was safely hidden at the Kiers'. But Lindsay was an open target. He'd go after Lindsay first and use her to get to Nicole.

How could he have been such a fool?

He'd been so consumed with Kendall that he'd ignored a critical danger. He'd made the same mistake he'd made with Debra all those years ago, when he'd underestimated his brother-in-law's rage.

The Guardian felt a rush of panic as he tightened his hands on the steering wheel. He had to think. Think like a hunter. What would he do with Lindsay if he were Richard?

He might kill her in front of Nicole as some sort of lesson. Richard would need a secluded place. The scenarios made the Guardian sick but also gave him hope. There might still be time.

Nicole was at the Kiers' and there was the possibility he could beat Braxton there. He dialed the Kiers' home number.

"Hello."

He suspected the young voice belonged to Zack's sister, Eleanor. She was a sweet kid and Lindsay had great affection for her. "This is Dr. Begley at the hospital. I'm calling to speak to Lindsay."

"Lindsay's not here."

"Is her friend Nicole there?"

"She's in the bathroom."

Good. She was still there. "Don't bother her. I'll just call back."

"Okay."

He hung up and threw the car in drive. He still had time, but how much he didn't know. He raced out of the parking deck and cut through city traffic and onto I-95 north.

His heart pounded as he wove in and out of the traffic. He couldn't screw this one up. He couldn't.

Twenty minutes later, he pulled onto the rural road leading to the Kiers' and slowly drove past their house. He parked in a driveway down the street, climbed out of the van, and hurried through the woods that separated the houses. Staying low, he moved toward the house. At first he saw only Mrs. Kier, who was at the kitchen sink washing dishes. He needed to move closer to get a better look but feared being detected.

His pulse raced. "Get out of the way," he whispered.

And then she stepped aside and he was able to see into the kitchen. Nicole was at the table playing cards with anther woman and an older man.

He breathed a sigh of relief. There was still time. He hurried back to his van and prayed Braxton hadn't hurt Lindsay.

The drugs in Lindsay's system made it hard for her to concentrate. She was aware of strong hands supporting her as she stumbled forward. She couldn't seem to lift her feet or keep her balance.

The area around them was quiet. Wherever they were was far from the main road. She opened her eyes and saw she was being taken toward an old barn.

The air was thick with humidity and sweat had dampened the back of her shirt. "Where are we?" she muttered.

The man holding her laughed. "We are in a very private place. Where no one will bother us. Where no one will hear you scream."

Lindsay swallowed her rising terror. "Why are you doing this? Who are you?"

"I'm someone who doesn't appreciate you sticking your nose where it doesn't belong."

"Who are you?"

"Christina's husband."

Christina. Nicole. "Richard Braxton."

"So she's talked about me?" Hate and resentment laced the words.

"Yes."

Braxton kicked open the rickety barn door and pulled her inside across the dirt floor. When they were in the center, he let go of her. She crumpled face-first into a heap. She tasted dirt and tried to spit it out of her mouth as she rolled onto her back. Above, she saw sunshine peeking through the slats of a room. In the distance she heard birds.

Lindsay moistened her lips. She felt so dry. There was little doubt that Richard planned an awful death for her. She remembered what Zack had told her he'd done to Claire.

She opened her eyes. Her vision was blurred but she could make out dark hair and a square face. She tried to sit up but he roughly pushed her against the hard ground. He straddled her body. She felt his erection press against her belly and she thought he was going to rape her.

She wanted to fight but found her body drifting as if she were on a raft floating out to sea.

Instead, he pounded two stakes into the ground above her head and then roughly grabbed her hands and lashed them tightly to the stakes. His weight lifted and he moved to her legs. He yanked her legs open wide and tied them to more stakes, then hammered them into the ground.

She tried to pull her hands free of the stakes, but they didn't budge. The hemp cut into the tender flesh of her wrist.

Through the haze, Lindsay understood that she needed to do something to save herself. She drew in a lungful of air and screamed as loud as she could.

Richard cursed, drew back, and slapped her hard across the face. "Shut up, bitch. I don't have time for this."

Pain rattled through her head.

He slid his hand to the flat of her belly and up under her shirt. He squeezed her breast painfully. She struggled in vain against her restraints as her stomach heaved at the thought of what was to come.

Richard put his lips next to her ear. "I don't have time for you right now. I have to go get Christina. I want her to watch what I'm going to do."

Abruptly he got up and left the barn. She heard the engine of his car fire up and gravel kick up under the tires as he drove off.

Tears burned in her eyes.

She was not going to die like this. She started to work on the restraints on her hands and ignored the way the rope sliced into her wrists.

* * *

Nicole was lost in thought as she sat at the kitchen table across from Eleanor and Mr. Kier. The pregnancy test she'd taken this morning had been positive. She was carrying Richard's baby.

At first she'd been so numb that she'd not been able to leave the bathroom. She'd sat on the floor and cried.

And then Eleanor had called out to her. So she'd dried her tears and come downstairs.

She laid down her hand of cards on the kitchen table. "Gin."

Eleanor frowned and leaned forward to study the hand. "You don't have gin."

Absentmindedly, Nicole glanced down. "I don't?"

"No. You can't have a straight with mismatched suits."

"Oh."

"Geez Can't anyone play a decent game?"

The phone rang and Audrey came into the kitchen and answered it. "Sure, just a minute. Nicole, the phone is for you."

Grateful for the distraction, she left her cards and moved to the wall phone.

Audrey smiled as she handed her the receiver. "It's a policeman."

Tension rose. "Thanks. Hello?"

"Christina."

Richard's smooth voice raked down her spine. Her grip tightened around the receiver. "What do you want?"

"I'm outside, parked at the edge of the driveway. I want you to smile to the nice people and then walk out the front door, come down the drive, and get into my car. If you don't, I'll be forced to do some very nasty things to your friend, Ms. O'Neil."

Nicole glanced over at Eleanor, who laughed as her father came into the room and tickled her. Audrey stood at the stove working on a pot of sauce.

"Don't keep me waiting, Nicole," Richard urged.

Steel cut through the silk. She *knew* Richard. He would do exactly what he said. "I'll be right there."

She hung up and managed a smile. "I think I need to get a bit of fresh air."

Audrey frowned. "You look pale, Nicole. Are you all right?"

"I'm fine. Just need some fresh air."

Kier lifted a brow. "Who was that on the phone?"

"Detective Warwick," she lied. "He wants to interview me again."

"I'll go outside with you," he said.

"No, no. Challenge Eleanor to a game of gin. I've been a bad opponent so far. I'm going outside for just a few minutes." The lies tumbled off her tongue so easily.

Mr. Kier studied her. "All right."

She turned and stiffly walked out the door. Before she went outside, she stopped at the entryway table, where she'd left her purse. She grabbed her cell phone and a vial of mace and put them in her pocket. Richard wouldn't expect too much resistance from her. And hopefully she could use that to her advantage.

As she reached the country road just out of sight of the house, she saw a dark Mercedes. Black and sleek, it looked out of place.

The tinted passenger window rolled down. Richard sat behind the wheel looking so calm and relaxed. "Good to see you, Christina. If you're thinking about running, I thought I should tell you that I have your friend Lindsay stashed in a very unpleasant place. If anything happens to me, she'll be long dead before anyone ever finds her."

Nicole opened the door and slid into the front passenger seat. "Let her go, Richard. You have me. Just let her go."

His eyes darkened. "Close the door, Christina. *Now.*"

Woodenly, Nicole closed it. If she made a move for the mace and did subdue him, what would happen to Lindsay? She had to wait for the right moment.

The doors locked immediately. He started to drive. "You've cut your hair. I don't like it."

She didn't know what to say to that and decided to stay quiet.

"But hair grows, doesn't it?" He frowned. "Put your seat belt on, Christina. I don't want you getting hurt."

She swallowed and tried not to let her fear show. "Where are we going?"

"Home, eventually. But first we have a stop to make."

"Where?" she demanded.

White teeth flashed. "You'll see."

Lindsay had trouble shaking the effects of the drug. Her mind wanted to drift and her eyes to close. She wanted to float and let the drug take her.

But as seductive as the drug was she knew if she gave in to it she would die.

She had to keep her thoughts focused. To get free of the ropes binding her was a challenge. To keep herself awake, she started to talk.

"Mom, if you're up there, I could use some help. Zack's a great cop, but I don't think he's going to figure this one out."

She'd managed to loosen the binding around her right hand, though she'd not freed her hand completely. Her wrist was raw from the constant rubbing and pulling against the rope. She focused on the pain in her wrist and the stones on the ground that now dug into her back.

It was hard to judge how much time had passed. But she knew she had to hurry. Time was running out. She moistened her dry lips and opened her eyes. She shook her head from side to side.

"Remember how we dreamed of driving to California?" She kept twisting her right wrist, ignoring the pain. Blood ran down the wrist. "Remember how we'd pore over the maps and imagine every step of the route?"

The silence was her only answer, and it was a stark reminder that her mother was gone and that she was so very alone. Terror burned inside her. "Help! Help!" She screamed until her voice was hoarse.

The odds were stacked against her and it would be so easy to give up.

Above, blue sky peeked through the slats of the roof. For just a moment, Lindsay felt as if something touched her hair. Like a caress.

"Mom . . ." The word felt wrenched from her.

There was no answer. Whether it was her mother or just a trick of her imagination, she didn't know. But the sensation was enough to calm her a little.

She drew in a deep breath as she had done so many times in yoga when she felt overwhelmed and scared. She kept breathing deeply. Her mind started to calm and refocus. "Don't panic. Don't panic. I can do this."

She swallowed and started back on the binding. "Where has Richard taken me?" She sucked in a deep breath and released it as she shook her head. "The sun is high above, so it can't be much past noon. He couldn't have taken me far. Mercy is in the center of the city." She was willing to bet he'd taken her east.

The heavy scent of dirt, cow dung, and hay mingled with the heat. In the shadowed corners mice squeaked.

"I'm in a barn. East of the city. Farmland east of the city. It's abandoned."

She thought about the new mall that was going to be constructed soon in the far eastern end of the county.

The farmland had been purchased and the owners had left months ago. Now the land waited for the bulldozers. It would be a perfect place to take her.

Just imagining where she was gave her a sense of control. She tried to pull her right hand free. It slipped a little in the binding but she couldn't quite free it.

She wasn't sure how much more time she had, but she knew if she didn't get her hand free before Richard returned he would kill her.

Richard had brought her here because he wanted to make sure that no one interrupted him when he returned. She guessed he was going to bring Nicole back so that she could watch what he did to her. Her death would be the death he would use to terrify Nicole into submission.

Ignoring the pain in her raw wrist, Lindsay started to jerk harder on the rope. "That son of a bitch is not going to win."

Somehow she had to get herself and Nicole out of this.

The Guardian stayed several car lengths behind as Richard moved onto the four-lane highway. When Richard reached the interstate, he headed east toward the airport. It made sense that the bastard would take his wife back to San Francisco. Familiar territory.

Once Richard left Richmond, finding Lindsay would be almost impossible. He couldn't let that happen.

Tightening his hands on the wheel, he considered ramming Richard's car. But even if he got his hands on the bastard there was no guarantee that he'd say where Lindsay was.

There were so many variables. He had to stay the

course and keep his cool. "Stay close and he will lead you to her."

Then Richard made an unexpected move. He drove past the airport exit and continued on until he reached the off-ramp for Route 33. The rural route cut through the town of West Point and then snaked into the countryside. Where the hell was Richard headed?

The fear and exhilaration had made the Guardian forget the pain of his cracked ribs. This was his moment to redeem himself. He would save the child when he hadn't saved the mother.

"God has brought me to this moment. This is my test."

When Richard pulled down a gravel driveway, the Guardian continued on past until he reached another driveway a quarter mile down the road. He turned the van around, and when he reached the driveway where Richard had turned, he stopped.

He glanced down the long driveway. He didn't know what awaited him. Richard very well could have marshaled an army. And as much as he wanted to kill Richard all by himself, he didn't want to risk Lindsay's life. He dialed Warwick's number.

Warwick answered it on the second ring. "Warwick."

"Jacob."

A tense silence followed. "Pete, we need to talk."

Jacob was upset. It took a lot to rattle that kid. "You've found the basement."

"Yes."

Pride mingled with sadness. He'd never wanted to hurt Jacob. He didn't need to share DNA to know the boy was his son. "You were always a smart one. I'm not surprised you figured things out. In fact, I'm glad it was you. The collar will look good on your record."

"Jesus, Pete, where are you?"

Pain and sadness resonated from Jacob's words, but

Mary Burton

he didn't dwell on the whys. He understood that questions like "Why?" didn't matter until the quarry was caught. Smart kid.

"I need you. And I need all the firepower you can put together."

"What are you talking about? We're after you."

"I don't matter anymore. Richard Braxton is in the city and he has his wife and Lindsay." He gave Jacob directions. "Just come. I'm going to try to catch him alive but I don't know if I'll be able to do it. It's more important to save Lindsay and Nicole."

Pete hung up. He checked his watch. There wasn't time to wait for Jacob and Zack. Richard wouldn't waste time. Pete got out of the van.

A small plane buzzed over and circled to land. There had to be a private airstrip close by. It made sense that Richard would have his own plane.

His ribs tightened around him like a vice. It hurt to walk, to breathe. But he wasn't going to let Lindsay or Debra down. *Not this time.*

He hurried down the long gravel driveway that disappeared into a grove of trees. The heat of the day made him sweat, and soon his shirt was soaked through. When he spotted the Mercedes parked under an oak, he slowed and moved behind a bush.

On the property was an old farmhouse. At one time it had been painted white, but the elements had long ago stripped the paint. Now it was a faded gray. The wide front porch had collapsed in on itself. The windows on the first and second floors were broken.

The house was too dilapidated to hide anyone. But as Pete stared at the house, a deep sadness caught him by the throat. The place looked like the home where Debra and Lindsay had lived with that bastard Hines.

The first time he'd stood on Debra's porch it had

been twenty-seven years ago. Lindsay had been two and she had hugged her mother's leg and stared up at him as he'd argued with Debra. He had seen the problems in his sister's marriage then and had begged her to leave. She had defended her husband and had ordered Pete to leave and never come back. A few years later he'd tried to help her a second time, but she wouldn't leave her husband.

And, God help him, he'd given up on her and her daughter.

The last time he'd returned to Debra's house, his sister was dead. Lindsay had run away from her foster care home. That bastard Hines had shot and killed himself in a hotel room.

Pete had been so full of rage and anger. He had burned that house to the ground, believing the flames would singe the sadness from his soul. He'd tried to track Lindsay down but hadn't been able to find her. She'd been lost to him.

And then this past May he'd seen the article on Lindsay in the magazine. He had stared at her blond hair and blue eyes and immediately had pictured Debra. All the memories had roared to life. And he knew God had given him a second chance to set things right.

"You are not alone, Lindsay," he said. He frantically began to search the grounds.

Nicole stumbled when Richard jabbed the gun in her back. "Move."

Nicole had been afraid enough times in her life. Richard had seen to that. But this time the fear cut bone deep. Today wasn't about saving only herself. It was about saving her baby. And Lindsay.

"Open the barn door," Richard ordered.

Nicole refused to make this easy for him. "Where is Lindsay?"

Richard's eyes narrowed. Nicole braced, ready for the hard slap that usually came when she questioned him. However, this time he smiled. He reached around her and pulled the door open. "She's inside."

His acquiescence was more frightening than his ranting. Still, she didn't advance. She thought about the mace in her pocket. If Lindsay was here, she could save her. Her hand slid into her pocket.

Richard was too fast. He grabbed her hand and jerked it back, twisting painfully until she dropped the mace. "You've learned a few nasty habits that I'll have to break you of, Christina. Now, get inside or I'll blow your friend's kneecap off," Richard said.

Nicole knew he'd do exactly that. She had to swallow the rage and play along until she thought of something else. She reached for the rusted lock and pushed it up. The door swung open slightly farther. Hinges squeaked as she pulled the rotting door open.

The large room was lit only by the sunshine peeking in through the rafters, which stretched high up to a peak above them. The floor was compacted dirt. A rusted sickle and an old harness hung from a peg on a post. Mice squeaked in a dark corner. The room had a foul smell, as if something had recently died there.

"Lindsay!" Nicole shouted.

There was no answer.

"Where is she?"

Richard pointed the tip of his gun to the northwest corner. In the shadows, she saw Lindsay. She lay on her back, her hands and feet tied to stakes on the floor. She moaned, a sign she was still alive.

Nicole met Richard's gaze. "What are you going to do with us?"

Richard closed the barn door behind them as if he had all the time in the world. "Lindsay has caused me almost as much trouble as you have, Christina. And now it's time she learned a lesson, like the one I taught Claire."

"Claire? What did you do to her?"

He laughed. "We had quite a bit of time to chat. She's a strong woman. Or rather, *was* a strong woman. She had a high threshold for pain."

Nicole felt sick. Poor Claire. She'd been so kind and had given her hope when she'd been so afraid. "Richard, spare Lindsay, and I'll go home with you. I'll be a good wife again. You don't need to hurt anyone else."

Richard pulled a set of handcuffs from his back pocket and clicked the first cuff on her wrist. He dragged her to the north side of the barn and clicked the other manacle to a wooden workbench. Driven into the center of the bench was a newly purchased ax.

Tears burned in Nicole's eyes. "Let her go, Richard. *Please.* I'll never run from you again."

"I wish it were that easy, Christina. I really do. But you brought all this on yourself. I want to be gentle and kind but you keep pushing me." His face hardened. "You need to be taught a lesson."

"Richard, please don't hurt anyone else. I'm the one that you're angry with."

"You drove me to this, my dear. You have only yourself to blame."

"I won't ever leave you again. I'll be a good wife."

A smile tipped the edge of his lips as he pried the ax free of the workbench. "I've spent the last weeks covering for you and telling everyone you were in Europe. Do you have any idea how humiliated I was for having to spin those lies knowing my wife had abandoned me?" His eyes glittered as he tested the tip of the ax blade with his thumb. The sharp edge sliced his skin and the tiny wound began to bleed. He smiled. "I did everything for you. I treated you like a princess. And you left me."

Richard was a monster. He was truly insane. Nicole had to keep talking to him so he'd believe she'd surrendered. "I understand now how much I hurt you, Richard. I shouldn't have run. That was so wrong of me. But I was afraid."

Richard stared at her. Sadness darkened his eyes. "Why were you afraid? I rubbed salve into your muscles. I bandaged your cuts."

That had been a truly horrible time. She'd laid battered and bruised on her bed and he'd tended to her injuries. She remembered how good the salve had felt. And how much she had loathed his touch. "You were good to me."

He nodded. "I gave you everything. I molded you into the woman you are today."

If she could just connect with him, perhaps she could spare Lindsay. There was no hope for herself. She would have to return with him. But if she could just save Lindsay . . . "I didn't see that at the time. I should have."

Lindsay groaned as if she were protesting, but she made no attempt to rise.

Tears spilled down Nicole's cheek. "I love you, Richard."

He closed his eyes for a split second as if he were overcome with emotion. "I've waited a month for you to say that."

Her knees wobbled but she faced her husband. "*Please* forgive me." The words tasted bitter.

For a moment his features softened. He looked at her tenderly. She thought she had him. She was going to find a way out of this mess.

And then a switch inside him flipped. His gaze hardened to ice. He advanced on Nicole in two steps and hit her hard across the face. She dropped to her knees. Tasted blood. The handcuffs cut into her wrist.

"You are a lying bitch," he spat. "You need to learn a lesson."

She cupped her stinging face with her hand. "What are you going to do?"

With the ax in one hand, he moved toward Lindsay. "I think the world needs to know that Lindsay's precious protector turned on her and cut off her hand."

Nicole screamed and scrambled to her feet. "Richard, leave her alone. *Please,* I beg you. I'll do whatever you want."

"Oh, you'll do whatever I want. But first you need to learn a lesson."

Lindsay's mind had been crystal clear as she had lain on the hard earth and had listened to Richard rant and Nicole cry. Anger had roiled inside her as ants had crawled up under her shirt and started to bite her but she'd kept her eyes closed. She hadn't made a coherent sound or moved as Richard had badgered and threatened Nicole. It had taken Lindsay all that was in her to keep her temper under control as Nicole had begged Richard to spare Lindsay's life.

Just before Richard and Nicole had arrived, she'd been able to work the binding on her right hand loose so that she could slip her hand free. But she'd not had the time to loosen the ones on her other hand or her feet.

As Nicole had pushed open the barn door, Lindsay had had only had moments to scoop dirt up in her fist. Now, she needed Richard to get close so she could throw the dirt into his eyes.

Richard knelt beside Lindsay and ran the cold steel of

the ax blade over her narrow wrist. "I wonder how many chops it will take to remove her hand? I'm willing to bet it hurts like a bitch."

Nicole wept. "Don't do this, Richard. *Please*, have pity."

"I have no pity for traitors. And that's what you are, Christina. You're a traitor."

Lindsay peeked through the slits of her eyelids. Richard had turned to face Nicole. This was her chance.

She drew in a deep breath and in one violent jerk pulled her arm free and threw the dirt into his eyes. The dirt caught him directly in the face. He yelped, dropped the ax, and staggered back. He rubbed his face and hollered like a banshee.

Lindsay quickly grabbed the ax and cut the binding on her other hand. Her heart hammered in her chest as she sat up and sliced through the bindings of her ankles.

Nicole yanked on the handcuffs as if she were possessed. "Lindsay, run. Get away from him."

Lindsay scrambled to her feet and ran to Nicole. "We're both getting out of here. Now stretch out your arm so I can cut the chain."

Nicole's hand trembled as she pulled the chain taut.

Richard fumbled for the gun in his waistband and swiped the dirt from his eyes. "Bitch!" He pointed the gun at Nicole and Lindsay. He cocked it and fired. The bullet whizzed past Lindsay's head and cut through the side of the barn. Sunlight shone through the hole.

Lindsay froze. Her fingers gripped the ax handle.

Richard pointed the gun at Nicole. "Drop the blade or I'll shoot Nicole in the head."

Lindsay stared at Nicole. Tears streamed down Nicole's face and her eyes pleaded for Lindsay not to give up.

Richard jabbed the gun in the air. *"Now."*

Lindsay laid down the ax on the workbench.

"Clever," Richard said. "Toss the ax over in that corner. I don't want you to be temped to try something again."

Lindsay threw the ax in the corner.

Richard laughed. "You couldn't save Mommy and now you won't be able to save Nicole."

Years of buried fury rose up in Lindsay. "You don't know anything about my mother."

He moved closer to Nicole. "I know a lot. Your friend Claire Carmichael had a lot to say as I sliced the flesh from her face."

Sweat trickled down Lindsay's back. "Screw you."

Enraged, Richard fired the gun. The bullet bit into the dirt by Nicole's feet, barely missing her. "If you refuse to accept your lesson, Lindsay, I'll kill Christina."

Nicole shook her head. "Don't do it, Lindsay. Don't make it easy for him. I'd rather die than let him hurt you."

"Shut up!" Richard shouted. He fired again.

This time the bullet nicked Nicole in the arm. He wasn't toying with them. She screamed in pain and grabbed her arm. She stumbled back but managed to stay on her feet.

Richard's face twisted with fury. He raised the gun to Nicole's head. He was going to kill her.

"Richard!" Lindsay shouted. "I'll get down on the ground. Just leave her alone."

Richard's hand shook as he held the pistol at Nicole's head.

"What do you want me to do?" Lindsay asked.

Richard didn't take his gaze off Nicole. "Go over by the ax and lie down on your belly. Stretch out your arms."

"Okay, just don't hurt her."

Mary Burton

Blood seeped from the wound in Nicole's arm. "Don't do it, Lindsay."

"Shut up!" Richard shouted. He held the gun steady. "Hurry up. Lie on your stomach and stretch out your arms in front of you."

Lindsay moved across the barn and knelt down. She stretched out trembling arms. She thought about Zack. He'd wanted a second chance and she'd been too afraid to give him one. God, if only she had a second chance.

Richard walked toward the ax and picked it up, then moved beside Lindsay. Glancing at Nicole, he steadied his grip on the ax handle. "This is what happens to bad girls, Christina."

"Don't do this Richard, *please*," Nicole said. "If not for my sake, then the baby's."

His gaze didn't waver. "What baby?"

Nicole swiped a tear from her face. "Your baby. Our baby."

Richard's gaze narrowed. "You're lying."

"I'm not. I just found out."

Lindsay drew in a breath. Maybe they could use the baby to connect with him. "It's true." She started to spin lies. "It's a boy. The ultrasound just confirmed it."

"A son?"

Tears streamed down Nicole's face as she slid her hand protectively to her belly. "Yes. A son. Yours and mine."

"A simple test will prove if you're lying."

Nicole lifted her chin. "I'm not lying, Richard."

Richard's gaze glistened with pride. "All the more reason to get rid of her."

Pete knew he had to act now. There was no telling when the cops would arrive. He had to save Lindsay. She had to know that she wasn't alone.

Swallowing the pain, he held his gun straight. In a split second he took in the scene. Richard had grabbed Lindsay's hair, yanked her head back, and was pressing the ax blade to her neck.

In that moment, Pete pictured Debra's last moments. She'd been alone. Afraid. He raised his gun. This was his moment of redemption. "Let her go."

Richard's gaze snapped up. "Back the fuck off or I'll kill her." He pushed the blade against Lindsay's neck, slicing her skin. Blood trickled.

"Kill her and I'll kill you and your wife," Pete said. He moved into the room so that the wall, not the door, was to his back. He didn't want to kill Nicole but he would.

"No!" Lindsay struggled to get free.

Pete didn't take his eyes off Lindsay. "You come first, Lindsay. If she has to die, then so be it. I came to save *you*."

Richard heard the sincerity in Pete's voice. He hesitated, understanding that Pete would kill his wife and child. "Who the hell are you?"

"I'm Lindsay's Guardian." Pride welled inside him. He'd waited so long to say those words.

Outside, police tires screeched to a halt. Footsteps raced toward the barn.

Richard sneered and lowered his gaze to the blade. He was going to kill Lindsay.

The Guardian fired.

Guns drawn, Zack and Warwick burst into the barn as Pete's bullet whirled past Lindsay's head and struck Richard in the face. Blood and brains splattered Lindsay's face and body. She screamed.

Warwick's face twisted with anguish. "Pete!"

Pete backed up, his gun still drawn.

"Drop your weapon!" Zack ordered.

Lindsay turned away from Richard's body. She didn't chance a glance down at his body. Instead, she looked at Pete. "You're my Guardian?"

Pete's gun didn't waver. "Yes."

Understanding dawned in Lindsay's eyes. "My mother's brother."

Pete nodded. "I wasn't there for you when you needed me then. But I'm here now."

Zack inched closer. "Pete, drop the gun. Give Lindsay a chance to get to know her uncle. It doesn't have to end for you."

Warwick's face looked carved from stone. "Please, Pete. Don't do this."

For an instant, Pete's stance relaxed a fraction and it looked like he might give up. Then he shook his head. "This is the end of the line." He raised the gun at Nicole, ready to fire.

Warwick hesitated.

Zack didn't. He fired. His bullet hit Pete in the chest. Pete dropped to his knees, the gun still in his hand. He turned his face toward Warwick. "You're a good kid."

Warwick froze, his weapon pointed forward.

Pete raised his gun a second time.

Zack fired again. This time the bullet struck Pete in the head, killing him instantly.

Adrenaline pumped through Zack's veins. For several seconds he didn't move. He wanted to run to Lindsay to take her in his arms, but he resisted the urge. He swept the room with his gaze. There didn't appear to be anyone else there.

"Lindsay, is anyone else here?" Zack asked.

She shoved her hands through her bloody hair. "I don't think so."

Zack looked at Nicole. Her skin was as pale as porcelain. "Anyone else?"

Nicole shook her head. "Richard said he'd come alone. He didn't want anyone to know where I was."

Outside the distant sound of sirens began to grow louder. Backup would soon arrive. Still, Zack let his gaze roam over the rafters and in the shadowed corners.

Warwick cleared his throat. "I'll cover you."

"You can handle this?"

Warwick looked like he'd aged a decade. "Yes."

Zack searched the room, and only when he was satisfied that the danger had passed did he holster his weapon and go to Lindsay.

She was covered in so much blood that he was afraid he might hurt her if he touched her. "Lindsay, are you all right?"

Green eyes locked on his. Tears filled her eyes and streamed down her face. "Yes." She wrapped her arms around him. "I thought I'd never see you again."

Zack held Lindsay tight. "It's okay, baby. I'm here."

Warwick, careful not to look at Pete, moved to Richard's body and searched his pockets for the key to the handcuffs that held Nicole. Finding it, he moved to her and unlocked them. He had a white-knuckle hold on his control and he wouldn't be able to hold it forever. He guided Nicole out of the barn.

Lindsay stared at Pete's body. "How did he know we were here?"

"He's the one who had been watching you on the cameras. There are cameras at Ruby's house too."

"My God."

Zack wrapped his arm around Lindsay and held her tight. Her heart beat rapidly against his chest. "Let's get out of here."

"Yes." In the harsh sunlight, Lindsay squinted and tucked her head against his chest.

As the backup cops arrived and fanned into a tight perimeter, he kissed her. "Lindsay, I love you."

She clung to him. "I love you too, Zack."

Chapter Twenty-Nine

Saturday, September 20, 1:05 P.M.

"That's the last of it," Zack said as he kicked the front door of the saltbox house closed with his foot.

"Still glad I'm moving in?" Lindsay said as she eyed the stack of boxes and furniture in the living room.

Zack set the box down and pulled her into his arms. Light from the transom above him shone into the hallway, giving the house a bright, cheery feel. He kissed her long and hard. "Absolutely. You're exactly where you belong."

Lindsay snuggled close to him. In his arms everything felt so *right*. After her nightmare experience in July with Richard Braxton and her uncle, Pete Myers, she'd realized just how much she loved Zack. No matter what their problems had been, she'd known she'd work with him to solve them.

Together, they'd gone into marriage counseling and had started to work on the issues that had kept them apart. The sessions weren't always easy. There were tears and some anger, but through it all they kept communicating and trying to find their way back to each other. And they had. Their relationship wasn't perfect, but then no relationship was. They both still had busy, demanding work schedules but they both understood that no matter what, they belonged together. Their love would carry them through anything.

Lindsay laid her head against Zack's chest. She savored the steady thud of his strong heartbeat against her ear.

So much had happened in the last couple of months. Kendall had survived her injuries. For reasons no one understood, the Guardian, Pete, had not cut off her hand. He'd left her to die, expecting her to bleed out. But because Zack and Warwick had found her in time, she'd survived the gunshot wound to her shoulder. She had lost a great deal of blood and was near death when they'd found her. It had had been touch-and-go for Kendall for a couple of days. Lindsay had visited her daily, feeling an odd connection to the woman who'd nearly been killed by Lindsay's own flesh and blood. When Kendall had awakened for the first time, she had been surprised to see Lindsay. She had been even more shocked by Lindsay's concern. However, as the days had turned into weeks and Lindsay had continued to return to the hospital, Kendall and Lindsay had forged the beginnings of a friendship.

The news media had swarmed all over the story. Their coverage had been relentless. Kendall was used to covering events herself and had hated being the center of attention. Ironically, Lindsay was one of the few people who understood how wrenching such coverage could be.

"I don't like this," Kendall said as she laid in her hospital bed, her right arm in a gray sling. She was pale and drawn, fragile even, but still held her chin up as if she were queen of the world. Lindsay had to give the woman credit. She was a survivor.

"Another story will come along," Lindsay said. "You'll be forgotten soon enough."

Kendall's face tightened as she absently plucked at a loose thread on her blanket. Tears welled in her eyes. "I'm sorry."

Lindsay frowned. "For what?"

"I wasn't fair to you when I was covering the Guardian story." She smoothed long fingers over her thigh. "But I've had a taste of what I put you through. I've been *the* story for the last month and it's not been pleasant. I was willing to sacrifice you for my career. I'm sorry."

"You were doing your job. I understand that it wasn't personal." Lindsay was trying her best to let go of her anger.

Kendall shook her head. "I was doing my job a little too well. And no, it wasn't personal, but that kind of media coverage can be hurtful. I see that now." An awkward silence settled between them.

That one apology had banished a good bit of her resentment. She managed a soft smile. "How's the shoulder?"

"Stiff and it really throbs at night. I'll be in rehab for months." Kendall wiggled all ten fingers. "But I'm very grateful to have both my hands."

"When does rehab start?"

"Two weeks. The doctors are pretty sure I'll regain full range of motion." She smiled. "I've heard my physical therapist is the best, but other patients say she can be a bit of a sadist."

Lindsay nodded grimly. "It's going to be her job to make your arm move in directions it doesn't want to go. I'm sorry it's going to be so painful."

She shrugged. "The pain doesn't bother me. It will just feel good to have my life back."

"Are you going to take that job at the New York televison station?"

Kendall shook her head. "I don't know. I don't have to make a decision for a few weeks. By the way, how's Nicole? I hear she's back in Richmond."

Lindsay gave her the recap. Nicole was also moving on with her life. Her bullet wound had been superficial and had not impacted the baby. She'd chosen to carry the child to term but hadn't ruled out adoption. Her biggest fear was that she could never love Richard's child.

Nicole had flown back to San Francisco to reclaim her life. With Richard gone she was free to reclaim her old studio and the bank accounts she'd not been able to access. But she'd quickly discovered that the city no longer felt like home. There were simply too many bad memories. So, she had returned to Virginia within weeks and had announced she was reopening her business on the East Coast.

Kendall nodded. "She's welcome to stay with me. I've got a huge house to myself."

"Thanks, I'll tell her."

Later, Nicole had agreed to room with Kendall, knowing she'd not be able to make any firm living arrangements until she decided about the baby.

When Lindsay thought back on all that had happened she still felt overwhelmed. But what always brought her down to earth was Zack. "I love you, Zack Kier."

"I love you, Lindsay O'Neil." He kissed her on the forehead. "I have something for you in the kitchen."

"Please tell me it's lunch," she said, teasing. The appetite that had eluded her this past year was returning. "I'm starving."

He grinned. "I'll grill us some hamburgers in a minute but first I want to give you this." He guided her into the kitchen. He reached in the drawer beside the sink and pulled out a small black box.

Her heart thumped wildly in her chest as she accepted the box and cracked it open. Inside was a ring. It was a thick gold band with three small sapphires and two diamonds embedded in it. "Wow."

Zack took the ring from the box and slipped it on her ring finger. It fit perfectly. "When we got married, we never bought rings. I thought it was time I gave you a proper wedding band."

Tears glistened in her eyes. For so many years, she'd felt an emptiness that had cut to her bone. Now, her life and heart felt so full. "It's stunning."

"You really like it?"

"Yes."

"I knew you wouldn't want anything fussy, but I wanted the ring to have some sparkle."

Emotion tightened her throat. "It's gorgeous."

He pulled a second ring out of his jeans pocket. "I picked up one for me as well."

Grinning through tears, she took the ring from him and slipped it on his ring finger. His hands were warm, calloused, and already she was imagining them on her naked body. "I guess this makes us official."

He laughed. "I want the world to know we're married."

She had come so far. There'd been a time when she had feared marriage, even love. And now she embraced them both.

Lindsay's counseling sessions with her therapist had focused not only on her relationship with Zack but with her uncle, Pete Myers. Police investigations had revealed that Pete had retired from the military twenty years ago and had settled in Richmond. He'd opened his gym and had become a foster father to Jacob Warwick. By all accounts, he had been a model citizen and father to Jacob. What no one realized was that Pete had harbored bitter disappointment and guilt over his estrangement from his sister, Deb, Lindsay's mother. When Deb had been brutally murdered twelve years ago, Pete's mental health had suffered a severe blow. Jacob was in the army and there'd been no one to ground Pete.

Pete had traveled to Hanover searching for Lindsay. When he'd discovered she'd run away he'd gone to the Hines house and burned it to the ground. From then on, Pete's mental health never fully recovered. All outward appearances suggested he was fine, but video journals found by the police revealed that he had a very troubled mind.

In the video diaries, Pete had ranted about his dead brother-in-law, about his own rage and his need for revenge. In fact, arson investigators were able to link several unsolved fires to Pete.

Seeing Lindsay's picture in the May article in *Inside Richmond* had snapped Pete's hold on reality. He had believed the article had been a sign from God for him to become Lindsay's Guardian. He had planted the cameras in Lindsay's town house and had obsessively followed her. His surveillance had alerted him to Sam Begley. Pete had surreptitiously known of Sam's obsession with gambling and it had been easy to lure him into a couple of bets on boxing fights. Pete had seen to it that Sam had lost. And then he'd used the doctor's debts to force him to supply confidential information about patients. Police later found Sam's body in the back of Pete's van.

In the end, Pete's obsession with Lindsay had destroyed Sanctuary Women's Shelter, the haven Lindsay had created as a tribute to her mother. But ironically, she'd not have been alive today to rebuild another shelter if not for Pete's fixation on her. If he had not been following her that hot day in July and figured out where Richard had taken her and called Jacob, Zack would never have found her alive. Richard would have brutally killed her, as he'd killed Claire, and Nicole and her baby would be back in California suffering under Richard's iron hand.

Even the loss of Sanctuary was only temporary. A month ago, Dana and Sanctuary's board of directors had given Lindsay the go-ahead to find a new location for another women's shelter.

Lindsay stared down at her ring, and despite her best efforts to remain positive, thoughts of the teenage boy who had died because of Pete haunted her.

Zack detected her shift in mood. "What's bothering you? Is it the ring?"

"No, it's perfect." She blew out a breath. "I still think of those boys my uncle shot." One had survived his wounds but the other had been buried. The wrenching funeral had attracted more than 500 mourners including Lindsay, Zack, and Jacob. "I just wish I could have stopped Pete from going over the edge."

He tucked a stray strand of her hair behind her ear. "You hadn't seen the guy in over twenty years. How could you be responsible?"

"Intellectually, I get that. Emotionally, I feel awful about what happened." When she was close to Zack, she felt as if she could get through anything. "I saw Jacob yesterday. He opened up a little about his feelings, but I can see the guy is a wreck."

"I'm glad he at least talked to you. He's gone to the department shrink but I don't think he's saying anything more than he has to. He needs someone to trust."

"Trust is a tall order for him to fill right now. His mother left him scarred and Pete shattered what little trust he'd regained." She shook her head. "It's odd. If my uncle had found me right after Mom's death, Jacob would have been a kind of foster brother to me."

Zack laid his hands on her shoulders. You're good at getting people to open up. Keep talking to him. He's going to need you."

"We've pieced together some of his life but not all of it. Peter Henry Myers was a complicated man."

"He cared about you both."

"Yeah." Lindsay felt the need to talk about something cheerier. "Enough sadness. Today is a happy day. Let's get those burgers on the grill. I'm starving."

He smiled warmly. "And after that, I vote we bag the boxes for today and try out that new bed."

She glanced out the kitchen window onto the deck to the only splash of color in the backyard. He mother's clay planters that Zack had rescued were filled with pansies and ivy. "Sounds good."

Zack collected the burgers from the refrigerator. "Mom called this morning."

Lindsay grabbed the hamburger buns from the bread basket. She and Audrey had shared a pleasant lunch last week. It felt good to be back in the Kier fold. Even Malcolm was warming to her. "And?"

"She'd like to throw us a wedding." He shrugged. "She doesn't want to put any pressure on us, but she'd like to see us married in a real church. She even wants to throw a reception at Zola's."

"That's very generous. I'd love to renew our vows, Zack, but finding the time to plan a big event is going to be kind of hard now. We have the house and we're both busy with work."

"Mom wants to do the whole thing for us. It's her gift to us. She'd wanted to do it after we first eloped but . . ."

"We didn't last long enough." Lindsay felt touched by her mother-in-law's offer. "That's really sweet of her."

Zack grinned. The smile softened his normally serious features and gave them a boyish quality that had her heart skipping. "So that's a yes?"

A soft breeze blew through the kitchen window and cooled her skin. "To remarrying you in front of all our friends and family?" She nodded. "That's a definite yes."

"And the party?"

"It sounds fabulous. I'm ready for a whole new start."